THE UNLOVED ONES

In Northern Chad there is a wild fastness of rock and
sand known as the Tibesti. It is the place (so the Arabs
say) where the wind was born; it is part of the vast,
dying Sahara, where every year the water in the *gueltas*
is a little lower and the grass a little more sparse. It forms
a gigantic, desolate background for the action of this
taut story of eight men and women who intrude
momentarily into its brooding silence. Bitter and dis-
illusioned, this 'bunch of liars and cheats', without hope
of love, each have their own—sometimes secret—reason
for their presence: blind Lady Teefer, nonsensically
searching for the body of her pilot husband, long dead;
her 'seeing eye' girl, Susan, 'rescued off a garbage heap';
Bert Bowdrey, desperately ill, frantically photographing
rock carvings; his wife, Ann, who has the eyes of a virgin;
Lassiter, the guide, who dreams always the same dream
of death. Menaced by marauding Touareg and continuously fighting amongst themselves, these 'unloved
ones' come face to face with destiny in this almost
unbearably exciting story, with its unexpected twists and
turns, that could only have come from the masterly
pen of Jon Burmeister who ranks among the top fiction-
writers of today.

THE
UNLOVED ONES

*

JON BURMEISTER

THE
COMPANION BOOK CLUB
LONDON

This edition, published in 1973 by
The Hamlyn Publishing Group Ltd,
is issued by arrangement with
Michael Joseph Ltd.

THE COMPANION BOOK CLUB

The Club is not a library; all books are the
property of members. There is no entrance fee
or any payment beyond the low Club price of
each book. Details of membership will gladly
be sent on request.

Write to:
The Companion Book Club,
Borough Green, Sevenoaks, Kent

*Made and printed in Great Britain
for the Companion Book Club
by Odhams (Watford) Ltd.*

600871576
1.73/257

This one is for
RICK and **PENNY**
from their proud father

AUTHOR'S NOTE

OFFICIAL RECORDS seem remarkably silent on the point of how le Clerc paid his magnificent native troops after hiking them nearly clean across the 'top' of Africa to join the British for the assault on the Mareth Line. If, therefore, I have taken somewhat of a liberty in suggesting that le Clerc's pay-roll, or at least part of it, came to grief in the Tibesti mountains, at least it can be said in my favour that I am not refuting history but filling in what appears to me to be a blank space.

If I have added to history I have also slightly embellished the geography of the Tibesti. In other words you will not find Zufra on a map, but it is typical of an oasis of these parts.

Some readers may query the present-day value of Metropolitan francs issued so long ago, but they are in truth perfectly valid tender. They were replaced, of course, by the 'new' franc; and naturally the franc also devalued, but nevertheless a pay-roll of the size involved in this book would be well worth seeking.

As always, I am indebted to people for really helpful advice during the tedious months required to research and write *The Unloved Ones*. My thanks go to my good friend of many years, Les Kietzmann, and the French Bank of Southern Africa Limited, for their helpful assistance in relation to currency matters; Ray Weir, who has forgotten more about aero and other engines than most people know; and a host of others who helped in small but important ways.

JON BURMEISTER
East London, South Africa

GLOSSARY

CHECHE: A linen cloth used wound about the face for protection against sand, wind, etc.

ERG: Soft, dune sand.

GUELTA: A pool, often rock-bound, usually small.

GUERBA: A water container made of the skin of a goat, suitably stitched.

GHUSSUB: A sort of gruel which is the staple diet of the Touareg, especially those living in the more remote areas.

HAMMADA: Hard, stony terrain.

LITHAM: The face-piece of the Touareg veil.

OUED: A narrow dry river bed or defile, called a *wadi* in Libya.

REG: Hard, firm sand on which vehicles can obtain surprisingly high speeds.

TAKATKAT: The Touareg cloak.

SOUS-PRÉFET: A sort of District Officer, with considerable powers, who administers a specific region or area.

TOUBOU: The indigenous but nomadic inhabitants of the Tibesti, markedly different from the Touareg and for that matter other Sahara peoples. Basically Negroid in appearance, it is possible that they stem from the original first inhabitants of the country.

TIFINAK: The Touareg language.

PROLOGUE

THE PLANE had the circling, idle, predatory stillness of a vulture. It had come down from six thousand feet, perpetually dropping its sharp nose, howling in brief bursts of power but mostly droning on the lap of a warm updraft of air. Then it seemed to home. It tightened its orbit until after fifteen minutes what had been a loose circumnavigation became, on one triumphant bellow of exhaust, a downward swooping upon a central point so precise that its movement had the neatness of a circus ring.

The circle broke momentarily. The plane drummed away, quite low and never losing its decision. There was no element of uncertainty about it. It gained a little height, then came back in a tight turn, lowered its wheels like claws, dropped the light feathers of its flaps and touched down in a shower of sand that left behind the slight churn of its passing. It slowed, nosed about a moment, then taxied into the mouth of an *oued*, swinging about quickly behind the silvery disc of its propeller so that it faced the way it had come.

The motor cut. The propeller feathered. In almost the same moment the pilot's door opened and he got out; stiffly, because the years were telling. His nose resembled the beak of an eagle, his black hair only slightly flecked with grey. His belly was board-flat, the legs under light tan trousers lean and athletic. But the stiffness lay in the nearly fifty years within him. He flexed his shoulders, wound his arms around a few times. He looked about him, at the hard *reg*, the firm sand of the Sahara, upon which he had landed. He studied the gnarled brown outcrop of rock that tiered on one side, the climbing dune on the other, that made an exclusive gully of this *oued* that sheltered his plane. He smiled, showing very white teeth. Then he spoke aloud to the silence of the Sahara.

'You don't make the same mistake twice. Hello, Dolly. I don't like you any more than I did last time.'

It was very hot. His mouth was dry for two reasons. The

9

heat and his excitement. He lit a cigarette all the same, because he never smoked when he flew and he had some hours behind him. He let the grey dull smoke roll over his palate for a moment. Then he walked back to the plane, clambered on to a wing and stared into the brittle bright distance. That way. He jumped down and peered through a window into the cabin. He could see in the shadowed interior the disembowelled radio that he had personally destroyed. This was an unauthorized flight and he had ripped its guts out shortly after leaving Tamanrasset. It had been a silly action which he now regretted, something done in the heat of the moment so that he wouldn't have to listen to them yelling at him in French to come back. *Sorry chaps, my radio packed up.* To hell with the French, anyway. They didn't really care. They were pulling out. Algeria was a big sore inside them and they were in the process of giving up all the *Territoires du Sud.*

He shrugged. Too late now. 'Let's go,' he said aloud, concealing the excitement within him. He began to walk, out of the *oued* until he got past the flanking rocks. Then he swung to his left, trudging over country. The rock, the sand, even the sprinkling of vegetation away behind him in the distance wasn't green, it was grey. Might be a *guelta* that way, he thought idly, but it was a thought lost in the torrent of his excitement. *She's over there somewhere. I saw the old bitch from the air. Always thought I could find her.*

He walked for little over a mile, an incongruous figure trudging all alone through an eternal vastness in his casual but expensive clothes. He was very aware of the silence which was absolute except for the faint scuffle of his shoes. It frightened him a little. That other time: it was one of the things he still remembered.

The mouth of an *oued* intruded. He stopped, his heart beginning to thud. Hell, it looked so narrow. But this was the one. He was positive. His sense of locality had always been faultless. He looked along it, his quick, sharp airman's eyes jumping from rock wall to rock wall, all the way along the *oued*'s two hundred yards of length until they slammed up against its closed end, instantly seeing the angular and unnatural jumble of deeper brown there.

He had to restrain himself. The inclination was to bound

forward, hallooing his delight, hearing his voice bound from wall to wall. *Twenty-four years and I found it, first try.* But he muzzled this instinct. Instead he looked down at his slim, expensively-clad feet. He talked to himself for a moment, regulating his breathing, eventually hearing his heart slow down. Then he took a slow, deep breath and began to move forward in regular, measured strides that took him down the *oued* without the drama and exertion of his first impulse. Halfway down he came upon a segment of wing lying up against the rock face. Its ragged edges sparkled where the paint had been knocked off, they twinkled with points of reflected sunlight. Nothing rusted in the desert. God knows, he thought, how I got her in here, but there was nowhere else to put her down.

A little further on he discovered footprints. They were quite clear. One set was neat and distinct, the other slightly blurred. They went on a parallel course, heading out of the *oued*. It gave him a small fright until he turned about and fitted one of his feet into the clearer pattern. Then he realized that the footprints were his own, made twenty-four years ago. His fright, if anything, increased. *Mine; mine and the kid's.* God, nothing changed in the desert, these footprints were frozen in time. He shook his head and walked on.

The Dakota lay hard up against the end of this natural cul-de-sac, concertinaed from the force of the impact, moulding its camouflage with these desert browns. He reached it and stopped. He was suddenly uncertain and uneasy. It could have crashed yesterday. There were tracks around the open doorway in the fuselage that culminated in four small mounds a few yards away. They were graves. At the head of each was a small clumsy cross, hastily made from bits and pieces of metal tied with cord. He knew; he'd made them himself. Two for the guards, a brace of young infantry lieutenants whose names he had never known. He had buried them complete with their dog-tags and the Webley revolvers they carried that had white lanyards attaching them like umbilical cords to the men who wore them. Both the lieutenants had died on impact, lying broken and twisted amongst the jumble of seats. The third grave was for the navigator, whose neck had been broken. The fourth—the last—was for the co-pilot whose head had been smashed open by the buckling instrument panel. He had been eyeless and noseless, but it had taken him three hours to die.

The pilot sighed. He had known neither of these men, they'd been a scratch crew thrown together for one solitary operation. He tried to force himself out of the grip of a sudden depression but the mood was strong. After he had buried the men, he and the kid had simply walked out. It sounded so easy, but the kid had four broken ribs and a badly sprained ankle. Progress was a deadly snail-like crawl of hours that lengthened into days, baking under the giant brass hand of the sun and freezing in the desert's icy night air until the water ran out. Then the kid became delirious and time and direction were gone; until one day when they were reduced to crawling on their bellies he found himself staring at the hairy two-toed foot of a camel, six inches from his eyes. He had looked up slowly, disbelievingly, ever upward it seemed into the dark, astonished face of a *goumier*, who had taken them back to his patrol. The water had tasted like nectar and . . .

He shook himself abruptly. He said aloud, sharply, 'Come on!' and moved forward to the wreck, stooped and entered through the open doorway. At once the sun was cut off and he was in a hot gloom. Prickly sweat had broken out all over his body. He could feel it running from his armpits down his sides under the light shirt. Slowly, stumbling over bits and pieces of wreckage, he made his way aft to the tail section, seeing the tarpaulin still there, crumpled, feeling his heart miss and thud with excitement. Then he had reached it, wrenched it aside to expose the two large leather suitcases lying next to one another. They had broken their lashings and slid forward on impact, that was all. They were undamaged. Bending, he fumbled at the catches, his sweating fingers sliding off the smooth silver metal, scrabbling at them until it dawned upon him that they were locked. He cursed savagely and stood up. There were plenty of makeshift jemmies lying around. He could have smashed the locks with ease but he did not want to. And he knew where the keys were, anyway. He turned abruptly and was gone through the doorway into the sun, returning after fifteen minutes shuddering over the horror of what he'd had to do. Fate had played a grim trick. It had been the second of the two lieutenants who had had the keys, so that he had been forced to open two graves. And the bodies had been partly mummified. . . .

But he had the keys. They lay shining in his shaking palm, frozen in furbished brightness by the dry desert. Fumbling, he fitted one to the first suitcase and opened the locks. Immediately, this time, the latches flew up under the pressure of his thumbs. Quickly, he snatched up the lid.

'Christ!'

The suitcase contained money, a beautiful rectangular sea of notes bundled and banded and as crisp as the day they had left the mint.

He shook. He picked out some of the packages, riffled them like packs of cards, put them back again. Francs, French franc notes, all of high denominations. He made quick mental calculations while opening and checking the other suitcase. About a hundred thousand quid all told, perhaps more. Lying here twenty-four years, waiting for any wandering nomad Toubou hunting a lost camel, a patrol of *goumiers* or *Maharistes*. He shuddered at the possibility.

Elation, oddly, made him calm. He scrubbed sweat from his forehead with a quick purposeful swipe of a nervous forearm. Time was pressing. He had a long way to go. It took a moment to lock the cases and pocket the keys. Then he stood up, holding them firmly, surprised at their weight. For a moment he was tempted to go forward and inspect the cockpit. It would be interesting to know by what miracle he had been left unscratched in his pilot's seat when the others had been injured or killed. Then he shook his head. No. There simply wasn't the time.

Carrying the suitcases, he left the Dakota and headed out along the *oued* back towards his plane, leaving a new trail of footprints beside those others that were twenty-four years old.

It took him an hour to walk the mile. The elation rapidly gave way to a sudden and surprising exhaustion. He had to rest often, dropping the suitcases heavily upon the sand, sweating unnaturally even in this desperate heat, snorting through his nostrils like a played out horse. But eventually he reached his plane. He wanted to slump in its shade but he had never been one to do things in half-measures. For five minutes he toiled, heaving the cases into the cockpit and then sliding them down to the tail section where he covered them with blankets and his own gear. He knew that at Tamanrasset all he would get was an official strip torn off him; it was only in Algiers that there would be any cause for mild concern but he was not particularly worried. He had a contact there. The right money in the right place and he could get away without an inspection. Damn it, he was Sir Peter Adair Teefer, baronet, and this alone would go a long way towards stilling suspicion. His French was perfect. His manner would be one of calm and rather guilty frankness. *Just a quick dip into the interior, old boy. Couldn't resist it. Flew there during the war, you know. Pranged once and had the deuce of a job getting out.*

He grinned with strong confidence. No more playing the gentleman Virginian, polo and all that, while his rich bitch of a wife counted his allowance and cut it whenever she caught him making out with somebody's pretty daughter. I'm on my own, he thought, independent at last. I did a dirty job in London for Jane which will ensure her everlasting gratitude and on top of that I can cut loose without worrying about the fact that when she dies her money is going to go to a lot of idiots I've never even met.

He was very tired, but at the same time content. He went back to the cockpit, slumped in his seat, fished out his water-bottle, drank greedily. He switched on the ignition, tried the starter. The engine caught at once. The propeller swung, hesitated and became a bright shining disc before him.

Sir Peter Teefer smiled. *Good old cow. Never let me down yet.* He was ready to taxi out of the *oued* when he began to shake in his seat. For a fraction of a second he had a moment of intense personal fright because he thought his heart had given in and was trying to jump out of his body. His body was juddering, it was being flung about. The desert beyond the wind-screen was rocking, jouncing, tumbling.

It came to him, then, that there were two engines—his and the plane's. At the same time he heard the ugly, smashing, rending sounds from without as though the plane were trying

14

to tear itself apart. He realized that the aircraft was rocking as though in a great, wild sea. He saw the instrument panel and the fittings in front of him blue from the incredible violence of the vibration. In that moment he knew, and instinctively cut the ignition, leaning forward weakly, hearing the death-throes die away until there was a stillness that was a part of the desert itself.

Long moments passed. Then he sat up. He passed a fore-arm across his forehead to wipe away the sweat. He looked back at the dark after part of the body where the suitcases were stowed and shook his head in a brief, desolate bitterness. 'Oh my God, not now. Why now?'

He got up slowly, all his movements stiff and mechanical. He rummaged around, found the tool-kit, opened the cabin door, jumped down on to the smooth hot sand. He walked like an animated dummy to the cowling, opened it, delved for the necessary tools and slowly and without haste removed the rocker cover from the number one piston.

There was no tension in the exhaust valve spring. The body of the valve was dangling loosely. He knew, after one touch of a long exploring finger, exactly what had happened. He was not expert on engines, but it was patently obvious. The valve head had broken off. There was a latent defect somewhere, some-thing no one, not even the most expert of mechanics, could have picked up before this crisis came. The valve at normal operating speeds heated up until it glowed cherry-red; the cooling of the engine in the three hours he had been away would have allowed for the last bit of expansion which would cause the valve head to snap like a carrot upon re-starting. His mind traced the logical pattern: the valve head would drop into the cylinder and be smashed up and down, causing irrevocable damage to the piston and connecting rod.

There was no need to examine any further. It was one of those things, that was all. He dropped the wrench he was holding so that it fell with a clang upon the rest of the tool-kit. He looked up at the desert sky, very slowly, studying it, think-ing how nearly he had been a part of it. He walked away from the ruined engine, out into the heavy brittle beat of the sun. He put his hands on his hips and shook his head.

'What an utterly unbelievable balls-up.'

It was typical of him that his first inclination was to laugh. Things had gone too well. If he had stopped at any time, he thought, and listened carefully, perhaps he might have heard the Gods laughing.

He was at a loss for a while. Automatically he checked his supplies. All he had was a two-gallon jerry-can of water in addition to his half-empty water bottle, two small tins of condensed milk, a packet of bouillon cubes and a tube of Lifesavers. There was a lot of instant energy around, he thought dryly, and as far as water was concerned he was not particularly worried. That trace of vegetation a few miles away made him fairly certain that, even with his limited knowledge of the desert, there would be a *guelta*, a rocklined pool fed from beneath by a spring, somewhere in that direction. In any case, the French would find him soon. The only immediate difficulty was the money. How the hell could he transfer two suitcases containing a hundred thousand quid to a rescue aircraft?

The thought made him shrug. So it was his gear. They would hardly be likely, in the circumstances, to make a sort of impromptu customs inspection on the spot. Far from it. He would trudge across to the arriving plane, sling his suitcases in and join them as part of one movement. He'd carried off this sort of thing before. The Teefer family, for all its lineage, had not been well-heeled for more than a century and was renowned for its ability to handle tight situations which were usually of a financial nature.

He had a meal of sorts: half a cup of water and two Lifesavers. He wasn't hungry anyway. Then he sat in the artificial shade cast by one wing, smoked a cigarette and let the time run by. He was a relaxed man, mostly, with a mind that did not project. But he was far from stupid and as the afternoon ran by he began to toss small equations into his mind: he had made an unauthorised flight from 'Tam'. So he was gone, somewhere, but the French wouldn't know where. They were very good with their administration, even if they were pulling out. They would try to find him, especially knowing who he was, but it would take time. They would have to piece together information from their desert patrols, this in turn possibly garnered from nomads and camel-herds and oasis people. It dawned on him with a small fluttering in his belly that rescue was not an automatic thing, an Alouette dropping from the sky and a crew running towards him with Gallic cries of welcome.

He realized this rather slowly, because a shallow mind is often slow, but when he accepted it, it was to his credit that he did not in any way surrender to panic. Instead he reacted practically, tramping out, for more than an hour, a huge S.O.S. panel on the sand. After that he got back into the plane and, forearmed by the horror of his experience twenty-four years before, built a snuggery behind the seats out of the two blankets he had, a small canvas and bits and pieces of gear. It would hardly suffice, he knew, but it was better than nothing. He might not be warm but at least he would not freeze.

After that he had time on his hands. Immediately he became aware of a quickness of breath, sweat on his palms, a tight feeling in his chest. There was no point in a perpetual squint at the gunmetal heavens so he found his log-book, sat down under the shade of a wing again and wrote firmly on a blank page: WHAT A BLOODY SHOWER. I WILL NOT WALK OUT AGAIN. TOO GHASTLY LAST TIME.

He read this, then heavily underscored the last two sentences. He put the book down, thought a moment, then accepted the fact that he was undoubtedly agitated. So he got up and found the small medicine kit. It consisted of nothing more than two bandages, burn jelly, iodine, a tube of lip-ice and some aspirin. He took three aspirin with a swig of water and settled down under the wing again with a rolled blanket as a pillow.

Sleep came unexpectedly. Prolonged excitement had led to exhaustion, and fright coming on top of the exhaustion had greatly increased it. So he slept heavily, helped by the mild analgesic of the aspirin, until he awoke freezingly cold and saw by the pattern of stars overhead and the graveyard luminescence of his wristwatch that it was ten o'clock. He crawled miserably into his snuggery in the plane but he was still frantically cold and sleep now came only in fitful dozes accompanied by frightful nightmares. He welcomed dawn, emerging into a grey monotony of landscape, lighting a cigarette and tasting the bitterness of the tobacco upon a jaded tongue. He felt stiff and depressed. Half a cup of water

17

and a cloying mouthful of condensed milk did nothing to ease either condition so he sat under the wing, smoked another cigarette and stared out of the *oued*.

He was surprised at how quickly the day passed, considering that he did nothing except wait for rescue, a rescue which he knew logically, could not yet be expected. And yet in no time the night was back and he had to face another few hours in the torture-chamber of the plane. This time he ripped the coverings off the seats and added them to his bedclothes. He slept hardly at all.

The morning of the third day brought a small mental deterioration. He was perfectly sane; but he was inclined to speak out loud, small grievances mostly connected with the inefficiency of the French. He caught himself doing this in the afternoon. He stopped suddenly, got into the plane and looked at himself in the mirror. He was astonished at the haggard face staring back at him, fuzzed with three days of black beard. The eyes seemed small, set above puffed pouches of swollen skin. He had a razor, of course. Taking quite a lot of time, he produced this, brought out the jerry-can and discovered that it was empty. He had been replenishing his water bottle from it. Going to the water bottle, he shook it and heard its contents sloshing shallowly around the bottom.

He spoke aloud again. 'That's bloody nice,' he said. 'That's bloody marvellous.'

It was three-thirty. He simply snatched up the jerry-can and the water bottle and walked straight away from the plane, heading for the tracery of vegetation in the far distance. He was gone a very long time. He returned only at about one o'clock in the morning, staggering, threading his way back along his footsteps by the light of an obliging moon. But the jerry-can and the water bottle were full. He had found the *guelta*, drunk from it until he was heavy with water, flung himself fully clothed into it despite the cooling of approaching dusk.

But most of this benefit had been lost on the return trip of ten miles or more and his pace had been distressingly slow.

Despite the cold, he slept heavily for six hours and woke in sunlight. He was weak and his middle-aged body felt bruised. He got up slowly, stood on the sand outside the plane and said aloud without any emotion. 'If they don't find me soon I'm finished.'

This was the fourth day. Again it passed without incident, except that at about five o'clock in the afternoon he felt compelled to do something and wrote in his log-book: SHIT, THIS IS BORING.

That night he suffered more than ever from the cold and slept a total of about two hours. He had nothing to read and he knew that if he had, he would have found it difficult to concentrate. The morning brought about a change in his attitude. Weakness gave way to a small sense of exhilaration because his body had rid itself of all its toxins. But this did not last. In the afternoon he began talking out loud again and was not aware of it. He pottered about the aircraft making silly little adjustments which were of no consequence. He drank a great deal of water and in the evening consumed the rest of the Lifesavers as if they were a meal and then finished a complete tin of condensed milk.

He made another trip to the *guelta*, renewing his water supply. But he struggled home at nearly three o'clock, the instant energy of the milk and the sweets completely burnt out by his effort. He collapsed in his snuggery and did not sleep at all, lying there shivering until the sun broke out and he realized that he was not prepared to look at himself in the mirror.

This was the fifth day. He made a small fire out of wooden fittings ripped from the plane's interior, boiled water in a tin cup and added one of the bouillon cubes. It was heavily salted but delightful, replacing without his awareness much of the salt he had lost from constant perspiration. Finishing off his meal with some condensed milk as a sweet, he felt greatly restored, so much so that in the middle of a cigarette he made a sudden, impulsive decision. He jumped to his feet, found his water-bottle and headed out abruptly in a ground-consuming stride, aiming west, whereas the *guelta* lay due north.

'Tomorrow,' he said aloud to the great emptiness, 'I'll try the south.'

It was nearly midnight when he returned. He was mumbling and exhausted, staggering like a drunk, yet obviously caught up in some considerable excitement. He got into the plane, fumbled on the interior light in the cabin, found the jerry-can and drank greedily. Then he got out his log-book and wrote in rather shaky capital letters: SHADES OF P. C. WREN!

He appeared to want to write more. But total weariness overcame him. His eyes drooped, his head nodded. He let the log drop, crawled into his meagre blanket nest and fell asleep.

On the sixth day he saw the jet. It boomed overhead, a needle-nosed Mirage with French markings, leaving a long brown contrail of waste gases that marred the faultless purity of the sky.

Teefer ran out from under the wing where he had been boiling water for another breakfast of bouillon. He tossed the tin cup aside, howling at the jet as it dwindled, screaming imprecations when it became a tiny speck and finally disappeared, leaving behind only the lingering thunder of its passing that rolled amongst the mountains in the distance.

He was more normal, at this stage, than he had been for three days. He returned briskly to the fire, kicked it out, took up his water bottle and strode without hesitation to the *oued* where the Dakota lay in crumpled isolation. This time he did not pause at the strange timeless magic of the place. He went directly inside, came out with a jagged but stout piece of metal and gouged a great hole in the starboard fuel tank, jumping aside as the high octane spattered out in a silver shower. Hastily he took out his matches, lit one, and tossed it into the sand at the end of the spurting torrent. In the same moment he was turning away, running, hands about his head while the petrol-stink filled his nostrils. He was still running when the tank went up with a giant 'woosh' of sound and a force-wall flung him down on the hot sand. But he lay there, grinning, feeling the violent heat of the fire searing his skin, his eyes not on the plane but on the tremendous column of black petrol-smoke that was climbing directly into the heavens.

There was no need to stay. It was too hot there, anyway, in the narrow confines of the cul-de-sac. He walked back to his plane and watched with great satisfaction the way the smoke climbed and climbed, filthy-black with carbon, rising a thousand feet or more.

It was only eleven o'clock in the morning. The Dakota burned and the smoke rose constantly while he watched it with an almost paternal eye; it was *his* plane, and its funeral pyre would bring help from the planes that were now obviously in the area. It rose while noon came and he consumed the rest of the second tin of condensed milk, his eyes alternating from the smoke column to an almost microscopic searching of the heavens. It rose until three o'clock in the afternoon. Then it unexpectedly tailed away and died. The last treacle-coloured puff drifted away in the direction of the Libyan border. And an hour later he heard the chuffing sound of a helicopter somewhere up above.

He ran out into the bronzed sun-beat, instantly seeing it like a drowsy dragonfly over to the north just beyond the *guelta*. It was an Alouette, a big one, stoutly puffing over a rim of hills. He waved and shouted but it went on and was finally gone.

For the first time in more than thirty years, Peter Teefer wept. He cried great globules of tears, turning his face to the sky as though it were rain beating on his face and crying, 'Oh Christ, you have deserted me!'

From that moment his mental deterioration became rapid. He crouched under the wing until the sun had gone. When it grew cold he ripped more wood from the plane and made another fire, standing tensely about it, prowling out into the darkness momentarily and returning shivering. He jittered about, rapidly smoking the last five cigarettes left to him and becoming more and more excited. He burst out suddenly into a recitation of Kipling's *Never the Twain Shall Meet*, reciting it more or less faultlessly from the memory of some long-gone classroom until he broke off quite aberratedly and began to sing. This went on for some time. Finally he retreated out of animal instinct into the den behind the seats, where for hours he carried on a rambling and angry conversation with some phantom figure of his mind. In the end, sleep took him.

The seventh day was unknown to him. He sat crouched during daylight under the wing, totally silent, his eyes staring blankly across the desert. He did not eat. And when nightfall came he retired to the plane and fell into a sleep that was semi-consciousness.

On the morning of the eighth day he was sane. The *cafard* had left him but he suspected its occurrence and guessed that he had lost a day, perhaps more, to madness. But although his senses had returned to normal his spirit had gone. He had no more food. There was water but he did not have the energy or the inclination to fetch it. He had, in every sense of the word, given in. The search was over. There would be no more planes. Influenced by that event twenty-four years ago, he had made the wrong decision in staying by his plane.

He took the blankets from the plane and sat on them for more than an hour in calm and silent conjecture. Then he took his log-book and wrote, with a small smile: IN HIS LAST BINN SIR PETER LIES.

He propped the book on the blanket nest, dragged the suit-cases out of the plane and dropped them on the sand. Then from his jacket which had been lying on one of the seats he took a manilla envelope, extracted a set of photographic negatives and burned them methodically. When they were gummy ash he said reflectively, 'Well, there you are, Jane'. Then took the lip-ice from the medicine kit and, at last giving way to some sort of emotion, wrote with it on the windscreen in sweeping strokes: I'VE HAD IT.

He dropped the lip-ice on the sand, picked up the two suit-cases and walked away from the plane, striking due west the way he had on the fifth day.

CHAPTER ONE

THE LAND-ROVER LURCHED. Its wheels spun. It dug quickly into the soft sand. But it had a small measure of forward momentum and in this moment Lassiter shoved the gear lever into extra low. He let the clutch out with a thump and fed petrol heavily to the engine. The big vehicle hesitated for a fraction of a second. All four tyres spat and in angry showers. Then they found purchase and it barrelled its way across the patch while Lassiter, relieved and concerned at the same time, signalled frantically out of the window to the truck behind him, a stiff arm waved up and down that meant *fesh-fesh*, powder-soft sand. But even while he signalled, his rear-view mirror showed the second Land-Rover burrow in and root like a hog, its wheels settling while sand spun silver in the sun like metal particles flung from a grindstone. The vehicle bogged. Its engine gave a few little grunts of expended exhaust and then cut out.

Lassiter stopped on hard sand and got out. He trotted back a way, sinking up to his ankles and heaving his way to the second Land-Rover. There he thrust his sweating, angry red face into the driver's window and said very loudly, 'John-oh, won't you ever learn sense?'

Dark eyes glared back at him. 'Lew, you know you can't tell *fesh-fesh* until you're in it. You signalled too late!'

Lassiter scrubbed sweat from his forehead with an irritable forearm. 'Nobody had to signal me.' He turned away, heading back for his own vehicle. 'Let's get the ladders.'

The occupants of both vehicles began to alight. From John-oh's came Lola Nailand and her two children, Catherine —called Thrin—and Neil, followed by their step-father, Joe Nailand. Lassiter had only two passengers: Lady Teefer and her companion, Susan Shields. These two met him as he reached his Land-Rover and began to unstrap the metal ladders from the roof.

'This is the third time today and it's not noon.' The older

woman's voice was sharp, strongly American. 'Where in tarnation are your goddam eyes, Lassiter?'

Lassiter had a headache. His mood was ragged. The first ladder came loose and the hinge in its middle pinched his finger. His temper boiled over. There was a collection of very rude words on his tongue and he was about to let them go when he saw the small sideways movement of Susan Shield's head. So instead he cursed silently and let the sand ladder drop recklessly with a metal rattle on to the sand. Then he said abruptly, 'It's John-oh's car, ma'am, not mine.'

Lady Teefer looked directly into Lassiter's face. But her eyes were dull and clouded. They appeared to gaze beyond him somewhere into the distance. She smiled a little. Animation came into the face but the eyes stayed the same. 'You were gonna swear at me, Lassiter, weren't you? And then Sue told you to hush.'

Lassiter made an obscene 'V' out of two fingers and held them a foot from her face. 'I wouldn't swear at you, Lady Teefer.'

Her face tightened. 'You're sayin' one thing and doin' another. I can tell.' She put out a beringed fist and punched him lightly on the chest. 'Down, Lassiter. Down, boy. I don't like my dogs a-jumping up at me.' Then she turned away and walked unsteadily towards the other Land-Rover. Joe Nailand came up and took her arm. She shook it off but he began to talk to her quietly.

Susan Shields moved up until her shoulder touched Lassiter's arm. 'When you t-talk the way you just did, she sus-suspects. She knows you're not humble like that. She sus-suspects that you're being an insincere b-b-bastard.'

Lassiter looked down at her. She stood ten inches shorter than his craggy six-feet-two. She had a girl's body and a small neat face. That and the slight stammer gave her a mark of childlike innocence until you looked into her eyes.

'I have my sincere days and my insincere days.' He kicked at the ladder. 'Would you mind bringing me some aspirin?'

She wanted to say more. Instead she shrugged. 'All right.'

Lassiter watched her go. John-oh came up. 'You want to handle this one, Lew?'

'No.' Lassiter looked back at the bogged vehicle. 'I'll drive.

You can do it with that lazy bastard Nailand. Better get going. The old bag is getting impatient.'

'You're telling me?' John-oh picked up the sand ladder. He turned to go and then hesitated. 'I'm sorry, Lew. I should have been more careful.'

Lassiter smiled. That was the trouble with John-oh. He was always sorry. Sorry I farted, sorry I knocked over the salt, sorry I was born. 'It's okay. I shouldn't have torn a strip off you, either. I've got a headache.'

The dark eyes in the swarthy face were soft like a woman's. 'I know. Take it easy tonight, Lew.'

Lassiter's face straightened. 'Don't presume upon a beautiful friendship.'

John-oh went away with the sand ladders. He said something to Nailand who scowled in Lassiter's direction. Then Nailand shrugged and went with John-oh to the back of the bogged vehicle. They got out spades and began to dig away the sand smothering around the wheels.

Lassiter lit a cigarette and studied the group around the other Land-Rover. He thought about Algiers, where John-oh had joined them. They had stayed there only three days and then flown to Tamanrasset in a rattle-trap Dakota crammed with peasant women and a cock that crowed loudly for half an hour and then died of a heart attack.

Tamanrasset, and a memory mainly of the great Hoggar mountains. This was where he had started to learn about his party, because until then with the exception of John-oh they had been just names attached to faces. One night there, a very good meal in the *Café et Restaurant du Hoggar* where Nailand had succeeded in eating himself into a state of dull-eyed torpescence and become quarrelsome over after-dinner cognacs and called his wife a bitch. The children had watched in their ever-silent, inscrutable way, and John-oh had got up in the middle of his drink and walked out.

Lesson One learned, and this crazy expedition not yet really started. The next day, a long hop from Tamanrasset to Djanet, where John-oh had arranged for the Land-Rovers to be waiting, a bumpy flight in the same Dakota during which Nailand vomited messily and Lady Teefer had to have heart pills.

Djanet: more memories. Lordly Ajjer Touareg, immensely tall indigo-clad men, veiled to their light-coloured eyes that looked out upon the world with self-complacent superiority, feudal masters of the Tassili plateau. Daylight, paying off the Algerian drivers and getting the Land-Rovers ready. Joe Nailand seated in a camp chair taking colour photographs, barking at his wife who carried and pushed and loaded, red-faced and sweating like the rest of them, meekly hewing wood and drawing water the way Nailand wanted. John-oh watching Nailand with his dark eyes. The children helping, but disturbingly silent, too mature in their inscrutability.

Night-time, too much to drink, the filtered moonlight of a palm grove, a conversation with Susan Shields that was a conversation one moment and an embrace the next, a consummation in him of fierce for ever loneliness, a joy, a deep wanting, a desire to stop time.

Lessons and memories. Lessons Two, Three, Four and Five, learned. Daylight, and the deepest depression he had ever known. A memory of beauty, a memory of apparent innocence, a knowledge of innocence gone.

Daylight, depression, and the Tenere to face. The Tenere: about seven hundred miles of desolation abandoned by God and only reluctantly acknowledged by the Prophet because it contained some few thousand of his subjects.

Lassiter flicked away the cigarette. How the hell did we do it, he asked himself. But they had. The seven hundred miles were gone behind them in a blur of innumerable days, of fast exhilarating travel on *reg*, slow blundering through the dune country, *erg* as it was called, break-downs, digouts, the long freezing nights that made the clock crawl.

In these days of Independence you could try to cross the Sahara on a mo-ped or powered billiard table. The authorities didn't care a damn. But even in the rigid not long-gone days of French control, the Teefer expedition would never have been permitted to start. Its equipment was superb; it was its members that made it odd: three men, two children, two younger women and a woman of fifty-four who not only had a heart condition but a distinctly greater disability that would have made the French embargo the expedition categorically and unequivocally.

Lady Teefer was totally blind.

They had got through because of two things: luck, and John-oh's unerring sense of direction and knowledge of the desert. Lassiter sighed. It was all rather hard to believe. But the real purpose of the expedition had not yet even begun.

Susan Shields came back. She extended two white tablets on a smooth palm. 'Your aspirin, master.'

'Thanks.' He threw them back with a mouthful of water from the cup she gave him. John-oh was signalling to him from the bogged vehicle. The sand clogging the wheels had been cleared away to make deep channels in front of them. The ladders had been placed into position in the channels, rammed under the curve of the tyres. Everything was ready.

Lassiter gave her back the cup. 'You've got about seventeen years on me. Think you could lend a hand with the pushing?' She never did much unless she was asked. But she nodded indifferently and they went across together.

Lassiter walked into the group. He was quick now in his movements. He touched Lola Nailand lightly on the shoulder. 'You'll push, Lola, won't you?' He looked down a little. 'Neil and Thrin, too.' When he smiled at them his face changed. It softened. 'John-oh, you handle the starboard ladder, Nailand the left.' He got into the driver's seat, holding the door open with one hand. The motor started and he gunned it. 'All right? Let's go!'

The Land-Rover lurched forward. Sand spat in two fat fountains from its rear wheels, spraying the little group behind as they staggered along, slipping, standing again, arms outstretched, bodies arched, heaving at the vehicle's flat back. Nailand and John-oh waited on either side, squatting, eyes screwed up against the lesser sideways shower. The big tyres rolled the full length of the ladders, grinding them into the sand. Immediately Nailand and John-oh sprang forward, scrabbled for the ladders in the sand, dragged them out, rushed forward and flung them under the rear wheels again. Just in time, the tyres bit and the forward momentum continued.

Lassiter was looking back. He had one hand on the wheel, one keeping open the driver's door. He had to shout above the engine noise. 'Once more! Once more and we'll be okay!'

The tyres reached the end of the ladders. Again the two men snatched frantically behind the spinning wheels. John-oh got his ladder out, darted forward and rammed it into place. But Nailand tripped and fell sprawling. Gripping on only one side, the Land Rover began to slew.

Neil darted around from the back. He was small but correspondingly quick. He hurdled Nailand's prostrate body, heaved at the sand ladder, dragged it along beside him and flung it under the sinking wheel. There was a moment of agonising hesitation. Then the left tyre gripped. The big treads sank into the steel rungs. The Land-Rover straightened and lumbered the length of the ladders. Its front wheels found purchase on hard sand. With a triumphant roar of engine it clambered out of the patch and pulled up alongside the other truck.

The group came up panting and threw themselves on the sand. Lassiter got out. He was grinning. He went to Neil, bent, held him around his small bony shoulders. 'Well done, kid. I'm proud of you.'

The child looked into Lassiter's face. He had elephant-grey eyes like his sister. Something changed in them. It was a kindling of warmth. But he nodded, nothing more.

Nailand arrived. Sand had stuck to the sweat on his cheeks and chin so that he looked absurdly bearded. He went directly to Neil and pushed him roughly in the chest. The child staggered and went over on his back.

'You little bastard, you tripped me!'

Neil's face contorted momentarily. He stared at his step-father. His mother said nothing. Thrin said sharply, 'Neil!'

Neil looked at her. 'Come away, Neil.' She took his hand and pulled him to his feet. 'Let's look for flints. There might be some about.' Neil's face cleared instantly and they wandered away.

Lassiter said distinctly. 'Nailand, you tripped over your own flat feet.'

'All f-four of them.' It was Susan Shields. Normally she had little to say that did not concern her directly. Lassiter was mildly surprised.

Jane Teefer turned her sightless, clouded eyes on the girl. 'Have a care, young woman. You too, Lassiter. That's

28

my kin you're talking to. If their mother can't stand up for those two brats I don't see why you should.'

'Somebody has to.' Lassiter looked at Lola Nailand. It was a tragedy, he thought, that her beautiful statuesque body and lovely ageless features should be inhabited by a timid and cringing mentality.

She was fussing at her husband, dusting at his shirt ineffectually. Lassiter could see the fear in her eyes. She was afraid because Nailand was angry and might vent it on her.

'I'm sorry, darling. Is there anything I can get you?' Afraid and sorry. Always sorry. Sorry to be around, sorry to be alive, like John-oh.

Nailand pushed her away to stop her useless beating at his shirt. 'You can get me some water to wash this bloody sand off my face.' He turned his furious eyes on Lassiter and pointed an accusing finger. 'Some day you'll go too far, Lassiter.'

'Up yours.'

'Cut it out!' Jane Teefer got up slowly, her breathing short and quick. 'I can't stand this goddam quarrelling. You cause any more trouble, Lassiter, and I'll . . .'

Lassiter began to smile.

'You'll fire me?'

She considered this for a moment. 'All right. I get you. But leave Joe alone. He's my cousin and I respect him. He's got a damn-sight more brain than you'll ever have.' She fiddled in a pocket of her slacks, found a cigarette and lit it unerringly with a gold lighter. 'Now let's get going.' The dead eyes looked straight into Lassiter's face. 'When do we reach base? We're nearly there, aren't we?'

'More or less.' Lassiter looked at his watch. 'It's noon now. We're on the edge of the Tibesti. By about three this afternoon we should reach a *guelta* which is the axis of the probable area in which your husband came down. We can set up camp there.' He hesitated. 'That's the idea, anyway. We've left Zouar and gone south. We've swung short and wide and north-west of Bardai. But there is another oasis about sixty-five miles from the *guelta*. It's called Zufra. There's water there, fuel, a radio, even law and order in the shape of a *Sous-Préfet* and about twenty soldiers.' He tried to infuse a little enthusiasm into his voice. This goddam, crazy expedition. 'I still think it would be better to work from there. You have to consider the state of your health.'

She studied him from the depths of her world of darkness. 'We got enough food? Enough fuel?'

'Yes.' He made the admission reluctantly. 'Enough to make the daily probes which will be necessary to find your husband's . . . plane.' He deliberately avoided the word 'body'. 'For the return journey, though, we will need to call in at Zufra for fuel.'

'These probes.' She drew on her cigarette. 'How you gonna work them?'

Lassiter wished he could draw in the sand to show her. 'We will use the *guelta* as a hub, the way I have described. Each day the two Land-Rovers will drive out on a parallel course. They will go outward for half the day, then move across and probe inward again during the afternoon. It's a box search. John-oh and I have discussed it very carefully. As far as we can see it's the only way we can blanket the whole area. If we don't find Sir Peter's plane then it's covered by *erg*.'

'Like hell. It's there. I know it. I can feel it in my bones.' She blew out smoke that hung in the windless air. 'And if we set up base at Zufra, the way you recommend, then we've got to travel sixty-five miles every day before we even start work. Right?'

Lassiter nodded. 'Yes. But——'

'No buts.' She dropped her cigarette. Lassiter watched while her foot came out, circled a moment and then dropped on it, grinding it into the sand. 'We'll use the *guelta*. To hell with Zufra. Enough time's been wasted. Hell, my Peter's been lying out here four years. It's time we gave him a decent burial!' She put out a hand that reached up to his shoulder and squeezed it. 'Isn't that so, Lassiter? Isn't it time we gave Peter a grave?'

He shrugged away the hand. There she stood, slim as a girl in neat white slacks and white blouse with a red scarf tucked in at the throat. She belonged at a bridge table, or a meeting of the Daughters of the American Revolution, not standing here telling him for the hundredth time of the obsession that had brought them some thousand-odd miles across a dying land for a pointless and ridiculous purpose.

'Yes.' He said the words obediently, out of loyalty only to the handsome salary she was paying him. 'If we find him. The French couldn't.'

'Ahh, the hell with the French. They couldn't find their own ass-holes, the way they handled it. It was a token search. All they did was pin him down to this area of the Tibesti.' She hitched at her slacks. 'Girdle's killing me. I wouldn't wear it but there's nothing worse than a woman with a drooping backside, even an old bag like me.' Her voice sharpened. 'Come on, now! Get those kids back, somebody, and let's go.'

Lola Nailand was mopping the sand from her husband's face with a wet cloth. Neither of them paid any attention. It was Susan who called the children. They were fifty yards away but they turned at once, instantly obedient.

Lassiter waited until they arrived. 'Before we break up, there's something I'd like to mention.' He was mildly diffident. 'Did any of you see a camel rider last night, watching us from a ridge near the camp? It was dusk, but I was sure enough to wave him over. Instead he turned away and was gone.'

There was a common, contemplative silence. Then Jane Teefer said, 'At dusk, Lassiter, you were telling us the story of the little boy and the duck. It took you half-an-hour, and you kept losing the punch-line.'

There was another silence. Lassiter felt his face flush. 'Forget it. Let's get aboard.' The group broke up and scattered towards the vehicles.

Susan Shields walked next to him. 'You shouldn't have st-stuck your neck out. But if it's any help, I saw the man too.' A small smile tugged at her lips. 'It's not the D.T.s, Lew. Not yet.' Then she touched him lightly on the arm and was gone across the sand to guide Lady Teefer to the Land-Rover. The two Land-Rovers pulled up together about a quarter of a mile from the fort. Their eight occupants got out and stood momentarily silent, staring at the yellow building that crouched ahead of them beyond a stretch of open sand.

'I wouldn't have believed it.' Susan Shields was standing next to Lassiter. 'Where's Gary Cooper?'

'It's real, all right.' John-oh came up with a pair of

31

binoculars. He trained them briefly. 'No name that I can see. But there are many of these scattered around the Sahara. I have been in one, Fort Pacot near Chifra.'

'Is this one on the map?'

Lassiter had the map in his hands. He unfolded it with a dry crackle of stiff paper. 'No. The map is new and this place is obviously abandoned.'

Jane Teefer was holding Susan Shields's arm with her white hand. The sun threw tiny white points of fire off the rings on her fingers. There was so many of them, Lassiter thought, that she might have been wearing hand armour. Sterling, gold and diamond knuckles. But not brass. Not for Lady Teefer.

'What's it like, dammit?' She squeezed the girl's arm. 'Everybody yuck-yucking and nobody tells me a thing!'

'Ever read *Beau Geste* before you went blind? Ever see the movie? Or *Under Two Flags*, or *Morocco*, or *Garden of Allah*? There were er-er d-dozens of them. I saw *Under Two Flags* on late-night TV.'

Animation came to the face surrounding the blank eyes. Jane Teefer chuckled. 'Yeah, I saw *Morocco*. And the other one too. It was Victor McLaglen, wasn't it?'

The girl shrugged. 'I wouldn't know. But it's that kind of fort.'

Jane swung around. 'Where are you, Lassiter?' She was looking directly at him. It never failed to amaze him, this incredible sense of hers.

Lassiter said, 'I'm right here, Mrs Teefer.'

Jane bared her teeth. 'Don't you "Mrs Teefer" me! You know my goddam title. Use it.'

Lassiter pretended meekness. 'Yes, milady.'

The older woman growled in her throat. 'God, Lassiter if I had eyes! Stop taking the mickey out of me. Now where is this fort in relation to the *guelta*?' Lady Teefer stabbed a finger ahead of her straight at the gates.

'I'd say the *guelta* is about fifteen miles east-north-east from the fort.' He made a small conversion in his mind. 'About twenty-five kilometres, eh, John-oh?'

The dark young man thought about it, then nodded. 'Yes, about twenty-five kilometres. That's more or less the distance.'

Jane Teefer was pleased. 'Well, then, why can't we use the

fort as the central point—the hub, as you call it? Can't make much difference. And there'll be rooms there, and shade, places where we can sleep and eat without being jammed together next to some goddam water-hole.'

'That's a good idea.' Lassiter's eyes were on the fort. 'It may even have a well. If it hasn't it wouldn't be too much trouble to supplement our water from the *guelta*, whenever we need to. The thing is to go and have a look, isn't it?'

They got back in the Land-Rovers and accelerated across the four hundred yards or so of open sand, passing a few stunted and dying trees in a sad row and a small straggle of pallid vegetation before they slowed down and eased cautiously through the gates. John-oh revved his engine and switched off. He pointed excitedly through his open window as Lassiter drew up alongside. 'We got company, Lew!'

They alighted and joined together in an uncertain group, regarding with caution the shabby Land-Rover with its raised bonnet.

'It's from Algiers.' Nailand pointed to the registration plate under the rear fender.

'God knows how it ever got here.' Lassiter looked around, trying to fight off a feeling of unease.

Jane was frantic with impatience. 'What's it all about? Who's here? What's from Algiers?' She gripped Susan's arm fiercely. 'Earn your keep, girl!'

'There's a Land-Rover parked in the courtyard.' She had a way of droning graphically when she translated vision into words for her employer. 'Like ours, but about er, er, t-ten years old. Rusty, t-tattered. Somebody's been working on the engine. The bonnet's open. Tools scattered around on the sand.' The note of her voice changed. It became sharper. 'A man has just come out of one of the doorways. He's thin, sandy. Late forties, I should say. He's standing there s-staring at us. Now he's holding his chest. He's beginning to cough. You hear him cough, ma'am?'

The sandy-haired man coughed into the silence, on and on. Then he spat, wiped his mouth, straightened. Everyone stared at him. He said at last, hoarsely, 'Welcome to Fort Masuril. My name is Bowdrey, Bert Bowdrey. I'm an archaeologist of sorts.' He rubbed his chest with one freckled hand. It was a spasmodic movement. Then he dropped the arm and stood there, staring at them.

Lassiter took a step forward. He could sense the wave of resentment flowing across the sand. 'We're the Teefer expedition. We are——'

'I read about it. In the papers, before we left home.' Bowdrey had a broad north-country inflection. His eyes switched to Jane Teefer. 'You won't find your husband, madam, or his plane. I've covered this area with a toothcomb in the course of my work. If the plane is here it has been covered by the dunes. You should pack up and go back. You're wasting your time and endangering your health.'

Lassiter felt irritation wash over him. 'I think you should let us be the judges of that, Bowdrey.'

'Leave it, Lew.' Jane Teefer took a step forward. She looked stricken at what Bowdrey had said. But anger over-rode her shock and her disappointment. 'Mister, I never take what anyone says for granted. You haven't been looking for a plane, you've been digging up old bones or arrowheads.'

Bowdrey said quickly, 'We've been photographing rock carvings. The Tibesti are full of them.'

'So what? Carvings, schmarvings. How long you been here, huh?' She barked the question.

He hesitated a moment. 'Ten days.'

Jane produced a monkey-like grin. 'Then you haven't done any toothcombing, brother. I've seen the map. In relief, I mean, so I could feel it. In ten days you wouldn't have covered half of this area, with all the hundreds of canyons and arroyos and dried-out watercourses. They've got funny French names but that's what I call them. We're staying, mister.'

She lost some of her animation, developing a dogged rather blank look. She could have been reciting. 'I said I was going to find my Peter and give his bones a decent burial. Four years, he's been out here. I thought about it long and hard before I made my decision. I made it long before the papers got hold of it. And I intend to abide by it.'

Without warning she began to pant. Her skin paled visibly. 'Sue, get my pills. Quick.'

Lassiter dropped back. He took her arm. 'Come and sit down in the shade. You're dead beat.'

Jane shook herself loose. 'I haven't finished yet.' She talked to Bowdrey again. 'Something else. Do you own this fort? Did you buy it from the Republic of Chad?'

Bowdrey became visibly angry. 'That's a damn stupid question to ask——'

'Don't get rude!' Nailand bristled forward.

'Shut up, Joe.' Jane sucked for breath. 'So you don't own it, eh? Okay, do you mind if we move in? You haven't offered, so I've got to ask. Should be plenty of room if it's like the forts I've seen on the movies. Enough for a garrison of soldiers. And there's only eight of us besides you.'

Bowdrey began to tremble. 'We got here first! You've no right to barge in here, shoving us around because you've lots of money and a title to go with it! Why bugger it——'

'Stop it, Bert!'

Bowdrey was cut off in mid-sentence. He subsided. All of them swung their heads. The woman stood in an arched doorway a few yards away. She was very composed and quiet. Hair like pale young corn hung below her shoulders. A silly apron partly covered a cheap cotton frock. She was barefooted. But she had an instant dignity. To Lassiter, absorbing her, she gave the impression of being able to let life have its pauses when she wanted.

Joe Nailand broke the silence bluntly. 'Who're you?'

The woman came out into the sun. Her bare feet were tanned the same light biscuit of her arms. 'I am Ann Bowdrey. Bert's wife.' Her eyes flicked quickly to him where he stood sullenly silent. Then she spoke to Jane. 'Of course you can move into the fort, Lady Teefer. We couldn't stop you. But you're welcome anyway.' She paused, looking at each of them in turn. 'I think we've all said enough. Would anyone like some tea?'

CHAPTER TWO

QUICK DARKNESS HAD COME. Night was a black oblong in the doorway, the lazy hiss of the Coleman lamp, a smell of curry in the cold air.

Ann Bowdrey snapped off her torch as she entered the room.

She came silently across the eddied sand on the floor to join the seven people who sat on camp chairs in a loose ring about a paraffin heater.

Susan Shields said politely, 'Thank you for stacking the dishes.'

'It was nothing.' Ann Bowdrey sat down next to her husband. 'Bert and I very much appreciate Lady Teefer having asked us to join you at meals. Our stocks are rather limited.'

Bowdrey was full of good food and unaccustomed whisky. It had mellowed him. 'Aye. It was a kind thought, Lady Teefer.'

Jane smirked. 'A drop of kindness never did any harm. John-oh!'

The dark young man leapt from his chair. 'Yes, ma'am?'

'Break out some more liquor, you goddam Ay-rab. Where your manners?' Her dull eyes circled the group. 'We're all gonna have another round.' She smiled a little threateningly. 'Anyone who don't want to join me can git the hell outta here.'

Joe Nailand laughed. He had eaten and drunk heavily. 'You're the essence of politeness, my dear Jane.'

The older woman turned her blue-dyed head and looked directly at him. 'Don't presume, even if you are my kin.' To the Bowdreys she added, casually, 'No offence. It's just my way.'

John-oh came around the circle with a tray of drinks. Bowdrey took his. Ann, slightly flushed, shook her head. John-oh muttered, 'You heard Lady Teefer,' and pressed the glass into her hand.

Against the cold of the desert night she had changed into a tweedy skirt, neat woollen cardigan, socks and flat-heeled brown lace-up shoes. She still retained the settled calm of the barefooted girl in the courtyard, she still held her body with a passive, loose authority. But in the more formal clothes, with the flaxen hair clubbed at the neck, she had lost that look of a blonde Brünnhilde of the dunes. Her eyes had developed warmth and her cheeks were flushed.

'Your good health, Lady Teefer.' She sipped her drink.

'Toasting me ain't gonna improve it.' Jane raised her glass

in a beringed hand. It was here her age showed, in the tiny deep ugly creases that extended to the fingernails. It showed here rather than in the smooth white face with the dead eyes that gave a false look of youth. 'I'm blind and I've got a heart condition. At fifty-four. I reckon the Lord was looking the other way when he passed out bodies and mine came by.'

There was a small silence. Ann Bowdrey said to Susan, 'I would like to help you wash the dishes.'

'Forget it. It's all part of the job. It's in the contract.'

Jane cawed. 'Contract, schmontract. Talking of jobs, what's your husband do, Mrs Bowdrey, when he's not digging up the ruins of Babylon, huh?'

'He—he's a schoolteacher.'

'And you?'

The blue eyes went to Bowdrey, who shifted in his seat. 'I'm a housewife.'

'Yeah?' Jane thought about this. 'You don't sound like a daffy-headed housewife to me, honey.' Then she shrugged. 'None of my business. We're a mighty mixed lot ourselves. All you know so far are names. You don't know where everybody fits in, so I'll tell you. John-oh!'

'Yes, ma'am?' John-oh came scurrying.

'You always keep your eyes in that place, son? Set 'em up. Doubles. Give him a hand, Lew.'

Lassiter rose. 'Yes, madame.'

Jane crackled hoarsely. 'Goddam Lassiter, always taking the mickey outta me.' She put out a hand to touch Susan, sitting next to her. 'Susan is my eyes. Tried a guide-dog once and it bit me. So I got to have Sue. She opens my mail, reads the papers to me, pays my bills. Gets a rake-off from the butcher, the baker, the candlestick maker. And the man at the drugstore supplies her with the Pill for free.' She grabbed Susan's arm and shook her, chuckling. 'How's that, Sue? Cap fit?'

The girl looked out poker-faced across the room.

'I'm lots of things but I'm not dishonest.'

'G'wan. Everybody gits a rake-off from a rich old bitch.' Jane turned back to the Bowdreys. 'Sue is twenty-two. This is probably a lie. She's more likely a year younger. But she's packed an *awful* lot of life into a few short years. Haven't

37

you, honey?' She reached across and prodded the girl again. 'Come on, now. How old are you really?'

Susan's face did not change. 'One hundred.'

Jane slapped her knee. She laughed until she choked. All the others looked at the girl. 'Where in hell are those drinks?'

'Coming.' John-oh arrived and passed around glasses. Lassiter, having helped pour, resumed his seat.

'You pour doubles, brown man?'

'Yes, Lady Teefer.' John-oh looked at his feet.

Lassiter said, 'Why don't you go to bed, Madame?'

'Nuts. And cut out that act of yours or it'll be the worse for you.' Jane Teefer dragged at her drink. She found and lit a cigarette with her usual incredible dexterity. 'I'm telling Mr and Mrs Bowdrey about *us*.' A hand waved to her left where Nailand slumped. 'This is my cousin Joe. From the British side of the family. My aunt, my mother's sister, married a Limey way before the war and settled there. Joe started to correspond with me about—how long ago, Joe?'

Nailand shrugged. 'About ten years.'

'No. It was more. Thirteen, maybe fourteen. Anyway I was mighty pleased. Only living relative I know of. I was an Appleby and we Applebys stick to our kin. Then when Joe heard of what I was planning he came across with Lola and her kids. 'We can all go, we can all help,' he said, which was mighty nice of him. My thanks to cousin Joe Nailand.'

Nailand grinned fatuously.

Jane produced a calm smile. 'Perhaps he was influenced by the fact that his business had gone bust. He was being bankrupted in the British courts and there were warrants out for this and that but——'

'Damn it, you didn't have to raise that!' Nailand's face suffused with blood. 'Why the devil . . .'

'But I wasn't going to listen to malicious tongues wagging that Joe had ducked the law and flown for help to rich cousin Jane. No sir.' She finished as though he had never interrupted. 'As I said, he brought across his wife and her kids. Lola and Joe have only been married two years. She was a widow before that. First husband, name of Brown, died of cerebral haemorrhage in 1966.'

Lola sat two chairs away from Jane. The blue-dyed head

tracked her down. 'It was lucky Joe came along, Lola, huh? I mean, considering what was happening.'

'I don't understand.' Lola's lovely face was blank.

'You seldom do.' Jane leant forward. 'I mean, honey, how all your friends' husbands, husbands of your pals from the bridge club and the P.T.A. and the goddam Laundromat, were coming around to give their regrets and were overstaying their welcomes because a certain somebody had just never learned to say no. Get me?'

Lola stared at Jane, at the downturned meanness of her lips. Into the silence she said tremblingly, 'What do you do? What do you do when they won't go, and then they . . . they get all funny and you can't make a fuss because the neighbours might . . . I mean . . . all that unpleasantness and explanations to your *friends* . . . surely rather just . . . what do you do?'

'You kick them in the crutch and to hell with explanations to their wives!' Jane slammed a hand on the arm of her chair, her jaw-muscles rigid, her bottom lip thrust out. Quite unexpectedly, the milky eyes filled with tears. 'God, to think kin of mine had to saddle himself with this. . . .' She shook her head. 'You got pumpkin pips in your head. Nothing else. Shake your head, honey, let's hear those pips rattle.'

Lola stared at her husband. 'Joe, please . . . I. . . .'

Nailand hunched forward 'Shake your bloody head!'

Jane's voice was suddenly like honey. 'Shake your head, Lola, we're just funning.'

Lola stared desperately around the circle. She bit her bottom lip. Then quickly, violently, she shook her head so that the chestnut hair bobbed against her cheeks.

Jane's cawing and Nailand's guffaw filled the air. Ann Bowdrey was getting up, saying, 'I must be going to bed. I'm afraid——'

'Afraid?' Jane's laugh cut her off. Her mouth shut like a steel trap. 'There's nothing you're afraid of. I can tell. Now you do me a favour before you go. Ask your husband whether he wants to go with you.'

Ann crouched, half-erect. She turned to Bowdrey. His face was slack with the liquor he'd consumed. He was staring, fascinated, at Jane. Abruptly he said, 'No. I'll stay.'

Jane grinned. 'There you are. He's interested. Now sit down, Mrs Bowdrey.'

Slowly, Ann settled back in her chair.

'That's better. Have a sip of your drink, honey. You're lining them up.' She stabbed a homing finger at the foot of the girl's chair where two full glasses stood propped in the miniature dune there.

Ann Bowdrey breathed out her disbelief and picked up one of the drinks.

'Lew!'

'Yes'm?' He smiled through the cloudy haze of his cigarette.

'Tell the Bowdreys where I found you, Lew.'

'I was attending a conference of Eagle Scouts in Williamsburg at the time.'

Jane's laugh was a scream. 'God, Lassiter, you'll kill me! I swear to God you'll kill me!' Then the lips turned down suddenly. She slapped both hands on the nylon wicker arms of the chair, making a flat popping noise like a small explosion. 'Now tell them the truth, you bastard. You've only had half your money. Want the rest? Then you tell 'em where I found . . .'

'In a gutter in London.'

Jane crowed. 'Yes, but how, Lassiter, how?'

He was watching the flush mount in Ann Bowdrey's cheeks. He was thinking of Germany and the bite of the night wind in the Alps and a girl with the same slender biscuit-tanned calves that were smooth but hard with muscle, he was feeling a stirring within him. . . .

'Lassiter!'

'I was having a hassle with some cops,' he said flatly.

Lady Teefer laughed again. 'That's more like it. In the gutter, with the slime of it over his clothes, and these demonstrators all around him with their beards and their signboards and the British bobbies swearing like hell—Jesus, Lassiter, I tell you now, I would have walked right past you, but I heard you say——'

' "God, if I was in Libya now",' Lassiter droned across her words.

'That's right. I hauled you out and took you to my hotel

and while you were still half-cut you told me some of your history. Like the bridge in Zambia. That was before Libya, Lassiter, wasn't it? I paid the flatfeet off and you told me about this bridge, and the way it closed up around the scaffolding like a slow-motion movie and you could see these black guys tumbling off it. . . .'

Lassiter sat up straight. 'They cut every place they could. They under-mixed, they murdered that job because the goddam Portuguese in their cute little jungle suits were watching from across the boundary laughing like hell because they knew the moment the bridge was up they would blow it, anyway. It was a pride thing, that bridge. So when it folded they said sure, the Portuguese paid you, you bastard, the proof of it is in your white skin. . . .' He shrugged. 'So I got ridden out of there on a rail.'

'Yeah, but it helped, Lassiter, you having a bottle for a head. It made it easy for them, didn't it?' Jane lit another cigarette.

Lassiter shrugged again. 'Maybe.'

It was as though Jane sensed this. Lassiter didn't care a damn. He wasn't worth baiting. Her mind moved on. 'John-oh!'

The young man cringed in his seat. 'Yes, ma'am?'

'Tell Mr and Mrs Bowdrey your surname.'

'Franc.'

'Franc. *Franc!*' Jane shrieked. 'Worth exactly that, too. About a quarter in American money. Except you got a good nose for the desert, hey, John-oh? Knows his way around the sands, this Ay-rab, although God knows how. Tell them where you grew up, brown man.'

John-ho was staring at his feet. He said nothing but his body quivered.

'No answer, huh? Well, I'll tell 'em. He was raised in a place where he learned perfect English and French, better than any smart Swiss school. You know what it was? It was a——'

John-oh jumped to his feet. Sweat had burst out all over his face. He shook his fist, shouting at her in a torrent of French. Then he looked wildly around the circle, gave a groan of anguish and ran from the room, his feet scuffing on the sand, his body swallowed up by the seeping blackness of the doorway.

'It was a whorehouse!' Jane was also on her feet, screaming after him. 'Why can't you face it? It was a goddam brothel, you yellow bastard!'

There was a silence into which her heavy breathing fell. Then she said slowly, panting, 'Time's moving on. Work, tomorrow. Let's get to bed.' She was suddenly old, withered, feeble. 'Here, Sue, give me a hand. My ticker's playing up.'

The girl got up, supporting her with a firm arm around her waist. They began to leave the room, but in the doorway Jane stopped. She was too tired even to turn her head, so she spoke out into the night. 'Lassiter, you can talk French. What did Franc say?'

Lassiter tossed his glass away so that it fell on the sanded floor. He got up. 'John-oh said that the badness is locked inside you. He said you can't get it out through your mouth and your eyes can't express it, so it's going to stay there.'

In silence, he pushed past the two figures in the doorway and went out into the night.

*　　　*　　　*

Susan had felt the mood coming on for an hour or more. When it happened she became greatly afraid and tried to concentrate on other things, and because this sometimes worked she went at it with the desperate determination of an insomniac trying to sleep or an inhibited person trying to urinate.

She was standing in the kitchen of the fort. It had a drunken door; sand was piled on the floor. The French had left behind a derelict deal table, a rickety shelf above it, and on the far wall a ten-year-old nude calendar. There was a stove on the table. A basin filled with sudsy water stood next to a pile of stacked dishes.

Her hands had begun to shake. She noticed it while she lit a cigarette. It's coming, she thought. Doggedly she lifted her eyes to the shelf that contained the Bowdreys' provisions and the stocks of the Teefer expedition, with a neat diplomatic division between them. Her mind babbled, striving to keep occupied. On my left, she thought, we have Bert and Ann

Bowdrey, who are broke and buy baked beans, corned beef, canned pilchards, sugar, coffee, tea, some powdered milk and a small bag of flour. Basic essentials. On my right we have Lady Teefer, weighing in at about one million bucks, with a different kind of shopping list: rock lobster, shrimps, herrings in various sauces, smoked oysters, turtle soup, clams, half-a-dozen choice canned meats.

> Hark, hark, the dogs do bark,
> The beggars are coming to town,
> Some in rags and some in bags
> And some in velvet gowns. . . .

The nursery song flowed through her mind. We're the ones in velvet gowns, she thought. I'm getting like Lassiter. Lassiter is the one who grins and baits a blind woman and barks commands that people obey. And then at night he gets drunk and the liquor brings out the fatal pity, the tenderness, the softness, the loneliness that Lassiter would feel even in a crowd. Lassiter was two people: the day-time, competent, incredibly efficient Lassiter; and the Lassiter of the darkness whose warm heart and shielding words were part of his nightly drunken beauty. Oh God, Lew, she thought, in a way I wish you could stay drunk, even slurring your way through the story about the little boy and the duck, and losing the punch line, but with the leaping fire showing the flashes of animation on your face and the new, soft way you look at me without the bitter condemnation of ugly morning, as though each night you discover me and lose me again somewhere around daybreak.

Her mind was suddenly empty and afraid again. She struggled against a dreadful lightheadedness. She jerked away from the table, dropping her cigarette, moving quickly across the sandy floor to the calendar on the other side of the room.

Mademoiselle Janvier of 1960 had small breasts with tiny nipples. The face was small, the features regular, the eyes big and brown, the dark hair worn long. Very French. She's rather like me, Susan Shields thought. Except there is more life in her two dimensions than in my three. She sparkles. I do not.

Why? She shut her eyes. She trembled suddenly, fighting

43

a terrifying influx of depression that threatened to hurtle like an avalanche into her mind. It would push aside reason, smother control, destroy hope. And she knew what she would do then.

God, hope! While there's hope there's life. An icy wind occupied her. It raged, it wrenched her away from the photograph and sent her across the sandy floor to the derelict table. She clung to it, feeling the wind grow, shaking her like a whipped branch. God, send hope, send . . .

Lassiter stood in the doorway, a glass in either hand.

She heard a voice say, 'Oh Lew. My lovely, d-drunk, night-time Lew!'

'Not so fast.' Lassiter came calmly into the room. He put the drinks down on the old table. 'What's the matter?'

'Nothing, now.' She went against him, her arms around his waist, her head against his chest. 'Not now that you're here.'

His body was warm. 'What happened? Was it Jane—what she said?'

She spoke with her lips against his shirt, muffled. 'Maybe she started it. But every now and again I find myself walking in the desert of my mind. There is nothing ahead and nothing behind. Th-then this wind comes and it blows into me. It is a wind of despondency and I know that in a second or a minute it will engulf me because there is no hope, no desire, no anticipation; and I grow afraid because it is a monster wind of suicide and I am er-er af-af-afraid that it will . . . consume me.' She lifted her head. 'How do you live without hope?'

Lassiter kissed her. She wanted to cling to him but he took her arms and gently held her away, full of night-time mellowness and beautiful thoughts. 'You go outside, out of the gates of this fort. You'll find a little tree there. It is stunted and grey. And you say to it: "tree, why do you live? You are misshapen and ugly, you struggle for survival, you will not even reproduce in this barren desert womb." And the tree will say: "once a year it rains. I wait for the rain. The rain is my hope" ' he smiled. 'Such a little thing to live for, isn't it? One shower of rain a year.'

She felt her throat begin to constrict and said out of her knowledge of life, 'God, I'm being a stupid child.' But out of

44

the fact of her youth it went on constricting so that she could not say any more and her vision blurred.

'There's no shame in crying. The old bags cry, too. It's a sign that there's still hope. Tears are not desperation. Desperation is dry-eyed. You've still got hope, Suzie.' He held her hand hard. 'You just thought you'd lost it.'

'I hope so.' She pulled away gently. She smiled.

'Hey, that's better.'

'I'm okay.' She turned to the table, facing the neat pile of washed plates.

He came from behind and put a warm arm loosely around her shoulders. The other one appeared in front of her, holding a glass. 'Here. You've forgotten your drink. Cheers, Suzie.'

'Cheers.' Relaxing even more, she rested her head against his solid body. 'Why did you let Jane humiliate you tonight?'

'Did I?'

'Yes. Why didn't you give her hell and w-walk out, like John-oh?'

'Oh, I don't know.' He leaned over her shoulder and put a bristly cheek against hers. 'I don't care, that's all. John-oh has got pride. What's pride? All it does is make you fall.'

She thought about this, nestling her head against his chest. 'That's true, I suppose. But if you don't care, you must have hope. What's *your* hope, Lew?'

She felt him move. 'Hey, now. Never ask a schoolteacher how he learnt the sums he teaches you.' He kissed her neck. 'You are beautiful. I love you. Old Lew loves you.'

She could not prevent the involuntary spasm of the muscles across her stomach and the rush of warmth there. But she shook her head stubbornly. 'Sure you do. At night. Everything is beautiful to you at night. I've learnt that. I also know what happened at Djanet is irreversible. You think about it every night when this happens to you and every morning you want to forget it.'

He emptied his glass. 'I told you I was a bum.'

'Stop feeling sorry for yourself.' She felt him pull away and was instantly contrite. 'Hey. Where're you er-er-going?'

At this time of the night he was good looking. There were none of the dents and furrows of his day-time tension. And by his smile he clearly bore her no resentment. 'I'm going to find the kids. Nobody, most of all their mother and step-father, could care a holy hoop where they are or what they're doing.'

She picked up one of the dishes. She began to dry it. 'Lew. Those kids. I've seen the way they look at you. Don't s-slur. You will bend an image.'

He went to the doorway. 'Hope can be the next night's drink. Or perhaps I'm waiting for the rain, like the grey tree. I won't s-slur, I promise.' Then he was gone.

I hope he doesn't fall down the well. She picked up a dish and began to dry it, realizing while she rubbed that the well was full of sand, anyhow. Then she put the dish down with a small clatter on the table she had christened the French Inheritance.

She was better now. Lassiter had swept away the attack of suicidal depression. Her thoughts were no longer jumbled and she was able to look back without that terrible fear, and remember the teenage girl who had lived in a hippie commune and become a main-line heroin addict at the age of seventeen and been institutionalized and finally cured. The only trouble was that the main-liner had been left with an intermittent stammer and desperation in her soul.

She picked up another dish and slowly began to dry it.

*   *   *

The children had chosen a room very close to the great open gates. They had prowled awhile, glorying in the arrogance of standing on the ramparts of their own fort and looking out over a moonlit desolation that was theirs by right of conquest. But the freezing cold of the night had driven them inside eventually. They were sitting on their lightweight aluminium camp stretchers with blankets wrapped around their legs and a cheap, battery-powered lamp for illumination.

'It's frightfully cold, isn't it?' Thrin scratched at her chest. 'You wouldn't think the desert could get like this. I mean, everyone pictures people pouring sweat all over the place and . . .'

'We're high.' Neil hauled at his blanket. 'The higher the colder.' He paused a moment. 'Where's Mummy?'

'Gone to bed with Joe. Did you enjoy the curry?'

46

'No.'

'Suzie made it. Do you like her?'

'No.'

'John-oh brought it. Do you like him?'

'Yes.' The words came out in a sigh.

'Let's talk to someone. We haven't for a while. Don't you think we should?'

'Yes.' He was pleased and crawled out of his blanket nest. 'Come on. Now.'

'All right, give me a chance.' She fiddled on the sand floor next to her bed. 'We must sweep some of this away tomorrow. Okay, I've got it. I'm ready.'

Both of them got out of bed and sat on the uneven grain surface of the sand. Neither appeared now to notice the cold. Thrin unrolled a piece of cloth about a yard square. It was linen, and contained a very worn picture of Christ on the cross.

She spread it flat with firm, competent hands. 'You sit with your hands on that corner. I sit with my hands on this corner. Now who's going to talk and who's going to answer?'

'I don't think I could talk.'

'All right.' Thrin rubbed her chest again. 'I'll talk, you answer.'

He frowned. 'Why do you keep scratching like that?'

She shrugged. 'I'm getting tits. And they're itchy.'

He was quite diplomatic. 'Do you think you're going to have big tits, like Mummy?'

'I don't know. Come on, let's talk to someone.'

'Yes.' Neil closed his eyes. 'Don't forget Lew.'

'I won't.' She also closed her eyes. She let a small silence go by. Then she began: 'We're frightfully sorry to bother you, but we have a few things to discuss.'

Neil, with his eyes shut, said, 'He says, okay, carry on.'

Thrin said, 'We would like you to protect Mummy from that bastard she's married to. Mummy is looking worse and worse.'

Neil's head nodded. 'He says he will, but watch your language.'

'I'm sorry!' She put a thin forefinger to her mouth. Then she inclined her head. 'Let me put it this way. Mummy is

47

stuck with Joe. Joe is bad. We would like Mummy looked after.'

Neil rocked. His legs were crossed, his eyes closed. 'He says he will do his best, but some people are . . . are . . . weak.'

Thrin rocked too. 'We are worried about John-oh, also. John-oh is very nice but he is humble like Luke the coloured chauffeur at Lady Jane's home in Virginia. We would like John-oh looked after.'

'He says. . . .' Neil swayed. 'Er—he says he will do his best.'

Thrin nodded. 'Good enough.' She paused for a long time, thinking. Then she said, 'We like Lew Lassiter very much. We do not think there is any bad in Lew, but at the same time there isn't much——'

'Much what?'

Both children opened their eyes. Lassiter was settling cross-legged into position at the third corner of the cloth, his long knobbly fingers already spread out and touching it.

He had grey eyes rather like theirs, except his lacked the crispness of their youth.

'Would you mind if I sat in?'

Thrin studied Neil. Then she said, 'No, Mr Lassiter. You're welcome.'

But they were awkward. They did not know how to go on. So Lassiter shut his eyes. He lowered his head, showing the circly pink of an embryonic bald spot. He had been listening at the door but they did not know it.

'There's a little grey tree outside this fort. It means a lot to me. Let's find out what's going to happen to the little grey tree.'

Neil shut his eyes. He had the pink blot on Lassiter's scalp in his mind. He liked Lassiter and wanted very much to tell him something about the tree, something different. He tried desperately, thinking of Lassiter's lowered head. That hair, he thought, needs water to grow. . . .

He opened his eyes. 'Why,' he said, 'it's going to rain more this year and the little tree is going to green a bit and grow. . . .'

* * *

Bert Bowdrey missed his footing in a small runnel of sand. He lurched up against his stretcher, lost his balance and sat down on it heavily. From there he looked up at Ann out of bloodshot eyes.

'Schoolteacher! My God! From now on that old blind bitch will be examining every word I say with those dead microscopic eyes and if I slip up with my grammar . . . don't let her fool you when she talks like a Hill Billy, she's a shrewd and clever woman. Why the hell couldn't you tell them the truth, tell them I teach motor-mechanic apprentices in a trade school?'

She still stood this way, her slender legs slightly apart, in supreme command of her body. 'You've had too much to drink, Bert. Let's leave it until tomorrow.'

'Aye and so have you, you bloody mealy-mouthed pledge-signing Methodist!' He glared at her.

'I am not a Methodist, Frank, I am a ——'

'What does it matter what you are!' He got up, quivering. 'Who cares a damn? You saw how she read those people—sightless, and she read them like a book. And them sitting there, taking it, including her own cousin. And getting you to drink three, four; ah hell, God knows how many whiskies when you've never touched a drop in the time I've known you. Me, too, held like you in the cupped palm of her hand. He shook his head. He was both befuddled and bemused. 'She's got some kind of radar. A sort of built-in system. She's the most dangerous person I've ever met and I could blow her over with a hard breath, sick as I am.'

Ann sat down on her bed. She studied him while he stumbled across the sand-eddied floor and slammed a hand against the stout mud wall. 'God dammit! Hasn't she got enough? Can't she rest content with her millions and leave the rest? And why wait four years—four years the snooty bastard's been dead and gone and now she comes, with the stink of money in her nostrils. I——'

'Have you got a cigarette, Bert?'

He stopped abruptly in mid-breath. He stared at her. Then he fumbled in his pockets and produced a crumpled pack. In quite a different voice he said, 'I've never seen you smoke. Didn't think you smoked at all.'

'I used to now and then. On night duty, when things were quiet.'

'Ah well, then.' He came across and gave her one, took one himself and lit them with a trembling hand. 'You do this. You cut across my thoughts right in the middle of a——'

The blue eyes showed their first flash of fire. 'You were only railing, Bert. Wasting words. You whine out of your bitterness. That accomplishes nothing. There're a few things you haven't thought of.'

He had begun pacing again. Now he stopped. He went still, turning to study her. 'Oh? How's that?'

'Why did she wait four years? Why did she come at all if she's so rich?'

His face went ugly. 'Greed. I don't think you can argue that. Rich people want more. It's common knowledge. As for the other question—who knows? Domestic problems, maybe. Maybe waiting to find somebody like Franc and that Lassiter chap. She couldn't have done it without them, or that dead-faced popsy who leads her around. She's only had the girl for a short while, I gather. And she needs them all. Probably it took time to get them together. And she needed Lassiter most of all.'

She drew on her cigarette. Because she smoked so seldom it tasted rich and nutty on her tongue. It made her think of the dutyroom off the wards, filled with grey layers of smoke that fogged the icy air and the staff nurse coming in saying, 'Mr Bowdrey's playing up, sister, I think you should . . .' and the cigarette ground out into black tobacco ash and his tortured face looking up at her from where she stood above him, with her professional voice coming out even and firm, 'Now, Mr Bowdrey, what's it this time? . . .'

She said, 'Yes, I think she needs Lassiter. She hates him really, don't you think? And he probably hates her too, and yet there seems to be a strange respect between them.' She became thoughtful. 'There's something else you hadn't thought of, Bert, when you were striding about slapping walls and bewailing your fate. . . .'

'I've waited a hell of a lot longer than four years!' He shouted the words, ridiculously twisted in half-stride, looking back at her.

'I know. But has it occurred to you that she is searching for an entirely different plane?'

There was a pause of a moment, not more. 'That's a blind. Sir Peter came down very close to the Dakota. The French established that. So she says she's looking for *his* plane, to find the poor bugger and bury his bones—my arse—but it's the same thing. There's a strong probability that the two wrecks are not more than a mile apart. Ahh, God, if only I could remember!'

She got up without a word, went to her suitcase and brought out a stainless steel container.

'You reckon I need it?'

'Yes. It's the liquor making you feel good.' She assembled a hypodermic with quick and expert skill, sank the needle into a small rubber-mouthed ampoule. 'The streptomycin is still necessary.'

He shrugged. 'Okay.' He sat down on the bed, hauled up the sleeve on his left arm. She did the injection, daubed the spot with a swab of ether-soaked cotton wool.

'Bert?' She had her back to him. She bent, returned the hypodermic set to the suitcase.

'Well?' He rubbed impatient fingers over the hard burn of the injection.

'This chap Lassiter. He's a strange one, isn't he?'

'Aye, he's strange.' He thought for a moment. 'There're things about him. Like this bridge you heard them mention. People died there, it seems. And Lassiter doesn't care.'

'Oh, he cares!'

'You reckon?' He squinted at her with a sudden measure of wisdom.

'He cares. Behind it all he cares. It's hidden. He's weak and he's strong.' She was in the courtyard of the fort, muffled against the cold. All the lights were out. Lassiter came up to her. She felt a wash of excitement, a terrible trembling in her limbs, a . . .

'Ann!'

She blinked. 'What's the matter?'

He came to where she stood next to the suitcase. He was awkward. 'Lassiter. Are you attracted to him?'

She stared at him. He could sense her quick anger, the

51

race of her heart-beat, the dislike which she showed. 'It's my life! It's my life! Leave it alone!'

He was already wheeling away, shaking his head. 'I'm sorry. I . . . had no right.' He became quite wise, quite cynical. 'But there's that Coleman there, wheezing away, and we've got to go to bed now. It's not *entirely* your life. I'm involved. How do you want it? Who goes to bed first? And do we put the light out now or afterwards?'

She was still angry. 'You're the sick one Bert. I'll turn my back. Get into bed.'

'All right.'

She went to the far corner of the room while he flung off his clothes and clambered into a pair of warm, old-fashioned, candy-striped pyjamas, adding a heavy sweater over the top. Then he scrambled on to the stretcher, pulled the blankets over him and said gruffly, 'I'm ready.'

Ann came back. He had his back very obviously turned to her. She shrugged. Her fingers twisted the knob on the Coleman. It gulped out its air and died. In the dark she began to take off her clothing.

Bert Bowdrey's body was rigid. He breathed very slowly and very quietly. That's her skirt, he thought. That slight overhead noise is her blouse coming off. And that whisper, that whisper of sound upon the sand, that is her bra and her panties. She is naked now and if there is any moon shining through the doorless doorway it is smiling upon a perfection of ivory skin that no man . . .

He buried his face in his pillow and fought desperately for sleep.

*　　*　　*

Joe Nailand glowered. It had all the humour of a blunt-toothed shark. 'So you had to sit there and squirm like a bloody teenager and look at her with those stupid cow-eyes of yours and admit that you got screwed by half the neighbourhood because you didn't want to upset your friends! Can you believe it!'

She was naked, her nightgown held limply at thigh level. In her hands it had all the glamour of a dishcloth, but her body shone with the lustre of eternal youth. Even her face was young. It showed only a few tiny hair-thin lines around the eyes. She looked twenty-five. And she was thirty-eight.

'Joe, you knew! You knew even before you came to live with me.' Her voice lacked timbre. It had a breathy quality.

'Christ, don't tell me, do you think I can forget it?' He slapped his forehead theatrically.

'But you said then . . .' she let the nightgown swing away in one hand, dangling loosely, quite unaware of her body, rather like a child in query, '. . . you said it didn't matter, you said you understood, you said you wanted me for what I was, I clearly remember you said that, and then you said something about how I had been too sheltered, it wasn't my fault, it was——'

'Ahh, God, that was another time, another place. And in any case I remember bloody well I was drunk when I said it. Don't remind me.'

They were in their room, half-lit in leaping lights and shadows from a lamp that was losing its pressure. Nailand sweated even in the cold, the permanent unhealthy sweat of his overweight. And he rushed everything, he gulped his food, swigged his drinks, driven for ever by the riding tension within him that made him pop his knuckles in a series of hideous cracks.

'She made a fool of you, too.' Lola Nailand said it timidly, the way she said everything. 'You sat there while she told the Bowdreys and everybody else that you'd been bankrupted at home and that there were warrants out. . . .'

He lit a cigarette fumblingly. 'It was no fault of mine that I got cheated on what looked like a sound investment. Damn it, money is nothing to me. I have a brain for money. It's a commodity, after all. I can buy and sell money every day.' He pointed the cigarette at her, stabbing it at her. 'I've told you a thousand times a man has got to stick his neck out. I don't want money when I'm seventy! I want it now! So bugger bank overdrafts and mortgages and loans.' He half-closed his eyes. His full mouth turned down. 'I'm not little Billy bank-clerk, putting his little bit in the kitty every night, scraping and saving while it grows so terribly slowly in a building society at six or seven per-bloody-cent. Money must turn over, it must multiply, if you've got five thousand, now it must be ten thousand a month later, don't you see?'

She produced wisdom, the more accurate because it was so simple. 'But Joe, surely wouldn't it be better to be Billy bank-clerk, and know that the money is there, growing, even if it is slowly, rather than stick your neck out the way you say, and go broke again and again and again because something . . . misfired.' The green empty eyes met his. 'In the two years we've been married it's happened how many times—three? four? And then this bankruptcy thing. And I suspect that you've been bankrupt before. Each time you seem to find some more money and go on.' She took a deep breath. 'Joe, I don't think you have a brain for money at all. I don't think you know anything about money.'

Nailand's temper boiled over. He dropped his cigarette on the sandy floor, trod across it as he strode towards her.

'Joe!'

'Joe hell, you bitch, you've got it coming.' He reached her, thrusting his round face at her so that she could see the sweat beaded on his upper lip and smell the sour tobacco of his breath. 'Listen to me. Get something straight. I don't need you. I don't know why the hell I married you. The only reason I brought you along was because you know too much about my affairs, dull as you are. But I want you to understand that you are a woman, that's all. And that means you exist to cook for me, clean for me, wash for me, lie on your back when *I* need you.'

She found the courage to say. 'You don't even do that any more.'

His face twisted in contempt. 'For God's sake, are you surprised? Grind, grind, grind away with you lying there like a lump and then in the middle you say "I forgot to hang out your washing, Joe." ' He had rather small hands for a blocky squareness of his body. He waved them at the roof. 'That I can do without, thank you. But let's get back to the point, and the point is that you are a woman and the definition of that word excludes *thinking*. I know you find the process difficult. But has this penetrated through that bovine skull?'

Fear and a foreknowledge of pain, a sort of childish antici-pation of hurt, misted her eyes. 'Joe, you're not going to——'

'Yes, I am.' He grinned when she cringed. 'I'm going to give you a beating, Lola. In the soft spots so no one will notice.'

'Joe!' She flung herself sideways awkwardly, her long legs still trailing off the stretcher.

'It's no good ducking. And you can't get out of the room. Where would you go, anyway? To Jane? She'd probably help me hold you.' A devil came into his eyes. 'Come on, Lola, be a good girl. Face the music.'

Still she cringed. She buried her face in the blanket and whimpered. Nailand let out an oath. He bent, dragged her upright.

'That's right.' He ignored the hands that fluttered about her face like a trembling fan. 'Hold still, darling.'

His fist came around in a short, vicious arc.

*　　*　　*

John-oh had left his jersey in his room. He was wearing only his day-time light cotton shirt and drab slacks and the cold was stinging. He bounced up and down like a fighter, shadow-boxing until the burn in his biceps stopped him. Then he jogged about the courtyard silently on his toes, his arms dangling loosely at his sides, a broad-shouldered young man whose fitness showed in the bounce of his springy calves and the even rhythm of his breathing.

He moved about the courtyard this way, circling it, crossing it, sometimes doing a figure-of-eight with the well as the centre, apparently sternly engaged in an abstract and aimless training routine. In reality it was an attempt to remain warm while he kept a patient and pathetic vigil.

John-oh was watching Lola Nailand's room.

It was one of the few with a door that functioned, so that all he could see was a wan and lustreless wash of light that seeped from the narrow strip at the bottom. But it was enough; he made this his homing-point in each tour of the courtyard. And after twenty minutes, as he neared it, he heard the smacking sound of flesh against flesh and Lola's muffled cry.

He reared to a stop, instantly panting, instantly cold and shivering although the hot fire of hatred boiled through him like lava. He stood a moment in an isolated world that consisted of him and the door and the sounds beyond.

55

I will break it down, he decided. I will smash it down with my body and then I will smash *him*. He set himself. He leaned forward, his burly shoulders angled into the warhead of an explosive human battering-ram. A moment went by. It was a moment that to him was endless in time. Then he shook his head. He straightened. No. Not that way. Briskly, he strode across his sandy Rubicon to the door. He raised one hand, clenched his knuckles and briskly brought them down towards the peeling wood. But at the last fraction of a second the fist quivered to a halt.

I am not related in any way, he thought. I'm just the guide. There is no tie between us. No affinity. I have no real right. It would be ridiculous. Perhaps I should cough.

Yes, he would cough. He breathed in deeply, holding the air in his chest. Then he let it out in a sigh. No. They will say I'm a peeping Tom, they will say. . . .

John-oh shuddered: He let his arms drop to his sides and walked back with his shoulders slumped, back across his bridge of indecision.

When he was at the starting point he heard a second blow and another whimper of pain.

This time fury took him. He charged across what was now a launching-pad of determination, his strong young body tensed to hit the door. But with one yard to go his mind suddenly contradicted him: she is twelve years older than you. She should be able to look after . . . she made her choice . . . they would laugh . . . Nailand is tough, Nailand would beat you to a . . .

There was only one way to stop himself. He flung his body out so that he slithered along the sand, plunging absurdly on his hands and knees right up against the door, cringing away from it as he felt his left shoulder actually touch the wood. Sweat burst out all over him from this frantic last-minute restriction.

Slowly he got up. He walked with dragging steps past the little circle of scuff-marks in the sand that marked the beginning and the end of his resolution. He walked on to the gates of the fort standing wide. There he stopped and studied the night sky without seeing it.

She said I am a coward. That's what she said when I ran out of the room. You yellow bastard, she said. Maybe the old bitch was right.

He turned abruptly and began to trot along the courtyard to his room. When he passed Nailand's door he put his fingers in his ears and ran on.

*   *   *

Susan Shields watched the alarmed fluttering of the methylated spirits in the tiny container. When it began to die she closed the air-vent on the Coleman and pumped the handle. A white light, startlingly bright, blossomed out of the mantle. The lamp began to hiss contentedly.

She took off her clothes rapidly. Lady Teefer was a blue-dyed dandelion in the other camp stretcher a few feet away, smothered in blankets. Shivering uncontrollably, Susan scrambled into ski-pyjamas and a sweater, then flung herself into bed and reached for the lamp.

'Where you been, honey?'

She jumped with fright and twisted around in the bed. The sightless milky eyes watched her from across the way.

'I'm sorry. I didn't mean to wake you.'

'I haven't been asleep, yet. Can't see a light when you're blind.'

Susan's hand came away from the lamp. It was something to which she simply could not adjust, this being with a person whose day and night remained the same.

'Are you all right?'

'Yeah. Took a couple of heart pills. You haven't answered me yet. Where you been?'

'Washing the dishes. Stacking everything. Preparing a few things for tomorrow.'

'Took your own sweet time, didn't you?' When the girl didn't answer she went on, drowsily. 'Been thinking about Peter. Kinda nice, meeting a British baronet when you're a widow of thirty-five and blind to boot. Not that I wasn't good-looking, mind you. Figure like Lola's, I had then, if not better.' She seemed to consider for a moment. 'Even so, even bearing in mind the Teefers had been broke for two hundred years, and he married me for my money, Peter was good to me. He was my eyes, the way you are now. Took

57

over in Virginia, ran the estate, made the staff respect him. And I'd been Mrs Barnes Marlow, don't forget, wife of a power in the land; a Timber King, he was. But when the old boy was dead and gone and Peter came along, Lord, he had everybody eating out of his hand.' Her voice sharpened. 'You listening, girl?'

Susan's eyes drooped. To keep herself awake she lit a cigarette. 'Yes, Lady Teefer.'

The older woman went on as though there had been no interruption. 'And then what Peter did for me right at the end, in London. That was a grand gesture, don't you think? Pity he had to combine it with this crack-brained scheme to cross the Sahara. And of course I didn't know until it was too late. Nothing I could do then, could I? The French were looking for him.'

'No, Lady Teefer.' Susan blew smoke out into the sharp air.

Jane sounded suddenly biting. ' "Yes Lady Teefer, no Lady Teefer." ' There was a small, reflective pause. 'You mad at me? You figure I was hard on you tonight?' There was a sudden quick, honey-like inflection in the voice.

Susan stubbed out the cigarette in the sand next to her bed. 'It just doesn't matter. I don't care.'

'You won't tell them, girl, why we're really here?' The voice was quiet and reasonable. 'You're the only other one who knows. You're my eyes. I need you. And I'm mighty sorry if I hurt you tonight. Had too much to drink.'

You hurt a lot of people, she thought. But aloud she said, 'I told you, it doesn't matter.'

This time she put the light out. Darkness came to her world. Minutes passed and Jane's breathing became heavy.

'Lady Teefer?'

There was a startled movement in the other bed. 'What in hell? I was asleep.'

'I'm sorry.' There was no sorrow in her voice, only a sudden questing. 'Do you think I can live? Do you think I c-c-can live again?'

'Hell, I don't know, honey.' The rounded accents came to her out of the darkness. 'Depends what you mean. Do you mean if you live so much, the way you have, if you cram such a span into so few years, more'n I ever did—and boy

I sure lived—can you start as though it's all a fresh new day? With you there waiting for the doorbell to ring and this guy standing there goggling holding a bunch of roses. Is that what you're meaning?'

'More or less.'

The reply came like the fall of an executioner's axe. 'I don't think so, Suzie. No. I sure as hell doubt it. You made your bed so far back. Now I reckon you got to lie in it.'

There was silence. Jane's breathing deepened and became even. She was asleep. Susan lay shivering under the blankets staring at the nothing of the darkness. *Come soon tomorrow, Come along quickly. Night has the quality of death.*

When sleep came she dreamed of rain.

CHAPTER THREE

THE TWO LAND-ROVERS had driven in a tight bumper-to-bumper circle around the courtyard rather like grumbling elephants in a ring. Now they faced the gates. Lassiter pulled up next to John-oh's vehicle and switched off. He got out, fumbled a pair of sunglasses out of a pocket and put them on. Sweat was already showing in a dark patch on the back of his drab shirt.

John-oh came over, carefully unfolding a map that was more than a yard square. 'What's the time, Lew?'

'Eight o'clock. There's been too much frigging around. Let's get going.' Lassiter touched the map with a long fore-finger. 'We're here.' The finger moved slightly. 'The *guelta* is about here. I'm going to sidetrack just a little to see if I can hit it. Nice to know where the water is.'

'That means you're going to go straight out of the gates and head slightly north of due east.'

'Right. You drive south for two kilometres and then parallel my course. Keep going for five hours. Then turn at right-angles, run off six kilometres and come home again. I'll swing across into the middle of the slot you've left open. That way we'll grid eight kilometres in the day.' He wiped his forehead. 'And if we find that plane I'll eat your jockstrap.'

John-oh nodded. Against Lassiter's crisp authority he was more than usually nervous and subdued. 'I've got it.' He lit a cigarette. 'It's a job. We're being well paid.'

'Sure. Let's see how long we can make it last.' Lassiter reached through the window of the car and sounded the hooter in two impatient blasts.

The Teefer group straggled out of doorways and bunched at the cars. 'John-oh will take the Nailands. I will take Thrin and Neil.' Lassiter's glance went to their mother. 'If it's all right with you, Lola.'

The woman shrugged. She was puffy-eyed. 'If you don't mind having them.'

The group separated. Susan Shields was left alone. Lassiter went to her. He lifted his sunglasses. 'I didn't slur. Want to come along?'

What she saw in his expression seemed to satisfy her. 'I'll ask Jane.' She trotted across the sand and disappeared into a doorway. But in a moment she had reappeared. 'It's okay. Jane's got some reading to do.'

'*Reading?*'

'In Braille. Conan Doyle.'

Lassiter shook his head in weary disbelief. He put his hands lightly on the shoulders of the children who stood on either side of him, turned with them to get into the Land-Rover and found Bert Bowdrey blocking his path.

'Going to photograph some more carvings?' He found it impossible to relax with Bowdrey. The man was so permanently tense. He was so instantly aggressive. It showed in the tight planes of his narrow face, in the tiny convulsive tic that pulled at a corner of one eye.

'I might be.' Bowdrey stood his ground. He blocked the way to the Land-Rover.

'The best of British luck to you. We have to get cracking as well,' Lassiter began to push past him. He reached for the doorhandle but fierce fingers gripped his arm.

'Mr Lassiter. May I ask the course you're taking?'

'You may.' Lassiter looked him meanly straight in the eye. 'But first take your flipping hand off my arm.'

Bowdrey let his hand drop. 'I'm . . . I'm sorry. It's just that I feel we shouldn't clash. My work takes time. It needs quiet

60

and solitude. I'm sure you'd no more like me messing around in your path than I would you, in mine.'

'I can't see that it would make any difference at all.' Lassiter's patience was getting out of hand, on top of which he had the feeling that if he were hit hard he would shatter. He surveyed Bowdrey dispassionately out of mildly bleary eyes. 'I don't quite follow. Why the solitude? All you have to do is find a carving. Then you point your camera and give it three rounds rapid. I don't understand why you have to go into an artistic trance, standing on one leg and chanting.'

Anger suffused Bowfrey's face. He stepped back, trembling· 'Mr Lassiter, I asked a civil question. There's no need to bloody-well——'

'Bloody-well what?'

Bowdrey lost some of his fire. 'To—to make fun of me.'

'Have it your way.' Lassiter lost interest. He was tired and the day had not yet begun. He flung out an arm. 'That's east. I'm heading slightly north of that. Franc will parallel my course. By nightfall, moving across, we hope to have gridded approximately five hundred square kilometres in a fairly narrow oblong.'

Bowdrey studied the pointing arm. He looked sick. He looked stricken. 'Thank you.' He stepped back.

Lassiter got into the Land-Rover. He waited until Susan Shields and the children were aboard. Then he signalled to John-oh. Both trucks roared back into life, and trumpeted out through the gates in a shower of flung sand.

Bowdrey stood for a moment staring after them. He let the sand settle on his hair, his sweat-sticky face, his clothes. Then he turned and half-trotted to the doorway of the kitchen.

'Ann! Ann!' He burst into the room so suddenly that she was startled. 'They've gone east. East, do you understand?' He pointed a quivering arm. 'They are probing country we *haven't even looked at!*'

She put down the saucepan she had been holding and gave him her full attention.

'That's terribly bad luck, Bert, isn't it?'

'Bad luck? Bad luck?' He put a hand across his face and laughed without humour. 'For crying out loud, what a way to put it! We're cursed, lass. God, why does it always have to be me? In and out of hospitals and institutions for half my life. And when I finally get out here, after those years of frustration, what do I do? I take a blinder and head in the wrong direction!'

He found himself looking into a pair of angry, unsympathetic eyes. 'Stop bewailing your fate. Stop whining. If anyone has cause for complaint it's me, stuck with a broken reed like you to work with!'

He was utterly shocked. 'I've never heard you talk like that. Can I help being sick? Can I help——'

'Oh, it's not your health I'm talking about and you know it.' She gave him a look of contempt. 'It's here.' She tapped her forehead. 'That complaining, injured, mournful, bitter mind.'

He stared at her for long moments while she held his eyes. Then he said, 'You've forgotten one more word. And it's one we have in common. We share it.'

She was still angry. 'What is it?'

Bowdrey said it slowly and deliberately. 'Greed.'

Their glances were locked. He saw the anger go out of her face. It was replaced by something else. She let her breath out in a small sigh. 'Yes.' The slender body turned so that he could see only the back of her cheap cotton frock, the smooth nut-tanned legs and bare feet. She was dressed the way she had been yesterday, when the Teefer group had arrived.

'This was a last chance, this thing.' She spoke looking at the wall where *Mademoiselle Janvier* displayed her lightweight Gallic charms. 'I want no going back empty-handed. I don't want to see the days following one another like cards flipping over. I don't want to see the buds and know it's spring, the rain and know it's autumn, the snow that tells me winter's come. I've had winter too long, and nothing ever different.' She spun about.

'It's such a terrible thing, don't you realize? I'm twenty-nine and the years are all the same, they've been the same for so long. But I don't want that any more. And only one thing will change it. The money.'

She reached out a hand and gripped his arm fiercely. 'Call it greed! Sure, it's greed. But I want that money, Bert, I want it as much. I want it more than you do and if I don't get it there will be no going back to all the other winters. I'll stay here dead and you can bury me in that sand-choked well out-side and there will be no worrying, chaffing spirit about this hot Sahara air. All of me will die.'

There was a passion between them for a moment, a vibrating, trembling, non-sexual lust. They were locked with it, held by it. He was made almost afraid by it. Then she let his arm go. She shivered and turned away, staring down at the kitchen table with its aeons of tiny scorches, its myriads of knife-cuts. 'Get the money, Bert. I don't care how. Just get it. That's why we're here. Follow Franc. He's the outside man to Lassiter. Drive on Franc's right, to the south of him. That way you will still be covering new territory except for the small area they will search today. It's unlikely that they have that kind of luck. Go now, Bert.'

He studied her as though he had never seen her before. 'You're not coming?'

All the intensity had gone. She was her usual settled, calm, competent self. 'No. Susan Shields wanted to go with Lassiter. So I agreed to stay behind and give Lady Teefer her lunch. And also I'm honour bound to prepare the supper tonight. It's my turn.' She smiled very briefly. 'That's the other me. The one that belongs with the sameness of winter sliding by.'

There was no arguing. He knew it. He hovered a moment, watching her although her back was turned. Then he shook his head and went out and after a while she heard the ragged beat of the old Land-Rover starting up, roaring courageously and finally fading into diminishing distance.

*   *   *

The defile ran at an angle, north-east in the direction of the Libyan border, and the *guelta* was an eight-yard streak of greeny-brown water not far from the entrance.

Lassiter stopped the Land-Rover. He let Susan and the children out. Then he went through the complicated process of turning the big vehicle in the confines of the close rock walls, finally joining them and idly toeing a tyre-mark in the sand.

'See that? Worn smooth. Obviously Bowdrey gets his water here.' He turned to the children. 'Why don't you swim, you two?'

63

'We haven't got bathing costumes.' It was Neil's realization and Thrin's face went solemn.

'This is the Sahara not Brighton.' Lassiter slapped the boy gently on his backside. 'You swim in your underpants, Thrin in her panties.'

Neil said, 'Suits me,' and became lost in his shirt as he tugged it off over his head. Thrin remained still, apparently studying her feet.

'Come on, toots!' Lassiter thumped her cheerfully on the arm. But still the girl looked woodenly down.

'Thrinny!' Lassiter grabbed her, ready to wrestle and make a lighthearted issue of it.

'Lew!' Susan said the words so fiercely that Lassiter instantly looked up. 'Come here.' It was an urgent command, done with sharp authority.

Lassiter let Thrin go. He loped over. 'Lew!' Susan hung on to an arm, hauled herself up on her toes to hiss at him. 'The k-kid is growing up. She's er-er-developing. Goddammit she's bashful, she's sh-shy of you!'

Lassiter half-turned his head to where Thrin stood, her back now turned, kicking at the sand. Neil was sitting, taking off his sandals.

He took Susan's hand gently. 'Come.' He led her a few yards along the rock wall to a jumble of rocks that were blue in the shade. They sat there perched on the hard cool-warm stone and Lassiter drew on his cigarette for a moment. Then he called, 'Thrin!'

The child turned her head only a little, using mostly her eyes with which to survey him unreadably. She said nothing.

'Be careful. There's sharks in that *guelta*.'

A moment passed while she studied him across the small distance, examining his face with great care. Then she made her own decision. The small hands crossed, took the bottom of her blouse. In a smooth movement she pulled it overhead and turned, standing full-faced to Lassiter, letting him see the rosebud sweetness of her new breasts while she smiled with a beauty that cradled a trembling embryo of womanhood.

It lasted only a moment. Then she was in the *guelta*, she was crying out that it was cold. Neil had joined her in a whirl of arms and legs, she was ducking him and she was a child again.

Susan thought: to live again. Oh God, if I could live again.

'We can't stay long.' It was the day-time Lassiter, shifting into first-gear competence.

'What's the time?'

'Exactly noon. We'll eat now, then go on for another hour. After that we swing south and start the homeward leg.'

They moved out of the shade into the blast of the un-tempered sun. 'Do you think we'll find the plane?'

'No.'

'John-oh doesn't think so either. Why?' They reached the Land-Rover.

He turned. He put his back against the car and then leapt away again as the hot metal hide seared his skin through the shirt. 'Because the French didn't. Because the Toubou haven't since. And there have been other expeditions passing through this area. Mapping parties. Archaeologists like Bowdrey. U.N.O. study teams. Idiots who write books about how they crossed the Sahara in a wickerwork wheelchair pulled by a team of twelve-year-old prostitutes from Aghades.' He was irritable. 'None of them found Teefer's plane. Why the hell should we?'

'Then where is it?' She opened the back door of the Land-Rover and got out the basket of food.

Lassiter shrugged. 'The French might have been wrong. High up in the Tibesti is some of the wildest, most rugged country on earth. It could be there.' They began to walk to the shaded rocks and Lassiter whistled the children out of the pool and waved a commanding arm. 'Or it could be covered by *erg*, shifting dune-sand. There isn't much around here. It's mostly *reg* and *hammada*, firm sand and stony stretches. But it's a possibility nevertheless. One nice big hefty windstorm and you wouldn't find Teefer's plane in a million years. He sat down. 'I told Jane in London that she was wasting her time. You heard me. When we joined John-oh in Algiers he said the same thing. And Nailand is still telling her. But he doesn't make much of a fuss about it because he's in trouble at home. The old bag turns a deaf ear to everyone. Why?'

Susan looked away. 'Call it an obsession. She wants to find Sir Peter's——'

'Ah, don't give me that crap.' Lassiter was annoyed. ' "I

sure am gonna find my poor Peter's bones and bury 'em." '
It was quite a fair imitation of Jane's drawl. 'God, how many times have I heard it? And I still don't believe it, especially because it's *her*. I could accept it from a woollyheaded old dear who kept cats and collected potted plants but not from that vicious old bitch who's got some sort of dirty rot inside her.' He regarded her thoughtfully. 'Is there anything about this expedition that I don't know?'

When she simply shook her head he grabbed her by the shoulders. 'You're lying!'

'I can lie the balls off a brass monkey, Lew.' The girlish lips said the words casually. 'Don't try to get anything out of me. And the children are on their way.'

He let her go. Neil and Thrin came up. They were dressed now, slick-faced and streaky-haired from their swim. Susan passed out biscuits and tinned ham and orange squash from a thermos. They ate quickly. Susan ignored Lassiter. The children murmured about the *guelta*. It took only ten minutes. Then Lassiter slapped his hands and said, 'Let's go,' and got up.

The children trotted ahead to the Land-Rover. Susan picked up the basket. She put out a hand to stop Lassiter as he began to move. 'Lew?'

'What is it?' There was impatience riding him.

'Have you children of your own?'

He looked at her out of a face totally devoid of expression. 'No.' Then he turned and walked away. She followed him and they got into the Land-Rover. He switched on the ignition, started the big engine, eased off the handbrake and let the vehicle nose its way along the defile to the entrance. He had done all this in an impenetrable armour of silence. But now he stopped and let the motor idle. A full minute passed. Then he said, 'They're dead,' and at last turned to look at her.

There was nothing in his face. She began to breathe a little quickly. She was uncertain, wanting to speak but unsure of herself. So he anticipated her.

'There is nothing to say.' He put the Land-Rover into gear again and drove out of the defile, turning quite sharply and forcing the car's blunt nose obediently back on to the compass point of its course.

Susan looked out of the window. It is dead, this world, she thought. It died a thousand years ago and we are as dead as it, this man and I, we live and yet we are dead like the yellow-brown land around us.

The Land-Rover roared on, its noise consumed by the empty silence of the desert.

*　　　*　　　*

John-oh drove tensely. His arms burned from the way they strained between him and the wheel. His hands were slippery with sweat and sweat had made dark patches under his armpits and on the front of his shirt. It had collected under the bottom rims of his sunglasses so that when he lifted them momentarily tears of it ran down his cheeks.

He wiped his face with a rolled-up shirtsleeve. Let go, he told himself. Relax. You're like a nervous racehorse. But he could not, and he knew it even while he was urging himself uselessly. If he hits me on the back once more, he thought, just *once* more, I will fix him. I will reach around, I will take off my sunglasses and show him the menace in my eyes. I will say to him: there are other ways of getting me to stop the car. Don't do that again. That is what I will say. And then, should he dare to touch me again, I will——

It came unexpectedly. A flat-handed clout on the shoulder, stinging him through his shirt. And Nailand's quacking voice: 'Stop, driver.'

John-oh reared. He stamped on the brake pedal so that the vehicle lurched and stalled. He writhed in his seat, struggled within himself. Then he let his hands fall from the wheel into his lap and studied them, seeing how they trembled. Desolation passed through him like a draining vacuum, leaving him limp. Then a small voice followed. That was not *quite* the right moment.

But the next time. . . .

He turned his head and said tonelessly, 'Which way?'

'Right.' Nailand got out. 'I'll search left.' He had a pair of binoculars slung around his chest. Now he lifted them and quartered the bleak terrain while John-oh repeated the movement on the other side of the car in the opposite direction. They did this for a full five minutes.

'Anything?' Lola asked the question from within the artificial gloom of the Land-Rover.

Nailand dropped the glasses against his chest. He pointed an arm thick with biceps, the hand incongruously small-fingered like a feeler. 'Over there. A tiny trail of dust. That's Lassiter leaving the *guelta*. Otherwise nothing.'

Lola strained her eyes. She searched a vista of pale yellow *reg* flecked here and there with the brown blot of a dead or dying bush, beyond that a pale grey stretch of *hammada*, rough with stone, then a whiteness of what was probably loose sand. 'I can't see it.'

Nailand didn't bother to turn. 'Of course you can't, you stupid bitch. The naked eye won't pick it up. But that's old bottle-head, all right.'

John-oh turned and looked at him across the bonnet. 'Lassiter is my friend.'

Nailand pointed his fingers and fluttered his eyelids. 'Oooh, *naughty* John-oh!'

'Joe, please.' Lola said it feebly. 'Leave John-oh alone.'

'Oh, so it's John-oh now, is it?' Nailand sucked in his belly, producing a chest that was mainly bulging diaphragm and over-developed pectorals run to fat. 'Still got the old beef, there. So don't get too familiar, darling, or I'll ruin the little bastard's good looks.'

Nobody said anything. Nailand and Franc got into the Land-Rover and it moved off slowly. They were a little higher than the ground on either side, moving along another stretch of rock-strewn *hammada*.

'Take it easy, don't rattle our teeth.' Nailand said it to the back of John-oh's neck. He and Lola sat behind, with John-oh alone in front, chauffeur-like.

They went on for a kilometre. The stony surface gave way to a mixture of sand and rough gravel and the going became faster and easier.

Lola was limp from heat exhaustion. 'Joe?'

'Why do you begin every sentence with that inevitable, whining, "Joe"?' Nailand's mood had soured like the food in his stomach. They had eaten earlier than Lassiter's party and he had crammed himself with four different kinds of canned food and water laced with brandy.

68

The limpid eyes showed no particular hurt. 'What happened with the last business, Joe? I never fully understood. You seemed to be doing so well and then——'

'In the middle of the Sahara she has to ask a question like that. And the stupid Arab can hear.' Nailand watched John-oh's neck grow red.

Lola leaned towards her husband. 'But what I mean is, well, one moment you were driving a Jaguar and then the next there were bailiffs at the door and we were running to catch the night Boeing. . . .'

'That was the crunch.' Nailand looked straight ahead of him. 'The final crunch. It was the accountants' fault. How was I to know the thing was running at a loss when they were too stupidly incompetent to pick it up? I'm not an accountant, I'm a businessman, I make money. I stick my neck out. Money is a commodity, it——' he broke off and belched. The sour stench of it caught her in the throat. 'In any case, I told you. You're not here to think. Do you want another going over?' He was losing interest. Something had caught his eye, a wink, a flash of silver somewhere to his right and already behind them.

'Stop!' He forgot even to hit John-oh on the back. Twisting his neck he could see it still through the rear window, a tiny twinkle of sunlight reflecting off something shiny.

'You go left.' John-oh was already getting out of the car. 'I'll take the right this time.' He flicked his head back. God, it was still there but it was nothing big, it wasn't more than a hundred yards away.

John-oh had seen nothing. He was miserably polishing his sunglasses with the short tail of his shirt. 'All right.'

'Keep those binoculars working.' He was full of crisp authority suddenly. 'This ground on my side rises a bit. I'm going to the crest.'

John-oh turned away disinterestedly and Nailand headed off. He walked rapidly, panting in the heat, following the beckoning mirror-shine that seemed never to grow nearer. Twice he lost his footing on a stone and nearly fell, cursing hoarsely each time, feeling the mess in his stomach churn. His heart thudded from excitement and the unaccustomed exercise.

69

He walked for another five minutes, reached the rocky crest and looked briefly over it to an endless sameness of landscape on the other side that stretched out from thirty feet below. When he turned back the twinkle was gone. He stopped abruptly, swearing low in his throat, crouching forward as though stalking a stag. God, it was here somewhere. He had lost the angle of the sun's shine.

The only thing to do was to circle. If he had the right place, and of this he was certain, then he must at some point of the circumference again catch the reflection of light off whatever it was he had seen.

He started to do this, moving in a broad curve. After a minute, when he was beginning to tell himself that it had been imagination, the sun seemed to blaze more brightly. Instantly the shine was there again, only a few yards away, blinding him with its intensity so that he could not tell what it was until he had scrambled up to it and picked it up in his shaking hands.

A cigarette case.

'God,' he said aloud, 'God almighty.' It was so hot it burned his fingers but he did not notice. It was untarnished, unmarked by the passage of time. Nothing rusted in the desert. The initials were there as clear as the day they had been engraved: P.A.T.

'Peter Adair Teefer.'

He heard his voice say the names. But he stood in a trance, still staring at the case. So the eagle-nosed bastard had been here after all. The French had been right. Jane had been right. He'd been here. He'd dropped the case or put it there as a sign. And then he'd gone off somewhere. But where? And where was the plane?

Awareness returned. He swung his body in a startled circle, staring back at the Land-Rover a hundred yards away and below him. But John-oh had slung his binoculars. He had his head in the window, talking to Lola. They had seen nothing.

Nailand trembled. He put the case into the back pocket of his slacks, making sure the button was fastened. Then he returned to the crest and searched the stretching arid desolation of the country to the south until his eyes ached. Nothing. More *hammada*. More *reg*. A wild tangle of rearing brown rock that would conceal a dozen *oueds*.

He let the glasses drop and worked his way back to the Land-Rover, his mind jumping over the significance of his find. John-oh heard his coming and walked around to the driver's door.

'See anything?'

Nailand's mouth opened and shut like a trap. 'Nothing. Let's go.'

They got back into the car and moved off steadily eastwards.

* * *

Ann Bowdrey's hands and arms were tanned the same biscuit colour as her legs. They moved quickly but without haste, slender and strong and competent. She was doing lunch for Lady Teefer and herself: Parma ham, potato salad, butter beans with a vinaigrette dressing, baby beetroot.

She stopped and admired the two plates. They looked rather nice, especially with the bold splash of red thrown in by the beetroot. It was wonderful to have the Teefer group's fantastic range of foods from which to select. And everything was out of a can or a bottle.

Her watch was square-faced, with a black ribbon strap. Durable, plain. Like me, she thought. It told her that the time was twenty-five minutes past twelve. It was not yet quite time to eat, so she collected the empty cans and bottles and placed them in an orderly pile on the sand in a corner of the kitchen. They were out of the way, but they nevertheless looked messy and she sorrowed a moment that there was no waste-bin of some sort; even an empty cardboard container would do. She would ask John-oh Franc, or Lassiter.

There was nothing much to wash. The can opener, minutely soiled; a measuring jug; a spoon and a knife. Yet they could not be left. Her training forbade it. She took a plastic basin from the shelf, picked up a jerry-can from near her feet and poured water into the bowl.

Rain. That was what it looked like. Heavy splattering rain. Rain coming down in sheets outside the windows and gurgling in a drainpipe. Cold. Winter coming on soon. Coal glowing in the grate. Her father slumbering in front of the telly, slack-faced and senile. Her mother fussing, pottering. Ann herself glowing after a hot bath, warm in a woolly robe and slippers,

71

loose and relaxed after the long hours of duty. She was heading for the chair at the hearth, a book in one hand. The telephone never rang any more. The dates had fizzled out into the occasional stop-gap request which she invariably refused. It was no use hoping. Hope was gone. Life was just her work, this kind of night, and a succession of winters that seemed to last so long.

Then the tap at the door. Her father waking, spluttery and bleary-eyed. Her mother's 'Goodness, who can it be at this hour?' And it was only eight o'clock. She answered the door herself, thinking that her parents had been dead for years and that she was dying, too.

The man who stood at the doorway had no raincoat. His cheap suit was so drenched it was sodden. The rain had plastered his thinning sandy hair to his skull and made tear-drops that hovered on his eyelashes and plunged and ran on down his wet face.

'Sister Anderson?'

'Yes?' She hovered, half-hidden by the door. It was something unconsciously copied from her mother.

'I doubt you'll remember me. My name is Bowdrey. Albert Bowdrey. I was in your ward in——'

'Oh, Mr Bowdrey!' She knew him, now. 'Come in, please.'

Still he hovered. 'It must seem strange, my coming here like this. It's just that I have something to discuss with you. I mean, not having seen you for nearly six months and then suddenly turning up like this . . . you must think it's funny.'

'Mr Bowdrey. There is nothing we can discuss with you standing drenched and shivering on the door mat.' The nurse in her had risen to the surface. 'And there's nothing funny about exposure, with your condition.' She took him firmly by an arm. 'Come in. I'll dry you out first. You can tell me what's on your mind afterwards.'

In the end she had to clothe him in a spare suit of her father's and put him next to the fire and give him two large gins from a bottle so seldom used that it had collected dust on its square sides. All this took half-an-hour, while her father stared at Bert Bowdrey in outraged hostility and her mother whimpered, flapping about with a feather duster in the background and Bowdrey himself clenched and unclenched his hands in unremitting tension, alternately staring into the black and rosebud colours of the coals and looking up at Ann where she watched him with a passive, composed curiosity.

When she judged that he was ready she stirred and said, 'Now Mr Bowdrey. You're looking better. I take it that what you want to talk to me about is private?'

'Aye.' He rose awkwardly.

'Well, we can't discuss it here, then.' She measured her father's rheumy-eyed hatred at having his tiny world disturbed, her mother's fluttery uselessness. It was the first time she had looked at them objectively in many years and she was astonished to find nothing within her; no pity, no sympathy, no sorrow. There was only a quick flame of excitement. Bowdrey, for all his illness, had a look of business about him. And why should he come to her after all this time? She had always realized he was clever. Even in hospital when he lay flushed with the fever of his advanced tuberculosis, she had felt that there was a good brain behind the angry, frustrated, yearning exterior.

She made up her mind. 'There's only one other place. We can't disturb the old folks. Come with me, Mr Bowdrey.'

Her mother's mouth fell open to show her false teeth. 'But Ann! that's your——'

'Yes.' She nodded firmly. 'My bedroom. Exactly. Come, Mr Bowdrey.' She took his arm, feeling how thin it was under the bag of her father's suit. 'It's this way. . . .'

The plastic bowl overflowed. Water spattered on to the deal table and clustered in fat teardrops on the accumulated grease of its surface.

She stared at them. Like the teardrops her mother had shed when she had left, begging her in the drawing-room to stay, whimpering, 'Darling, what have you done, you've broken Daddy's heart,' Daddy with his india-rubber unbreakable heart bellowing at her from the stairs as she opened the front door, 'You silly young bitch, giving up all this, the security, a job you'll never get back. . . .' She had stared into the ferocity of the old eyes and wondered how, somewhere along the line, love had turned into dull acquiescence, a forelock-tugging, grace-saying, sickeningly dutiful obsequiousness, and from there into a heartless awakening that had the shock of icy water. She had said nothing. She had simply closed the door behind her and gone down the steps towards the taxi that waited. And she had left no single part of her behind.

A trickle of sweat ran out of her hairline, hesitated a moment and plunged down one cheek. That seemed so long ago. It wasn't, it was only weeks. But her world had opened so much; there was so much now for which to strive. No more rain, no more endless winter, just the dry baking air of the Sahara and the wild grand desolate whirl of the Tibesti going ever upwards somewhere north-east of her.

It was time for lunch. The practical square face of her wristwatch told her so. She picked up the two plates.

'Thought I'd find you here, honey.'

Jane Teefer stood in the doorway, one beringed hand holding a whisky glass. Two milky eyes studied Ann across a few feet of sand.

The plates clashed once like cymbals striking. Then she had put them down again on the table. 'You startled me.'

'It's the sand. Muffles your footsteps.' Jane sipping her drink. She was wearing navy slacks and a crisp white jacket with a navy scarf at the throat. For fifty-four she was as trim as a girl. The years showed only in the wrinkled white hands with their blotches of age-freckle.

'Your lunch is ready, Lady Teefer.' Ann clenched her hands.

'I'm kinda breathless today. Don't know that I much feel like it.' The trim shoulders shrugged. 'We never learn, do we? Too much booze last night. I'm panting.'

Ann observed the rapid rise and fall of the older woman's chest. 'It's a tachycardia, Lady Teefer. You'd better take it easy. Lie down and take one of your heart tablets. I'll bring you your lunch in a while.'

Jane began to smile. 'A tachycardia, huh?' She took a step into the room. 'A tachycardia, Mrs housewife Bowdrey?'

The girl's own heart thundered. 'I . . . had an uncle with the same condition.'

'Oh, really.' The voice was dry. 'Is your husband out taking pictures?'

'Yes.'

'What's he use?'

74

'Use?'

'Camera, girl! What kind of camera does he use?'

She hunted desperately in her mind. 'It's a—a—Japanese make. Very good.'

'Size, girl. What size film?'

'Oh . . . I think . . . thirty-five millimetre.'

'Strange. Two-and-a-quarter square would be better.' She advanced another step. Her rings chinked against the glass. 'You go out with him mostly, I figure. Today is an exception. You mostly go out with him, watch him work, help him?'

'Yes.'

'How's he do it—colour or black-and-white?'

'I . . . both, I think.'

'Must be interesting. I used to fiddle a bit with photography before I lost my eyes. Never took pictures of rock carvings, though. Working in the bright sunlight like that amongst the canyons must be difficult. I figure Mr Bowdrey would have a setting of say 5·6 at a 25th, huh? That about right?'

'Yes.' She let her breath out in a quick sigh.

'It's wrong, girl. It's all balls.' The neat figure closed in. The voice sharpened. 'Why you keep walking back? Why you keep walking back, Mrs Bowdrey? You got something to hide, girl?'

'No.' It was a soft, breathy, trembling word.

'That's good. You see, I got no eyes. I have to see with my ears and my hands. All I've seen with so far are my ears, and I'm just a little bit puzzled. Can't quite figure you out. So now I want to see with my hands. That's the way I got to know Lola properly, that's what I did even before I hired Suzie.' The voice became honey-like. 'Now you can't have any objection to my touching you, can you?'

The girl struggled within herself. 'I . . . I don't know. It's not——'

'Proper?' The lips had a tracery of wrinkles under the lipstick. 'We're both women, aren't we? What's not proper about it?' She shrugged. 'Course, if there's things you don't want me to know——'

'There are not!' Sweat ran down Ann's cheeks. 'There's nothing. Nothing at all.' She panted. 'Go ahead. Touch me if you want to.' The words burst out of her. She shook.

'That's better, girl.' The woman moved in. 'Much better. I can see so much with my hands. I feel skin, I feel sweat, I feel the fever in people, I feel a calmness or a clammy hide. And then I know.'

She came in close, throwing the glass carelessly aside so that it landed with a soft thump on the sand near the table.

'Now.' The white hands came out like feelers. They reached out, touched the face, quickly moved on to the hair, followed it down below the girl's shoulders. 'Nice. What shade?'

'Pale blonde.'

'Goes with your voice. You got a blonde voice.'

Now the hands touched her face, outlining it. 'Heart-shaped. Good nose. Colour eyes?'

'Blue.'

Fingers flickered lightly across her lips. Ann writhed involuntarily. Jane chuckled. 'You don't like me. Not one little bit. It figures. Good mouth. Wide, generous. And your neck . . . no turkey wrinkles. You're about twenty-eight, right?'

'Twenty-nine.'

Again the chuckle. 'Not bad.' The hands came down and touched Ann's shoulders. 'Good frame, so far. You're wearing a dress. Light linen. Cheap. It's my guess you were wearing one yesterday, too. Why not slacks, honey?'

'It's . . . against my . . . my beliefs.'

'Oh.' The word was drawn out, dry. 'Now the picture builds. You're one of those. One of those sects, huh?'

'No. I'm a——'

'Doesn't matter.' There was no change in her voice when she said the next words. 'Take your frock off, Mrs Bowdrey.'

'Off?' Ann stared.

'How in hell you expect me to see?' Now the voice sharpened. It crackled like a whip. 'What you hiding under there—diamonds?'

'It's ridiculous. Quite ridiculous.' The words tumbled over themselves. She put up an aberrated forefinger and thumb and squeezed her bottom lip, her terrified eyes locked with the milky discs in Jane Teefer's face.

'Girl, you've got to understand something.' Jane let her hands fall to her sides. 'I'm just an old lady. I'm blind. How do I see you in my mind? What picture do I use? So far there

76

is just a face, with nothing below. Come on now, honey. We women got no secrets from one another.'

'I . . . don't know.' Ann trembled in indecision, confused by the sudden wheedling tone.

'Please. For a blind woman.'

Ann's hands fluttered like the beating wings of a bird. Then she reached up, undid the zip fastener on the dress, pulled it over her head and let it fall to the sand. She quivered. She put her hands across her front.

'That's better. Now turn around.'

Ann turned. She was facing the back wall, staring at *Mademoiselle Janvier* whose parted lips and wide eyes appeared to look back in fascination.

'*No!*'

She was too late. Two steely fingers had unhooked the bra and it was gone.

'No need to worry, honey.' The fingers came out, smoothed their way down her bare back. 'Good. Lovely skin. I figure you are five-six, weight one-eighteen. Right?'

'Yes.' The word tumbled out of her dry mouth. She stared at the French girl on the calendar. The brown eyes watched her with their two-dimensional wisdom.

'Turn around girl.'

Dumbly, she faced about.

'Don't be so shy. Lemme see.' One white hand reached out like a striking snake. The fingers hooked clawlike about the girl's wrists exactly where they crossed over her bosom. A steely, irresistible strength hauled them down and held them imprisoned. The other hand touched, explored, felt.

'Very good. No sag. You got the body of a teenager. You're lucky.'

The wrists were released suddenly. Ann let her hands swing to her sides. Her legs felt weak. Her vision was blurring. She closed her eyes, felt the warm wall touch her back.

'That's better.' The voice came like a warm purr. 'Relax. Relax, Ann Bowdrey. I got some more to find out. There's something else I gotta know, something I suspect.'

The hand came quickly, forcibly. The breath was quick, see-saw, ragged, the old body was close up against hers.

Ann's eyes flew open wide in horror. She shrieked. Something in her exploded and Jane Teefer was pitched half-way across the kitchen, tumbling, sprawling in a slither of sand on the floor.

'*Get out! Get out! Get out!*'

It was her own voice calling out of darkness. She felt the yielding sand under her and a dark moment lost in time. Then her eyes opened and she began to sob, the sobs tearing her throat while she crawled in her abject nudity to her clothes and clutched them, holding them against her.

Calmness came eventually. Calmness and a sort of peace. She dressed, facing the wall. And when she finally turned around the other woman was gone. And so was one of the plates.

Lady Teefer was having lunch.

*   *   *

Lassiter's Land-Rover had fitted neatly into the empty slot left by Nailand's extended swing south. It was two o'clock and both vehicles were now returning on the homeward probe, parallel to each other and approximately three kilometres apart. As near as possible, taking into account irregularities in the ground, their sweep converged; what was not within the compass of one group would be covered from the other side. The maximum range of their binoculars met, so to speak. Each party also searched its outside: in Lassiter's case, his glasses ranging north covered the terrain deliberately omitted by the other group, while Nailand's maximum southern coverage would be marked on the map. Tomorrow, the trucks would move across and start again two kilometres beyond this point.

The scheme was as thorough as Lassiter and John-oh could conceive and had been hammered out to finality in Algiers. It was tiring, exacting work with many stops. It would become more difficult, too, with course deviations to inspect *oueds* and defiles and detour impassable ground. These would have to be covered on foot. It would take time, possibly more time than they had at their disposal. But if Sir Peter Teefer's plane had come down within the rectangle they were ultimately going to transcribe, and was still visible, then theoretically they would find it.

It was a good theory, Lassiter thought. But they were banking on the French having pinpointed the general area of Teefer's disappearance and the French might have been wrong. He braked and let the engine idle.

Susan was pale from the furnace heat. 'Another stop? My eyes are aching.'

'Mine too.' Lassiter got out. 'I'll sweep south. You do the north.'

Susan raised her binoculars and began to sweep the desolate ground, seeing up close a patch of grey *hammada*, an area of gravel, some sand, more *hammada*, more sand, firm yellow sand out of which straggled two bushes. One of them had a look of blueness to it.

She took away the glasses, wiped her eyes quickly and impatiently on the sleeve of her shirt. Strange, that. A blue bush. Crazy tricks the mind played. She raised the binoculars, found the patch again. Blue? God, it *was* blue.

'Hey!' Her forearms quivered with the effort of trying to keep the heavy glasses fixed.

'What you got?' Excitement jumped into Lassiter's voice. In a moment he was next to her, brushing against her. Their eyes met. He looked almost fierce. 'What is it? Where?'

'Follow me.' She held the binoculars with one hand and pointed a slender arm. 'Eleven o'clock. There's a guy out there. A man. And something else. A brown blob. I thought it was a bush at first.'

'Got it.' He spoke holding the binoculars to his eyes. 'That's a camel lying on its side. But I'm not so sure about the man. Looks like a blue bundle.' An idea came to him. 'Thrin, blow the hooter. Twice.'

There was a pause while Thrin scrambled away. Then the Land-Rover's horn shattered the silence.

'It's a man, all right. He's standing up, looking our way.' Susan lowered the glasses. 'Can we go get him?'

'Yes. The ground between looks all right.' Lassiter was already moving away. He got into the truck and started the engine.

It took them fifteen minutes because of the terrain. They had to crawl over a stony stretch and avoid a beckoning, treacherous-looking *oued*. Lassiter stopped eventually some

79

fifty yards from their goal because there was a patch of soft sand between. Then the four of them alighted and clustered in front of the Land-Rover, momentarily uncertain, staring at the figure that walked slowly towards them, stopped, and then considered them over a small distance.

Susan's mind went back to Djanet, and the lordly blue-veiled figures that stalked the palm-groves there. This was a Touareg, a man swathed in cloth like armour so that only his feet and ankles, his hands and his eyes were visible. The eyes were grey, level, heavily made-up around the lids with kohl the way a woman would use mascara. The hands and feet were as slender as a girl's, the body, even under the encompassing blue headcloth, veil, cloak and baggy white pants, had the narrow leanness of a stripling.

'Touareg,' she whispered.

'Yes.' Lassiter spoke conversationally. 'A true desert Touareg. Young. No more than sixteen. His eyes give it away. His camel is dead.'

Lassiter had been right both times. The eyes were the eyes of a youth, not a man, and the camel stretched out beyond him had the awkward stiffness of death. 'Can you speak to him?'

He shrugged. 'I don't know Tamahak. John-oh does, I think. But if this kid can speak a bit of French we can get along.' He took a step forward, put his hands on his hips smiled to put the still figure at ease.

'*Parlez-vous Français?*'

Only the head moved, the most fractional inclination.

Lassiter shrugged. 'A man of few words, this chap. *Comment vous appelez-vous?* I'm asking his name.'

'T'ekmedhin.'

'*Où sont les autres? Ou êtes-vous seul?*'

A hand no browner than a heavy tan made a loose, vague sweep of the country to the north. '*Ils sont de l'autrecôté. Mon chameau est tombé malade. Je suis resté en arrière.*' The French was slow, rusty. The voice lacked manhood's timbre. It established his youth. But the lack of fear in his light eyes was ageless. They rested now on the children, who stared back with solemn, fascinated interest.

'*Pourquoi ne sont-ils pas revenus vous chercher?*'

'*Je pensais guérir le chameau moi-même. Ou peut-être ilse sont perdus.*' He stopped, then seemed to consider that this needed further elucidation. '*Ici c'est le Tibesti. Ce n'est pas le pays d'Imo-chagh.*'

Lassiter said to Susan: 'His camel died and his band are lost. What bothers me is what they're doing out here. The Tibesti is essentially Toubou country and the two groups cordially detest one another. He has admitted that he is not on home ground.' To the youth he said in French. 'Are *you* lost?'

A small pride came into the eyes. '*Pas exactement.*'

'Well then, you will know there is an oasis, Zufra, about two, maybe three days march away. Why did you not strike out for there?'

It was impossible to tell, this time, what went on behind the indigo veil. So little was visible in the narrow gap that was like the driver's slit in an armoured car. Except, Lassiter thought, that this boy is armoured only in cloth and pride. 'Because the camel has only been dead one day. I was waiting to see whether my people would return.'

'And will they?'

There was a pause. 'Not yet.'

Susan Shields's growing impatience gave way. 'What the heck's going on, Lew?'

Lassiter put a hand on her shoulder. 'One more question, first.' And to the Touareg: 'What is your band doing here in the Tibesti?'

The slim, blue-cloaked shoulders shrugged. 'I do not know. I am not of age.'

'Like hell.' Lassiter studied the clever eyes. Then he turned to the girl. 'He won't admit that he is completely lost. And he won't say what his group is doing in these parts. He says he hadn't struck out for help yet, because he thought his people might come back for him. Now he's not so sure.'

'Surely that doesn't concern us?' Susan studied Lassiter critically. 'Why are you being so cautious? This kid is stranded. He's in need of help. Surely we can load him into the Land-Rover, take him back to the fort and keep him alive until his tribe or whatever they call it, return?'

For Lassiter indecision was a rare thing. But he showed it now. 'The Touareg can be very tough. I know little about them and what I do know John-oh told me. But this is a shrewd, smart kid with a lot going on behind that *litham* that I would like to be able to see.' He thought a moment. 'Let's have a look at that camel.' He swung to the boy. 'I wish to examine your camel.'

There was the smallest inclination of the head. Then the robed figure turned disinterestedly about and led the way to the dead beast.

Even in death the camel had that look of sardonic humour which is so much part of them and which the Arabs attribute to the fact that whereas humans know only ninety-nine names of the Prophet, the camel knows the hundredth. It was stretched out quite stiffly on its side, and up against its neck were three black-smeared bowls in the sand which Susan realized with sudden revulsion were lined with dried blood. She shuddered. But Lassiter, bent over with his hands on his knees, displayed great interest, nodding his head repeatedly while the Touareg's voice went into a long monologue in French. Then he straightened and turned to her.

'I've been told about this sort of thing. The beast died of something peculiar to camels known as "blood in the head". Nobody really knows what causes it. The animal begins to stagger. It developes a glazed look in the eyes. Then it runs round banging its head against anything solid it can find. Eventually it falls down and dies of a stroke. But if you're quick you can cure it.' He pointed a long forefinger. 'You make three bowls in the sand with your cupped hands. That's a form of crude measure. Then you cut the jugular vein in the neck. Dark blood comes out first, changing colour as the flow continues. When the bowls have been filled, the cut in the neck is closed with a wad of hair. If you're in time the camel will recover quite soon.' He stood up. 'In this chap's case he was too late, although he says he didn't think he would be.'

For a minute all of them studied the dead camel. It would lie here for a thousand years. Then Lassiter shifted impatiently. He made up his mind. 'It seems to be genuine. I suppose all we can do is take him along with us.' He turned to the Touareg. 'You wish help? We can take you with us to our camp. It is not far.'

The boy nodded. '*Oui.*' And then after a pause, '*Merci.*' He turned and picked up the light Touareg saddle with its slender crucifix pommel, a leather bag, a blanket roll and the single-thong leather rein, all of which lay neatly stacked nearby. He advanced with them towards the Land-Rover, hanging back as the doors were opened on the left side and Susan and the children got in.

Lassiter grinned. He said, 'Get in,' pointing to the back seat next to Neil. 'I doubt that this bloke has ridden in a car before but he's not going to let on. I don't like the kid. But he's got plenty of guts.' Then he went around to the driver's side, got aboard and started the engine. The Land-Rover bumped away, back on to its original line of travel.

Susan lit a cigarette and stared through the windscreen. The Touareg sat directly behind her. He must be uneasy, she thought, and frightened, even terrified at this unaccustomed ride. But he is too proud to show it. She felt a vague desire to reassure him.

She turned quickly and in doing so caught him off guard. Because the eyes she met were not afraid. They had the red ferocity of a wolf, and mixed with this was a look of jeering and malevolent triumph.

She jerked around to face her front, trembling and afraid. It is going to be a very long trip home, she thought.

CHAPTER FOUR

THE SOUS-PREFET OF ZUFRA was a neat man with a strong sense of order. He was also inclined to be impatient. Thus it irked him in two ways to have to squat in the sand on the edge of the oasis, listening to the unending dribble of execrable French that flowed from the gummy mouth of the horrible, dirty old man sitting next to him. In the first place there was the strong probability that the *Sous-Préfet* had already dirtied his neat, light-khaki uniform. The eight Toubou had been camped here for three hours and all sorts of things might be lying around, apart from the inevitable camel dung. And in

83

the second, the old man was bordering on senility and prattled ever on with the loquacity of second childhood.

Only one thing kept Lieutenant Pierre Goru squatting there, nodding as though he had all the time in the world and wasn't worrying whether his backside might not have connected with some piece of stray foulness: it was the importance of what the old man was saying. He was called Khoum and although he was in essence a Toubou he was in reality a mixture of breeds and had spent some years with the Touareg.

Khoum even counted like a Touareg. He had finished enumerating the camels and now he was busy with the men, detailing the *iklan*, the *bellah*, the youths, the noblemen. To do this he drew a rectangle in the sand, and as he talked he made strokes near it with a forefinger. Each time a row of strokes reached ten, he put an additional stroke in the box he had drawn. It had been an interminable process but now it was finished. The *Sous-Préfet* counted the lines in the box: ten. That represented, therefore, one hundred.

'One hundred? You're sure?'

He received a toothless grin and a nod in response. 'Ask my friends. They will tell you.'

The other seven Toubou were a line of white robes and black faces in the darkness. Their heads moved in ragged unison. '*Certainement, c'est vrai.*'

'One hundred Touareg. One hundred and twenty-seven camels. That is the largest party I have ever heard of. From whence do they come?'

Khoum shrugged and his silent choir followed suit. 'The Hoggar perhaps. Perhaps Air. Or maybe Tassili. Their camels are a mixture. It is difficult to tell.'

The *Sous-Préfet* wiped sweat from his chocolate-coloured face. He was a Negro from the south, a Christian, unhappy and strange up here in this dry world of Islam.

'No women, no children. Just the *iklan*, the *bellah*, their Touareg masters. It can't be a *razzia*, a camel-raid. Those days are gone. And the party would never have been so big anyway. Did you notice their weapons?'

Khoum produced another wizened, monkey-like grin. 'Bolt-action rifles.' He made the motion of slamming home a bolt-action rifle. 'One to every man. Plenty of ammunition.'

Dominus Christus nostrum. Goru crossed himself. He was very devout. A twinge came to his belly. It was partly fear and partly indigestion. He over-ate regularly.

Out of the turmoil within him he readily produced irritation. 'What are they doing in *my* district?'

'I don't know.' Again the gummy smile, the shrug.

The *Sous-Préfet* smouldered. 'The leader's name. Do you know it?'

The walnut-wrinkled face went solemn. 'Jedren.' There was a sigh from his choir.

The twinge inside Goru became a solid ache in his solar plexus. God, Jedren of all people. He got up stiffly, replaced his puce-coloured beret, saluted.

'Thank you. I am glad you found your lost camel.' That was how it came about, all this information. The camel had gone astray and they had searched the lower parts of the Tibesti for it. It was nothing to search for a missing camel for a month or more. A camel represented wealth and time meant nothing. Absolutely nothing.

The seven-headed choir nodded and Khoum waved farewell. They would be gone in the morning and he might not see them for three years.

The *Sous-Préfet* walked rapidly through the oasis, leaving the small jungle of palms behind. He crossed a bleak area of open ground to a line of five small flat-roofed buildings. All of them were crumbling. Some looked almost derelict. It was this way since the French had left. No money, no interest, poor administration.

The best of the buildings was used as a radio shack. Lieutenant Goru entered, crossed the room and stood next to the sergeant who was crouched at the set.

'What are you getting?'

The man looked up. He was a Negro like Goru and when he smiled his white teeth were an island of blazing enamel in the black sea of his face.

'The news from Fort Lamy.' The trooper shook his head. 'Not good. The rebels ambushed a truck and killed nine of our men. The Legion pursues.'

'Ah.' The *Sous-Préfet* made a sound of disgust. 'Always the Legion pursues. And gets nowhere.' God, to think they were so weak that they'd had to ask Paris, 'Please, send back the Legion. Let us pretend it is the old times and lend us the Legion to fight our dreary, deadly little war for us.' About the only reassuring thing was the fact that this ugly internal strife was further south. But even then, he reasoned dismally, if the Government eventually topples, so do I. The Government was a Christian, Negro government and if it went it would be replaced by Moslem rule. Then down will come Goru wife, soldiers, Zufra and all, he brooded. He knew some English and he remembered the nursery rhyme which he had learnt but never understood, so many years ago. Now it seemed particularly applicable.

He rubbed his belly. It bulged against the light khaki shirt. 'If you hear anything more, let me know.'

'*Oui, mon oncle.*' The sergeant was, in fact, Lieutenant Goru's nephew.

The *Sous-Préfet* had reached the doorway. 'I have warned you before. Call me "uncle" again and I will remove those chevrons from your sleeve, personally. We must have discipline.'

The smile on the other chocolate-coloured face died away. *Oui, mon Lieutenant.*'

Goru walked on through the darkness. He reached the main village, skirting square mud houses with their flat roofs and tiny patches of greenery until he reached his own. Here he hesitated a moment, checked the trim fit of his uniform shirt, then swept aside the bead curtain and entered through an arched doorway.

'*Pierre, mon cher.* You are late.' Camille was waiting for him, dressed especially for him in colourful lamé. She did this only on certain occasions and Goru felt a small stirring of excitement.

It was overshadowed, though, by his problems and preoccupations.

'I have been talking to Khoum.'

'Khoum?'

'A Toubou I know. He and his group have been hunting a lost camel in the Tibesti. Khoum had some rather interesting things to tell me.'

'Trouble?' She studied him while he took out a neatly-folded khaki handkerchief that matched his uniform. He mopped his face.

'Trouble—hah!' Goru's irritable glance went from her face to *grand-mère* sitting in a corner rocking her body from side to side and mumbling a senile, toothless dirge. She was about a hundred years old and Camille was her eighteenth child. Camille was also the only one of them still living.

'Must that old bitch——' Goru stopped himself. His eyes slid to the crucifix on the wall and the very old, very cheap print of the Madonna and Child. He crossed himself. 'I'm sorry. It's just that . . .'

'You're upset and tired.' Camille brought him a big glass of rose wine. 'When a man gets like that he must first drink, then talk. In that order.'

'Bless you.' His warm eyes studied her. She was mostly Negro, but a little of some other blood showed in the narrow-bridged, hawklike nose and thin lips. Camille was very clever. She had been married to a French Captain who had died of dysentery in 1965. This gave her much status. I am very lucky to have her, he thought.

Half the wine was gone. He felt a glow in his body and the howl in his belly had stopped. 'I have four problems. He finished the wine and extended the empty glass. 'More, *ma chérie.*'

Camille poured. 'And they are?'

Goru took the glass. 'First of all, the trouble . . . in the south.' He made his voice quite confiding. He even flicked his head in a southerly direction. 'The rebels have scored another success. Nine men killed in an ambush.'

'There is absolutely nothing we can do about it.' Camille was so categorical she became almost loud. 'Nothing whatsoever. All we can do is go about our work here and hope and pray that things come right.'

'Perfectly true.' He shrugged, drank some more. 'One can't help worrying about it, nevertheless. The other problems, though, concern me more directly.'

'Such as?'

The *Sous-Préfet* put his glass on a small table. 'I can't help thinking that the three are interconnected.' He put one forefinger across the other, beginning to tick off points. 'First,

87

those infernal Bowdreys. You'll remember them. They came here to buy petrol. We had them to lunch.'

Camille nodded. 'The woman had the eyes of a virgin.'

He refused to be sidetracked. 'They bother me, those two. Desperately poor, with the most shocking equipment. And yet they come all this way to photograph the rock-carvings of the Tibesti which both you and I and anyone else who has gone to the trouble to find out, know have absolutely no archaeological value. Why?'

'They are fools,' she said softly. 'The world is full of fools.'

'All right. Let us accept that they are fools. I don't think so for one moment, but nevertheless for the time being they are fools. Now, Khoum tells me that the Teefer expedition has arrived. Two Land-Rovers, six adults, two children.' He remembered Khoum's strokes in the sand, with nothing in the box this time because none of the rows had reached ten. 'It must be them.'

'The blind woman, searching for the body of her husband?'

'Yes, that's the one. There was a piece about her in *Paris-Match*. And apparently *both* these groups have established themselves in Fort Masuril.' He sighed and reached for his drink.

Camille said, 'There was a fourth problem.'

Goru lowered the glass. 'You have heard of Jedren?'

He saw the quick alarm in her eyes. 'The Touareg? You know I have.'

'He is also in my district.' He leaned towards her to make his point. 'With one hundred men and more than that in camels!'

They watched each other carefully. Then she said, 'He would go through Zufra like a wind. We would not stand a chance.'

'Of course not.' He thought for a moment. 'To sum up, we have the following position: a strange man and his wife, without money, who hunt carvings that have no value. A blind woman who seeks the bones of her husband, at much expense, with the purpose only of burying them. And finally a Touareg bandit, a mystery-man of the Sahara about whom we have heard a lot and know very little. All of them, within days, arrive at almost the exact same spot. Two have nonsensical reasons for their presence. The third does not need a reason because he is a law unto himself.'

He shook his head violently. 'I do not like it, Camille.' He called her this only when gravely troubled. 'It stinks, it smells. It has the stench of the carrion that brings three strange jackals to the same water-hole.'

'You have a solution?'

'No. But I feel I must not wait for things to happen. A thunderstorm will break over our heads. I must act quickly. I must cut out the sore before it reaches a head and poisons the body.'

She studied him wisely. 'Do not force it. It will come.'

'I hope so.' He had drunk the entire bottle of wine. He felt warm and loose.

Camille put a thin dark arm around his thickening waist. 'When a man cannot find the answer to something, he bottles up like a volcano. Let us release the lava.'

Goru grinned. 'I think that is an excellent idea.' He went over to *grand-mère*. It was impossible to tell whether she was asleep. He took her apron in his hands and flicked it lightly over her head. Then he joined Camille in the curtained sleeping alcove.

She made love with a brilliant Gallic fervour that she had learned from her late husband. Afterwards, in the darkness, Goru lay on his back staring at the low ceiling. He was completely at peace with the world.

'I have not found the solution as yet. But I have reached a decision. And that is almost as good.'

She whispered, 'What is it?'

He turned over and lay on one elbow, looking at the dark form next to him. 'Tomorrow. Tomorrow I will go on a tour of inspection. And I will visit this place called Fort Masuril and see why the jackals have gathered there.'

He turned on his back again and in a minute he was asleep.

*　　*　　*

The three Land-Rovers returned to Fort Masuril within minutes of each other as dusk was giving way to night. The tired and thirsty crews of the two Teefer vehicles scattered to their respective rooms, Lassiter deviating from his course only long enough to offer the Touareg boy water and food, both of which was refused. So Lassiter told him in English to go to hell and then in French to find himself a place to sleep and amuse himself how he liked as long as he kept out of the way. Then he went on, to find that Lady Teefer was having an early-evening nap and therefore the reports that he and Nailand were supposed to turn in would have to be delayed until everyone met in the Mess for supper.

When Lassiter reached the room he shared with John-oh, the younger man had poured two hefty whiskies and added reasonably cool water from a *guerba*, a goatskin container that had been kept in the shade. John-oh was pacing.

'What's the matter?' Lassiter took off his shirt on which the sweat had turned cold and splashed water over his face and neck from a basin in an aluminium stand.

'It's Nailand.' John-oh grabbed his drink as though it were Nailand's neck. 'He treats me like offal, like a piece of camel dung you kick out of your way as you walk. "Hey, Arab!" "Stop, Arab!" "Start, Arab!" ' He glared across the room. 'I can't stand it!'

Lassiter gave each armpit a one-second burst of deodorant from an aerosol container. He found a clean shirt and struggled into it. 'There's something eating that guy. You're just a safety valve. So is Lola. He works out his tensions on the two of you.'

John-oh said, 'Well, I've had it. If he does it again I'm going to cut his guts out. Damn-it-all, Lew, you know I'm not aggressive. I just want to be left alone.' He swung his head from side to side. 'But a man can take so much and no more. If he does it again, I'm telling you I'll cut his guts out.'

Lassiter said roughly, 'All right, then, go ahead and do it. Don't just threaten when he's out of earshot.'

John-oh put his glass on the light camp table. He placed his hands carefully in his pockets. 'Lew?'

'Huh?' Lassiter was sitting on the edge of his stretcher, unlacing his canvas shoes.

'I'm chicken, aren't I?'

Lassiter let one shoe fall. Then he turned to look at John-oh. 'There are degrees of cowardice. And there is circumstantial cowardice.' He smiled with a degree of compassion the others would have found surprising but John-oh, who knew him, had seen that smile before and sometimes relied upon it. 'There's the fellow who sat all night in his tent waiting for his first battle. He was afraid that he would prove to be a coward; so eventually his blew his brains out. Silly, wasn't it? And then you take me: I'm terrified of heights. A thousand feet above a gorge, building a bridge, sometimes I'd freeze. Nobody ever knew; I learned to live with it.' The smile turned into a grin. 'Some of the girders on the bridges I've built, sonny, they've got my fingerprints on them, etched into the steel.' He kicked off the other shoe, got up, fetched his drink. 'Forget about Nailand. All bullies are the same. They enjoy knowing they're riling you.'

'It's not all that easy.' John-oh was thinking of Lola. He picked up his drink. 'What is it that's eating Nailand?'

'I don't know. I'm developing a feeling that there's a lot I don't know about this expedition.'

'Such as?'

'Such as Jane's real reason for coming here. Do you honestly believe she came all this way and spent all that money to find and bury Sir Peter's bones?'

John-oh considered this. 'When you contacted me to come along, I was not really in a position to question her motives. In fact I didn't care a damn what her purpose was.'

'Likewise. I was broke and in trouble with the flat-feet after a lost weekend. If she'd said that she wanted to cross the Sahara because she was a freak and needed sex with a camel, I'd have gone along. But now . . .' Lassiter pointed a long bony forefinger at John-oh, closed one eye and aimed along it, '. . . now I'm thinking.'

John-oh was interested. 'But what else would bring her here?'

'I don't know.' Lassiter fiddled with his empty glass. 'But when people—*if* people—use a front to disguise their true intentions, the reason is often . . . financial.' He winked. 'Get me?'

'Yes and no.' John-oh produced cigarettes. 'No, because there is no gold here, no oil, no mineral. . . .'

Lassiter was shaking his head. 'I have no more idea than you, what else it could be. Just let's keep our eyes and ears open.'

'Another drink?'

Lassiter looked at his watch. 'No. Time to go to the Mess. Jane will be installed by now and waiting to hear the results of Probe One. Let's go.' He slapped John-oh on the back. 'I'm down to my last clean shirt. Your turn to do the drip-dries tonight.'

'Okay.' John-oh shrugged into a jersey. He waited while Lassiter did the same and changed his socks and shoes. Then they started out of the room.

In the doorway Lassiter stopped.

'Something else. Just so you know the score. I did a bit of general reading about the Tibesti before we left London. Do you know the archaeological value or significance of the carvings friend Bowdrey is going to such lengths to photograph?'

John-oh shook his head. 'No.'

'Nil.' Lassiter put his arm around John-oh's shoulders. 'Absolutely bugger-all.'

They walked out into the darkness of the courtyard.

*   *   *

Bowdrey, having lone-wolfed it all day, was eager to report to Ann. But he was very tired and this brought on a bout of coughing which raged on for minutes, ending only when he produced another mouthful of blood-speckled phlegm and lay back, exhausted, on his stretcher, looking at her out of eyes that seemed deep-sunken in their sockets.

She gave him his streptomycin injection, straight-faced and automatic in her movements.

'What's wrong? Something's happened to you today.'

She shook her head. 'It's nothing. We all have our ups and downs. Lady Teefer is very trying.'

Tired as he was, he boiled immediately. 'Has that old bitch been at you?'

'No, Bert.' Although she shuddered inwardly at the recollection, she knew how useless and how dangerous it would be to tell him. 'How did it go?'

He propped himself up on his elbows. 'Nothing to report. They drew a blank. I will shadow Nailand again tomorrow because he is the outside man.'

'That's good.' She was remote, detached from him. He sensed this and had a fragmentary recollection of sitting at the hearth in her parents' home, in a borrowed suit, while she brought him gin.

'Are you coming to the Mess?' She was looking at her watch.

He realized suddenly the extent of his exhaustion. 'I don't think so. Could you bring me a couple of drinks, lass?'

She ignored the silent plea in his eyes. 'You managed very well without liquor before the Teefer group arrived.'

He became irritable, and envious of the firm, healthy body at the foot of his bed. 'Only because we didn't have the money to bring our own. If the drinks are available, bring a couple for Christ's sake and don't lecture me.'

'I'm not lecturing you.' They sounded, she thought, as though they had been married for years.

He sat up. 'Then what's on your mind?'

'There is only one thing on my mind, Bert. You know what it is. I don't want to see you lose your drive. So far we are keeping your T.B. at bay. But liquor could destroy you.'

Her expression made his mouth twist wryly. 'If we found the money. And then, after that, I went on the booze. What then? How would you feel?'

She moved from the foot of his stretcher, looking with the socks and the brogues as though she were headed for a grouse shoot. 'I would not care a damn, Bert. Not a single, solitary damn.'

She walked to the door. Then casually, over her shoulder: 'I will ask Franc or Lassiter to bring you two whiskies. No more. And some food. That's just as important.' Then she was gone, out into the courtyard.

* * *

Nailand had washed by stripping naked and sponging his body with tepid water. He dried himself enthusiastically, pulling the towel hard across his back and shoulders in a sawing motion while he admired his reflection in a travel mirror Lola used for her make-up.

'Not bad for forty-two, I must say.' He sucked in his belly and shoved out his fatty pectorals.

'Joe?'

'Joe?' he mimicked savagely, bending and studying his face in the mirror.

'Who is Pat?'

'Pat?' He saw himself frown.

'Yes, on this . . .'

He understood suddenly and wrenched his body around. She was standing next to his bed, holding his trousers in one hand and Sir Peter's cigarette case in the other.

'Christ, you bloody meddling bitch!' He leapt across the room, striking her brutally in the face with one hand while he snatched at the case with the other, Lola, who normally accepted his blows on the basis that she was automatically at fault, this time began to cry, sniffling and knuckling at her eyes like a child while the skin on her neck developed the red blotchy patches of emotion.

'I'm sorry.' It was so unusual for him to apologize that she dropped her hands and stared at him. But he had at all costs to reassure her, and with his composure returning he gave silent thanks for the fact that her feather brain had not grasped that those were initials on the case, not a name. She had not noticed the tiny full-stops between each letter or the fact that all the letters were capitals.

'Pat was someone very special to me.' He fumbled for ideas in a relatively unimaginative mind. 'We . . . we were very nearly married. This was years ago. She spent a night in my flat and then the next day she flew to Rome for a fortnight with an uncle who was somebody in the Embassy there. Except that she never arrived. Her plane came down in the drink. I found the case only after I knew she was dead.'

Tears returned to Lola's eyes. Only they were tears of genuine pity.

'I'm sorry. You've never mentioned her before.'

She was so incredibly forgiving, so generous with her emotions that she could weep over a rival who had never existed. For a moment he felt the tiniest, most fragmentary spark of tenderness, instantly extinguished in the flood of triumph that swept over him at having deluded her so easily.

'I'd be glad if you didn't mention this to anyone.' He dropped the case into an open travel bag, zipped the bag shut. Then he looked at his watch, satisfied that loyal, stupid Lola would remain mute. 'We'd better get a move on. It's time we went through to the Mess.'

He began to dress, busy with his thoughts while Lola applied extra make-up to conceal the slight swelling at the corner of her mouth that had been caused by his fist.

*   *   *

T'ekmedhin had finished half an hour with John-oh, a question-and-answer session which had left the guide with a lot of words but very little fact. Now he stared after John-oh's retreating back and said very softly, under his breath, '*Haratin!*' It was a generic term applicable to the slave class of the Sahara and he spoke the word with great contempt.

It was full dark and they had been talking in the courtyard. As soon as John-oh's figure reached the open doorway of the Mess, the Touareg turned away and drifted across to the kitchen. There was a lamp hissing softly on the table but the place was empty. He went in, stopped at the table and looked around. His eyes hovered on *Mademoiselle Janvier* for a moment, reflecting nothing. Then he studied the shelf with its stack of provisions. After a while he took down a can of grapefruit. The picture on the label intrigued him. He put his right hand into the broad left sleeve of his *takatkat*, his robe, and brought out his arm dagger from its sheath there. Lamplight glinted on the straight six-inch blade as it stabbed down into the can. Juice bubbled out through the gash. He pulled his *litham* down a little to expose his mouth, raised the can and drank some of the liquid. His lips twisted at the bitterness of the stuff and he flung the tin carelessly into a corner. No wonder they looked so miserable, these people.

He went out into the night again, crossed the courtyard quite briskly and climbed to the north-eastern watch tower. Here lay his saddle, blanket-roll, his leather bag. He took up the bag and perched on a buttress. Out of the bag he took an earthenware bottle and a big flat square of cheese. This was his supper. The bottle contained *ghussub*, millet flour mixed with water and powdered cheese to the consistency of gruel. He drank some of this, then ate sparingly of the slab of cheese which was made out of equal parts of goat's and camel's milk.

It took him less than ten minutes to finish his meal. Then

he stood, stretched lithely, checked the rising moon. It was time. He trotted very lightly down the steps, and moved across the courtyard, keeping well away from lighted doorways. Out of the Mess came the sound of music, voices loudly raised in talk, the smell of alcohol and burning tobacco. Under the *litham* his lips twisted in contempt. They were offal, these people. Only the tall man who had found him represented any real threat and this man also consumed the liquor that destroyed the senses.

He shrugged and moved on, reaching and passing through the gates. He walked steadily until he reached a small rise in the ground. Here he stopped. Despite the moon he could not see very far. Darkness encompassed him.

The voice he was expecting came softly from the top of the rise, mocking gently. 'You are late. Does T'ekmedhin enjoy the company of his rescuers so much?'

'Enjoy!' The boy put heavy, ironic emphasis on the word. 'They are like braying asses. They fight and quarrel amongst themselves all the time but no blows are struck.'

The voice had a hint of laughter. 'You must tell them our proverb: "Kiss the hand you cannot cut off".'

'They would be too drunk to understand.'

'Do not underestimate them.' The voice became serious. 'They are like this, the Franks. But they can be unexpectedly strong.' There was a pause. Then. 'No news yet, I suppose?'

'Nothing. I will speak to you again this time tomorrow.'

'All right. Peace.' The voice trailed off into the night.

'Peace.'

T'ekmedhin walked quickly back to the fort, climbed to the watch tower. He unrolled his blanket and lay down but his senses remained alert, listening without comprehension to the noise from the Mess. After a while he sat up and delved in the leather bag, smiling under his *litham* as he brought out a shining, modern Beretta automatic. Then he lay down again, contented like a child, and began to wipe minute specks of sand from the weapon.

*　　　*　　　*

From canned meat and vegetables Ann Bowdrey had managed to produce a very palatable stew. The pot stood steaming on the same table as the bottles of liquor while the group, minus Bert Bowdrey and the children, ate in a circle around the paraffin heater with their plates on their laps.

'So you drew a complete blank.' Lady Teefer neatly loaded her fork, put the mouthful between the wrinkled red lips and chewed firmly. 'That's the net result, huh?'

'Yes.' Nailand didn't bother to look up. He was attacking the mountain of food on his plate as though afraid it might escape. Both cheeks bulged and gravy dribbled down his chin. 'There was bugger-all to see. That right, Lassiter?'

Lassiter nodded. Then he remembered again that Jane was sightless. 'That's right. The country today was fairly open, madame. But it's going to close up and become more difficult as we move across. You were on the outside, Nailand. Did you notice how the ground changes?'

Nailand belched loudly and coarsely. A spasm caused by some internal conflict passed across his face. He cured it by quickly drinking half his whisky, but this in turn made him choke. Everyone waited while he coughed and heaved, purple-faced, eyes bulging, bits and pieces of stew and saliva raining in a disgusting spray from his mouth. Eventually he was able to say hoarsely, 'Yes. There's a tangle of *oueds* and defiles mixed up with wild rock and *erg* as well, which is going to be hell to sort out.' He cleared his throat, rather like revving an engine before putting it into gear, and renewed his assault on the stew.

Jane was surprisingly complacent. Lassiter had expected tantrums or at the very least some of her inevitable hellishness, but tonight she was proving unpredictable. She said quite calmly, 'Well, we got plenty time,' and lit a cigarette while the empty plate balanced on one scrawny thigh.

John-oh appeared in the doorway and hovered there uncertainly, rubbing his hands against the cold. Immediately the blue-dyed head turned.

'That you, Ay-rab?'

'Yes, ma'am.'

'Well, don't stand there like goddam Banquo's ghost. Come in, get yourself a drink, get yourself some grub.' She turned away. 'This brown man is always acting like something's gonna sting him.'

John-oh entered. Lassiter said, 'Find out anything from the Touareg kid?'

'Not much.' Jane's insults, unlike Nailand's, mostly rolled off John-oh's back. He joined the circle, holding a fresh drink. 'He repeated everything he told you, Lew. And it was a hell of a job to screw any more out of him. All I can add is that his party is a big one—about a hundred, all told. Mostly noblemen, with a sprinkling of slaves and one or two youths. There are no women or children. When I asked him where they came from he waved a hand in a westerly direction. That could be anywhere: the Hoggar, the Tassili, maybe even Air. When I asked him what their destination was he said he was not in the confidence of his leaders.'

'He said the same thing to me.'

'The kid is playing it very dumb.'

'Not dumb.' Lassiter was quite sharp about it. 'That little bastard knows a hell of a lot more than he lets on. I don't like him.'

'Nor do I. He's got bad eyes.'

'A group that size is unusual, isn't it?'

'Heck, yes.' John-oh gulped at his drink. 'Especially here. No women. No kids. I haven't heard of such a thing in years.'

'Did he name the leader?'

'Yes. Jedren. It's a Touareg name one comes across.'

'Mean anything to you? I mean this chap particularly.'

'No.' The younger man shrugged. 'Don't forget, it's a year since I was in the Sahara at all, and then before that, Libya, with you.'

Jane Teefer moved astutely to the point. 'Ay-rab. In a nutshell: does this Touareg boy and his group represent a danger to us?'

Lassiter answered before John-oh. 'I'll sum it up for you, Mrs Teefer.' This time Jane chose to ignore the deliberate barb although the tightening of her face showed she hadn't missed it. 'Such a large number of Touareg, far away from their stamping grounds, can only be a battle group. This is a very rare thing in modern times. These men are not camel-raiding or feuding with the Toubou. That's also largely a thing of the past. If they were, they wouldn't be more than ten, maybe twenty in number. The idea was always travel light, get in quickly, get out quickly. They didn't even kill unless they had to. No, it's not that. They're not flea-bitten desert robbers. They would not be interested in three Land-Rovers and some bits and pieces of equipment. Under normal circumstances we would be entitled to ignore them. They would turn up here today or tomorrow, pick up T'ekmedhin, and we'd never see them again.

'Well, then.' Jane was pleased. She dropped her cigarette and trod neatly on the butt. 'What's all the fuss about? Let's forget it.'

'No, Lady Teefer. Not yet.'

Ann Bowdrey was leaning forward in her chair without her usual passive calm. 'I think you should make yourself clear, Mr Lassiter. You use the words, "under normal circumstances." This indicates that there is something here which might not be normal, something which might interest the Touareg quite apart from our vehicles and equipment. Am I right?'

Jane produced her monkey-grin. 'Very astute, Mrs Housewife Bowdrey. I missed it. Come on, Lew. What in hell you getting at?'

'Well, madame.' Lassiter made them wait while he lit a cigarette. He winked at Susan. 'If the reason for the presence of one of the expeditions at Fort Masuril is something other than it purports to be and this reason could prove . . . of benefit, shall we say, to the Touareg, then the circumstances would be abnormal, wouldn't they? And the Touareg would have every reason to be interested in us. Or in some of us. The Touareg have virtually followed in our tracks because the Bowdreys used almost exactly the same route as us: Djanet, and across the Tènèrè. First the Bowdreys. Then the Teefer group. Now Jedren and his boys. Amazing coincidence, isn't it?'

Colour rose into Ann Bowdrey's smooth cheeks. 'We were the first here. You are implying, in no uncertain terms, that Bert and I are not here just to photograph the carvings of the Tibesti!'

'And what about me?' Jane had developed a dangerous calm. 'He said *one* of the expeditions. You better speak up, goddam Lassiter, and say what's on your mind.'

'I already have. You asked whether the Touareg represented a danger to us and I've given my answer.'

John-oh said quietly, 'Ma'am, there is one possible explanation for the presence of the Touareg that might satisfy everyone.' He looked across at Lassiter. 'Lew, why can't these people be moving slowly south to take part in the rebellion against the central Government? It is something that would appeal to them, to try their hand against the Legion once more after all these years.'

Lassiter shrugged. As he often did, he seemed to have lost interest in the subject. 'Could be.'

'You're a clever boy, Ay-rab. That's it. Subject closed.' Jane held out her empty glass. John-oh took it, filled it, brought it back to her.

Ann Bowdrey had not lost her anger. 'Nobody likes to be falsely accused. I wish to reiterate that Bert and I are here for the sole purpose of——'

'I said subject closed, Mrs Housewife Bowdrey.' Jane sipped her drink. 'You've made your point. And everyone knows why I'm here. Let's leave it at that.' She reached across the gap between her chair and Susan's, found the girl's wrist and squeezed it.

Nailand spooned up the last of his stew and plugged it into his left cheek. 'That disposes of the Touareg but not my appetite. We growing boys must eat.' He extended his plate to John-oh. 'Get me some more food, Arab.'

The shadows on the opposite side of the courtyard mantled him in an enfolding darkness from which he could observe the Mess doorway that beckoned to him like a yellow-lit keyhole. He moved very slowly forward, making no sound at all.

'T'ekmedhin!'

He whirled, his right hand streaking to the dagger inside the sleeve of his cloak. But he was confused, his eyes slightly blinded by the light. His head swung, seeking the voice.

'We are here, T'ekmedhin, near the gates.'

The slow, schoolboy French, the light unbroken voice, the sudden glimpse of two small forms linked together by their hands and palely outlined by a wash of light from their doorway. All the tension went out of him in a sigh. *Les enfants.* He walked towards them quite openly now, stopping a yard or two away with his hands at his sides.

'Come.' They were smiling, beckoning him into their room. He considered a moment; the sick man, the one who coughed, was asleep in a room near the far end of the courtyard. The remaining seven adults were alone. It was safe. He followed the children inside.

The room did not alarm him. There were only two low lightweight beds, a mat, some clothes scattered around. A battery lamp gave pale illumination. It was not much different from a Touareg hut.

Then he saw the snakes. There were at least twenty of them, large and small, and although he knew snakes, never had he seen creatures of such wondrous colour; startling reds, vivid greens, indigo like the cloak he wore, some patterned with diamonds, some with stripes, some plain, but all thickly and venomously curled about each other and the ladders that were propped in amongst them on the board. He was fascinated.

Both children were smiling. The older one, the girl, had beginning breasts and was good-looking. He regarded her with a mild interest while she studied him in fascination.

Neil held up the die. 'Look.' He showed T'ekmedhin the red dots that glowed like round coals on the slick ebony surface.

Then he rolled the die on the board. It came to rest showing a three.

'*Un, deux, trois.*' Neil took up a counter from the first square and moved three places on the board. He struck the foot of a ladder and shot up it so that he was now twenty places ahead. He and Thrin crowed to demonstrate their delight. Neil rolled the die again. This time it showed a five. He counted off the spaces and was immediately swallowed by an impossibly purple puff-adder, sliding the counter down its thick coils while he and Thrin groaned in mock despair.

T'ekmedhin started forward. He snatched the die from Neil and rolled it across the board. Obligingly, it showed a three again. T'ekmedhin took another counter and prodded it heavily across the squares and then up the ladder. There he released it. He crossed his arms. The light eyes flickered with triumph.

'Ahah?'

'Ahah!' They chorused it after him.

He might have smiled. A slim brown hand shot out, rolled the die again. A single red dot winked amongst the ebony. T'ekmedhin moved the counter one square and was consumed by a short, desperately unhappy-looking green snake.

'*Diable!*' The eyes flashed. But he was nevertheless pleased because he was still ahead of Neil.

'*Diable!*' they laughed. Neil removed both tokens from the board. He and Thrin squatted on the edge of the bed, on one side of the board. She motioned to him to do the same. After a moment's hesitation he perched, straightbacked, opposite them.

Neil struggled with his French. 'You begin. Then my sister. Then me.'

Mahogany-brown fingers took the die and rolled it. A six came up so they explained to him that he must throw again. The second roll produced a three. The total of nine squares took the Touareg up a long ladder at the top of which he released his counter, put his hands in his lap and said calmly, '*Bon.*'

When Thrin took the die, she thought that this time, almost certainly, there was a smile in his eyes.

* * *

It was the fag-end of the evening and Nailand was showing the effects of some steady drinking. It was visible in the slack planes of his face and the wickedly red-shot eyes.

'One more drink and I'm off. I'm taking my wife to bed.' He held his glass out to John-oh. 'Scotch and water, Arab. Large. What's the matter, Arab? Have I offended you in any way?'

John-oh took the glass. 'No.' He went across to the table and poured the drink, came back and gave it to Nailand. Inevitably his eyes met Lola's.

'She's good-looking, huh, Arab?' Nailand gulped at the drink. Some of it ran down his chin.

John-oh said nothing.

Into the silence Nailand's flat voice prodded him again:
'I said she's good-looking, Arab. Don't you agree?'

John-oh stared down at his feet. He quivered. Jane said
sweetly, 'Answer him, brown man.'

'Of course she's good-looking!' John-oh said the words
convulsively.

'That's right.' Nailand adopted a reasonable tone. 'Then
why do we have to drag it out of you?' He pretended a sudden
discovery. 'I know what it is! The Arab doesn't like the idea
of me taking my wife to bed.' He shook his head. 'That's very
naughty of you Arab. It's all quite legal, you know. We're
married.'

'Joe, please.' Lola's big empty eyes, moistly green, studied
John-oh.

'Joe, please!' Nailand mimicked in falsetto. He didn't bother
to turn his head. 'I feel for you. I really do. Damn it, I'm
tempted to lend her to you for the night.'

John-oh's head jerked up.

'Ah, you'd like that, wouldn't you? Come on, tell us.
Wouldn't you?'

'Thinks something's gonna sting him,' Jane observed.
'Always does. Come on, John-oh, in that whorehouse you were
brought up in you musta had plenty of dames. Lola's got a
fanny just like them.'

'Lady Teefer!'

'Shut up, pumpkin pips. I wasn't talking to you.' She
blandly considered John-oh. 'My advice is take the offer, kid.
Lola's got a hell of a body on her. I oughta know. I felt it
myself.'

'No, it's too late.' Nailand slapped his hands together. 'He
who hesitates gets lost.' He got up grinning,. 'How's that for
a new saying, Arab?' He wagged his head. 'I was only kidding,
mind. Never would have done it. You know why, Arab?'

'No.' John-oh whispered the words.

'Because you smell. You pong.' He mouthed the words
with exquisite relish. 'And as the day wears on you get more
fruity. Now you wouldn't want my wife to smell like that,
Arab, would you? And nor would I.'

There was a very long silence, an acute silence in which
everyone stared at John-oh while he studied Nailand in

fascinated horror. Sweat burst out on his forehead and rolled into his eyebrows where it clustered like diamond-shining dew, hesitating, trembling there until finally it fell, plunging in salty irritation into his eyes and producing the catalyst that sent him hurtling out of his chair, bent like a held spring and quivering with the force of this restraint.

'You pig. You stupid stuffing pig.' The words rolled inexorably off his tongue.

Nailand bent his upper body. He closed up, his silly small fists crossed neatly across the conversely big arms. 'Well. So there is some guts there. Let's see the length of your intestinal fortitude, Arab.'

John-oh retreated. He skittered like a crab out of the circle of chairs. Sand went flying in a spray lit golden by the lamp. He put a hand into a pocket. When the hand came out it brought with it a metallic click. Four inches of erect silver steel off which white points of light flashed.

'I'll cut your guts out.' The strange voice came from between John-oh's chattering teeth.

Jane squealed with delight. Her short white fingers bit into Susan's arm. 'What's happening? What's happening, girl?'

'John-oh's got a er-er flick-knife.'

Jane leaned forward. She screamed like a virago, 'Kill him, Joe!'

Nailand had considered the flick-knife and gone pale. Then he looked at the anguished face behind it and laughed. 'God. I should have guessed. You bloody Dago. All right. Come on. Cut my guts out.' He began to walk forward.

John-oh retreated. His feet scattered sand. 'Keep away!'

'But you were going to cut my guts out.' Nailand advanced. 'Why do you retreat, Arab?'

John-oh slashed pathetically with the knife. He was so strong that the blade hummed through the air. 'Keep away.' He said it, this time, while his body shook in a palpable ague.

'You're so frightfully chicken.' Nailand put another cautious foot forward, well aware of John-oh's cowardice but afraid nevertheless of the desperate random slashing of the blade. He gained a yard on the other man. He was about to increase it, when his body shuddered to a sudden agony that began in the long muscle on the left of his spine and ran like fire through him, making him drop his arms. He said, 'Ahh, Christ!' quite involuntarily.

Lassiter came past from behind him, holding a fresh drink in one hand. Lassiter said, 'Give me the knife, John-oh,' and collected it in passing, without argument, casually as though it were the post. Then he lowered himself into his camp chair, put the glass down carefully on the sand and looked at Nailand for the first time.

'Like fowls, we are developing a pecking order. You are below me on the ladder. Now behave yourself.'

Nailand stared at him while the agony still filled him. Lassiter returned the look with his composed, friendly, night-time face. As though to stress his amicability he released a gentle whisky burp and smiled.

The liquor that Nailand had taken all night finally caught up with him. He became confused. The room rocked. His blind gaze went around the circle. This was all a crazy nightmare. It was a Sahara Mad Hatter's tea party. He was mumbling, telling them about it. Lassiter was the Mad Hatter and that still-faced girl was Alice and Jane was the Queen, screaming for heads. Even now the Queen was saying, 'What happened, girl? Come on for God's sake. . . .' And Alice was standing up, her lips red in the white still face, and Alice was saying, 'The Mad Hatter stabbed the Knave of Hearts in the back, with his finger, and took away the Turtle's tea-cup, your Highness. . . .'

There was sand in Nailand's mouth. Sand and blood. In a vague way he realised that he was lying on the floor. He felt desperately weak and very drunk.

Jane was cawing, 'What was all that about the Mad Hatter and Alice and. . . .'

'I don't know.' Susan went to Lassiter. 'He said you were the Mad Hatter.'

'Does it fit?'

'I don't know. Yet.' She turned and began to walk out of the room, looking straight ahead.

Jane heard her go. She fumbled erect. 'Wait for me, girl. How am I gonna get to bed without you? What am I gonna do?'

Susan stopped in the door. The slight shoulders rose and fell in a small shrug. 'Get lost, I suppose. That's cousin Joe's new saying remember? "He who hesitates gets lost." Well, you hesitated, Lady Teefer, madame, your Holiness, so just do that. Get lost.'

She said it all very quietly. Then she turned her back and went on out of the room.

*   *   *

The night sky, still palely lit by the moon, was lighter than the solid dark bulk of the fort's wall so that as the boy came up the steps to the catwalk his body was outlined in faint silhouette. He moved like a ghost towards the crenellated watchtower, where his saddle and blanket and other belongings lay. He walked confidently until he was only a few yards away. Then he slowed and stopped. For a fraction of a second the slim body hesitated, the sharp eyes stabbing the gloom inside the tower. Something was wrong. There was a bulkiness, a liveness there. The right hand had flashed to left sleeve and moonlight threw fire off the dagger as it arced back like a trailing comet, paused flashing, trembling, ready for the vicious down-swing as the body set itself like a lance for the forward lunge.

'*Attention!*'

It was not just that one sharp word in French that stopped him. He would have ignored the warning with contempt. But it was accompanied by a sharp metallic sound that he instantly recognized.

It was the cocking of the hammer on his Beretta.

For a long time T'ekmedhin stared at the tall figure seated on his own blanket. He lowered the dagger and they regarded each other with mutual interest. Then Lassiter got up and smiled and said, 'Keeping those sharp peepers of yours working hard, kid? That's the way. Do your job properly. But just remember one thing: all the time you're watching us, I'm watching you.'

He spoke in English, deliberately, to taunt the Touareg. Then he eased himself out of the tower on to the northern catwalk.

Out of the darkness the Beretta clattered at T'ekmedhin's feet and Lassiter's voice followed it, this time speaking in

French: 'Children should not be allowed to play with dangerous toys.'

The boy could hear only fading footfalls, and after a moment these ceased. He stared into the blackness. His fingers gripped the dagger so hard that the hilt bit into his palm. Then his rage and humiliation erupted in one single expletive which he spat viciously out into the night.

'*Merde!*'

He heard Lassiter's chuckle float up to him from the deeper darkness of the courtyard.

*   *   *

Ann Bowdrey stood braced against the cold in the darkened doorway of the empty kitchen.

'Mr Lassiter!'

The tall figure stopped abruptly. 'Things that go bump in the night. Don't do that to people with weak hearts. Where is your husband?'

'Asleep.'

'And you taking the fine night air, begorrah. It's eleven o'clock. The bar is closed.'

'I was waiting for you.'

'Were you ever in Eichstadt?'

'Where's that?'

'The Bavarian Alps. I was up there on a construction job. It was very cold. We were in a *brauhaus*. There was a big fire in the hearth and this girl sitting by it. She was blonde like you and tanned like you. I was going across to her but then the disaster hooter went and I was running for the bridge . . . I never knew her. The next day she was gone.'

'I wish it had been me.'

'Make it you.'

'I can't, it's too late.' She was so close he could feel the warmth of her breath against his face. 'You are so lucky. All your winters have been different.'

'And yours? The same . . .?'

'All the same, like train windows in a station blankly sliding by.'

He put his hands on her shoulders. 'But now. Winter's gone. . . .'

'For ever. I will never have winter in my soul again.'

He pulled her against him and kissed her. She clung to him, she ground her body against his. He put a hand on one jersey-covered breast. She gasped and trembled, then kissed him with sudden fervour, putting her arms around his wide chest and holding him fiercely. When she put her smooth face against his cheek her breath was coming so fast that her voice was a light fluttery thing, a lacework of words: 'What happened to the bridge?'

'Avalanche hit it. Destroyed it.'

'And you built——?'

'Another one.'

'That same winter?'

'Winter and spring.'

'And the girl . . .?'

'Never came back.'

'It *was* me.'

She trembled. And in the coldness of the night there was heat. Then from the distance came the soft pulpy sound of coughing and Bowdrey's muffled petulant voice calling: 'Ann. Ann, where are you?'

She pulled away. For a moment she looked into his face. Then she said quickly, 'Good night, Mr Lassiter.'

He watched her merge with the darkness.

CHAPTER FIVE

AWAKENING FROM SLEEP should be a gentle process. But with Susan Shields it was not like this. If was fright, it was glass shattering. She whimpered once, opened her eyes and figured out that she had been alive 7,832 days. After that she got up.

She dressed quickly in bra' and panties, slacks, blouse and open sandals. Then she lit a cigarette and went outside into the courtyard. Lassiter was standing at his Land-Rover. He raised a hand and she went over.

'Sleep well?'

'So, so.'

'I had a good night at the movies. Wide-screen and stereo. Hell, death and damnation.' He managed to look reflective and morose at the same time.

She gave him her cigarette. 'Suck on this.' Lassiter was best left alone for a while. She walked off.

'Where you going?'

'To make coffee for Lady T.'

'Make me a cup.'

'Say please.'

'Please? Go to hell.' He turned his back.

'Shoosh.' She lingered, trying. 'Smiling doesn't hurt.'

'I smile more than you. But I smile at night.'

'You're telling me! And you hate yourself every morning.'

'Where's Nailand?' He was talking to the gates of the fort.

'I don't know. Nursing his head, I suppose. And his back.'

'He's going to work today. By Jesus he's going to work.' Lassiter relished the words. 'Go and make that coffee.'

She went into the kitchen and stared at the stove. She wondered whether Lassiter dreamt about his children or the bridge in Zambia or the time Lady Jane found him in the gutter in London. Lassiter would have an endless sequence of dreams available. He would be able to move in and out of them at will like one of those non-stop moviehouses.

She made the coffee and took him his cup. He had the map spread out on the truck bonnet and his head lowered over it. She put the cup next to the map and went on. But when she was at the door of her room she heard voices and turned.

Nailand had emerged. He was wearing shorty pyjamas and trudged barefooted across the still cool sand with the slogging, woeful air of a man with a desperate hangover. He leant his head on one side to accommodate his injured back and held his small hands out ahead of him as though parting the air.

He was talking all the time, waving his arms within the prescribed area allowed by his torn muscle. But Lassiter was talking too, stridently, advancing towards Nailand. They met and Lassiter's voice overrode the other so that the girl heard the words, 'You'll work, by Jesus,' and Nailand's 'But. . . .' until suddenly Nailand was running, scuttling away with his hairy belly showing, clutching at the pants of his pyjamas, with Lassiter swinging kicks at his backside until Nailand reached his Land-Rover, jumped inside and slammed the door, peering out with blood-red eyes and baying for help.

The girl ran into her room. Jane was sitting up in bed brushing her hair.

'Coffee.' Susan gave her the slopped-over mug. Then she sat on the edge of her stretcher and put her head on her knees. She wanted to relieve herself. She started to laugh and she laughed on while Jane's angry questing voice battered at her, until the laughing turned into sobs and she produced huge fat anguished tears and finally fell silent.

'Now what in hell was all that about?'

She got up unsteadily. She had wet her pants. She began to change. 'We're all mad. We're all insane. There's not one of us normal. We're going to die. We surely must. We can't be allowed to go around using up all this good clean air.'

'Shut up, girl. Now. What started all this?'

'Joe Nailand didn't want to work today. He's badly hung and on top of that Lassiter hurt him last night. He came to tell Lassiter. But Lassiter chased him into his Land-Rover and now he's keeping him there until we leave, in his pyjamas.'

'In his pyjamas?' This seemed to offend Jane more than anything else. 'By God! That Lassiter!' She scrambled out of bed. 'Can't treat my kin like that. Gimme my gown!'

She wrapped herself in the robe and forced her small white bunioned feet into mules. 'Here. Take my arm.' She was puffing. 'Get me out there.'

They reached the door. Then Jane stopped without warning.

'What did Lassiter use last night when he hurt Joe?'

'His finger. Don't you remember? I told you.'

'His finger!' She turned unexpectedly and started back for her bed. 'Do Joe good, being bullied around by Lassiter. Been getting bumptious lately. It's an Appelby failing. Got to be kept in check.' She sat down. 'Gimme a smoke.' Then after the click of the lighter she released a sudden cackle. 'Hell, it musta been funny, Joe running away with Lassiter——'

'Swinging kicks at his backside that missed by miles.'

'Hah, God. And Joe with his fat belly. . . .'

'It was showing because his pants were slipping down.'

'And I'll bet talking all the time but. . . .'

'But you couldn't hear him because of Lassiter shouting so much.'

They laughed heartily. Susan's eyes watered so that they looked weak.

In the middle of a squawk Jane stopped. 'You in love with Lassiter?'

Susan stared at her. She took a cigarette away from the child-red lips. Then she said, 'Love? What is love?'

'Huh?'

'What is love?'

Jane pondered. 'You got a damn good question there. I don't know.' There was a pause while they considered each other. Then she shrugged. 'Come on. Help me with my clothes. I feel good today. Going to go on the probe with you and Lassiter.'

* * *

At seven-thirty Lassiter brought John-oh out to the Land-Rover so that they could agree on the dimensions of the box-search for the second day's probe. He did it with an ulterior motive, because Nailand, trapped inside his own vehicle for half an hour, had spent this time of his imprisonment waking up, plumbing the depths of alcoholic depression and doing some serious thinking. At this stage he got out of the Land-Rover and stood musing on the now hot sand, feeling tiny and insignificant, useless and unmasculine. When he said, 'Lassiter, I did some rather heavy drinking last night and behaved like an ass. I'm sorry,' Lassiter produced one of his rare day-time smiles and pointed a long arm and said, 'Go and get dressed.'

He felt no particular triumph. In his time he had worked with two-legged animals and at least Nailand had a veneer of culture. And at forty-odd you didn't change overnight, or after being fried for half-an-hour in a closed car. Give Nailand ten hours and five drinks and he would be Nailand. But he would walk very carefully from now on and he would leave John-oh alone. By and large, Lassiter was pleased. There was no longer any doubt about the names on the ladder. The pecking order had been finalised.

By eight-fifteen the second probe for Sir Peter Teefer's body was ready to start. By this time Lassiter was growlingly impatient. But there were one or two strings left untied from the day and night before and although it did not follow that they had to be tied, it worked that way.

Bert Bowdrey appeared and Lassiter provocatively gave him their course for that day down to the last detail. He insisted even on outlining it on the map. Bowdrey took it all in silence, red-cheeked, uncertain of Lassiter's flinty-eyed co-operation and unwilling to plumb it, the way one would skirt a cave inhabited by a nasty-tempered bear. He marched away, clutching his cheap Japanese camera under one scrawny armpit.

Lady Teefer emerged on Susan's arm. The Nailand children got into Lassiter's vehicle without question. Joe Nailand, now properly dressed, came out with Lola. He boarded John-oh's vehicle and sat staring at his knees with heavy eyes.

John-oh started his engine. Lassiter, about to follow suit, remembered his sunglasses. He went to get them and found Ann Bowdrey in his way, just inside the arched doorway to his room.

He had clear memories of kissing her, and rather vague ones about what he had said. She stood with passive purpose in the calm-bodied way he had first seen on Monday.

'Mr Lassiter.' The smooth arms hung relaxed, the slender tanned hands were loosely clasped below her waist.

Lassiter said, 'It wasn't a hell of a big bridge, anyway. I mean, it was nothing to worry about.'

Her eyes flickered. 'I don't know what happened last night. I can't explain it.' She was deliberately facing what had happened. It was like an unpriestly confession. It was as though she enjoyed wounding herself.

Lassiter said, 'Why don't you rather forget——'

She interrupted. 'No, Mr Lassiter. I prefer to remember. That way it won't happen again. I waited for you last night for a specific reason.' Her mouth simply obeyed her mind. It lost its softness. 'I wanted to tell you that my husband and I are very devoted, very dedicated to what we are doing. We are photographing the rock carvings of the Tibesti. And to pry and search, or examine our motives, would be needless, time-wasting and foolhardy. If we are poor and misguided, even if what we are doing is ridiculous, it is our business.'

Lassiter began to understand. 'What if you've discovered the Big Rock Candy Mountain?'

Her expression remained minutely the same. 'Mr Lassiter, you're being well paid to lead the Teefer expedition. I would suggest that in those circumstances you let us cut up The Big Rock Candy Mountain and sell the pieces at Brighton.'

Lassiter lowered his head in thought. Then he said, equably, 'Okay. For the time being. Let's leave it like that. So you carve up the Big Rock Candy Mountain if you find it. But I'm left with nothing except running for the bridge and trying to hold back the avalanche at Eichstadt.'

The thermometer dropped a degree. 'Go back to the *brauhaus*. The girl might have returned.'

Her eyes lifted beyond him. He turned. The group from his Land-Rover had alighted. All of them had their backs turned. They were looking towards the gates.

Three black men wearing khaki uniforms and puce-coloured berets, mounted on large whimsical camels, were riding into the courtyard.

*   *   *

The *Sous-Préfet* of Zufra was hungry. Breakfast was an unhappy memory of coffee and a biscuit in the cold of dawn. Each time he belched, which was often, he tasted a great foulness of gases, so that he pictured his stomach as a dark pit about which the greedy and unslaked digestive juices washed. It was a frightening thought, aggravated by an ache in his lower back which was caused by the hideous see-saw motion of riding. In truth, he admitted, he made a poor cameleer, and although his immediate wish was to rest his back and eat something, he stayed mounted because of the slight compensation offered by the effect of surveying these surprised Franks from a height which lent a lordly dignity to the unexpectedness of his arrival.

All of them had gone still. This gave him the opportunity of one or two minutes of inspection. He recognised the Bowdreys. The immensely tall, thin man standing with the Bowdrey woman would be Lassiter, of whom he had heard. In his short time in Libya, Lassiter had managed to create something of a legend about himself which had penetrated even to Fort Lamy. Regarding him with interest, Goru wondered how anyone who resembled an ostrich could have such a reputation. Then Lassiter smiled at Ann Bowdrey and the *Sous-Préfet* understood. Lassiter began to come across the sand towards him, so he made his camel kneel. It obeyed with a hollow and unearthly groan which was in keeping with Goru's mood.

Lassiter arrived as the *Sous-Préfet* dismounted. They shook hands and introduced themselves, with Goru surprised and pleased at Lassiter's fluent French. Then Goru surveyed the assembled faces and said rapidly and unexpectedly, '*Bonjour. Je suis le Sous-Préfet de Zufra.*' To the Bowdreys he added in English, 'Meester and Messus Bowdrey. I 'ope that you are well.'

Both of them nodded and Ann Bowdrey smiled. Camille had been right, he thought, she did in fact have the eyes of a virgin.

Into the brief silence came Jane's voice, loud and cawing; 'Earn your keep, girl, what in hell is happening?'

'I gather that the *Sous-Préfet* of Zufra has arrived, Lady Teefer.'

'What's he? Some kind of big-wheel burrhead?'

Goru walked across to them, smiling and saluting.

'Lady Teefer, I presume?' This was a phrase that had taken his fancy when reading about the original encounter between Stanley and Livingstone, so it came out fairly well. But the rest was terrible. 'I 'ave come to see 'ow you are. Best wishes from the Government of the *République du Tchad.*'

'Gee, thanks.' Jane put out her hand and they shook. 'We're doing okay.' It was apparent that she enjoyed the felicitations of bureaucracy. She called up Lassiter and between the two of them they introduced Goru to the rest of the group. He said formally, '*Comment-allez vous?*' each time, and with the children, patting their heads, '*Quels beaux enfants les Anglais ont!*'

After that he was taken on a brief tour of the fort by Lassiter and Susan. Jane, who was feeling the pace, went to wait for them in the relative shade of the Mess.

Goru's tour came to an abrupt end in the kitchen. He strode heavily across the threshold. His eyes alighted on *Mademoiselle Janvier*. Then, like radar, his head turned and he found himself surveying the stacked magnificence of the Teefer commissariat.

Goru belched sharply and involuntarily. It was as though his stomach had irritably reminded him of how it was feeling. Warm saliva filled his mouth. He turned limpid, beseeching eyes on Susan and said thickly, his tongue awash, 'I am 'ongry.'

It took him fifteen minutes to work his way through three tins of herring, a small bottle of stuffed olives, some smoked oysters and a mound of *paté de foie gras*. Then he burped gently into the hollow of his fist and said in a soft, happy voice to Susan, 'Tell all to go to Mess. I wish to speak to them. Rapidly, please.'

He watched her retreating back until she had swung out of the doorway. 'In Paris, they make some of the women like that, like sticks.' He had switched to French, knowing Lassiter was at home in it. Now he lit a Gauloise. 'I have been to Paris.' Then his eyes changed, they changed like the smoke he blew in whirls across the still heavy air of the room. 'So Monsieur Lassiter. Today, maybe, you find the bones of poor Sir Peter.'

Lassiter considered the *Sous-Préfet* before he answered. Goru had eaten at the old deal table, seated on a backless camp stool. Now he had swung around, using the edge of the table to prop him up and accommodate his aching sacro-iliac. Lassiter was perched stork-like on the end of the same table, so that in a way they studied each other from the side, a little cagily. Goru's body was in profile, so that Lassiter could see the round ridge of pendulous pectorals under the khaki tunic and the strong bulge of his belly. But the chocolate-coloured face was turned fully towards him and while he watched, it split in a smile that had in it a hint of crocodile. This was a new side to Lieutenant Goru, this small sign of menace. Lassiter, seeing it, was pleased.

He showed it. 'She pays me. Well. I do not question her motives. You are paid by the *République du Tchad*. Do you question the motives of your Government?'

When Lassiter smiled it made Goru, also, think of a crocodile. So they were different, these two men, but there were things in them that were similar.

Goru got up slowly, grunting, holding his back. 'Two answers, *mon ami*. Firstly, the Government does not have an ulterior motive, which your employer may indeed have. And secondly; if it did have, then although I might not question this with a Ministry and get myself fired, I might confide in an outsider.' He winked. 'You follow, of course?'

Lassiter took the hint. 'Of course. I agree, it is remarkably odd, this quest. It bothers me, too. But I simply cannot find an alternative. One must remember that she is getting old, and sick and blind, and has more money than several rich men put together. At this stage I can only shrug and say perhaps she loved him very much and would like to see his remains decently interred.'

'Hah!' Goru prodded him speculatively in the ribs as though he were testing the prime of a side of beef. 'I am a Christian. I die in due course. Do I care that the jackals may scatter my bones and howl to the desert moon over my worthless carcass? No, I do not, because my soul is now in the hereafter. My body is clay and although I would prefer a burial decently given I do not think that I, or any other Christian, would be greatly disturbed by the lack of it. Because of the soul departed, I mean.'

Lassiter nodded. 'That's true.' The *Sous-Préfet*, in addition to his intriguing latent menace, was shrewd as well.

'Is Lady Teefer a Christian?'

'No. Lady Teefer has a foulness within her.'

Goru smiled again. Gently, this time. 'We begin to understand each other.' His eyes probed Lassiter's. 'Not all Christians are to be found wearing out their knees on a hassock.' There was a short silence. Then, abruptly: 'Monsieur Lassiter, I put it to you bluntly. *What is it that the old woman wants here?*'

Lassiter shook his head. 'I wish I knew.'

Goru sighed. 'You conceal nothing. This I can detect. But the others'—he wagged his head—'to extend my metaphor I am reminded of jackals, with a smell of carrion in their nostrils.' He straightened up, trying to become brisk in the blossoming heat of the day. 'All this *préfecture*, this district, is called Zufra. So let us go to the Mess, Monsieur Lassiter, and talk to these jackals of Zufra, shall we?'

*　　　*　　　*

Jane had somehow been impressed by Goru. When the *Sous-Préfet* arrived he found all the others waiting for him under the authority of her command. Lady Teefer herself was smoking impatiently and tapping a sandalled white foot deformed by the enormity of its ugly bunion. Bowdrey glowered, sunk deep in one of the camp chairs with his camera and two books about the Tibesti carvings nestling on his lap like credentials.

Goru took up a position before them and Lassiter stood nearby. The *Sous-Préfet* reverted to his own version of the English language.

'Lady Teefer, Meester and Meesus Bowdrey, uzzers all. Today Lady Teefer seeks the bones of her 'usband. Maybe not find and 'ave to look long time. Ver' important, Lady Teefer, eh? Much expense, time, travel, to bury a man four years dead. And Meester Bowdrey continues to make pictures of the Tibesti carvings.' He smiled with encouraging relish. 'Much— er—plaudits—when you get 'ome, Monsieur Bowdrey? Books, films, loud clapping of hands?'

To Bowdrey the *Sous-Préfet* was purely a black man who spoke shocking English. But he was an armed black man in an inexplicable position of authority; so he needed only appeasement, nothing more. He made no attempt to understand Goru. He was in fact incapable of understanding Goru.

He stood up. The books slipped from under his arm and he clutched wildly at the camera. 'Aye. That's right. It's research which could bring great rewards.'

Goru's eyelids fluttered. 'Meester Bowdrey, I learned my English in bad places. *Pardon, s'il vous plaît*, when I say unto you, sir, that you are talking the greatest crap. Those carvings you picture with your little thirty-five millimetre camera have no worth.'

While Bowdrey's mouth was still funnelling, digging deep for the bellow which would refute this, Goru's mild eyes switched to Jane. 'And Madame Teefer, I regret to say zat I find your story of burying Saint Peter's bones equally ridiculous.'

Jane, like Bowdrey, needed time to react. And although she began to pant while Bowdrey was still fumbling for words the *Sous-Préfet* gave neither of them a chance. In fact, he became suddenly quite abrupt.

'I wish to speak French. Monsieur Lassiter will interpret.' And he went on, quickly and fluently now, with Lassiter breaking in from time to time and giving them the English of it. 'Unfortunately I am not in a position to investigate. You are fools and I do not suffer fools gladly. But if you insist, my jackals, on gathering here for your obscure purposes, then it is my duty to warn you of a danger. There is a very large band of Touareg in this area. I think you know what Touareg are— the Imo-chagh, the Free Ones, they call themselves. They are the People of the Veil, the indigo men. They know no master. This band is led by a man called Jedren. No one knows from whence he came but he is more free-minded than all the rest of the Touareg put together. He makes his own laws and bows only slightly to Islam. He can shoot a fly off a camel's ear at one hundred metres. He can make you sob and he can make you laugh in the beautiful poetry the Touareg compose for games. It is something they leave largely to their women, but Jedren is a Touareg Shakespeare. I do not know him. All this I tell you, I have only heard. But I have heard it in Zufra, in the Tibesti, far from Touareg country, blown on the desert winds. So that the flesh-and-blood Jedren will be more deadly than I describe, because hearsay is the pale smoke from the start of a fire. I tell you that Jedren, if he felt it necessary, would cut you straight up the guts and pull out your hot moist entrails and make you hold them in your hands while you died.'

Ann Bowdrey shuddered. But none of them was really touched by it. The *Sous-Préfet* was merely telling them a story to frighten naughty children. It could not happen. Not here. Not now.

Goru went on through Lassiter. 'It is my duty to protect you, however foolish you may be. Therefore I am leaving my two men here with you. The sergeant will be in charge and he will report to me nightly by radio. If he sees fit, he and the trooper will accompany you on your probes into the desert.' His eyes flicked across the room. 'This applies equally to you, Mr Bowdrey.'

The words, turned into English by Lassiter, sank in fairly slowly. The seven adults in the chairs absorbed Goru's decision. They mulled over its full effect upon them. Then Jane, Bowdrey and Nailand were on their feet, loudly protesting.

Jane turned a dull ugly red; Nailand's angry tenor quacking filled the air, backed by the strident north-country bellow of Bert Bowdrey. Lassiter's amused glance moved from face to face, while the *Sous-Préfet* stood passively until they had talked themselves out, with Jane's '. . . this is un-American, it's an invasion of privacy. . . .' overridden by Nailand's '. . . don't worry, Jane, those two idiots outside are complete savages, they won't have an earthly about what's going on. . . .', finally trailing into silence.

Goru spoke briefly to Lassiter, who interpreted: 'The *Sous-Préfet* is not prepared to discuss the matter any further. It is his decision and it stands.'

Jane Teefer's voice grated like a rasp. 'You're just lucky you're God Almighty over a hundred-odd square miles of sand and stones, buddy. I've got to accept it, but don't think for one moment that I like it.'

Goru raised an eyebrow and spoke quietly to Lassiter, who reacted with intense pleasure: 'The *Sous-Préfet* disagrees that he is God Almighty. There is only One, and Lieutenant Goru does not pretend to such a high estate. He suggests, Madame, that when you make such free play with God's name, you should consider your position in the hereafter.' He raised a whimsical eyebrow. 'The *Sous-Préfet* does concede, though, that he has considerable authority. So much so that if the man with the voice of a duck uses the word "savage" again, he will take him out into the courtyard and have him shot.' Lassiter's pleased eyes settled on Nailand. 'That means you.'

Nailand went deathly pale. He was having a bad day. Then colour rushed back into his face. Words trembled on his tongue and fell out into the hot air. 'I'm sorry. I didn't mean. . . .'

Goru gazed at him sternly. 'You muz always say what you mean.' Then he turned his back and extended a hand to Lassiter. 'Goodbye, my friend.' He was talking French again. 'I am an old warrior, I have fought for France in the past. And when trouble comes I can smell it. Now I smell it here. Do you?'

A picture came to Lassiter of the children with their tattered praying mat and he pushed it irritably aside. Then he remembered how the girl talked of walking in the desert of her mind and he pushed that out too and sighed and said, 'Yes.' He knew what kind of trouble Goru meant. As if they didn't have enough of their own.

Jane had finally recovered sufficiently to make trouble. From behind them she said quite sweetly, 'Lootenant, Your Highness, before you and Lassiter burst into tears and pound each other on the back, did you new pal tell you that he is harbouring one of those mean Injun-type Touaregs right here in this Fort?'

Lassiter's mouth fell open. He had in fact forgotten momentarily the existence of the boy T'ekmedhin. Goru, in turn, was astonished.

'Is this true?' He looked reprovingly at the other man.

'Yes,' Lassiter said. Then he told Goru the exact circumstances of the finding of the Touareg. He told him in detail because Goru was now sharply alert, even angry, and Lassiter knew he would want detail. He told Goru even of his subsequent encounter with the boy in the watch-tower.

'You were charitable but foolish.' Goru was already moving to the door. 'Hell and buggeration, that little bastard could have walked four hundred miles carrying his saddle and everything else without turning a hair.' He reached the door and signalled to his men who were slumped in a slant of dark shade near the gates. When they failed to see him he went out into the courtyard in a series of heavy bounds that were fat but had an element of feline grace about them. A string of words rattled off his tongue, ending with a loud and thunderous, 'Cross-eyed bastards,' because he appeared to prefer to do his swearing in English.

The men sprang erect like animated marionettes. They grabbed their rifles and sprinted across the sand, arriving panting and at a sort of attention with their rifles at port. More words poured from Goru. He drew his revolver, cocked a speculative eye at Lassiter and said in French. 'If that kid is armed I'm not going to play the fool.' Then he was gone, personally leading a minute and thorough room-by-room search of the fort that brought him back twenty painstaking minutes later, his shirt dark-blotched with sweat.

'Nothing. Bugger-all.' He was panting slightly. He holstered his revolver with a faintly foolish air, ignoring the crowd at the Mess doorway and speaking directly to Lassiter. 'I would not have assassinated the child but I have a feeling that he might very well have tried to assassinate me. Anyway, he's gone. Bag and baggage, as you say in English. Which, surely, proves a point?'

'It does.' Lassiter was feeling rather foolish himself. 'I suspected, but I had no proof. What does one do—abandon a boy in the desert on a suspicion?' He managed to produce an eloquent Gallic shrug.

'No, no, of course not. I understand.' Goru grinned suddenly, a very human grin that made Lassiter like him more. 'Anyway, I was right about that old war-horse smell of trouble, wasn't I?'

He did not expect an answer. He simply snapped a salute, then walked away across the courtyard with his two soldiers. When he reached his camel he turned to the sergeant, his nephew. 'You know your instructions. Nobody knows that you understand English, including that lanky Frank. Listen to every word they say. And do not forget to report as instructed or it will be the worse for you.'

The sergeant produced something between a salute and a wave. '*Oui, mon oncle.*'

Goru's face swelled. The sergeant's eyes rolled. He went rigid and peeled off a parade-ground salute. '*Oui, mon Lieutenant!*'

Goru grunted. 'It is most fortunate that you remembered we are not related when it comes to military matters.' Then he turned away and sorrowfully got aboard his camel, his mind full of complexities but conscious too of the agony of the ride home. The camel, equally reluctant, got to its feet with a see-saw lurch and a hollow groan and stalked in absurd dignity between the gates of the fort.

*   *   *

Forcibly delayed by the visit of the *Sous-Préfet*, it was nine-thirty before the two Land-Rovers of the Teefer expedition thrust through the gates. They went with a clean healthy rumble, the immaculate and heartless precision of exact mechanical intercourse between piston and cylinder. Ten minutes later, like a pale shadow, the Bowdreys followed in a rattle of badly-adjusted tappets. They veered south, watching Nailand's dust-trail, nervously pursuing him in a dangerous game of hide-and-seek amongst the *oueds* and defiles that kept them rigidly tense in their seats.

By rote, it seemed, Lassiter had taken the children and Susan. The children had not asked their mother. They had simply got aboard. Jane went too, of course, and Goru's sergeant who crouched unhappily in the very back of the vehicle. He studied them warily while sweat rolled down his chocolate-coloured face from his forehead into the untidy folds of his *cheche*. He clasped his Lebel between his knees with sweat-wet fingers.

Jane sulked for the first few minutes. She resented the presence of the sergeant, whom she quite rightly maintained stank. Lassiter, studying the man in the rear-view mirror, saw his eyes narrow fractionally when Jane came out with this. And Lassiter, not altogether sure of his interpretation of the man's reaction, stored the thought away for further reference.

It was not like Jane to be quiet for long. At the first stop the mechanics of the search excited her. She got out with Susan, clinging claw-like to the girl's arm.

'Watcha see, girl? Huh? Which side you on?'

It was unlike her to become muddled with direction. 'The South. There's nothing so far but I've only covered about twenty degrees.' She lifted the big binoculars impatiently. 'Sand there is, in p-plenty. It's rockier than yesterday, though. The country is full of ups and downs. A few stunted bushes.' They made her think of the way she had first spotted the Touareg.

'And Joe? Can you see his truck?'

'No.' The girl shifted. She pulled her arm loose and moved a yard away out of the cloud of tobacco-fouled breath. The Sahara jumped into the eyepieces of the binoculars again. Again she marvelled at its deadness. At best it was dying, and only where it was dying would it support life. How much longer would that go on? Every year the *gueltas* were a little lower, the vegetation a little thinner, life a little scarcer.

They drew a blank. The big vehicle rolled off again for another mile, stopped, searched, went on, stopped, searched again. It was a monotonous, soul-destroying and exhausting process, especially when a dip in the ground had to be investigated on foot.

It was nearing noon when Jane said abruptly: 'Take me to this *guelta* of yours.'

Lassiter protested mildly. 'That's a long way off course. It will delay us.'

'Lew, will you stop goddam arguing with me? I told you before, I don't like my dogs to jump up at me.'

He gave in and started the engine. 'Thy will be done, Mrs Teefer.'

She ignored the prod. She even chuckled. 'Good boy. Let's go.'

The box search had moved surprisingly far south in only its second day of operation. What had been a short detour yesterday was now a long haul north. They drove in silence over good and bad stretches of country until the Land-Rover nosed between the walls of the defile and pulled up in the mould of its own tyre-tracks near the pool.

The beat of the motor echoed down the long rock corridor and died away. They got out in silence. The sergeant went immediately to the *guelta* and drank. Then he sat in a pool of shade. He produced a bag of dates and began to eat, his Lebel across his knees and his dirty-white *cheche* hanging untidily below his chin. The children swam again, this time without any hesitation on the part of Thrin despite the presence of the black soldier, who had his back turned and seemed plunged in thought.

Jane stood for a long time. She literally sniffed the air. She moved her head from side to side the way a good gun-dog will when the covey is still distant. She muttered, 'God, that black bastard stinks,' and moved a little further up the defile in the direction of the Libyan border.

'What's on my right—the pool?'

'To your right and s-slightly behind you. You're about fifteen yards ahead of it.'

'And on the left?'

'Just the rock wall.'

'If I keep my feet on sand will I be okay?'

Susan glanced about. 'Er, er, yes.'

'All right. Then get lost. Leave me alone. I got some

thinking to do. Go get Lassiter to play with your tits. He's done it before, hasn't he?'

The girl stared at her, poker-faced. 'I think, in your future dealings with me, that you should be a little more c-careful. You're not stupid. I'm your eyes and on top of that we share something. I can bl-blow you and you know it.'

Jane was never afraid. Now she produced a small, cunning grin. 'Threats, huh?'

'No. A straightforward warning.'

'This doesn't sound like the girl I picked off a garbage heap.'

'It isn't.'

They regarded each other for a moment like two cautious sparring fighters who have not yet made contact, thirty-four years and only one pair of eyes between them. Then Lady Teefer said softly, 'Honey, sometimes I'm foolish. Real foolish. I say things I regret. So I'm sorry.' A white hand came out and touched Sue's arm, squeezed it. 'Don't let me down, girl. And I'll look after you.'

The girl walked away. She went on past the sergeant, past the *guelta* where the children waved at her. She waved back. Finally she reached Lassiter who stood with his back to her and his hands on his hips, staring out towards the entrance of the defile.

'They waved at me.'

He turned. 'The children?'

'Yes.' She was pleased by it.

They were hidden slightly from the others by a bulge in the rock wall. Knowing this, he reached out and pulled her against him.

She said, 'Lew, I t-told you. . . .'

'*Lassiter!*'

They leapt apart. The hoarse, cawing cry came from far away, hallooing down between the high faces of stone. Jane was small from here, a tiny neat-suited figure standing square to them with her feet wide apart and her arms raised like a prophet.

'*Lassiter, he's been here! I tell you my Peter has been here! I can feel it. I can smell it. God and Jesus be praised, I tell you Peter was here!*'

It was a cry of hope and despair. It died away in echoes and Susan's skin crawled. She let Lassiter hold her again. 'Jane is mad. Absolutely mad.'

'I don't know.' It had frightened him too. They watched the figure, made so small by the distance, turn its back on them.

He shivered and looked down at the girl. As though to reassure both of them, he kissed her. He kissed her gently but she responded with fire and want. Then she pulled away. She studied his face and something changed in her expression. 'I know what you're thinking. I read you like a book. You're thinking that I'm not kissing you because I like you but because I'm randy. I've had it before and once you've had it you've got to go on having it, and Lassiter is the available male. You're entitled to think that way, of course. But if you're going to, then don't get so goddam tender the way you were that night at Djanet.' She turned away and began to walk back towards the *guelta*.

'Susan.' He reached out a long arm and grabbed her. 'Don't talk like that.'

She stared at him with hostility, pulling away. She backed up against the rock wall. 'I'll talk any way I like. All I'm saying is make up your mind. Don't treat me as a whore one day and a lady the next and then a whore again and then a lady because it's rather confusing and I. . . .'

'Shut up!'

'That's more like it.' She grinned with the tears making a glitter in her eyes.

He moved up against her. She wanted to slap him but he held her arms down and pulled her against him, holding her. The rock wall was close to him. Over her shoulder he read the letters carved into the stone two feet from his face.

P.A.T.

The steam went out of him. 'She was right.' He turned the girl gently. 'Look. Jane was right. See, there.'

They stared in silence.

Then she said, 'Peter Adair Teefer.'

'Yes.'

'Are you going to tell her?'

'No. Will you?'

'Not if you don't want me to.'

He put his arm around her and they began to walk back along the sand.

*   *   *

Bowdrey had got on to the roof of his Land-Rover. Looking up, Ann could see the sweat glistening amongst the golden-red hairs on his legs. He was wearing khaki shorts. What she could see of his thighs and the curve of his calves were hard and masculine and muscular. The body was practising an unfair deception, she thought, the legs were the legs of a whole man and yet there was this putrefaction in his chest.

'Where is he now?'

'About a mile ahead on our port beam, as the sailors would say.' He dropped the binoculars against his chest and got down awkwardly. 'They are searching quite thoroughly. That would be all Franc's doing, though.' He almost smiled. 'I don't think Nailand is feeling very well.'

She looked at him searchingly. 'And you? Are you all right?'

'Fancy that.' His face twisted. 'Do you mean you're actually interested in my health? But then you need me, of course. For the time being.'

'Don't be like that, Bert.' She turned away. 'Do you think Lassiter knows about the money?'

Her back was turned. He reached out to touch her shoulder and then brought his hand back, so that she was never aware of the gesture. 'No. Not after last night. He keeps implying that there is another motive to both the expeditions—ours and theirs—but he doesn't know what it is.'

'I'm glad he doesn't know. He's dangerous. If he knew he would search much harder. He would find the money. I know he would.'

'In other words he's more efficient than I am?'

'I didn't say that. But he would find the money. I know it.'

Bowdrey stared at the nape of her neck where the blonde hair parted in its downward cascade so that he could see a triangle of smooth skin. 'You have such faith in your dear Mr Lassiter. That's because you're on such personal terms with him, no doubt—out in the bloody cold at nearly midnight. Is that where you get your confidence, wriggling around in the sand of the courtyard with him?'

She swung around and hit him in the face all in one movement. She was a strong young woman and the open-handed slap had the force to knock him down. 'I've told you before, it's *my* life! Leave me alone!'

The marks of her fingers were coming up on his cheek. He just sat there, looking up at her. Then he began to cough. He coughed while she stood with her arms folded, looking down, unmoving. He coughed until the phlegm came up in a convulsive spasm and spattered on the sand with its many bright red specks of blood so that it reminded her of some jelly creature of the sea.

Finally she moved. She bent and took his hand, helping him to stand. 'I'm sorry. I don't like to lose my temper.'

He wiped his mouth. 'I don't blame you. What I said was unforgivable and I am sorry too.' He went to the door and opened it.

'Bert.'

'Aye?'

She hadn't moved. She had, more than ever now, that look of fierce and settled resolution that he had seen before. 'If they find the money before we do.' She spoke very slowly so that there could be no mistaking her words. 'If they find the money first, Bert. What will you do?'

He watched her for a time that seemed to stretch on into infinity. Yet neither moved. Then finally he reached beneath the dashboard on the right of the steering column and brought out a revolver. It was a British Army Webley, a big weapon with a tunnel of a muzzle.

Bowdrey held it up. He let the sun throw points of burnished light off it. Then he met her eyes again, studying her for another long moment.

'I will kill them.'

She said nothing. He turned abruptly, put the Webley back, got behind the wheel and started the engine. She came around to the passenger door and got in. Bowdrey put the truck into gear and they drove away.

CHAPTER SIX

GORU AWOKE with a sense of alarm and confusion. And pain. *Mon dieu, mon dos!* That filthy camel.

He swung his legs off the bed, blinked blearily at his watch. Six o'clock in the evening. God, if only he could have gone right through the night. But his sleep had lasted one hour. Anyway, it was drinking time and this cheered him. He had dreamed wildly that he and Lassiter had been holding off a vast army of Touareg led by a faceless Jedren whom Goru had shot countless times without effect. The battle had ended with the two of them running out of ammunition and throwing potatoes at the Touareg, and Goru being shot in the back by a small Touareg boy holding a Beretta. The lower back. Yes, that would follow, of course. His back was sore. But for God's sake, why potatoes?

'Camille!' He called more sharply than he intended. But she was there at once, pulling back the light curtain of the alcove and proffering a glass of cognac that reeked of its potency. Always, it seemed, she anticipated his needs. He smiled happily and patted the bed next to him.

'Here. Sit down. Let's talk.'

'It went all right, I presume?' She was a little offhand because of the way he had arrived home and flung himself on the bed with little more than a grunt. And also because she suspected that he was pleased with a decision he had made on his own, without her influence.

'Oh yes, it went all right.' He took a huge uncivilized gulp of the brandy. He was sorry in retrospect because it was bad manners, but pleased at the way it burned itself in his middle. 'They are a strange crowd, out there. The Bowdreys are false. You saw it immediately when they called here on their way and had lunch. Now I am even more certain. This sick little man with his cheap little camera and the woman who watches him with the eyes of a nurse, not a wife—ugh! He made a face. 'Then there is this man Lassiter of whom we have heard. Very strange. Very ugly. Long and thin with huge feet and the most pleasant freckled face but when he smiles I think of a crocodile opening its jaws. I become afraid. Then he speaks to me in perfect French and I think I have a friend. A very complex man, a most interesting man. He has seen the world in every way and yet I detect somewhere a hint of Puritan.' Why else should they end up throwing potatoes at his dream-Touareg?

Camille touched his hand. 'The blind woman. The one who pays. What about her?'

Goru shrugged. 'Evil. A dreadful, extremely clever woman. But limited by her lack of sight, of course. She has in her *entourage* a stupid bully whom I believe is her cousin and a girl with the eyes of a wise woman. I cannot assess them fully except that they do not amount to much.'

He fretted with his glass. 'It is Lassiter, Lady Teefer and the Bowdreys who enter into this puzzle. Lassister not because he knows anything—I'm sure of that—but because he is clever and if there is anything to be found out he will do it. The Bowdreys and the old woman know something, of course. They advance their different reasons for their presence but I reject them as so much crap.'

She prodded gently. 'You have not found out. But you suspect.'

'Oh yes, I suspect all right.' He drank again. 'Whether the Bowdreys and Lady Teefer are there for the same purpose is impossible to determine. But forget about Lady Teefer. Think about the Bowdreys. They are so poor; so patently badly adjusted between themselves; so abjectly dedicated to a nonsensical object. This, to me, smells of only one thing.'

'Money!'

The words did not come from Camille. They came from the corner of the far room, from the old crone whom Goru had for so long regarded as part of the furniture. She was right, of course, she was following his line of thought. But it was unusual for her to interject. Normally her gummy mumblings were part of the background. So he cursed automatically and began to heave himself to his feet. He had every intention of flipping her apron over her head, which acted normally with the same effect as a sharp blow on the skull. But Camille raised a restraining hand. This was in itself unusual; and the old crone, bright-eyed and very much aware of the proceedings, chuckled.

'I want to tell you, my son, about a money-plane. You are

worried about these people at Fort Masuril and I have been thinking, but so much was forgotten, lost in my youth, when I was in my late seventies.' This time she cackled. 'Now it has come back to me. But first I would like a full glass of cognac without any water and all that nonsense. Give it to me and I will tell you a story.'

Goru stared at her. She was not, for the moment, in that world of senile rambling in which she spent most of her time. Abruptly, forgetting his back, he got up, poured her a danger-ously strong glass of neat brandy and went across the room and pushed it into one hooked, claw-like hand. He stood over her.

'A money-plane?'

'Yes.' She drank deeply without spluttering. 'Ah, this cognac sends fire through my old limbs. I feel like a girl again, the way I was in nineteen-forty-two when General Leclerc was based in Fort Lamy. You remember him?'

'I will never forget him.' Goru rubbed his nose which had become frantically itchy. As though it scents things, he thought ridiculously. His eyes watered and he blinked at her through these false tears, blearily looking as though he were about to fall asleep, and aware of it, and becoming angry with himself through his mounting excitement. Presumably he would react similarly in front of a firing squad and go down in history as a hero when in actual fact he had been concentrating on the fact that he was passing water into his trousers and embar-rassed because he did not want anyone to notice.

His mind was leaping convulsively, in impulses, as though it did not want to hear. He struggled with it, concentrating, his belly fluttering, staring into the face that had the million wrinkles of a mummy.

'I did not serve with Leclerc. But I knew him by sight. He was a living legend. After he had cleaned the Italians out of the Fezzan he marched his force about 2,000 kilometres across the Sahara into Tripolitania and came in on Montgomery's flank in time to help break the Mareth Line.' He indulged in a slight flight of fancy. 'He was to Montgomery what Blucher was to Wellington at Waterloo!'

The old woman's rheumy eyes had begun to sparkle. 'There will never be another Leclerc. History does not permit this.

But I am telling you of a time of my youth, 1943, when I was about 74. At that time I was living in Fort Lamy. I had three, four children still alive, not only Camille.' She blew a kiss at her surviving daughter. 'I am at the airport at Lamy. It is dark, nearly night-time. I know all these generals and officers. They are friends of mine. That is why Camille married an officer. We are standing around in a circle holding drinks while three men pack two suitcases. These men are armed and they in turn are guarded by ten armed soldiers. Talk goes around. Leclerc, taking everybody who could march with him, is long gone. But he must have money to pay his troops. So an aeroplane belonging to the King of England sits on the tarmac and eventually the suitcases are filled and locked and they are handed over to the British, two lieutenants, with revolvers at their waists. They take the suitcases and go across to the aeroplane and it takes off.'

She faltered. Her drink was half gone but already she was blinking owlishly. Goru's heart had begun to pound. He was angrily impatient. Age might inure people to certain things but it also produced an increasing intolerance to alcohol. At the same time he could not hurry her. So he stormed across the room, fetched his own drink and came back. He gulped at it greedily.

'What happened?'

'The men got aboard the plane with the suitcases. It took off and was gone into the night.' The shoulders that were so thin they were like coat-hangers under the floral dress, swept upward in a shrug. 'We went inside and carried on with the party. The next day I hear the news—the plane never reached Libya. There was much searching but it was never found.'

Goru leant over her, his words tumbling out over his tongue. "These suitcases. You saw them packed. Obviously they contained a lot of money. How much?'

'About one-hundred-and-forty million old francs.'

Goru gaped.

'Were they metropolitan francs, or endorsed for use in North Africa only?'

'Metropolitan, very high denominations. I saw them myself. I suppose to pay the troops he was going to obtain smaller notes with the help of the British.'

Goru pondered, still in shock. God, no wonder they were there, those jackals at Fort Masuril. The plane must have come down close by. But how did they know? And why wait so long? Automatically he made a calculation and quickly produced the answer: twenty-seven years. And why should the Bowdreys and the Teefer group arrive within days of one another after so long a time? Was it some sort of concealed partnership disguised under the front of two separate and distinct expeditions?

His mind began to leap-frog over the equations, pushing aside possible answers while it threw up more questions. So he gave up. He turned away, holding his drink. The old crone was already asleep, her head tilted to one side as though her neck were broken, her half-finished cognac cuddled in her lap in two claw-like hands that were the size of a child's. Gently, he took away the glass and almost as an afterthought flicked her apron over her head.

Camille was watching him with a mixture of sympathy and interest. 'All day, the old one has been struggling to remember. She hears more than we realize. Only now the answer has come to her. She was a very clever woman in her day.'

Goru went back to the sleeping alcove and resumed his sitting position on the bed. He stared across the room. His mind had gone blank and he was in a state of mild shock.

'This money; it is a king's ransom. A dream-fortune. What are you going to do?' It was Camille, gently prodding him, her own mind already alight with speculation.

Goru blinked. 'The Bowdreys. The Teefers. The Touareg. In that order. All so quickly. And yet after so long. They know. All of them. I am certain. Jedren must be laughing up his sleeve. He has other people to do his searching for him. And whoever discovers the money will find Jedren at hand to dispossess him.' He became suddenly agitated. 'God, do you realize that with that money Jedren could turn North Africa into a burning torch?' He put his hands in his pockets as though he had gone cold. 'I shudder at the consequences.'

'Pierre.' Camille gave him his forgotten drink, refreshed now so that it was full again. She held it to his lips for him to sip. Her voice was soft, breathy, her lips almost against his ear. 'Always the others, you mention. What will they do, you keep saying, what will happen? But what about *you, mon cher*, what about you? It is so *much* money.'

His startled eyes met hers. 'What do you mean?' He knew what she meant.

'This money. It is a flat in Paris. It is a chalet in Switzerland, it is the Riviera. It is goodbye to the Sahara. It is goodbye to Africa, to the harshness, the dryness, to the sight of an ox slaughtered in the middle of Fort Lamy. It is farewell for ever to that meagre monthly salary you get. I've seen how your face twists when it comes. You think; am I doing all *this* for *that*?'

Goru pulled away. 'What you are suggesting is impossible.' His voice was husky. 'This is my country.'

A small smile touched her lips. 'And so it can continue to remain—to be visited for a short time at widely spaced intervals.'

Goru took the drink from her. His mind was beginning to project. It had started off on ordered lines but was now, reluctantly, veering away along the line of her thinking. My mind is like that buggeration camel I rode, he thought, I am not controlling it too well. Aloud he said, slowly, 'The money has not yet even been found. Do not build castles in the air. The drop would be a long one and you would hit the ground very hard. It might prove difficult to recover.'

'The money will be found. I have a feeling.'

'Hah! You women and your feelings.' He sipped the drink. But although he did not want to show it, he shared this sense of complete confidence. It was as though they could go ahead right now and plan. Perhaps it would be wise, anyway. 'What about Jedren?'

'You have twenty men armed. And a much better brain. We are not completely defenceless, Pierre.'

He was flattered without being deluded. She meant *her* brain. 'The money belongs to France. Or the *République du Tchad*. One or the other. I am not a lawyer. But it certainly does not belong to me.'

She showed a flash of fire. 'Nor does it belong to the Bowdreys or the Teefer woman or Jedren! Are you going to stand by and watch one of them take it because it's not yours?'

'No. No. No. I can't do that.'

'Then what are you going to do?'

Goru nearly lost his temper. He whirled, spilling some of his drink. 'I don't know! Will you stop nagging me, woman! At this moment I am a creature of indecision! Do you expect me just to go like that'—he snapped his fingers—'and tell you precisely what I propose doing when I have not yet fully recovered from the shock of hearing about this . . . this money?' He said the last word as though it was almost too much for him. Then he pouted. His stomach was crying within him at the injustice of being empty, and tense as well. Without knowing it, Goru was well on the way to a peptic ulcer. 'In any case, I'm hungry. And I cannot think when I am hungry.'

Camille responded instantly to his mood. A certain doggedness had come to his expression together with a glitter in his eyes that she had seen before and recognized as latent menace. It had never yet exploded into anything and she was not prepared to let it, if this was possible. In the three years of their marriage he had on a few occasions mildly frightened her. And this was one of them. It was as though he ceased momentarily to be the genial Pierre Goru and had become instead the *Sous-Préfet* of Zufra, an old war-horse, bulkily threatening, who knew what it was to kill.

'There is *coq au vin* for dinner. The last of the chickens.' She put her slender arm around his thick waist. 'Come, *mon bien-aimé.*'

Half an hour later Goru sat back in his chair and released a low, rumbling, purringly contented belch. He looked at her with soft eyes now that reflected like the gauge on the mirror of his satisfaction. He was full of chicken and awash with wine.

'Consider this.' He lit one of his Gauloises. 'I have at the Fort two men. They have a radio. The Sergeant will report every night. In fact, he is due to do so very shortly. These men are instructed to accompany the Teefers and the Bowdreys on their probes. The sergeant has been carefully told to listen to every word that is said. Now, all this was done *before* I knew anything about the money-plane. It was done on a small whiff of doubt, no more. Now *there* is insight for you.' He shrugged his heavy shoulders. 'And I ask you: what more is there to be done? If my men do their duty and I have no reason to doubt that they will, I will know—I *must* know—that the plane has been found *before even Jedren gets to hear of it.*' He had leant forward across the table, staring into her eyes to make his point. 'Then, at that stage, I will decide and act. Now this you must accept.'

She accepted the inevitable. Apart from which he was right. It irked her a little because usually she liked to have some say in his decisions.

'*Oui, mon cher.*' It was just a murmur. She looked away. Goru got up. He found his webbing belt and buckled on his revolver. His eyes, sharp and shrewd, rested on her for a moment. 'Is there anything else I can do? Have you any suggestions?'

The slim shoulders shrugged under the lamé.

'None.'

He grinned, turning away. Camille liked to meddle, and this time she couldn't and was a little hurt. It made him feel all the more confident. 'I am going to the radio room. *Bon soir, chérie.*'

There was only the murmur of her reply as he stepped out on to sand that was purpled with shadow in the many footprints of its surface, like pock-marks in a smooth skin. A high moon, round and brilliantly yellow, guided him through the oasis towards the low bulk of small buildings. One showed a square of light. The radio room winking an inviting eye.

He was nearly there when he heard the light scuffing on the sand, a rapid pulse-beat of footfalls coming through the grove of palms. He stopped, one hand going gently to touch the smooth reassuring butt of his revolver. It was so quiet tonight A butterfly fluttered feathery wings inside him.

One of his men burst out of the palms. Goru recognized him at once. The man was running fast, but there was something wrong with his gait. It was irregular, weaving. The trooper fell, sprawling, got to his feet again and floundered on. He saw Goru and veered towards him, stopped, tried to salute and then put his hands on his knees and let his lungs take over, sucking for breath.

It was difficult to wait. Goru gave the man half-a-minute. Then he pulled the man upright and peered into his face.

Blood was running from a contusion at the corner of his mouth. One eye was so puffed it was nearly shut. His beret was gone and his tunic was torn right down the front. All his buttons were missing.

'You are a disgrace.' Goru spoke icily. 'What the devil have you been doing?'

The trooper's eyes rolled. 'They called me out to where the Toubou were camped yesterday. I thought Khoum was still there. Then they attacked me, took my beret, cut the buttons off my tunic. They laughed. They said I must fetch you and tell you that I . . . I have been dishonourably discharged from the Army of Tchad.'

Goru's hands shot out like steel claws and took the man by his lapels. He dragged him close, grinding out the question. 'You son of shit. Who? *Who* attacked you? Who did this?'

'The Touareg.'

Goru's stomach spasmed. He pushed the man away from him so that he stumbled and fell on his backside, sprawling there and staring at Goru with shocked eyes.

'Consider yourself under arrest. Go to your quarters.' He turned away. His tiny force, so quickly humiliated. He was furious and frightened in turn. Jedren was out there, waiting for him. Jedren had sent a calling card. And such a clever calling card. Jedren must be gifted. He must be the most fantastic leader, he must. . . .

Goru stopped himself. He let his arms fall to his sides. He spoke to himself carefully and earnestly. Jedren is a man. I am a man. I have fought in battles of which Jedren has never seen the like. He took a deep breath, wiped at the sweat that had burst out on his forehead. Then he began to walk quickly through the palm grove, moving with measured, firm steps until the palms thinned out and the moon burst suddenly overhead, bathing him in betraying light and showing him the semi-circle of men fifty yards away who stood ahead of a line of silent kneeling camels.

He made himself stop. God, they were so tall, so fearfully tall. And so still. He breathed in and out a few times, deeply, through his nose. Then he called: 'Where is the one known as Jedren?'

He was answered in perfect French. 'I am here. May I speak

with you, *Monsieur le Sous-Préfet*?' The voice was accentless, light-timbred and smooth with mockery.

Goru took another deep breath. 'You said you *wish* to see me. And you have a strange way of sending for people.' He began to walk steadily across the sand, coming to a stop eventually about five paces from the curve of dark tall figures. 'You have committed a crime. You have assaulted one of my men. I regret that I shall have to detain you to face charges.'

There was movement, a stir, a faint murmur of amusement. One of the Touareg stepped forward. He was taller, broader than the others. 'The man was aggressive and abusive. Half-drunk, I think. He mocked us and called us heretics. Then he attacked us as though he were amok. We were forced to defend ourselves.'

Goru said shortly, 'That is not his version.'

'Possibly so. One who is full of guilt is always full of excuses. But we waste words.' Jedren's voice carried a hint of quiet laughter. 'If I were to *allow* you to detain me, these eight men here would tell what had happened exactly as I have. Nine against one. Are you not wasting time?'

Goru said stiffly. 'I will overlook it this time.' He had made his empty threat. He had shown them that he was not afraid. It was an *impasse* and he was well aware of it.

'I am sure you are being wise.' There was a small pause in which Jedren allowed the full weight behind his words sink in. 'I wished at first merely to give you my greetings and offer you some of our mint tea; I am in your district and it is only right that I should call upon you. But I am afraid that the incident of the soldier has rather spoilt that.'

'I readily agree.' Goru shifted his weight, his feet sinking in the soft sand. 'It would have been more civilized, perhaps, had we been able to talk in my quarters, or yours. To be blunt, though, because now we must: why are you in my Préfecture? You are very far from home.'

The indigo-cloaked shoulders rose and fell. 'Passing through, perhaps. Perhaps to buy some of your fine Tibesti camels. Is it illegal to be in your district?'

'No. It is not illegal.' Goru thought a moment. 'Jedren, I am being straightforward with you. It is a pity that you cannot reciprocate. But that is your business. Let me put what I have to say once, and then it is done: I know why you are here. I know of the Franks at Fort Masuril. I know what it is they seek. And I warn you. Leave them alone. Leave what they seek alone. It is not yours.'

There was a long silence. The Touareg crossed his arms. Goru thought of the dagger he would have up the left sleeve of his cloak and his hand strayed down, idly, towards his revolver. But Jedren only chuckled. 'And if I choose to ignore this warning?'

Goru said heavily. 'You know that I am the *Sous-Préfet* of Zufra. I have an armed force at my disposal. And also I have a machine gun, an FN which fires one thousand cartridges in every minute of time. I ask you to think, Jedren, I ask you to reason before you act.'

The soft voice answered him at once. 'It is regrettable that you should have to threaten me. We have a saying amongst the Imo-chagh, my friend, which you should remember: "reason is the shackle of cowardice". I reject your warning.'

'Very well then. I know where I stand.' Goru stepped back. He saluted stiffly and walked away towards the palms, showing them only his wide back.

'*Monsieur le Sous-Préfet.*' The words reached him as he was about to enter the grove. Goru stopped, keeping his back turned.

'Listen, *Monsieur le Sous-Préfet*, and you will know why I reject your warning.'

Goru stood still. Then he heard a sound that made the hair on the back of his neck bristle, while his skin crawled. It was the snick-snack sound of a rifle bolt being pulled back and thrust home again, repeated many times so that it seemed to echo again and again across the sand.

Slowly, Goru turned. Where there had been nine men, the sand was now black with them. All were still and silent, tall figures robed in indigo that was black in the night-light. And nowhere was a rifle to be seen.

'It would have been so easy.' Jedren's voice with its undertone of mocking laughter came clearly across the sand. '*Bon soir*, my friend. I hope you can sleep well.'

Goru broke away. He burst into the palm grove and began to run, forcing his way blindly through the whipping fronds.

It was his dream again, the sands teeming with the People of the Veil, gunfire reaching a cacophonous climax of sound, Jedren moving amongst them untouched, the pain in his back as the bullet from the Beretta hit it. He ran until the terrible fear had gone, and the radio room showed its warm welcoming window. He ran until he could stop and listen to himself pant and tell himself more calmly now that those men had been there all the time, hidden in folds of dead ground, and that Jedren was nothing more than a cheap showman.

He shook his head. Sweat showered like teardrops in the moonlight. It was no good bringing himself down to earth like this. It was still his dream. Those people out there had been real. And there was no machine-gun here at the oasis that could fire one thousand cartridges in one minute of time. That had been a lie, one of his many useless threats. He had only nineteen men, nineteen Lebel rifles, his revolver and a case of ammunition.

Goru thought about his dream again. He began to walk towards the radio room. His mouth curved in a wry grin. I hope, he thought, that Lassiter's throwing-arm is good, and that there are plenty of potatoes at Fort Masuril. Because there were none here.

* * *

Twenty years before, there had been amongst the nuns in the convent at Fort Lamy an English one with a hunch back who had an eye for spotting clever children. She had singled out a little chocolate-coloured six-year-old and, amongst his other subjects, taught him English. This she had done for the six years his schooling had lasted, so that the sergeant had gone into the world ignorant, young and largely uneducated. But he could understand and even speak a little English.

He thought about it now, leaning on the parapet of the fort, looking out across the moonlit desolation and listening to the snores of the trooper who lay wrapped in blankets in the same watch-tower where the Touareg boy had slept. His English, he thought proudly, was nearly as good as his uncle's. Good enough that he had been able to follow the general run of conversation while he fried in the heat of the Land-Rover. Good enough to know that the blind woman

139

had said he stank. He would not forget that. One did not forgive that kind of insult easily. She had said it without caring whether he understood or not, and he intended to do something about it if he got the chance.

It was nearly nine o'clock. Time to report. He moved towards the watchtower at the other end of the catwalk. The portable radio was here. But as he reached the entrance he stopped. Had someone called his name? He paused. Then it came again, quite clearly: 'Henri!'

That was his name. The voice was light, almost disembodied, and it emanated from outside the fort, from out there in the moonlit desolation.

He went abruptly to the parapet. 'Who calls?'

'It is I, Henri.' The voice floated out of nowhere. 'You know me well.'

The sergeant's eyes rolled. He began to shiver. He gazed desperately into the desert and saw nothing. 'I do not know you.' His voice was hoarse.

'Oh yes, you do.' Was it beneath him? He peered over the parapet, the hard mud pressing uncomfortably against his stomach.

'Henri!' The voice, this time, was behind him. It called from down in the courtyard, light and mocking in the shadows.

The sergeant whirled. His hands gripped the rough surface of the parapet while he quivered. His eyes were starting from his head.

'Who are you? What do you want?'

'Are you sure you don't know me?'

The sergeant said huskily, 'I am sure.'

The voice scolded him. 'You should be ashamed of yourself. I am one you treasure. One whose memory you adore.'

He was almost spreadeagled against the parapet wall. Sweat rolled off him in waves. 'Is it . . . is it. . . .'

'Henriiiiii!' The voice came from far out in the desert, floating to him in an eerie wail.

He shuddered. He blundered about. 'You were here. Now you are there. What are you?' His lips shook and his voice was a thin breathy thing.

'I am me.' The voice was mocking him again. 'Why don't you come down? Perhaps I will show myself to you.'

140

'No!' His heart was thudding as though it were going to break out of his body. 'I . . . I am afraid.'

'You must not be afraid, Henri.' The voice was behind him, down in the courtyard again. 'I am your friend.'

The sergeant fell on his knees. 'Merciful Mother of God, protect me!'

'There is no need for that.' The voice was quite strict. 'I will speak with you again. Tomorrow night, perhaps.'

'Good night, Henri.' The voice was out in the desert again.

There was a silence. The sergeant allowed it to go on and on. Then he burst to his feet and sprinted along the catwalk, reaching the trooper and grabbing him, shaking him awake. The man grunted and opened his eyes, staring up into his sergeant's sweating, anguished face.

'Quick!' Henri was panting. 'You must come and listen. The voices that speak to me out of the night.' He dragged the trooper to his feet. 'Come *on*, damn you!' He pushed him roughly to the parapet. 'Listen. Listen to the voices.'

There was no sound, only the sawing of the sergeant's breathing. The trooper shivered without his blankets. He turned worried eyes on Henri. 'God, sergeant, you must be careful. It can get you so easily, this *cafard*. It is a madness of the desert that destroys you.'

The sergeant put out both hands and dragged the man against him. The moonlight reflected off the frightened black face, showing the small pits of tribal scars.

'Ah!' He pushed the trooper away. 'I tell you, they were real. I'm saner than you are. Come, you must wind the generator, I have to report to the lieutenant.' He turned his back and headed back again towards the further watchtower.

*   *   *

'You lying so still anybody'd think you were dead, but I can tell you ain't sleeping 'cause your breathing's so light.' Jane's voice came out of the darkness and touched Susan lightly with a mixture of denture-powder and nicotine.

'I'm awake.'

There was a chuckle from the other bed. 'That's an Irishism.' The sound of her fluttery breathing came for a while. Then: 'Been thinking about Peter. About when I met him, I mean. I was blind already, of course. But although I couldn't see, I knew I was marrying one hell of a handsome man. I'd heard all about him. But there're handsome fairies who look like Greek Gods. I wanted to know about the other part. Was this guy a *man*? Well, it happened, of course. We were courting already and we weren't only gonna hold hands. But the first time I said to him, I said now looky here Peter I gotta feel, I haven't got eyes, I gotta feel and I mean with my *hands*. So he just laughed and he came to me and I felt, and by crikey honey, I tell you I let out a shriek and hung on, with him laughing fit to bust a gut. I just never had known that anybody could have a——'

'Shut up,' the girl said.

There was a short, breathy pause. 'What was that you said?'

'I said shut up.'

'That was what I thought you said.' A small hand drifted across and touched Susan's rigid body. Susan could feel the cold metal of Jane's rings. 'God, child, you're like ice, and hard as steel. I do something to make you mad?'

'No.'

'What is it then?'

'Nothing.'

'Nothing? Got to be a reason. Tell me.'

'Leave me alone.'

'Come on. Come on, now.'

'Is there a God up there?'

'Guess so. Still plenty of churches around. Why?'

'Because I'm going to pray to Him.'

'Tarnation. Ever prayed before?'

'I don't think so. Not that I can remember.'

'First time will be mighty hard. Maybe He won't be all that keen on listening.'

'The world is full of deaf ears, Lady Teefer. Now leave me alone. I'm going to clasp my hands and say my prayers.'

'You're awful bitter.'

Her voice had the hardness of steel. 'Leave me alone, Lady Teefer, I'm praying.'

*   *   *

John-oh let the Land-Rover idle to a halt and switched off.

He sat in deepest silence for a moment, then fumbled a cigarette from a pocket and lit it. The lighter glowed and died and he was left in a pale darkness, pale because the moon had slid away over the top of the defile but lit its topmost face. He could see the yellow blur of sand, the big crouching boulders, the sinister black oval of the *guelta*.

He got out slowly, went around to the back of the truck and took out two jerry-cans. He unscrewed the cap from the fresh water tank and let it dangle on its chain. Then he walked the few paces to the water, knelt, took the tops off the jerry-cans and plunged them under the cold surface of the water. They chug-a-lugged briefly and grew heavy. He pulled them out, went to the tank and emptied each in turn, hearing the water splash tinnily in the empty interior. It made him both angry and impatient, this sound. He would have to do about ten trips at this rate, maybe more.

He went back to the *guelta*, immersed the cans once more. They seemed to take longer this time and his hands ached from the cold. He looked to his left, along the narrow stretch of sand that wound towards Libya. It seemed to glow a little in the quarter-light of the reflected moon. Then he turned his head the other way and went quite still.

A camel stood in the entrance darkly silhouetted against the night sky, a dark camel carrying a man who seemed robed in darkness. And they were motionless, as though they were stone and had been watching this defile at night for a thousand years.

John-oh got up very slowly, letting the jerry-cans gurgle to the *guelta*'s bottom. He backed up against the truck, trembling, fighting a terrible weakness in his legs. He fought for his voice and at last found it.

'Who are you?' It carried in a tenor quaver that seemed to rebound all the way down the passage.

There was no answer. The statue cameleer was silent.

'Oh God.' His heart thudded as though it were fighting to be free of his ribs. He called again in French. 'I am from Masuril. I wish you no harm. I am collecting water.'

Again there was no answer. But the stone camel and its mute rider seemed to turn, to face towards him and begin a ghostly advance.

'No!' John-oh fell on his knees. Pure terror had overcome him. He put his hands up in an attitude of prayer. 'I am unarmed. Please!'

The camel seemed to grow huge, to block the defile from side to side. John-oh screamed. 'Christ, no!' He jumped up, gibbering, scrabbling his way along the side of the Land-Rover with his back to its icy hide, fumbling for the door and opening it from behind, almost falling into the seat. The engine burst into life, the lights probed long strong healthy yellow beams down the northern walls of the defile. There was just enough room to turn if he swung, reversed until the back wheels spun momentarily in the wet edge of the *guelta*, turned, cursing, reversed once more, heaving with his powerful arms at the heavy wheel, ramming the gears home while sweat plunged out of his hair and ran in frightened rivulets down his face, turning and reversing and turning again until suddenly the truck was straight, its blunt snout was pointing directly towards the entrance, the big bright beams of its lights throwing up the sand, the rock walls, even illuminating a little of the outside desert. Then John-oh cut the motor and sat staring straight ahead of him.

There was no camel. There was no rider. The sand showed harshly-lit ahead of him all the way to the opening. It showed in its yellow grains the tracks of tyres. His. Lassiter's. And nothing else. No camel-prints of the statue camel and its dark sentinel.

John-oh opened the door. He got out very slowly, as though he had become suddenly old. He went to the *guelta* and waded until he was knee-deep, feeling for the jerry-cans and bringing them out, taking them like an automaton to the back of the vehicle, pouring them into the splashy maw of the water tank.

It was never there. It was a figment of your frightened mind. The words fell in ones and twos into the exhausted emptiness of his mind. It is your fear of the Touareg. It is your fear of the dark. It is just simply, your fear.

The tank was full. Water bubbled out and made golden teardrops on the cap's chain. He screwed it shut automatically, slung the empty jerry-cans in the back, went around and started the motor. He drove slowly to near the entrance, studying the rocks on either side. There was not one that by any stretch of imagination could have resembled what he had seen.

He looked up. Between the high walls he could make out only one star that winked at him cheerfully from out of a millennium of night. I will draw strength from you, he thought. Perhaps Mrs Nailand was watching it too. The thought comforted him greatly. We will draw strength from it together, he told himself, and began to drive back through the bumpy desert to the fort.

CHAPTER SEVEN

BERT BOWDREY watched Lassiter's Land-Rover bump between the gates and head straight away over the level firmness of the *reg*, leaving a long trail of sand-smoke behind it. Then John-oh's vehicle came bulkily past him, blocking his view of Lassiter, spattering him with sand so that he had to spit grains of it on to the sleeve of his shirt. John-oh swung his truck to the right immediately, moving to take up his inevitable position as right-hand man in the box search. By this time Lassiter was gone, hidden by a small cloud that was the diminishing dust of his passage.

Bowdrey looked at the sand stuck to his shirt with the tiny cotton-balls of his spittle. He stared at it with absolute hatred.

'They're late again.' It was Ann, moving next to him with that silent force he had got to know so well. She wore the same cotton dress she'd had on when the Teefer group had arrived, and was barefooted the way she had been then.

'Aye. But they're covering ground.' He flipped his head so that drops of sweat were flung off. 'We'd best be going.'

'Lassiter is alone today. Just the sergeant with him. Did you notice?'

'Yes. The old blind bitch, the seeing-eye girl and the children have stayed behind.' He began to move towards the truck. 'Come, lass. There's no time to waste.'

It was suffocatingly hot in their Land-Rover. They opened the windows but it made no difference. The air of the courtyard moved with a sluggish indifference, leaden with heat.

Bowdrey ground the starter. It whined and throbbed. 'Come on, you old cow.' He tried again. The starter filled the silent square with its harshness. Bowdrey took his fingers away and dropped his hands in his lap. 'Oh shit.' Sweat ran off his nose. 'She's at it again.'

'Try again, Bert. That's only twice.'

Her even, level voice infuriated him. 'God blast, woman, I know her, I know when she won't go!'

She looked into the sun-scorched, chipped and freckled face with its dew of perspiration. 'Let me try.'

'Ah, for God's sake, what a typically idiot woman thing to say! What're you going to do, cast a spell over it? Oil the gear lever?' He got out raging, storming around to the front. The bonnet came up and cut him off from her view.

Ann struggled across into the driver's seat. Her sweat-wet thighs clung to her skirt and hauled it up high against her groin. Slowly with firm hands she tugged the dress into place. Then she reached out and tried the starter. Immediately, the engine caught. Its rumble coincided with the crash of the bonnet coming down and Bowdrey's furious appearance at her window.

'For Christ's sake! You could have cut me to pieces! How the hell did you know what I was doing?'

'It's running, Bert. That's what you wanted, isn't it?'

He said something under his breath and began to open the door but she stopped him. 'I'll drive. You're in too much of a state. You'll hurry and maybe do some damage that we can't fix.'

He met her eyes for a moment. His lips quivered. Then he stormed around to the passenger side and got in. He sat a moment, his fingers knotting and intertwining with the tremendous tension that filled him. Then he said abruptly, 'Well, get on with it!'

She turned with a deliberate slowness. 'Light me a cigarette, first.'

He watched her with a sudden care. 'You're doing this on purpose. I know it.' But he found cigarettes and lit them. He gave her one and said with primitive sarcasm, 'Now milady. Do you mind very much if we start our joy-ride?'

She drew smoke and sent it boiling against the windscreen.

146

Then she said quietly, 'No, not at all.' She put the Land-Rover into gear, took it easily through the gates, then brought it up to a fast neat clip along the *reg*, veering at right-angles to the lingering sand-smoke that marked the trail of John-oh's vehicle.

*   *   *

John-oh was doing a very thorough piece of searching. He was dogged and determined and for the first time he had Nailand off his back. They stopped, probed the surrounding landscape with their binoculars, stopped, probed again. They set off on stumbling, sweat-soaked hikes to *oueds* and defiles that the truck and the glasses could not reach. They worked in different ways—John-oh quiet and methodical, Nailand sullenly and uncommunicatively thorough. But they did well, unhampered by the silent trooper in the truck's rear seat, and it was two o'clock before they stopped for a poor lunch of canned herrings, some ham and a flask of coffee. The trooper, withdrawn and remote as ever, unwound his dirty *cheche* and ate a mess of dates. The meal was eaten in absolute silence in the oven-heat of the vehicle. There was only the sound of Nailand's nibbly gobbling, the clink of a can, the whoosh of the flask being opened. Then the meal was gone and Lola was still busy packing the remains into the picnic case when John-oh was going again, competently negotiating a tricky patch of *hammada* as he swung southward towards his allotted two kilometres for the backward leg of the search.

The country had got wild and rough. There was a little more vegetation, some grey-green bushes, a few clumps of grass that was so dry that it looked petrified. Once they disturbed a gazelle which dashed away in effortless bounds. They watched the graceful impulses of its flight and nobody said anything. They went on into a tangle of rearing rock, soft sand that the four-wheel drive took them through crab-like, as though they were swimming, little cul-de-sacs and defiles which when they were big enough had to be investigated. It took time, time enough for all of them to know they would be late the way Lassiter would be late, too, although his side of the box was not quite as rough.

John-oh had stopped thinking. He had become honed down

by the search, tranquillised by the analgesic effect of working his rigidly tense body into a state of muscular limpness. It calmed him unexpectedly, so that at the first stop after lunch, while Nailand was plunging through *erg* towards a defile, he turned around in his seat and looked at Lola. The words came without any pre-thought.

'Last night when I was at the *guelta* I thought I saw a Touareg. He was mounted on a dark Hoggar camel and he came towards me and I knew that he was going to kill me. I fell on my knees and I cried out for mercy. And then I turned the Land-Rover and found that there was nothing, not even the imprint of a camel's foot. I was afraid in the *guelta*, Mrs Nailand.'

She saw his strong young arm lying along the top of the seat. It would have been so easy to reach out and touch it. But she didn't. Her hands remained folded calmly in her lap. And with her, too, the words came so easily: 'I know what it is to be afraid.' Her eyes went away from him for a moment to the distant figure of Nailand sullenly stumbling his way back to them. 'One can be afraid of fear, even. I will come with you to the *guelta*, Mr Franc.'

'Thank you.' That was all he said. He turned around and started the engine. The vehicle moved off as soon as Nailand had got in.

*   *   *

Bowdrey let the binoculars drop so that they thumped heavily against his chest. Standing on the roof of the Land-Rover, he looked down at a foreshortened Ann.

'It's no use. We've lost them. It's an hour, now, that they've been gone.' He gave her a look of wild despair. 'We're cursed. We're star-crossed. We'll never find the money and we'll die out here in this God-forsaken place.'

'You act more like a fool with each passing day.' Her deep eyes held nothing but contempt. 'Get down and talk like a man.'

He jumped and fell sprawling. The leather thong of the binoculars wrenched at his neck. He jerked them off and flung them away, cursing. He got up panting, sand sticking to his wet forearms and to one cheek.

'I'm not a man and you know it. I'm a half-man.' The words came out quickly, bitten off by the short wheezing of his breath. 'It's just your flipping bad luck you got landed with me. But then I knew about the plane, of course.' He shoved his contorted face into hers. 'You're bloody-well stuck with me and why the hell can't you accept it!'

She put out her lean brown hands and took him by the shoulders. She shook him easily, without effort. 'Bert, stop tearing yourself apart! Don't *waste* emotion. That's all I'm telling you. This wild nervous energy of yours is so misdirected. Will rage find the plane? Will despair find the plane?'

He took her wrists. He squeezed them while a look of agony crossed his face. Then it was gone and he was saying softly, 'Ah, God I know. I know, lass. It's this bloody rot inside me. Knowing it's there, knowing there's nothing I can do about it, knowing I've got so much time and no more. The impatience —it boils like a volcano.'

She dropped her arms. She showed even a fleeting tenderness, gone so quickly he was not sure whether he had seen it. 'Come. Let's sit for a while. We both need a rest.'

They went to the back of the vehicle because the sun was westering and had stamped an elongated shadow-imprint of the truck on the sand. She took a flask with her and poured tea for them.

'That's better.' Bowdrey was slumped against the rear fender. He lit cigarettes for them and they sat and smoked and sipped the tea.

'What's the time?'

He looked at the wristwatch with its sweat-blackened leather strap. 'Half-past-three. We're going to be late getting back.'

'It doesn't matter.' She thought about the probe. 'This is their third search today. The box is moving south very well. John-oh Franc is very good, very methodical. He would by now have turned in exact parallel to the outward course he was running. You know what that is. All we have to do is follow. You don't *have* to see his dust trail. It's not imperative. It's impossible, anyway, the country has got so wild.'

Bowdrey shrugged. 'All right.' He was more relaxed, now. And his mind was following another pattern. 'Those Touareg.

I don't for one moment believe that they are doing anything more than passing through. That *Sous-Préfet*, or whatever he's called, is an old woman frightened by nothing more than rumour. But if they do know about the money——' He stopped in mid-sentence, staring at the ground between his knees, puzzled. Then he flicked his head to look at her. 'How the hell did they find out?'

She spoke carefully. 'Bert, there are many Touareg in Djanet. We spent the day there, you remember, and you had too much wine at the café and spoke very loudly. Anyone in the restaurant who understood English could have followed the gist of it.'

She remembered his flushed face, the sweat beaded on the freckled cheeks, the rough north-country voice over-loud with heady wine and excitement and the fever of the tuberculosis. In three damning sentences he had given away the entire object of their trip. Looking about her at the silent robed figures at the other tables she had prayed quietly that his quick words with their broad intonation had not been understood. And then again, in Chifra, in almost identical circumstances, there had been further indiscretions, small slips brought about by circumstances in which she could almost have forgiven him, but mistakes nevertheless that added up to a fairly plain indication of what they were doing.

'Nonsense, woman.' Bowdrey was obviously worried. His ever-present temper remained in control but he forced a sort of injured annoyance into his tone. 'Me. It's always me. Do you ever do anything wrong, you perfect person?'

She ignored him. She looked out ahead of her and drew idly on the cigarette while minutes passed. It was he who made the peace eventually. He cleared his throat and said quite con-versationally, 'This section is so wild that I don't think we need worry much, anyway. There's just no place where a pilot, even one as good as Sir Peter, could bring a big machine like a Dakota in without writing off everybody.'

Because they were at the rear of the truck they were looking back at the ground they had covered. He pointed. 'Even there, for example. There's about two hundred and fifty yards of nice, even *reg*. But fairly high rock to the south.' He angled his hand as though it were an airplane. 'He would have had to come in sharpish. Probably hit with one hell of a bang. About there.' He pointed south of the long line of tyre tracks. 'Then if everything was still hanging together he would go slithering along on his belly and fetch up with an almighty smack against the rock here on the northern side.'

'Or,' she said quietly, 'if he was lucky he would sail right through the mouth of that defile. Do you see it? It looks narrow from this angle but I'm quite sure it would accommodate an aircraft with the wingspan of a Dakota.'

'That would be stretching anybody's luck.' He was almost scoffing, raising his eyebrows when she got up and fetched the binoculars he had flung into the dust.

She came back and sat down again, her back against the fender. The defile was about a hundred yards away and some degrees to their left. Ann focused the binoculars on it. She studied it for what seemed an inordinately long time. Then she said, as though it were a very ordinary remark, 'The eastern wall has been damaged. Something has struck it about twelve feet up. You can see where the rock was scored and some of it broken away.'

Bowdrey snatched the binoculars from her. He seemed hardly to look. Then he was on his feet. They rose together, impelled by the current of their mutual excitement.

'Did you check that defile?'

'No. It was on your side. And in any case our last stop was nearly a mile back.' Her breathing was as quick as his, now. They panted the short quick words at each other.

'But you could have checked while I was driving!'

'Oh, for God's sake!'

She tore herself away and began to run, blindly, forgetting the Land-Rover in her excitement. Bowdrey hesitated and then cursed and followed her and so they ran together, the barefooted girl oblivious of the pain of her sand-scorched feet, the lean sandy-haired man unaware of the savage burn in his lungs, the way the hot air he sucked in greedily seemed to tear his chest open. They ran until they fetched up gasping, leaning against the western wall of the defile, staring down its length, seeing the section of wing, their eyes jumping beyond that to the bulk of the crumpled Dakota. Bowdrey cried out in ragged triumph and then they were running again, staggering in the pulverising heat along the defile, passing the chip of wing, ignoring it, obliterating with their scudding feet the two faint lines of footprints that might have told them something later. They ran until Bowdrey, staggering, stopped so suddenly that the girl cannoned into him and they lurched, clinging momentarily to avoid a fall. They were only ten yards from the wreck.

'She's burned! She's been on fire! God, oh my God, look at her.' His cork-dry mouth croaked out the words. He turned bright crazy eyes on her. 'Jesus, my baby has been cremated. My baby with all the money in her belly.' Then he was gone in a lurching run, crunching over blackened strewn metal, beating and fighting his way in a mad torrent of cursing through the twisted and charred wreckage until he could force himself through the open hatch in the fuselage. She saw him cut himself on his arm and the blood came out bright scarlet against the sooty carbon that coated the plane like a mantle. He was gone only a minute, but it stretched for ever into her time.

. He came back very slowly. He was as spent as an over-extended athlete, clay-faced beneath the red scars and chips of the sun. His legs trembled visibly. He had difficulty in speaking.

'There's nothing in there. It's a shell. Just a few cinders. The seats, the fittings. The suitcases. The money. All gone.'

It was for a moment impossible for her to grasp the finality of what had happened. She was in the grip of complete shock. She stared at the wreck, at the totality of its charred destruction. Some parts of the metal had melted. The sand had in some places glazed.

'Is this the right plane?'

It was a febrile grasping, a numb and dazed searching for a tiny thread of hope.

'Aye.' He pointed to the nose of the Dakota. Concertinaed up against the blind end of the defile, this part had escaped some of the more direct fury of the fire. Just below the smashed cabin, blistered and peeling, was a caricature of a hawk, a lop-sided grotesque bird with a beak out of all proportion to the rest of its body.

'That was Sir Peter's doing. Always said he looked exactly

like that. Told me about it after the prang. It's the right plane, Ann.'

'Then there is nothing more to be said. Except this.' She came close to him. 'I'm not going back, Bert. I'm not going back to the train-windows of my life, not when there could have been things like the *brauhaus* at Eichstadt and the snow and the sound of the hooter just as he was. . . .'

She turned and walked away, limping now, in pain now, pain of mind and body, showing him her slender body from which the calm resolve had gone.

He watched her go. Then he looked up at the gunmetal sky. His voice rolled up above the encompassing walls of the defile.

'God? God, you hear me up there? Why did you do this to me? Why did you plant rot in my body and hope in my mind?' And then he wept, and he cried the way Peter Teefer had cried four years before in this land of death, 'Oh Christ, you have deserted me!'

Only the silence answered him; and after a while he followed the girl out of the defile.

*   *   *

Jane Teefer's beringed fingers clinked against the glass. She lifted it to the wrinkles in her lips, sipped, pulled a face. 'Je-sus! Shades of bourbon and branch-water. This is Scotch and *guelta*. Any tadpoles in here, Ayrab?'

'No, ma'am.' John-oh was at the drink table. 'I put purifying tablets into the tank. That's probably the reason for the strange taste.'

'Well next time leave 'em out,' she cackled.

Lassiter was slumped back in his camp chair. 'Probe Three was unsuccessful.'

She frowned.

'Nothing, huh? The Ayrab too?'

'Nothing,' said John-oh from the drink table. His eyes met Lola's, held them for a moment. He was thinking of the *guelta*, of her being with him, and he was not afraid. The *guelta* had changed character in his mind.

'That's bad.' Jane put down her empty glass. 'How much longer, you figure?'

'It's impossible to say.'

'Well, you'd better find that goddam plane or there will be trouble.'

'Tomorrow you must lend me your magic wand, your Highness.'

It was all building towards trouble: Nailand said something under his breath; John-oh turned, interested, biased; Susan studied Lassiter with deep interest out of an over-still face; Lola surveyed everything with her limpid eyes. All of them waited, in their different ways, for the explosion. But it did not come.

Jane crumpled. Her face seemed to fall in upon itself. She put up her beringed hands and said through them in a weak and reedy voice, 'Leave me alone, Lew. I'm old and sick and I got a tachycardia coming on. That's no way to talk to a woman. Just leave me alone.' And then she began to weep softly.

The effect was shattering. Susan had never seen Lassiter so out of composure. He rose uncertainly, hesitated. He looked at Susan for help but she ignored him. Then he crossed the circle to Jane. But Jane with her blind woman's radar sensed his coming and slapped away his reaching hand. 'Don't comfort me. I don't need no comfort. I'm rotten. You're rotten. People like us don't need comfort, we don't need love. We're lost, Lew. There isn't one decent person in this place 'cept maybe those kids. And we're getting worse, all of us. I'm sick of the fighting and the bickering. Just find Peter and his goddam plane and then let's get out of here, this place is cursed.'

'I've found the plane.'

It was another voice intruding upon them. Six heads turned in complete unison to Bowdrey standing in the door, raggedly dishevelled, sick, and quite clearly drunk.

Their minds were not attuned. But four of the minds were quick; Jane, Lassiter, Susan and John-oh. These people, without completely accepting what he had said, grasped the arrival of something new and shocking. They accepted it while Nailand floundered drunkenly and Lola gaped.

'Come in, Mr Bowdrey.' Jane was unnaturally calm. The small fat white hands had come away from her face and she stared across at him with the milky perception of her blind eyes. 'You've found Peter's plane? Is that right?'

'No.' Bowdrey reeled in. He teetered to the middle of the ring of chairs, where his feet settled in the sand while his body weaved. He pointed a forefinger almost under her nose. 'I haven't found Peter's plane. I've found the plane you were *really* looking for. I've found the Dakota.' He laughed crazily, his eyes going from face to face and coming back to Jane. 'The *money-plane*, you old bitch, that's what I found, but it's no bloody good to you or Nailand or Lassiter or anyone else because it's been burnt to hell, it's been incinerated and the money with it.' He tottered around to face the door. Ann came in. Over the dress she had been wearing all day she had pulled a polo-necked sweater. Her feet were encased in cheap unglamorous carpet slippers. She limped as she walked, but she did not sit.

'Ask her. Ask her about the plane, Lady Bitch.'

Ann spoke mechanically, in a strange disinterested voice. 'I was there. I saw it. The Dakota has burned, and the money with it.'

There was a pause. Bowdrey staggered through a gap in the circle of chairs and helped himself uninvited to a drink. Jane Teefer's blind head turned.

'Mr Bowdrey. Please listen to me. I do not know what you are talking about. I'm feeling bad tonight. I'm sick and I'm older than my years. So just cut out the insults and tell us what this is all about. Because I give you my promise that I have not understood one word of what you have been saying.'

'Bullshit.' Bowdrey weaved his way back into the ring. He stared with drunken wisdom at the group. 'The money's gone. There's no need to lie, now. I got there first but I was too late. One dirty stinking Toubou, one match. That's all it probably took. The game's up. We can all pack and go home.'

Ann Bowdrey said, almost idly, 'I'm not going home.'

Jane ignored her. 'Mr Bowdrey, how in hell's name do I convince you? You talk about a Dakota. You talk about money. What Dakota and what money?'

Bowdrey laughed. 'Something has dawned on me. You think I found the Dak., snaffled the money and then set the plane alight. Shrewd old bag, you are.'

'We would have seen that kind of fire for miles.' Lassiter got up and stood facing Bowdrey. 'You don't have to believe Lady Teefer. But you can believe me. Do you think I knew about this money-plane? Do you really think so?'

Bowdrey considered him with a sort of bibulous caution. Finally he said, 'No. No, I don't think you were in the picture. The seeing-eye girl would know because the old bag is blind. Nailand would know because he's her cousin. But I don't think you and Franc were let in on the story. So seeing everybody else is playing it dumb, I'll tell you, Lassiter.'

He took a swig of whisky. 'You have heard of General le Clerc?' When he saw Lassiter's quick impatient nod he went on. 'You remember he dashed up from Fort Lamy into Libya at the height of the desert campaign? Right. Well, he left his money behind.' He laughed. 'The General had other things on his mind. So a plane was sent to fetch the cash. A British plane, a Dakota. It landed at Lamy at night. Two suitcases of money were loaded. They were guarded by two Army lieutenants. The rest of the crew were just a pilot, co-pilot, a navigator and an erk sent along to help load. The plane took off into the night but it never got to Libya. It came down in the Tibesti in one hell of a prang. Everyone was killed except the pilot and the young erk who was only nineteen years old.'

Bowdrey gave Lassiter a look of drunken cunning. 'Now let's play games, Lassiter. Who do you think the pilot was?'

'Sir Peter Teefer.'

'Clever boy. Clever Lassiter. And who was the young erk?'

'You.'

'Exactly. Not hard to grasp now, is it? We walked out of there, Sir Peter and I. A hundred bloody miles or more, with me delirious after a while, until the French found us and we were flown to hospital in Libya.'

Bowdrey finished his drink and wobbled the empty glass at John-oh who got up quietly and took it. 'There's not a hell of a lot more to say. We were in different hospitals. We were interviewed by intelligence officers. I had a pretty shrewd idea where we'd come down but I knew Teefer would be even more sure, being the pilot. So when the Dak wasn't found I guessed that he had played it as carefully as I had and was planning ahead, the way I was.'

John-oh brought him his drink. 'I tried like hell to keep tabs on Teefer. I found out he'd been sent home, so the money was safe for the time being. Then I was demobbed in 1945 and before I could do anything about going back I developed this bloody rot inside me.'

A weary bitterness showed on his face, even through the slackness of his drunkenness. 'The story of my life from then on was one hospital and institution after another. And even in between, when I was out because they reckoned they'd checked it, I had no money to finance the trip. So I gave up. I knew Teefer would go back for the money. Then four years ago I read that he'd come down in the desert. I couldn't understand why he'd waited so long, but I tell you, I sweated blood while the search was on. Then they couldn't find him and I realized he was dead and suddenly all the hope was back again, but still I was sick and broke. I dreamed and schemed for four years. And then I read that the old bitch was coming after the money herself. I couldn't wait any longer, and we beat you to it by a few days. It was Ann's money that got us here.'

He teetered around to look at her. 'I'm sorry, lass. It was a bad investment.' Then he shrugged at Lassiter. 'That's all there is to tell.' He walked to an empty chair and flung himself into it. In a strange way these last two drinks seemed to have levelled him off and he appeared less drunk now than when he had arrived.

Lassiter was interested. 'You've overlooked something, Bowdrey. We were searching for a different plane altogether. The second one, so to speak. And for all you knew it could have come down miles away from the first.'

Bowdrey shook his head. 'Listen, I followed the reports of the search for Teefer from a hospital bed. I read everything I could get my hands on. And I was bloody well aware of the fact that the French had pinpointed Sir Peter's crash close enough to the Dakota so that when I read about the Teefer expedition four years later I knew very well that the search for his body was a cover-up for the real thing—getting that money.'

Lassiter spoke as though to a child. 'If the French pinpointed Teefer's disappearance to an area very close to the Dakota, why does it follow that he *crashed*? If he'd got this far then there is every chance that he landed. See the difference?'

Bowdrey fumbled in his exhausted and confused mind. 'No.' But Jane leapt to the point.

'Now you're thinking, Lew!' She was triumphant. 'You mean he came down all in one piece, huh? He landed and walked away from it?'

'He might have crashed when he landed. Maybe that's why he couldn't get off again. But that he walked away from the plane I know for sure. Yesterday Susan and I found his initials carved into the wall of the defile at the *guelta*. Sir Peter had been there, alive.'

There was an electric silence. 'Why didn't you tell me?'

'I didn't see the point. All it would have served would have been to upset you, to make you dwell on the possible agonies he might have suffered before he finally died. Now, though, with what Bowdrey has told us, the circumstances are different.'

Lola spoke up quietly and unexpectedly. 'Joe and I also know that Sir Peter landed alive. On Tuesday, on the day of the first probe, Joe found this. It took a little while for me to realize whose it was, because Joe lied to me as usual. But I worked it out.' Her hand went to a pocket of the jacket she was wearing and produced the silver cigarette case even as Nailand jumped to his feet and shouted, 'You stupid bitch!'

Jane was panting. Her fingers bit into Susan's arm. 'Get it, girl. Bring it here. Now!'

Susan crossed the ring and took the case from Lola. She gave it to Jane, who held it between her palms. One stubby finger traced its way across the engraving.

'It's his. God, it's his. I gave it to him on our first anniversary.' She whispered the words. Then suddenly, she was shouting, loudly triumphant: 'You see, I was right, Lassiter! Didn't I say yesterday I could feel Peter in that *guelta*?' Yet again, her tone changed. It became flat and challenging. 'Joe, why in hell didn't you tell me about this?'

Nailand managed to look sullen and furtive at the same time. He shrugged. 'Same reason as Lassiter. What purpose would it have served?'

'Hope!' Jane shouted. 'Hope, goddammit! I was losing heart. I was nearly ready to give up. These things would have put heart into me!'

Nobody said anything. She smouldered for a while. Then:

'There have been some goddam questionable motives amongst people I pay and people I thought I could trust. I'm going to leave it for the moment, but come pay-day I'm going to think again. Let's hear some more, Lassiter. So Peter landed alive. What then?'

'I think he was alive for some time. He went to the *guelta* for water. Maybe more than once. The fact that he carved his initials there show that he was bored and had time on his hands. He was waiting to be rescued. His health must have been okay because the box search proves that wherever he crashed or landed it was a long way from the *guelta*. This is backed up by the discovery of the cigarette case. He either dropped it or put it where it was found in the hope that its shine might attract a rescue plane.'

Bowdrey shook his head with weary annoyance. 'You're wasting words, all of you. I agree, it looks as if Sir Peter did survive the crash. But he still wasn't found, so he still died. And the Dakota had burned and the money with it. He'd made the trip for nothing, just like us.'

Lassiter had become wearily patient. 'You like playing games, Bowdrey. So let's play another one. If it had been you, and not Sir Peter; if you had landed normally after spotting the Dakota from the air; if you had walked to it and taken the suitcases of money and brought them back to your plane; if you then found that it wouldn't start, or in trying to take off you hit *erg* and damaged the undercart; if you were stuck then, waiting for rescue, and you heard planes but they didn't see you. What would you do, Bowdrey?'

The answer came unexpectedly from another source. While Bowdrey, still fumbled, Susan said quietly, into the new silence, 'I would set light to the Dakota.'

'Thank you. Somebody is thinking at last.'

A change came over all of them. Bowdrey had sobered. 'That's speculation, all of it.' But he said it with a distinct renewal of hope.

'Mr Lassiter is right. I'm sure of it.' Ann Bowdrey had lost her look of almost alarming apathy. That same quiet driving purpose had flooded back into her. Her cheeks were flushed. 'There is a way of proving it, too. Those suitcases, Bert. Were they locked?'

'I saw them being locked. One of the lieutenants, the older chap, had the keys on his belt.'

'And you told me once that Sir Peter dragged the bodies out and buried them immediately, just as they were.'

'Aye.' He became excited. 'I was lying there with a twisted ankle and four broken ribs. I watched him. You mean——'

'If the graves have been opened, we will know for sure. The fire could not have entirely obliterated them. I doubt that Sir Peter would have smashed the suitcases because then he would have had difficulty carrying them back to his plane.'

She spoke so calmly of inspecting sundered graves. Lassiter felt a small stirring of revulsion. 'Before we go any further and start digging up corpses, Mrs Bowdrey. Just how much money is involved?'

She saw the look on his face, she read the meaning of the way he talked to her. But it meant nothing now that the money was back in her mind. 'Approximately a hundred thousand pounds.'

There was total silence that seemed to stretch into infinity. It was broken at last by John-oh's softly-breathed, 'God-almighty!'

Lassiter grinned wryly at Jane. 'No wonder you were paying us so well, madame.'

'As God is my witness I didn't know about the money!' The words exploded out of Jane. She jumped to her feet. 'I know nobody's gonna believe me. I'm just not that kinda person and I've got sense enough to admit it. But *I did not know.*' She glared around her as if she could see them, panting, her lips quivering.

'Lady Teefer didn't know. You have my promise.' Susan produced a very small smile which she directed at Lassiter. 'If that's worth anything, of course.'

'I knew nothing of it either.' Nailand grinned his shark-grin. 'If that's worth anything as well, of course. In our own way we're all a bunch of liars and cheats, aren't we?'

'That's the first sensible thing you've said since I've known you.' Lassiter turned from him to Bowdrey. 'If we find this money and of course it's a very big if, because it is in turn dependent upon finding Sir Peter's plane, then we're going to split it. I hope you read me loud and clear.'

'That will be the bloody day!' Bowdrey was on his feet, raging. 'That's my money and Ann's and nobody else's. If you're to be believed then you didn't even know it existed until, poor bloody fool that I am, I told you about it!'

'You're a liar and you're stupid as well. The money belongs to the French Government or the Republic of Chad.' Without knowing it he was using Pierre Goru's words. 'If we find it and we keep it, then we are stealing it. And in any case, you'd given up. Your cloddish brain took you as far as the burnt-out Dakota and from there it stopped working. We gave you back a shred of hope because it is still a shred after all. If we don't find Teefer's plane then we don't have the money.'

'Offer them a quarter, Bert.' Ann Bowdrey's quiet voice intruded. 'That money was written off long ago by the governments concerned, Mr Lassiter. It is ours by right of discovery. And I think my husband and I have a moral right to the larger sum.'

Nailand entered the picture. 'It should be divided equally into eight parts. There're six of us and two of you. Or six parts if you like because you and your husband, and Lola and me, can be regarded as single units.'

Jane's cawing overrode a sudden babble of voices. 'Like hell! You think I'm gonna take an eighth when it was my money that was poured into this expedition? God, think of the salaries, two new vehicles, the equipment! You've got one helluva cheek even thinking——'

'You'll be refunded your disbursements——'

'Never! I will not accept a penny under——'

Lassiter began to laugh. He laughed while he got up and walked out, and stood in the darkness until he was joined by Susan. They listened for a while. 'The *Sous-Préfet* called them the jackals of Zufra. He wasn't far wrong, was he?'

'It sounds like a pack, baying.'

He smiled. He put an arm around her small waist. 'There's a bottle of brandy in the kitchen. It's meant to be used for medicinal purposes. Let's go and make sure that it's safe for human consumption.'

They walked away into the darkness.

*　　　*　　　*

Thrin said, softly, 'You can come out, now.'

T'ekmedhin emerged from where they had hidden him. The light-coloured eyes studied both the children with complete lack of interest. But he saw the way the girl was looking at him. He put out a slender brown hand and touched her arm.

Her face lit up. 'Do you want water? Food?'

The Touareg shook his head. 'It is night.' His laboured French was slow. 'The grown Franks. Are they asleep?'

Neil answered. 'They've all gone to their rooms. There was a terrible argument in the Mess earlier on but I don't know what it was about. Mommy and John-oh have gone to the *guelta* to put water in the other Land-Rover's tank.'

T'ekmedhin relaxed. 'Where is the board with the snakes?'

They had it ready. Thrin pulled it out from under her bed together with the box of counters and the die. She set it out.

The Touareg perched at the end of the bed. His eyes flicked from one to the other, tense, secretive eyes. 'I will play first. Then we will play that other game I taught you.'

They laughed, both of them. 'Oh, that was fun.' Thrin gave him a counter and the die in its cup. 'Here. Throw.'

A brown hand flipped the die out on to the board. It showed a six, and there was for a moment sardonic amusement in the Touareg's eyes. 'I play again.'

Thrin's face glowed. 'Yes. T'ekmedhin. You play again.'

*   *   *

John-oh had waited until all of the Land-Rover's engine noise had echoed and re-echoed up the defile and complete silence had fallen save for the little ticking sounds of cooling metal.

'It is a terrible thing to be lonely. I am lonely even amongst people, Mrs Nailand. And it is because I am always afraid. I grew up in a whorehouse. I had my first woman when I was fourteen. They used me as sport when they were bored. It is a hell of a way to begin one's life. But with you I am not lonely and I am not afraid.'

They were in the front seat, together but far apart, leaning against their respective doors. And they made no attempt to close the gap.

'You heard the story of my life from Lady Teefer. I was weak, I know. But it is very easy to confuse issues, and lie on your back because you think that what is inside you is the love you so desperately need. Now, here in the quiet of this *guelta*, I know how wrong and how mistaken I was. All the fear and loneliness are gone. And it is because I am with you.'

He waited a little while. Then he said, wonderingly, 'I had hoped. I saw the way you looked at me. And it is truly wonderful to hear those words. But it is wrong, this thing. You are married and I am twelve years younger than you.'

'I am married to a sick-minded bully, Mr Franc. I don't think we need worry ourselves unduly about that. And as for the age difference, time is really a relative thing, isn't it? You see, people say I'm stupid but I have in fact had rather a good education. I can reason. It is only my fear that makes me seem dull-witted.'

'I never thought you that.' He spoke quickly in defence of her. There was a silence of some moments. Then he said, 'Between us, everything is possible. Life stretches ahead as a thing of great beauty, without the barrenness of this dead land. And yet, with you even this desolate place changes. It becomes enchanted in my mind.' He studied the beautiful face. 'I love you very much . . . Lola.'

Her lips parted. She breathed deeply, quiveringly. 'I, too. I love you, John-oh.'

He reached out and took her hand. She gasped. She brought her free hand across and put it on top of his so that she clung in this way, to this small part of him, straining like a tightly-drawn wire, vibrating all over her body with an uncontrollable ague, her hair tossed about her beautiful face, crying out faintly, and then going limp suddenly, her hands retaining his but softly now, caressingly, and her body slumping away from him against the door.

For a full five minutes she stayed like that, her breathing deep and even. And then she smiled at him with an exquisite wonder and tenderness. 'Mr Franc, I have just experienced absolute completion. For the first time in my life. And on only the touch of your hand.'

He gently tightened his grasp on her hand, fleetingly, then let it lie warm and loose within her caress. 'I have, too. Together we have had a thing of magic happen to us, here in the beauty of our sandy enchanted garden. I thought the

Sahara was death, a piece of dusty planet flung upon our earth. But it is not. It is life. It is our life. I will love you for ever.'

They sat in silence, satiated and content. Then after a while he started the engine and then drove out of the defile, leaving behind only the lingering echoes of their passing.

*   *   *

The fat luminous face of the sergeant's wristwatch showed nine minutes to nine. It was nearly time to report. He leaned with his elbows on the parapet, watching the minutes seem to crawl by. He was bursting with excitement.

Money. An aeroplane full of money had crashed many years ago here in the Tibesti. A long time later one of the crew had returned, found the money, removed it, but had himself been unable to take off and had died without ever being found. If the Franks found his plane, then they would also find the money.

Rehearsing these facts carefully in his mind, he nodded with satisfaction. Yes, that was it. It summed up what he had heard while he crouched in the shadows on the opposite side of the courtyard, listening to the loud voices from the Mess and laughing quietly at the foolishness of these people who quarrelled over money they did not yet possess. Nevertheless, it was exciting. They were thorough—certainly the tall Lassiter was very thorough indeed and there was a strong chance that they might succeed.

Henri looked at his watch again. Five minutes to nine. It was nearly time to wake the trooper whose snores again resounded from the watchtower.

'Henri!' The light voice came to him out of the desert.

He jerked erect and began to tremble. Mother of God. Not again!

'Henri!' The voice was more commanding this time, but still weirdly disembodied.

His voice was hoarse and it shook. 'What do you want? Who are you?' I insist that you tell me who you are!'

There was a chuckle. He froze, rigid, disbelieving. It had come from behind him. Slowly, ever so slowly as though in a state of partial paralysis, he turned. His terrified eyes sought the courtyard's deepest shadows.

'I beg of you.' His entire body trembled. 'Leave me alone. You will drive me mad.'

'Be calm, Henri. There is no need to be afraid.' The voice came from the desert again, light and teasing. 'Do you not recognize my voice?'

He stumbled around. 'No.'

'Think, Henri.'

'I cannot. Please go away.'

'Come down, Henri. Come down and I will reveal myself to you.'

His eyes seemed to start from his head. Sweat was bursting out of his skin. 'Never!'

'Henri!' The voice had switched to the courtyard again. 'Do not be a coward! You are a shameless coward.'

The sergeant lost all sense of reason. He snatched up his rifle, charged along the catwalk and pelted down the steps. His chest ached and his legs were weak but he hurtled into the courtyard's shadows, whirling the rifle like a club, swinging it about in a scythe-like movement that parted the cold secret air until he stopped, gasping, leaning on the weapon, head drooping, demoralized.

'Henri. I am out here.' The lonely call came from the desert again.

Like a madman he charged through the gates, storming a hundred yards out into the desert. Then he stopped because he was so obviously alone. There was only the harsh moon-like landscape and the sound of his hoarse breathing.

Very slowly, apathetically, he walked back to the fort. He climbed the steps like a man in a dream. It is the *cafard*, he thought, I have caught the desert madness and I am going to lose my mind. He shook the sleeping trooper awake and walked with him to the radio at the other end of the catwalk. He switched on, still in his mood of total apathy. He hardly heard the whine of the generator as it began to turn. Then, already holding the microphone, he noticed that the set had not come alive. He switched off and then on again, but the light on the console remained a dull and lustreless eye.

'Trouble,' the trooper said. He stopped turning the generator.

Henri nodded. He tried the switch a few times without

165

effect. Then, knowing nothing about the technicalities of the set, he did what most untrained people will do with any piece of stubborn machinery: he shook it.

Distinctly audible came the tinkling of smashed parts.

'Broken,' said the trooper.

The sergeant shook it again. It was worse than broken. It was smashed. The inside of the set sounded as though there were not one whole thing remaining.

'We have not touched the radio since last night.' The trooper looked about uneasily. 'How could this have happened?'

'The voices that call to me in the night.' Henri slumped down next to the set, his hands across his knees, staring down at the courtyard. 'They have brought about the death of this thing. There is death all about us and I am afraid.'

The trooper bent and put a hand on his shoulder. 'Sergeant, there are no voices. It is the *cafard* that has got you. In the morning we must collect the camels and go back because we cannot report.'

'There is no need.' Henri continued to stare at the nothing of the darkness ahead of him. 'When we do not report my uncle will come to find out what has happened. And in any case, I will die here. Now go to bed. I will stay by the radio.'

The trooper hesitated. Then he shrugged and moved back to his snuggery in the watchtower. The sergeant stayed where he was, wide awake, unaware of the biting cold. Soon, he thought, the voices will come back and I will ask them about the radio.

CHAPTER EIGHT

DURING THE NIGHT the wind had come up. It was a gentle wind at first, blowing in little puffs along the *oueds*, coasting over the firm sand of the *reg*, playing tag amongst the small stones of the *hammada*. But as the night deepened it seemed to grow tired of these little games. It grew resentfully fierce, puffing now, strong enough to lift a low sheen of grit off the *reg* with a force that could sting. In the *oueds* and in the sandy places it blew moonlit pennants of golden sand from the crests of the dunes.

From the high fastnesses of the Tibesti the power grew, for it is here that the Arabs maintain the wind is born. This wind had been an infant at first and then a petulant child. Now it matured into a raging and furious adult, a giant howling through the passes and the defiles like a discordant bugle blast, tearing at the dunes so that they writhed like smoke and were carried away to pile up in some distant place.

There had been a wind like it, four years previously. And now, out of hate for the memory of its dead but powerful brother, it undid the things that wind had done. It took away the wind's creations, destroyed them, dissipated them, disintegrated them.

And in the process it exposed a plane.

It took some hours. At first only a wing-tip emerged but soon the entire wing was bared; then the cabin, the fuselage, the empennage and the undercarriage, so that finally the plane stood quite naked with only its wheels still stubbornly submerged, quivering in the blast as though cold now after all these years and embarrassed at its new-found nudity.

The wind was noisy. Ann and Bert Bowdrey both woke. They heard each other's restless movements but neither said anything for a long time. If this wind, she thought, covers Sir Peter's plane, wherever it may be, then I will not go home. She remembered her father shouting at her from the top of the stairs and calling her a bitch. Bitch! My God, his bleary senile blunderings and her mother so much a part of the feather duster that they even looked alike. Them, and the broken sobbing of the rain in the drainpipe.

She said aloud, 'If we find the plane. Do you really intend to divide the money?'

His voice was dry. 'You must think I've gone soft in the head. That's our money, Ann.'

'Then how do you intend to ensure that it remains ours?'

It was easy to detect her total lack of confidence in him. 'You think I'm a fool, don't you? You and Lassiter. A clod, he called me.'

'Always, Bert, the emotion, the self pity. Let's try some facts, now.'

She lies there, he thought, in that gossamer night dress that encases the long burnished limbs and statuesque body. And she talks coldly about money. He trembled. He said with difficulty, 'I have an idea. Just for once, have faith in me. So many things could intrude to change it. That shrewd bastard Goru, for one. The Touareg for another. It is impossible to plan with exact precision.'

'Just so long as you're thinking and not ranting.'

There was a silence, then the sound of blankets being thrown back, his slight form darker against the darkness, and he was beside her. The bed gave a little to his weight.

'Bert! What on earth——'

'I'm cold. Jesus, I'm cold.'

His voice shook.

'Well, then, it's the height of stupidity to get out of bed.' She was still speaking while he was fumbling away her blankets, taking her so much by surprise that he was lying next to her before she could resist, his thin arms wrapping themselves about the firm warmth of her body, his hot breath roaring against her cheek. 'Bert! Get out of here! This is quite ridiculous! Get out of here at once!' Without knowing it her voice had the sudden frigid sharpness of her mother's, thirty years before under similar circumstances.

'It's been so long. Christ, it's been so long.' He had managed to get both arms around hers, trapping hers against her body so that she was reduced to an ineffective and undignified squirming. 'I need you. I want you. I need a woman I'll——'

'You need a woman, Bert? Just any woman?' Her voice cut across his like a knife.

He went still. They were both still, and yet as tense as wire under strain.

'I . . . I'm sorry. I managed that rather badly. I muck up everything, don't I? He withdrew his arms, sat up, swung his legs off the bed. He coughed a little, then straightened and began to shuffle across the sand.

'Bert.'

Immediately, he stopped.

'I know how you feel. Men get like that. And it's going to affect your . . . efficiency. You'll get edgy and preoccupied. So I'll help you, Bert. Come back.'

He came back slowly and uncertainly. Getting into bed with her, they were both all elbows and knees. He fumbled at her night dress, awkwardly touched one smooth breast. She pulled away instantly. Her voice came out of the darkness, level and unemotional. 'Don't do that again. I said I would help you. And I'm sure you realize now in what way. That's all. Nothing else.'

It took a minute. Just one minute. And on his way back to his own bed the thought came to him that if it had been the other way, the proper way, he would have made a muck of that anyhow.

*   *   *

Lola Nailand opened her eyes to the feel of sand on her neck. She lay afraid for a moment, the way she had been afraid of things for so many years. But then she heard the wind's shout and realized that the sand was coming through the hole in the roof. I found hope tonight at the *guelta*, she thought, stretching in pleasure, remembering. On the touch of a hand. Just that.

She got up lightly and moved her bed out of the way of this strange rain. Rather that than block the hole. She could never do that. Then she went to sleep again. And in her sleep she dreamed only of Jean Franc, not of John-oh the absurd.

At dawn the wind died. It died reluctantly, softening gradually at first, then becoming fitful and afraid as it realized that death was near. It dredged up a few puffing blasts that thumped with fading fury into the fuselage of the plane, making it quiver again but without the destructive violence of before. Losing even this strength, in dying it sought absolution and rubbed soft hands about the desert's dusty face as though in feeble apology.

By the time the sun rose, the wind was gone.

CHAPTER NINE

THE THREE LAND-ROVERS were in line abreast. Their blunt snouts pointed towards the gates of Fort Masuril. Lassiter and Bowdrey stood next to each other, bending over a map that was spread out on the bonnet of John-oh's vehicle. The rest of the Teefer group, and Ann Bowdrey, clustered behind them.

'So it's about there.' Lassiter pitched away his paper coffee cup. He kept one long forefinger on the map. 'We would probably have found it today, although, of course, it wasn't what we were looking for.' He grinned with that touch of early-morning menace that had intrigued the *Sous-Préfet*. 'Strange how you happened to be so conveniently south of us.'

Bowdrey, always so quick to flare, was unusually subdued. He reddened, opened his mouth to say something, then changed his mind and remained silent.

'Okay.' Lassiter folded the map and tucked it under one arm. From his shirt pocket he took his sun glasses and waved them in a semi-circle at the group. 'Bowdrey will lead because he knows the way to the place, although I could probably find it now that I have been shown the location. Once we get there our first object will be to investigate the graves, as suggested last night by our good friend and companion, Mrs Bowdrey.' He managed a sort of combination leer and sneer.

Ann Bowdrey returned his glance. She ignored the taunt, although colour crept into her tanned cheeks. 'And then?'

'I am presuming that we find the keys to the suitcases have been taken. Operating on this presumption we will know that Teefer spotted the Dakota from the air and came down somewhere nearby. He would certainly not make the same mistake twice, so he would have been careful about his choice of a landing ground, pretty positive in his own mind that he would be coming down on firm sand. Only, probably, he didn't; that's why he never got off again. Another thing: his flight from Tamanrasset was unauthorized, so he might have taxied into an *oued*, for concealment. That, again, might have been the cause of his trouble. So keep a sharp eye open. We will fan out in a star search, not a box. I will travel north, Bowdrey south, and Nailand west, almost back towards the fort. For the time being we must disregard the east because we have only three trucks and in any case the country over that way is impassable, he wouldn't have landed there unless he was in trouble.' He put on the glasses. 'The children don't want to go, Lola. How do you feel about that?'

Lola Nailand half-turned her head in the direction of the children's room. 'I've spoken to them. They seem happy to stay and Thrin is quite able to prepare lunch. Apart from which I gather that the sergeant also doesn't want to go, so they will have protection.' She spoke without her usual woolliness. It was unlike her. And she seemed calm this morning. Lassiter wondered about her but he had other things to occupy his mind.

He looked up at the watchtower. The sergeant was visible, standing next to his radio with his back to the courtyard, staring out over the desert on the south-eastern side. 'The sergeant has problems. But they're his, not ours.' He stopped, considering. There was complete silence, the silence of acute attention. He held them as securely as if they had been weights in the balance of his palm, and it would have been amusing if it were not for the memory of midnight's nightmares. He went on: 'I suppose we can go now. But just one more thing. The group finding the plane will have to let the others know. I've got an old ex-army three-oh-three in my truck. Nailand, if you have to, you can borrow the trooper's Lebel. Pay him for the hire, if you like.' He cocked an eye at Bowdrey. 'Got a weapon of some sort?'

Bowdrey simply nodded. Lassiter clapped his hands together, eager to get started. 'All right. Bowdrey's signal is two shots if he's in luck, Nailand three, my lot, four. Now let's go.'

They scattered to the three vehicles. The black trooper came down from the catwalk where he had been watching them and got into Nailand's Land-Rover. The sergeant had refused to speak to him. Without orders, he was simply blindly carrying out Goru's original instructions, and because he had ridden with the Nailands so far he was doing it again.

They took off in a long straight line through the gates and then separated to avoid each other's dust. The sergeant, high up in his lonely post at the watchtower, saw them go. He waited until they were specks, specks that moved apart, joined together and swerved across each other's tracks as they went into the rough country. Then he sat down next to the radio and studied it again intently, still shaking his head, staring at it as though willing it to work. Moodily, he lit a cigarette.

* * *

It was desperately hot in the cul-de-sac. Bowdrey came away from the long-dead funeral pyre of the Dakota with sweat streaming down his cheeks and blackening the front of his shirt in huge sodden patches.

'The graves of the two lieutenants have been opened. That's clear enough, although the bodies were completely incinerated.' He looked as though he had swallowed a lemon.

'Hyenas? Jackals?' It was Lady Teefer, very pale and leaning heavily on Susan's arm.

'Then why not the other two graves? They're untouched.' Bowdrey swiped with an irritable forearm at the sweat on his forehead. 'No. Sir Peter has been here, I'm sure of it. I remember which graves the lieutenants occupied. They were the first two, close to the plane.'

Lassiter looked at his watch. 'Nearly noon. We can start the search now. Unless somebody wants lunch.'

They shook their heads.

Lassiter looked along the defile towards its mouth. 'God, how he ever got in here. He must have been one hell of a pilot.'

'He was.' Jane turned away with Susan. 'He flew a lot, back home. The boys said he was one of the best.' She lit a cigarette. 'Let's get out of this hell-hole and find Peter.'

At this stage they separated. Lassiter drove off north with Susan and Lady Teefer. The Bowdreys were next, heading almost due south. John-oh, the Nailands and the black trooper pulled out last, negotiating a stony patch and then swinging the big vehicle back a few points south of due west.

They had driven for five minutes when Nailand said unexpectedly, 'Where the hell were you, last night? You must have come in damned late.'

'It wasn't late.' Lola smiled at the reflection of John-oh in the driver's mirror and saw his eyes light up. 'I was back long before the wind started.'

Nailand grunted. He said to John-oh's back, 'Can't you drive faster, Arab?'

'Lew said to go slowly.'

'Well, Jesus, he didn't mean walking pace.' Nailand looked to his left, across Lola. There was open ground here, a long, narrow, but firm strip of sand. Quite long enough on which to land a light plane.

'Stop!' He said it so sharply that even the trooper in the back stirred.

John-oh braked obediently. 'See anything?'

'Not yet. How far are we from the wreck of the Dakota?'

John-oh looked at his dashboard. 'Just over a kilometre. About one mile.'

'Jesus, even that's far for a man on foot.' Nailand studied the area a little despondently. It was ideally suitable for a light plane to land, but would Teefer have been prepared to walk such a distance, especially on the way back, with two heavy suitcases? He shrugged. On the other hand, they had turned up nothing so far. It was worth an investigation.

'There's an *oued* coming up.' John-oh pointed ahead and to the right. 'You can barely see the mouth of it. Rock on one side, dune on the other. Shall we take a look there?'

'All right.' Nailand glanced around once more. Then he lit a cigarette while John-oh eased the truck forward, letting her speed build until she was running nicely across firm sand towards the *oued*'s mouth.

It took a minute, and then they were there, stationary at the *oued*'s mouth. And facing them from inside it, also stationary, was Sir Peter Adair Teefer's plane.

It shone in the sun of high noon, it twinkled with a thousand diamond points of light that reflected off its sleek unrusted body. It sat very neatly with a look of eagerness about it, as though it was about to fly, waiting expectantly for the firm touch of its skyman master who was four years dead.

'Great God in heaven.' Nailand whispered the words to himself, so that they were barely audible. They stared, petrified with wonder.

A full minute passed.

John-oh had the quickest mind. He was able to see, to absorb, and to accept while the others floundered through thoughts of daylight delusion, hallucinations and mirage. Something gave way in him. He became filled with an

elemental triumph. He flung open his door. *'We've found it!
It's ours!'* He began to run towards the plane.

The hypnotic stillness of the others was broken. Like the
flicking of a switch the tableau broke apart. They swarmed
after John-oh, first Nailand, Lola and finally the trooper.
Nailand overtook John-oh. He pushed the younger man
violently in the back so that he fell sprawling. Nailand went
on, uncaring, rushing to the plane, gasping for breath, heading
for the cabin door until he saw the blanket bundle almost
covered by sand, that lay under the starboard wing.

He swerved in mid-stride and straddled it. He bent, grasping
it savagely with both hands, heaving it with a grunt out of its
shallow grave, expecting to bring something heavier with it.
But it was only the blankets, and the lightness was so unexpected that Nailand fell heavily on his buttocks. He retained
his grip on the bundle and with feverish hands began to open
it. Out of the corner of his eye he detected movement and
whirled around. John-oh was talking to the trooper in French,
gesturing towards the man's rifle.

'Not yet!' He glared at them from where he absurdly sat.
'No signal shots yet!' His voice was loud and frantic. He got
the bundle open but it was empty except for a book that
slipped out and fell on to Nailand's lap. It was a pilot's log-
book. He grabbed it, flipping the pages. Again, he half-saw
movement. This time John-oh was reaching for the cabin door.

'Keep away from that plane!'

John-oh stopped and stared at him. All of them regarded
the wild figure clutching the book. 'I am Lady Teefer's cousin.'
He was almost babbling. 'I will inspect the interior of the
plane before anyone else. Lady Teefer would expect it of me.
Now stay where you are and don't give me any more trouble!'

The younger man dropped his hand from the cabin door.
He looked at Lola and shrugged. The trooper leaned on his
rifle. There was silence while Nailand impatiently thumbed
his way past routine entries. Then he slowed down. He began
to read, turning one or two more pages.

' "In his last binn Sir Peter lies?" ' He looked at them with
his mouth open, shaggy-haired, slack-cheeked, confused.

'What do you mean?'

'That's what it says in the log. The last entry. There're

three before that. He must have been alive and stranded for a few days.' He got up and headed for the cabin, opened the door, and disappeared inside.

John-oh picked up the book. More cleverly, he started from the back and soon found Teefer's last few entries. He read them while Lola stood at his shoulder.

'Look here.' He pointed to Teefer's second entry, the rather crude reference to being bored. 'There're no dates. But he was obviously stranded for some time.' He peered into the plane through one of the windows, trying to see what Nailand was doing.

Lola took the book. 'Why "Shades of P. C. Wren"? And then this last one: "In his last binn Sir Peter lies." It's a line from a poem. I feel I know it. I've read it somewhere.'

'Come over here.' John-oh had moved around to the aircraft's nose. Lola tossed the book on to the blankets Nailand had discarded and joined him. 'Look at the windscreen. He wrote that with something like soap, and the sand has stuck to it and dried it like cement.'

' "I've had it." ' She read the words aloud softly, pityingly, wondering what sort of agonies the man had had to endure.

Nailand came out of the plane. He was strangely haggard. 'There's nothing. Absolutely nothing. No suitcases. No dead body. No clothing. Let's have a look at that diary again. Teefer obviously wandered off. He couldn't have got far. Not with those suitcases. He might have left some indication in the log.' He snapped his small fingers. 'Where the hell is it? I left it on those blankets.'

They moved around under the wing again. There was nothing on the blanket pile except a peppering of sand.

'I read it and put it back there.' Lola was bewildered.

Nailand's ragged temper flared. Sweat was coursing off him in floods. It was unnatural. It was almost alarming. 'You! You stupid bitch, you couldn't remember your own name for more than a minute!' He raged up to her, grabbed her by the shoulders. 'Where the hell is that log-book?'

He was behaving peculiarly. He seemed more anguished than anything else. John-oh interposed himself between them, suddenly no longer afraid. He actually pushed Nailand away with the force of his strong young body.

'The trooper has it.'

'*What?*' Nailand whirled, the soldier, standing a few yards away, smiled at him. He was holding the diary in both hands with his Lebel tucked awkwardly under one arm.

Nailand stalked towards him. 'Give that to me.' He said it in English and then in very bad French.

The trooper shook his head. '*Sous-Préfet.*' He nodded down at the log. '*Sous-Préfet.*'

'He wants to give it to the *Sous-Préfet.*' John-oh said something rapidly in French to the trooper and the man nodded. 'Yes, he says the *Sous-Préfet* must know what is in the book. He has confiscated it, so to speak.'

Nailand's fury boiled over. He pointed a quivering, commanding finger. 'Tell him this is his last chance. Tell him if he does not give me the book it will be the worse for him!'

John-oh translated quickly. The trooper became sullen. He took a step backward. '*Non!*' He shook his head decisively.

'Why, you black bastard!' Quite out of control now, Nailand jumped across the intervening space. One unskilled, whirling fist took the man on the side of the face and he went down on his back on the sand, staring at Nailand out of shocked, terrified eyes. Nailand, off balance, staggered to find his footing and then fell on top of the trooper. They scrambled around in the powdery sand, Nailand cursing, the trooper rolling and twisting away, clutching the book to his chest. He managed to slip out of Nailand's grasp, got to his feet and began to run out of the *oued*, staggering and weaving and painted with the sand that had stuck to his sweat-wet skin.

'Stop!' Nailand's wild eyes found the abandoned rifle. He snatched it up, worked the bolt and fired. Sand spurted near the running man's feet but he went doggedly on. Nailand fired again and John-oh heard the smack of the bullet as it tore its way through the trooper's thigh. The man collapsed and rolled on to his back. Head raised, he looked towards them, twisting desperately from side to side and crying out his anguish and his fear.

'Christ, I'll teach you!' Nailand began to run towards the man even as John-oh came across to cut him off. John-oh dived, missed, and fell sprawling. He got to his feet like a cat but Nailand had gained yards. He worked the bolt of the Lebel and

John-oh saw the empty case spin out in an arced streak of brass. Then he reached the trooper. He said in a wild, gasping voice, 'I said I'd show you, didn't I?' and shot the man in the chest.

Everything came to a halt. Nailand was still, Lola was a frozen statue under the wing. John-oh ploughed to a halt and stared down at the fallen man.

The trooper raised his dust-powdered head awkwardly and looked at his chest. He saw the blood welling there in rich scarlet. His eyes widened. They lifted to Nailand, rolled in terror, moved on to Lola and remained there. There was a beseeching in them like the eyes of a dying animal. He began to say something but the words gurgled in the torrent of blood that came bursting through his lips. His head fell back. His body quivering violently. His heels drummed on the sand in the midst of a petrified silence. Then he was still.

John-oh knelt. He took the man's wrist and felt for a pulse. Then he looked up. 'You've killed him, you stupid swine.'

Nailand dropped the rifle. He regarded the corpse as though it were the horrid property of a nightmare. His mouth opened and closed soundlessly while his chest rose and fell with the fierceness of his breathing. Then he shuddered convulsively, bent over, put his hands on his knees and began to vomit. They watched him, John-oh and Lola, both of them quite impassive until the spasm was spent and he turned to them with the shine of phlegm on his chin and tears running down his cheeks.

'I didn't mean to do it! Jesus oh Jesus, I didn't mean to do it!'

John-oh spat. 'That was premeditated murder, and you know it. You're going to hang, Nailand, or perhaps they won't bother with all that fuss out here. Possibly the *Sous-Préfet* will put you against a wall at the fort and shoot you. But either way, you'll die.'

Nailand fell to his knees. He raised his arms, his hands clasped in abject supplication. 'Oh Christ, forgive me! I didn't mean it. I went mad. I lost all sense of reason. I didn't know what I was doing.' He began to sob, still in his attitude of prayer, his shoulders heaving.

John-oh bent and crossed the dead man's hands over his chest. Then he said without looking at Nailand, 'That's not the way I saw it. I'll be chief witness at your trial and I'm going to love every minute of it.'

Nailand began to babble. 'You don't have to tell anyone! He's dead and nobody can bring him back. We can bury him. It won't take a minute. We can say he was demoralized by what has happened to the sergeant, and deserted. Or we can say that he ran amok and that we had to take his rifle from him and that the thing went off accidentally and killed him.'

There was a silence. Nailand stared at John-oh, at the new hardness of his face, the strange, dispassionate relentlessness of his expression. Then he whimpered and turned away. He crawled across to Lola on his hands and knees and put his arms around her legs, pressing his face against one calf. 'Lola, Lola, listen to me! I beg you. You're my wife. I don't want to die. Please, make Franc listen. You don't have to tell the others. It's just not necessary. He was only a silly black savage. Nobody's even going to miss him. Don't you see?'

She looked down at him with a strange dignity. 'He was probably worth ten of you, Joe.' Then she turned to John-oh while Nailand still clung to her, his sobs renewing. 'He has given me no kindness and no love. He has beaten me and humiliated me. He has made me do things you would not even believe. He has a mind which is the next best thing to a cess-pit. But at the same time he took me out of a kind of life I was living that would have destroyed me. And when he married me I think he was sincere for a very short time.' She shrugged. 'So I suppose I owe him one favour. And only for the time being. Just temporarily. Will you help me?'

They studied each other with deep seriousness for a long moment. She saw the incredible devotion in his eyes. 'All right. If you want it that way. But only temporarily, as you said, until we're away from this place. Then I am going to talk whether I am believed or not.'

Lola nodded. 'Thank you.' They were being strangely formal with each other in the presence of death and the absurd indignity of the man who had caused it.

John-oh looked at his watch. 'By coincidence, Nailand fired three shots. That's our signal for finding the plane. The others will be here at any moment. I think we had better make it look as though he ran amok. This happens in the desert. It takes different forms. Saharaitis, the French call it. Or *cafard*.' He turned newly stern eyes on Nailand, eyes that had seen the filth and dishonour of life since the whore's bed that had been his cradle. 'I will need help.'

Lola stepped out of her husband's grasp. 'I'm not afraid.'

They dragged the dead man from where he had fallen, back towards the plane. John-oh rubbed out the scuff-marks. Then he took a heavy wrench from the tool-kit lying on the sand below the opened engine cowling and forced it into the trooper's right hand where he lay on his belly under the starboard wing. He collected the three expended cartridges, put one in his pocket and dropped the other two on the sand a few yards away from the body. Finally he turned to Nailand. 'I think you can take an interest in the proceedings, now. The picture is this: the dead man had been behaving oddly for some time. When you found the diary he demanded that you give it to him. You said you would, but only after Lady Teefer had read it. I translated this but it had no effect. He pulled back the cocking-piece on the bolt and aimed the rifle at you. You dived for him, brought him down, and in the process the rifle went off. The bullet struck him in the thigh but he turned over, grabbed the wrench which was lying at hand and was about to throw it at you, at a distance of two yards, when you shot him again. Got it?'

Nailand nodded dully. Now that they had agreed to help him he gave no impression of gratitude, no sign of regret for what he had done.

'Here come the others.' John-oh had heard the first distant growl of an engine. In a moment Lassiter's vehicle nosed into sight, followed almost instantly by Bowdrey's. Lassiter nearly missed the mouth of the *oued*, where John-oh's tyre tracks swung sharply to the right. He stopped so suddenly that Bowdrey coming up frantically behind almost bumped him. Then both vehicles reversed, swung, and drove into the *oued*.

The reaction of the new arrivals was very similar to that of John-oh and the Nailands; first silent shock, then Susan's quick voice describing the scene to Jane, who clung to her and breathed so shallowly that she appeared on the point of collapse. Then Susan and Lassiter for the first time noticed the sprawled body on the ground. Lassiter walked over to it, knelt, put a hand to the man's chest.

'What the hell happened here?'

In the background, above his harsh voice, Susan was telling Jane Teefer in a hushed voice that 'the trooper with the Nailands seems to be dead'.

Nailand's glance was locked with Lassiter's. His voice came out timbreless, and dry with the rust of his fear. 'We found a diary. A log-book, really. Just that and some blankets. No body. No money. The log shows that Sir Peter was alive for some time. But the trooper wanted the book. I said through Franc that I wouldn't give it up until Jane had read it, but he wouldn't accept that. He cocked his weapon and I could see that he was going to shoot me. So I dived at him. We struggled and then the rifle went off. He fell. I could see that he was hit but he picked up that wrench he's holding and was going to hurl it at me. I had his rifle by this time. I can't remember even cocking it but I automatically threw it up and fired.' He gained confidence as he spoke, sliding back into the old Nailand and shedding the gibbering, crazed, uncontrolled man of only minutes before. 'I didn't even aim. I didn't mean to kill him.'

There was a long silence. 'You made a pretty good job of it.' Lassiter's eyes were on the two wounds. Then he turned to John-oh. 'Is that the way it happened?'

John-oh gave an indifferent nod. 'Yes.'

'Lola?'

She simply nodded.

'I don't like this.' Lassiter looked from one to the other. 'You two are behaving oddly. There's something fishy about all this.'

'Ah, the hell with it!' Jane's cawing voice broke in. 'So he's dead. So what? Probably went crazy like that sergeant of his at the fort.' Her voice sharpened. 'You're sure my Peter isn't here, Joe?'

'Positive.' Nailand showed visible relief at the change in topic. 'I've been inside the plane. There is no sign of his body or the two suitcases of money.'

The Bowdreys had been standing apart. Now Bert came forward. He, too, disregarded the trooper's body as if it had been so much wood. 'What now? What do you think happened?'

Lassiter got up. 'Where's the log-book?'

'Just a minute!' Jane's voice stopped Lola as she was in the process of bending to pick it up from where they had replaced it on the blankets. 'That's my Peter's book. It's mine, now. You keep your dirty hands off it, Lew.' She prodded Susan. 'Go get it. Tell me what it says.'

Susan fetched the log-book. Like Nailand had done, she flipped past the pages of routine entries and then read the four comments Teefer had recorded while stranded.

Jane began to sniffle. 'My poor Peter. How he must have suffered. Waiting, waiting every day for help that didn't come.' She managed to produce a small sob. Then she went back to business. 'Girl, search that plane. Look for clothing, notes, anything that might tell us where he went.'

'I searched. You're wasting your time.' Nailand sounded quite plaintive.

'Search, schmearch.' Jane was looking very ill. 'I got a seeing-eye girl and I want *her* to do the looking. Every business venture you touch, you go bust. You think I'd trust you searching an aeroplane? God, you might overlook the propeller.'

Nailand subsided. In complete silence Susan came forward, picked up the blankets and shook them. She felt in the sand underneath them, all the time describing to Jane what she was doing. Then she entered the plane through the open pilot's door and was gone.

Lassiter watched all this with a mixture of amusement and cynicism. Then he walked around to the cowling and called John-oh.

'What do you make of this? The cowling has been opened. Tools on the sand. Teefer must have developed engine trouble after he came back with the money. There's no damage to the rest of the plane.'

John-oh joined him. He poked his head into the engine and fiddled while the rest of them stood silent. It took him a few minutes. Then he straightened, wiped his hands on the sides of his trousers. 'Teefer removed the rocker cover over the first piston. He found that the valve head had broken off and dropped into the cylinder. This would cause hopeless damage to the piston and connecting rod. In fact, the engine would have juddered so much that it could have jumped clean out

181

of its housing.' He thought for a moment and then added reflectively, 'Teefer must have got one hell of a fright. The noise and vibration inside the plane would have been terrible.'

Jane broke in. 'He never had much mechanical knowledge. Always his rich wife paid for the mechanics. Could it have been fixed?'

'Not here.' John-oh was quite categorical. 'He certainly knew enough, ma'am, to find the cause of the trouble and identify it. After that it was just a case of waiting to be found. There was nothing he could do.'

Bowdrey pressed forward. 'Aye, and I know why he hung around, too. When we walked out from the Dakota crash, I can remember him saying, "Kid, we were fools to leave the prang. They would have found us." Even in my delirium I can remember him saying it. He repeated it over and over again.'

There was a short, reflective silence in which all of them in their different ways pictured Teefer's mental if not physical agonies. At this stage Susan emerged from the plane's cabin.

'Nothing, Lady Teefer.'

'You sure girl?' Jane's voice was sharp, probing. The milky eyes seemed to pierce Susan's frail body. 'No clothes, no wallets, no papers?'

'Nothing. The plane has been er, er, s-stripped bare. Even some of the wooden fittings have been ripped out.'

'That would be for fuel,' Nailand said, rather unexpectedly.

Lady Teefer seemed to crumple. Something went out of her. It was like a spark ceasing. Her shoulders slumped. She looked very ill and very old. 'So that's that. Where is he, then? What did he do?'

Lassiter shrugged. 'I can guess. But let's dispose of this chap'—he pointed to the body of the trooper—'first. After that I'll tell you what I think.' He turned to Nailand. 'You did the damage. Get three shovels from the vehicles. John-oh and I will help you bury him.'

Nailand looked away. Then without a word he trudged over to the Land-Rovers and came back with the shovels while Lassiter went through the dead man's pockets and collected a small handful of personal possessions.

It took ten minutes to bury the trooper. Nobody said anything. They simply studied the mound for a while and then Lassiter took them around to the nose of the aircraft so that they could study the gritted scrawl across the windscreen.

'There's your answer. Despair. Teefer must have hung around for days. He must have wandered about quite a lot. We know he found the *guelta*. He was waiting for the French. We know that his flight from Tamanrasset was unauthorised and Susan tells me that he had apparently deliberately damaged his radio, the bloody fool. Once he was stranded he couldn't get off the ground or even call for help. But eventually he decided to start walking.'

'Too late,' John-oh said. 'By that time he would have been in no condition for a hike.'

Bowdrey was gradually catching up with events. 'Aye, and clobbered with the weight of the two suitcases.'

Lady Jane's head swung like a swivelled gun. 'You and your goddam money. That's all you think about, isn't it?'

Bowdrey had got over a whole series of shocks—the plane, the dead man, the absence of Teefer's remains, the absence of the money. His natural aggression was rapidly returning. 'That's right, and I'll make no pretence of it. Teefer was nothing to me.'

'You're a rotten sort of Limey bastard, aren't you?'

'You're not much better yourself, you old bitch.' Bowdrey went turkey-red.

'Jesus Christ!' Jane clung to Susan's arm, panting. 'God, how I'd deal with you if I had eyes. You stinking mercenary sod!'

'Stop it!' The force of the strong, unexcited voice, the tremendous and controlled drive of the firm body—always, it seemed, these things made them listen when Ann Bowdrey spoke.

'Exactly what are you accomplishing by indulging in a disgraceful and undignified cursing-match?' She looked at Bowdrey because he could see. He could not only see, he could measure the contempt that lay there, a contempt made complete since last night. And as far as Jane was concerned, she could feel with that radar-like perception of hers the disgust of this strong woman.

'Lew, what do you think?'

183

'He walked. But he walked too late, as John-oh says. He wasn't going to leave the money behind, so he walked with two heavy suitcases.' He extended a long arm, deliberately a vague arm. 'And he could have walked in any particular direction because he might have been crazy by this time, but let's try and read him: south, possibly, in an attempt to reach Zufra; north because the *guelta* was there, it was a direction he knew; or east or west as well, if he was heading out aimlessly.'

'What do you think we should do, Lew?' It was Jane this time, already beginning to think again.

'I think we should resume the star search, but afresh from this point.' Lassiter tried to show more enthusiasm than he felt. 'I think we should search very slowly, at walking pace, thinking the same way a tired, half-starved man would think, looking for the kind of place a man in that condition would stop to rest a while in the shade, and maybe never get up again. That way, if the wind hasn't covered him, we'll find him.' He smiled artlessly at Bowdrey. 'And the money.'

'Then let's do it that way.' Jane's milky eyes swept around the semi-circle. 'Anybody got any other ideas?' When they remained silent she tugged Sue's arm. 'Get me back to the truck, Sue. Lew, you get these people organized. I sure am tired.' Slowly, leaning on the girl heavily, she moved away, almost disinterestedly, towards Lassiter's Land-Rover.

Lassiter pointed a finger at John-oh. 'Go south. Maybe you'll have some luck. Bowdrey, go north towards the *guelta*, unless you've got other ideas. I'm going to back-track a bit, back east.'

Bowdrey was resentful. 'I think we all know it's most likely he walked south, because of the oasis there. Why can't I take that route?'

Ann interrupted before Lassiter could answer. She took Bowdrey by the arm, coldly, impersonally. 'There'll be no arguments. We'll go north, Lew.'

It took a minute or two for everyone to get aboard. Then the Land-Rovers rumbled bumper-to-bumper out of the *oued*. They left behind the four-year silence of the plane, and the new mound of the trooper's grave.

*   *   *

The sun had sunk so low that already all of the courtyard was in shadow. It made a bloodshot eye balanced on the distant eyelid of the western horizon. The desert was going grey with the ageing of the day.

The sergeant was unaware of time. He stood at the very edge of the catwalk staring straight down at the sand twenty feet below him, his eyes fixed on a specific place. He frowned, puzzled, the way he had been for some minutes, because he had spent the day in a stupor, without food or water, and his mind was moving very slowly. Only with the unobserved passage of time, the hint of cold in the air, had he come alive, stretching, moving about, looking out over the parapet, waiting for the voices to come. He was anxious in fact that they would talk again tonight because he intended to take them to task over the destruction of the radio. He had also studied the courtyard with its deepening gloom, thinking that they might surprise him from this side; and in doing so, he had made his discovery.

The spot was directly below his feet, a neat indentation in the sand. Close by was a smaller one, tiny in comparison, but also angular. In both cases, the sergeant thought, it was as though something box-like had fallen there.

He lit a cigarette. Then he walked quite quickly along the catwalk, trotted down the stairs and knelt at the spot he had been studying. The children were playing hide-and-seek somewhere, their voices calling to each other, floating from one abandoned room to another. But he ignored them, suddenly tremendously excited with the importance of his discovery. His heart had begun to thunder. All the sanity that he had so strongly feared was departing, flooded back. He was a sharp, alert, trained soldier for the first time in two days.

He extended a dark forefinger, almost delicately, and without touching the sand he traced the outlines of the two depressions. Then he looked up, directly above to the catwalk, eyes narrowed, picturing in his mind something he could not see from where he crouched.

Abruptly he came to a decision. He rose quickly, trotted back to the steps, ran lightly up them and along the catwalk to the radio. He placed the generator on top of it and then picked up the console. Panting, struggling under the weight of the set, he went all the way down again to the courtyard, finally dumping his burden as near as possible to the two depressions. Then he stood up, looked around, spat out his cigarette because it was searing his mouth and getting in his road. He breathed in once, deeply. Then he stooped, picked up the radio and placed it in the larger of the two depressions.

It fitted perfectly.

The sergeant said something quickly and fiercely under his breath. He took the generator and tried it in the other depression. Again, the match was exact.

He was tremendously excited. He went slowly back to the catwalk and stood gazing out over the vista of a dying day. He lit another cigarette and tried to think on logical, fixed lines. So, the radio had fallen twenty feet while he had been out chasing voices in the night. But it hadn't jumped off. It had not taken sudden animation and sprung joyfully to the sanded courtyard below. It had been lifted, held poised, and then wilfully dropped. Then it had been carried back again and placed in its original position, all with such perfect timing that he would never have known unless those two depressions in the sand had not come to his notice, or, going further back, it would never even have happened if he hadn't been lured into running stupidly out into the desert . . .

His thinking ground to a halt. In the background almost subconsciously, he heard the children calling. They were playing the fool now, each trying to find the other.

'Cooooeeee!' That would be the boy.

'Cooooeeee!' No. That was the boy. But it wasn't. Thrin emerged from the kitchen and called again. Neil appeared, mimicking her. Their voices were identical. They ran towards each other, met near the gates and started to romp.

The sergeant stared down at them. His lips parted and his breathing came very quickly. If he had been a European his face would have gone dark with blood. Instead it seemed to puff out, and the veins at his temples throbbed. He turned like a cat, picked up his Lebel and rushed down to the courtyard, churning his way through the sand to come to a stop a few yards from them, his Lebel held across his body, his eyes wild, his anger bursting out of him. They looked up, saw him, and went still.

'*Vous enfants! Vous enfants terrible!*' He panted. Very slowly, he advanced, half-crouching, bringing the Lebel around so that its muzzle pointed like a single black eye. They got up. As he came towards them, so they retreated slowly towards the gates.

'So it was you!' He switched to English. 'You call to me at night, eh? "Henri," you call. First the one, then the other. You make me think spirits are coming. You make me think I am mad.' His fury overtook him. He screamed. 'You make me think I am losing my mind!'

He had them cornered, now, at an angle against one of the gates. He saw their fear. He wanted to rain blows on them, to frighten them out of their wits. But at the same time his brain, as if to make up for its forty-eight hour torpor, raced ahead remorselessly, reconstructing for him the way in which he had been deceived. The one, probably the girl, out in the desert, the boy concealed anywhere in the courtyard. Their routine must have been perfectly rehearsed. When he charged out through the gates the boy would have dashed up to the watch-tower, lifted the radio and generator . . .

His mind stopped. Time stood still. The boy was not strong enough. Nor the girl. He had himself found the set heavy. Then who. . . ?

His skin crawled. He opened his mouth to ask the inevitable question, and in the same moment he saw the two pairs of terrified eyes move beyond him, over his shoulders. He saw the eyes dilate, saw the girl's mouth open to scream. His face screwed up. His mind sent a racing message to his body to turn, but he was too late.

He never felt the wicked slicing of the knife as it whispered across his throat. He felt only a terrible weakness as blood gushed out of the gap and rushed in a scarlet torrent down his tunic.

The sergeant dropped his rifle. His knees began to give. He stared at the children out of round dying eyes. His lips framed the words: 'I never wanted to hurt you.' Then he fell in one straight movement face down into the dust.

*　　　*　　　*

John-oh had driven the last two miles over the firm sand

approaching Masuril with the needle hovering near seventy kilometres. It would be dark soon and he was tired. He looked to his right briefly and saw Lassiter's truck approaching, its park-lights already glowing yellow like a lion's eyes. They would reach the gates at almost the same time. He grinned, picturing the reaction of most of the group to the dismal failure of the afternoon search. In a way he was disappointed himself. The money did not mean a great deal to him—it was too remote, too uncertain in his own mind for real excitement, but at the same time it was treasure-hunting of a sort and the thrill lay in the chase.

He was nearing the gates. Lassiter barrelled in alongside and made rude signs at him which John-oh exchanged. Then he made a deliberately over-courteous gesture to Lassiter to go ahead and enter the fort first.

Lassiter waved graciously. He slid in ahead of John-oh's truck, enveloping the second vehicle momentarily in a fog of dust. John-oh had a fragmentary picture of the other Land-Rover moving at one moment and then suddenly and inexplicably slamming to a halt. He cursed and jammed one foot hard on the brake. The back of the other vehicle reared towards him through the smoke-like dust. It was too late to swing the wheel. He could only stare helplessly in what seemed like an eternity as his own vehicle's wheels locked, it lost speed, but slithered at a slowing momentum inexorably towards the other so that they finally crashed in a clang of fender striking fender and the innocuous popping of a head-lamp glass.

John-oh jumped out running. 'Lew, for Christ's sake what in the hell are you——'

He stopped. He had rounded the front truck and saw Lassiter crouched over the body lying between the gates. He trotted up as Lassiter turned the sergeant over and the hideous loose grin of the gashed throat became visible.

'Oh Jesus,' he said weakly.

Lassiter came to his feet like a released spring. John-oh, frightened and uncertain, reached out to grab him but Lassiter knocked him aside. He was running, running as fast as his legs could take him, heading in a tight curve for the children's room. He slithered on loose sand, half lost his footing, in the doorway, then plunged inside.

Thrin and Neil were against the far wall. T'ekmedhin was turning, the knife dull with the blood of its first victim, his white teeth bared in a snarl of hate, the eyes in the visor-like gap of the veil spitting venom.

Lassiter shouted, 'You bastard you!' and swung a big fist that caught the Touareg as he was moving. It knocked him over, but there was not enough power in it. T'ekmedhin somersaulted on to his feet, the knife gone, and slipped eel-like through the door.

Lassiter came out after him, fell again on the scattered sand, and lost ground. He came up bellowing. 'Stop him! Stop him, you bloody fools!' But the Touareg had already passed the body of the man he had murdered. He weaved around John-oh, who grabbed and missed. His flying feet took him out into the desert, his cloak streaming behind him as he ran.

Lassiter arrived at the vehicles gasping and wheezing. He stopped, realized the futility of the chase, put his hands on his hips and said all in one breath, 'Oh shit what a ballsup.' He looked around, suddenly saw the dead sergeant's Lebel. He cursed, stooped, came erect already working the bolt. In complete silence they watched while he put the rifle to his shoulder, lowered his head on to the comb, took first pressure. The running figure of T'ekmedhin and Lassiter's cocked body seemed joined together by the wand of the rifle barrel. Then Lassiter was straightening, giving the gun to Nailand and saying, 'The harm's done. If you want to kill him, kill him. You're good at it.'

Nailand took the weapon automatically. He studied Lassiter for a moment. Then he looked at John-oh and Lola, at Jane and the girl. He seemed to make up his mind. He raised the gun to his shoulder, settled over it. T'ekmedhin was more than a hundred yards away by now and within yards of dead ground, a tiny rise up which he was already racing. To Lassiter he was a doll-like figure by now. So that when the rifle exploded and the doll flopped over the top of the rise, all arms and legs, the rifle's noise seemed cacophonously loud. It was rather like killing an ant with a hammer or a sparrow with a cannon.

The smell of cordite hung in the air. Nailand turned, quivering, lowering the gun. 'Did I get him?'

'You got him all right.' Lassiter took the weapon and automatically ejected the spent shell. 'You're very good at shooting people.'

They began to walk, all of them, in a group through the gates to where the children stood still-faced, waiting for them.

CHAPTER TEN

THE SOUS-PREFET threw down the microphone with a clatter that made the orderly wince.

'Nothing. *Sacré Dieu*, Nothing. What is that stupid nephew of mine doing?' He was not remotely interested in the answer. He was simply being angry out aloud. 'Has he lost his mind?' He resorted to his favourite form of swearing, which was in English. 'The stupid bastard! Hell's shit! My own sister's son!'

The orderly remained absolutely still while Goru paced up and down. It was no use blaming Henri, of course. Goru knew this. Swearing at the boy was simply a way of letting off steam. His decision had always been inevitable. He had simply kept putting it off, telling himself that the radio could so easily break down for a variety of reasons. One valve, and—phht. So far, this had kept Goru at Zufra. But always, hovering in the back of his mind, had been the curve of Touareg on the sand outside the palm grove, Jedren's mocking voice, the click-clack of a hundred rifle bolts and the dream of the ineffectual bullets and Lassiter throwing potatoes.

Goru reached the far wall of the radio shack. He turned, winced, put his back against the wall and clutched his belly where a spasm of pain clenched briefly and was gone. He was wearing his puce-coloured beret and his uniform hugged his heavy figure. When he pointed a forefinger at the orderly he was all business.

'Corporal, you are not renowned for your efficiency. I know this and you know it. Do what I tell you properly and you will have a sergeant's chevrons by tomorrow.'

The man leapt to his feet, tingling. The old warhorse in Goru could still inspire. He had an eye for drama. 'Sir!'

'Assemble all the men. Full kit, rifles, fifty rounds of

ammunition each. Have the camels gathered, saddled, and made ready.' Inwardly he shuddered at the thought of the ride. Camille would have to strap him up, this time. Metres and metres of crêpe. He looked at his watch. 'I will give you one hour.'

The man flipped a salute and was gone. Goru sighed, lit a Gauloise, blew smoke across the empty room. The wind of the orderly's recent departure disturbed it, made it swirl.

In the French army, he thought, or the British or German ones for that matter, I would have given him fifteen minutes. One simply had to get used to a change of attitudes. For a start, camels could not be stabled. One had to let them go, and find them and catch them when they were required. They were lazy useless creatures who worked for only a third of the year and reluctantly at that. They were the prima donnas of the desert and one treated them as such. But for all their faults they would go where the four-wheeled vehicles could not, where the half-tracks could not.

To hell with the camels, he admonished himself, I am dodging issues. I am sidetracking myself when in reality I must face up to the fact that I have been a bad commander. Henri was not entirely a fool; the radio, unlike most of Goru's equipment, had been virtually new. When Henri did not report last night, Goru told himself, I should have accepted trouble and gone out to Masuril there and then, and only the horror of that see-saw trip kept me from it.

He dropped the cigarette and ground it into the dirt on the floor. He hitched the webbing belt around his waist, blew out his cheeks and left the radio room, casting one last regretful eye at the set. When he reached his own quarters he was inclined to be abrupt.

'A glass of cognac, please.' He could see Camille's disappointment. She was wearing her special lamé and he knew with a twinge of regret what had been in store for him. 'Then I want you to strap my waist the way the Touareg do it. Even they, the bastards, are cursed by hernias from these disgusting animals they have to ride.' Almost as a reflex gesture he flipped *grandmere*'s apron over her head to stop her gummy mutterings. 'Please hurry. I feel I have left things far too long and that there is trouble out at Masuril.'

'I know.' Camille splashed brandy into the glass and brought it to him. 'I told you, yesterday, that when Henri did not report you should have gone. I smelled trouble on that wind.' Always, Camille had to have her say. He simply shrugged.

'It is Jedren.' She brought him the glass, a hawknosed woman, Arabic more than Negro, beautiful in her own way and especially so to him. 'I think the money-plane has been found and Jedren knows it. So he isolates them, out there.' She brought her lips up and kissed him briefly. 'And why? Do you know why?'

'No.' Goru said stupidly. When Camille plotted he always got left behind. In any case he had drunk half the brandy and it was sending tongues of fire through his limbs and anaesthetizing the grumble in his stomach. He was experiencing a distinct up-surge of confidence.

'Because,' she said patiently, 'you are his only threat. He is inviting you to come. And on the way he intends to destroy you.'

Goru thought about this. It was rather clever, and renewed spasm gripped his belly despite the cognac. He shook his head. 'I see that. But how—I mean, there was the radio, there were Henri and his trooper. They were within the fort, armed, carefully instructed. I simply do not see how.'

'This is just my thought.' She had found a roll of crêpe bandage. 'Lift your shirt.' He obeyed and she began to strap him. 'I love you very much and I would not like to see you shot down in an *oued* because you are walking into the spider's parlour.'

Goru finished the brandy, holding his arms at shoulder level while she finished the strapping. He spluttered, slightly drunk. 'I will be careful, I promise. But I do not think Jedren —if it is him—will expect a night march.'

She finished off with a big silver safety pin. 'Avoid anything that smells of ambush. Skirt it. Look after yourself, my Pierre. You are all I have.'

Goru became emotional. Tears filled his eyes. God, what would she do without him, saddled with that old bag in the corner? 'I will look after myself,' he said huskily. Then he pulled down his shirt, tucked it in over his fat waist and walked blindly from the room, already shouting for the corporal as he reached the quick bite of the night air.

*   *   *

'A very thorough piece of work.' Lassiter stood with his hands on his hips surveying the mess in the kitchen. The others, including the Bowdreys who had just arrived, clustered silently behind him. 'I take my hat off to the little bastard.'

The stink of petrol filled the air. All packaged foodstuffs, anything in a container that was not made of metal, had been piled in the middle of the floor and doused with petrol. The flour, the powdered soups, the tea, the coffee, the powdered milk. Everything. Then the canned foods had been slashed open to join the reeking heap.

Susan had been explaining to Jane what they had found. Now she pushed past. 'He couldn't have destroyed everything. Surely something must have been overlooked, even if it's one or two cans.' She began to fiddle about, taking ruined food and tossing it aside.

'I'll help.' Ann Bowdrey joined her.

'Do what you can. I need a drink.' Lassiter turned away and the rest of them followed with Jane using Nailand as a prop. Lassiter looked down as he walked, at the silent, shocked children. 'How the hell did he get in there? That little lot must have taken him at least fifteen minutes to accomplish. Were you asleep?'

The shake of Thrin's head was the minutest movement. 'We were in our room.' The words were whispered. Her lips trembled. She stared straight ahead of her. Neil studied the ground, more apathetic even than his sister. Lassiter shrugged. He was tired.

They reached the Mess and went inside. It was newly dark. He poured himself a drink. Then he went and slumped in a camp chair. The children huddled near the doorway, afraid now to be alone.

'Give me a whisky, Ayrab.' Jane let herself into the chair slowly and fragilely, as though she might break. 'A double. Fix the others up with what they want.' She lit a cigarette. 'What do you figure this means, Lew? Where do we stand?'

He was tired, baggy-eyed and unwashed. 'Do I have to

spell it for you? It means we must get out. Right now. The Touareg don't want us in this place. Forget about the plane. Forget about the money. And forget about dear Saint Peter's bones, God bless them.'

John-oh brought the drinks, handed them out and sat down. They made a partly frightened and partly preoccupied semi-circle—Bowdrey, flushed and sick-looking, Lola, Nailand, Jane, Lassiter and Franc.

'What do you think, Ayrab?'

'Exactly what Lew says, ma'am. It is time to get out.'

There was another silence. Then Jane's lips turned down at the corners. 'The two tough guides, the Sahariens, those tanned strong men of the desert, turn out to be two chickens. I'll put a simple question to you, Lew: if the Touareg wants us out of this place so bad, why the hell don't they just move in and eject us?'

It was a clever question. Lassiter became uncertain and Jane's radar detected it. She was beginning to grin, that unpleasant, humourless, monkey-like grin, even while he spoke. 'There are two possible reasons. One is that they are waiting somewhere out there for T'ekmedhin to report. And of course he isn't going to. But they don't know that yet. This might delay them. The other reason is that they might be waiting for us actually to find the money.'

Jane was delighted. It was what she had been expecting. 'Then why destroy our food, huh? That would be a goddam stupid thing to do if they wanted us to stick around and do their work for them.' She drew on her cigarette. 'I'll tell you the explanation, Lew. You wanna hear it?'

'All right.' Lassiter shrugged. 'But I won't necessarily accept it.'

'You'll do what I goddam say!' She flared, but only momentarily. Then she toned down to being almost placatory. 'Look, the Touareg's feud is with the black men. With that fat bastard down in Zufra and the two soldiers he left behind. The Touareg boy killed one soldier and Joe killed the Touareg, so that's that. I don't think those tribesmen know about the money. I think their arrival was pure coincidence. They've been having themselves some fun. Goru told us how vicious they are. When T'ekmedhin, or whatever his name is, doesn't report back they'll wait for a while, then write him off and go on south to fight the Legion, which is where they were heading in the first place.'

'So you don't feel we should leave?'

'You're goddam sure I don't, even if one of the vehicles has to go into Zufra for more supplies. Dammit, if you're scared we can tell Goru and he can give us another armed guard. He can come himself if he likes.' She swung her head. 'Joe? Bowdrey? What do you think?'

'I think we should stay.' Bowdrey said it quickly and categorically.

Jane chuckled. 'Still got the stink of that money in your nose, eh? I would be brave, too, for a hundred thousand pounds. Come on, Joe, what about you?'

Nailand tried unsuccessfully to look thoughtful. 'Perhaps it would be better if we did go, Jane.' He patted her arm. 'In any case, haven't you spent enough on this fruitless search for Peter's body? And I am not just talking about time and money. I'm talking about the effect on your health.'

'Nuts, I'll be okay.' The short white fingers fiddled restlessly with the rings that cluttered them. 'And I don't regard the search as fruitless. We found the Dakota, didn't we? Sure, that was an accident, it was Bowdrey's pigeon, but it was a major discovery. And then, on top of that, we found Peter's own plane. That was more than just a major discovery, that was goddam fantastic.' She stared out across and beyond the circle of people. 'No, I can't call this search fruitless. On the number of days we've been here, the results have been amazing.' She shook her head. 'If you want to talk me out of staying on here, base your argument on the presence of the Touareg, not the so-called fruitlessness of our search. I can't and I won't accept that.

She was right, but Nailand chose to stick perversely and tiresomely to his present tack. 'All very well, Jane. But you've forgotten that we are now looking for one individual body in all this vastness. We have already tried to find it, and failed. What is the point of going on?'

'Plenty. A weak man, a staggering man, can deviate, he can wander off course. Lassiter said it. So we go back to the plane, alter course a degree of two, and start again. And we keep doing that until we find him. I put it to you bluntly, Joe, I'm not being frightened into giving up yet. I'm staying.'

She stopped, lit a cigarette, then deliberately turned her head around the circle, appearing to study each face with deliberate challenge. It was incredible. Then she came back to Nailand. 'Lassiter and Franc will stay, no matter what they say, because if they don't they won't get any pay, they will have breached their contract with me. Susan will stay for the same reason. So if you want to take Lola and the kids and get out, you can.'

'I'm staying.'

Lola said it so unexpectedly and so calmly that all of them looked at her.

'Even if Joe goes?' Jane cocked her head.

'Even if he goes.'

'Well, well.' Jane rubbed her hands and chuckled. 'Guts in surprising places. And not much connubial loyalty. What now, dear cousin?'

It dawned on Nailand suddenly that he was out of step. As Lassiter said afterwards, he could see the penny drop and hear the lavatory bowl that was Nailand's brain, busily flushing. He grasped at last that he was backing Lassiter and John-oh, opposing Jane and being deserted by Lola whose unexpected and unbelievable disloyalty made him stare at her out of shocked eyes. He turned a dull red and said sullenly. 'I was only trying to help. Of course I will stay.'

'More loyalty,' Jane said dryly. 'Okay, that's settled, then. Got the message, Lew?'

'Yes, madame.' Lassiter got up and stretched. 'John-oh, Nailand, you'd better come with me. We've got to bring those vehicles into the courtyard. I think it would be wise. And there's a dead man—no, two dead men—to dispose of.' He turned dispassionately to Bowdrey. 'You can come if you want to. An extra shovel would be a help.'

Bowdrey said stuffily, 'I've never refused to co-operate,' and got up. Lassiter laughed and the four men walked out into the cold of the night to the gates. They stood in a shivering group near the stiffened body of the sergeant.

'Let's get that Touareg kid first.' Lassiter got into John-oh's Land-Rover. He started the engine, reversed a little way, then swung the vehicle so that it faced out into the desert. The lights came on, bright, sending two parallel beams shooting out and cutting away the darkness, reaching and merging at the rise over which the Touareg had fallen.

Lassiter got out carrying his rifle. 'Just in case.' He worked the bolt to get a cartridge into the chamber.

Nobody said anything. They walked in line abreast, silent, preoccupied, casting giant bobbing shadows ahead of them. It was cold and their breath made little puffs of mist in the night-lit air. When they reached the small crest Lassiter went ahead. He stood at the top and pointed the rifle barrel downwards.

Then he laughed.

'You're a bum shot, Nailand. And T'ekmedhin is a good actor. Come and have a look.'

They crowded the crest, parting just enough to let the light through. There was no direct illumination below them but the drop was a short one. It was palely lit by the bounce-back of the Land-Rover's headlights and the wan golden wash of the moon.

There was no body at the foot of the crest.

Lassiter jumped down. He pawed around in the sand. Then he knelt and flicked his gas lighter, making a minute inspection. 'No blood. You didn't even wing him.' He scrambled back. 'Friend T'ekmedhin is well on his way to Jedren by now.'

'So?' John-oh stood leaning on his shovel.

'So let's bury the other poor bastard and go and have another drink.' Lassiter turned his back on them and walked back into the two bright eyes of the headlights.

It took them only ten minutes to dig a grave in the soft sand near the gates and bury the sergeant. Then John-oh turned his truck once more and both vehicles were driven into the courtyard to join Bowdrey's. After that they went back to the Mess.

Susan and Ann had arrived. Lassiter told them and Jane about the Touareg. The news was received in contemplative silence. Then he got a drink and sat next to Susan. 'Save anything from the wreck?'

The slender shoulders rose and fell. 'He missed a few things.

197

There are two cans of pineapple in syrup, one of tomato juice, two cans of meat loaf, a can of peas. Turns out Mrs Bowdrey also had some stuff in her truck. We've got enough for about two days if we take it easy.'

'That's all we need.' On the strength of a heart pill and three whiskies Jane's confidence and condition had both revived. 'We'll find Peter tomorrow. I got a feeling.'

None of them was inclined to talk. They sat quietly with their private thoughts, drinking without the abandon and aggression of previous nights. They ate sparingly after an hour, an unsatisfying meal of canned meat and biscuits prepared by Ann Bowdrey. And after that the group broke up and left the Mess, going their private ways.

*   *   *

Goru's back ached despite the strapping. The camels moved like bobbing dark ghosts in the night. He looked at his watch. At least there was not much further to go. About ten kilometres, more or less, to the fort.

The men rode silently, the white of their *cheches* cutting their faces in half, disembodying them so that the black upper half was lost in the night.

There was not much moon. But the light it gave showed the stretch of desert to the east and the looming rocks of a defile straight ahead.

'Halt.' Goru said it quietly and the forward movement stopped. He was thinking of Camille's words: *avoid anything that smells of ambush. Skirt it.*

'We will detour to the east.' Goru straightened his cramped body. 'Not through the defile. Forward.'

The men did not like it. A detour meant more time in the saddle. They were cold, miserable, homesick for the warm green and rain of the south from where they had been recruited. Homesick like me, he told himself.

The defile was on his left, now. The rocks that formed the outside of its eastern wall lay tumbled out, rearing up against the lighter sky like jagged teeth. It occurred to Goru suddenly and with stomach-gripping fright that he was being very obvious. And Jedren would delight in obvious people. If the defile was the perfect place for an ambush, then Jedren would lay his ambush outside it. Knowing, Goru thought in a last withering moment of despair, that I am a fool and will walk right into it.

He stopped so suddenly that his men crammed up against him. The hair on his neck prickled. He drew his revolver and pulled back the hammer. Looking back, he raised an arm. There was movement, the clink of metal as the men unslung their weapons, a rustling sigh of expectancy.

Goru breathed very slowly, as though even his inhalations might be audible. He began to inch forward, his sharp nervous eyes probing the deep shadows of the rocks on his left. It is coming, he thought, damn my eyes for listening to a woman, I should have trusted my own war-horse instincts. He held the revolver across his body, so that it pointed at the rocks. He was waiting in agony for what he knew was going to come. When it did, though, it took a slightly unexpected form.

It was the quiet, humorous chuckle he had last heard on the sand outside the palm grove at Zufra.

Goru squeezed the trigger and the revolver exploded with a deafening bang and a spat tongue of flame. He whirled his camel, crying out, 'Come on, come on, move!' but even as he was firing again into the rocks they came alive with the flashes of a hundred rifles and he heard the crying of his men as the bullets struck them, the groaning of the camels as they fell. There was sound and yet there was no sound. Goru moved in this sound-silence, sobbing, rushing into the rocks as his troopers milled, screamed, fell in dark bundles.

It is the dream, he thought. It is the dream but it has come too soon. He fired at the dark shapes ahead and they moved but did not fall. Ah God, the dream! He was thinking of it even as the bullets struck him and the camel simultaneously so that they pitched into the sand to lie as still as the pile of troopers behind. Sound returned to him, the last furious blast of the rifles from the rocks. The noise, he thought incongruously, was rather like the rattle of hail on a tin roof.

Darkness of mind came, and consumed him.

CHAPTER ELEVEN

THE HEAT in the *oued* was like an oven. Sweat streamed down the faces of the small cluster of people around Lassiter's vehicle. Behind them, Sir Peter's plane twinkled with light, shimmering in the haze as though it were about to flap its wings and take off.

Lassiter had finished giving them their routes. John-oh would go north, varying slightly from Lassiter's course of the day before. Bowdrey would go south. Lassiter would drive south-east on a bearing that would bring him out a few miles south of the fort. It was really Nailand's route of the day before, but again minutely altered.

'Let's go, for God's sake.' Lassiter checked his watch. He'd got them out here early, earlier than they had ever started before. It was hard to believe, he thought, that this was Saturday, that they had been at Masuril since Monday and this was the fifth probe. In a way, this crazy cockeyed expedition had accomplished far more than he had ever expected and if they went on in this blundering way, muddling through with a heavy helping of serendipity, there was even a mad chance that they might somehow find Teefer and his ridiculous suitcases of money.

He got into the Land-Rover and started the engine, drumming his fingers impatiently on the wheel until a hoot from John-oh behind him and then Bowdrey in turn announced that they were ready. He put the truck into gear, nosed out of the *oued*, checked his compass and swung south-east.

Susan was his only companion. Jane had elected to stay at the fort and so, surprisingly, had Lola and the children. There were therefore only six of them on this important probe, two to each vehicle.

'How's the world, today?' He drove very slowly, grinding along in low gear.

She smiled.

'I haven't been very talkative, have I?'

'It doesn't matter.'

'It does. You probably think I'm brooding. But I'm not. I'm thinking. And I'm thinking ahead.'

'So am I.' He left it at that, and they drove away the morning in the monotony of their task, talking only when it was necessary, when it involved the mechanics of their search.

At noon another tangle of rocks reared ahead. Lassiter stopped a quarter-mile away. 'There's a defile in there. We'll probably have to do some of this on foot, although I know we're wasting our time. If Teefer walked this far he was an Olympic athlete.' He checked both the compass and the map. 'We are directly across the line of the route from Zufra to Masuril, if one wanted to use the shortest way.' He extended an arm out of the window, pointing to his right. 'The fort is that way. About five miles, probably.'

She had quartered the ground to the south. Now she looked straight ahead of her through the windscreen, her hands trembling slightly from the weight of the binoculars.

'There's something strange at those rocks. Things are scattered about. They look like bundles but it's hard to make them out.'

'Not another T'ekmedhin?'

'I'm not fooling.' She gave him the glasses. 'See for yourself.'

Lassiter took them. He became very still. Then he handed them back and had the car moving in almost the same motion. 'Those bundles are camels. Lying down. And there are some other things, too. I wouldn't like to say what they are until we get there.'

Three minutes later they stood shocked, silent, disbelieving, amongst the heaped dead of the Zufra patrol.

There was no sound except the ticking noise of the Land-Rover's metal. The troopers lay at all angles and in all positions, sprawled, curled, flung out with their camels around them. The wine-red of dried blood was everywhere and flies buzzed busily.

It was very difficult to adjust, to believe that this was true. They were numbed by it for long moments, staring about, moving their hands aimlessly, not knowing what to do. Then the girl said, 'Oh dear God, no,' and began to go from body to body, stooping over each one, turning it if necessary, her hair falling across her face, heaving and tugging at the corpses, careless of the paste of half-congealed blood that began to stain her hands and clothes, increasing her pace all the time, eventually straightening and staring at Lassiter, begging him with her eyes. 'There must be one. Just one. Surely they can't all be dead!'

Then she went on again with Lassiter joining her, both of them studying the dead black faces of the young men who had been alive only hours before until finally they rounded a boulder and found themselves looking at the *Sous-Préfet* of Zufra, a grey-faced, blood-smeared Goru, still clutching his empty revolver, who smiled at them weakly.

'So nice to see you again. It has been rather a long wait.' He spoke faintly in French. 'You observe before you the remains of Pierre Goru's unsuccessful one-man frontal attack. Jedren out-smarted me and because I am a fool seventeen good men have died.'

Lassiter knelt next to him. 'You're not a fool. What could you do against a hundred Touareg?'

'A hundred?' Goru's mind rambled a little. 'There were a million, Monsieur Lassiter, and we shot them but they would not fall, so in the end you and I threw potatoes at them.'

Lassiter put a big hand gently on the *Sous-Préfet's* shoulder. 'We'll get you home and patch you up. No more talking.'

Goru's lips twitched. 'The first time you smiled at me, Monsieur Lassiter, I thought of a crocodile, yawning. There was so much latent menace there. Now I see much good.' His eyes moved on. 'And in the seeing-eye lady, too. Covered with the blood of my men, and she does not care.' His eyes closed. They lifted him with difficulty and carried him to the back of the Land-Rover, installing him there with Susan crouched next to him to stop him from being flung about. He was hit, she saw, in the neck, the right forearm, and the waist. His tunic was saturated with stiffened blood, making it crackle like starch when they moved him.

He was so silent on the journey to Masuril that Susan thought he was dead. Almost as though he had anticipated this, Goru at one stage opened a ruminative eye and said in English, 'There is life in the old dog yet,' and then lapsed into unconsciousness again.

The five miles to Masuril was an aching memory for her, a confused recollection of the Land-Rover bumping along its uneven course, the tiny grunts that came from the unconscious man when he was jolted, the pain in her arms from trying to hold him in one place, the knowledge that the wound in his side had opened again and was bleeding new scarlet blood over the maroon of what had dried, the recollection of Lassiter driving with one hand on the wheel, looking perpetually back at her over his shoulder and asking, again and again, 'How is he?' and the realization that in a few days a strange bond had formed between these two men who were so totally dissimilar in every way. *Lassiter likes Goru.* It was a warming thought that stayed with her right into the courtyard, where the others who had already returned from their probes gathered silently and watched while Goru was carried by Lassiter and John-oh to their room.

The thought was with her even when Ann Bowdrey followed them a moment later with a small case she had fetched from her room, met Lassiter in the doorway and said, 'I am a nursing Sister, Mr Lassiter,' and then went inside with him. After that Susan went to her quarters. She washed herself like an automaton and changed her clothes, then sat in a chair staring at the wall and smoking cigarettes until John-oh came to tell her she was wanted in the Mess.

They were all there, the members of the two groups, even the children who sat silently with their mother. Only Goru's and Ann Bowdrey's absences lingered like a question-mark.

She joined them after five minutes. She looked tired and creased. 'Lieutenant Goru is quite badly wounded. Frankly, I have never had to deal with gunshot cases before, but the position is that the ulna in his right forearm has been smashed by a bullet. I have done what I can, but he will need surgery very soon—what is known as an open reduction of the bone there. On top of that he has been hit in the trapezius muscle at the junction of the shoulder and the neck, the bullet damaging tissue and nerve and passing on through. And finally he has been hit on the left side. It is rather difficult to determine whether any organ such as the spleen has been damaged or whether the abdomen has been penetrated. I don't think so.'

A bead of perspiration appeared on her forehead, hesitated, plunged down into an eyebrow. She blinked and touched a forefinger to her eye, rubbing unconsciously at the irritation. 'Add to all this the fact that he spent some hours in the freezing night air, and you have the picture of a man who needs quite urgent treatment. I have given him an injection of an antibiotic I use for treating Bert, in the hope that it will help, but there is nothing more I can do.'

She subsided. She seemed to crumple a little. And it was not because of what she had had to do. It was the fore-knowledge of what was to come, the inevitable decision that must be reached, now by all of them. Susan saw this, she saw the purpose go and the desperation replace it in the strong body.

Lassiter said, 'Can he make it to Zufra?'

Ann Bowdrey nodded. 'I think so.'

Jane Teefer pursed her thin lips with their hairline creases and spat. 'Goddam cigarettes. Listen, all of you. I want to make something clear. What happened to that fat bastard was entirely his own doing. What about us? That's what we've got to decide, and we've got to decide right now.' She found Lassiter with her dead eyes. 'There is no doubt it was the Touareg, Lew, huh? And you saw these dead guys, you saw them with your own eyes?'

'You're even more of a bitch than I thought you were, you know.' Lassiter could have been commenting on the weather. He flicked his forearm to glance at his wristwatch. 'But the answer to all your questions is in the affirmative. If we don't get out of here soon we are going to have a visit which will end up with our throats being cut like the sergeant's. Jedren must know about the money. It's obvious. Otherwise he would never have taken an irrevocable step like annihilating Goru's force. Goru was his only threat, and he had to get rid of it. So he has, and it follows that we are next in line.'

Nailand said aggressively, 'How could he know about the money? How could he have found out?'

'Perhaps you blabbed in Djanet, when you got potted.' Lassiter's glance moved. 'Perhaps Bowdrey blabbed on the way here. You're both inclined to run over at the mouth.'

'Bert talked. Twice he said too much in the wrong places.' Ann looked at him with a mixture of hatred and contempt.

Bowdrey quivered. He had had enough. 'How do you know it wasn't Lassiter? He was pissed every night for most of the trip, so I hear.' He swung on the girl, shouting now. 'To think you'd say that about me in front of all these people! You condemned me as though I was a dog, without a shred of evidence!'

'Why don't you all shut up!' Jane's noisy braying overrode the rest. 'Let's leave the cat-calling for later, huh?' She waited until there was complete silence. 'I think Lew is right. We better go. And quickly, too. You get it organized, Lew.'

'If I go, I will wait at Zufra until the trouble passes and then I will come back.' Ann Bowdrey had a look of almost crazed sorrow. 'I will never go home. Not without the money. Never.'

'Do what you goddam like.' Jane turned away. You're a big girl now Mrs Bowdrey, even if you've never had it.' She took Susan's arm. 'Come on, honey, get me to the truck. We got to get moving. Hurry them up, Lew.' Slowly, holding the girl tightly, she left the room.

It was only the Bowdreys whom Lassiter had to goad. For the rest of them the memory of Goru's blood-caked body and the knowledge of seventeen massacred men was a sufficient spur.

Bowdrey had been the first to turn his truck and it stood squarely blocking the gates as though in bulky testimony to the bull-like obstinacy of its owners, who insisted on bringing out every item of their belongings. It went on in a seemingly endless procession between their quarters and their truck until John-oh and Lassiter offered to help but were rudely rejected. Bowdrey's thick north-country bellow filled the courtyard. He was carrying a bundle that consisted only of blankets, and yet it sagged in his thin freckled arms.

'I'll not be bullied and harried, y'hear?' Sweat was washing down his face in waves. 'I'm not a rich titled bitch. I can't afford to abandon things and nor can Ann.' He pushed roughly past John-oh. 'Now get out of my way.'

Lassiter, who had been hanging on to his temper, finally let it go. He reached out an arm, caught Bowdrey by the shoulder and swung him around. Then he knocked the bundle out of Bowdrey's arms, took him by the front of his shirt and hauled him up close to his own anguished red face.

'Bowdrey. Listen to me carefully. I'll give you one minute to get that truck going or I'll move it myself. Do I make myself perfectly clear?'

Bowdrey cursed in ragged foulness and spat into Lassiter's

face. Lassiter pushed him away so hard that he staggered backward, his arms windmilling until he finally fell sprawling. He sat there in the dust and began to cough, hating Lassiter with his eyes while Ann rushed in, stooped, gathered the bundle under one arm, swung the other in a looping half-circle and hit Lassiter open-handed across the cheek.

'Don't listen to him, Bert!' She was mad-eyed and panting. 'I put every penny I had into this thing and I'm not leaving any of it!'

'You bloody-well are, you know.' Lassiter was snarling, wiping the spittle from his chin with a subconscious horror of gaining Bowdrey's infection. 'I've had enough.' He began to storm towards Bowdrey's Land-Rover but the girl intruded across his path, blocking him with her strong firm body, her back turned to him, heaving him away while she shouted, 'Get up out of the dust, damn you Bert! They want to make us leave our things behind. Stop coughing and get up and help me!'

Lassiter grabbed her by the shoulder, his eyes filled with the closeness of her neck, the cascade of corn-coloured hair that swept down her back, the tensile and resilient strength of her. There was no want in him, just a violent anger mixed with a reluctance to hurt her. He was about to fling her to one side when she went soft in his grasp. It was the last thing he expected. It upset his balance so that he staggered and let her go. He nearly fell. When he came upright she was standing square across his path.

'Stop it, Mr Lassiter, leave me alone. You're too late.'

Lassiter was panting. 'Too late?'

'You're not deaf, are you? I said you're too late. You never would have been in time. Look at the gates, Mr Lassiter.' Her eyes glittered with a sort of perverse triumph. 'You've been too busy hounding us to see what's happening. Look at the gates! They're here, don't you see? The Free Ones, the Indigo Men. The People of the Veil. They're here and you're stuck with them. Deal with them, Mr Lassiter, like you dealt with the bridge at Eichstadt!'

Lassiter lifted his eyes. Over her. Beyond her. He went very still. He went very cold.

The *Sous-Préfet* had had a dream, he remembered. About

a million Touareg, and throwing potatoes at them. It is the dream, he thought, it is Goru's dream. Fifty yards out from the gates stood a line of camels that seemed to go on into infinity. Tall graceful camels ridden by tall graceful men armoured in blue cloth visored only enough to show their eyes. They sat their camels, their brown sandalled feet relaxed and crossed beyond the crucifix pommels, watching with quiet interest.

Lassiter let his arms drop to his sides. He moved slowly, almost idly, across the few yards of sand to the back of his Land-Rover and quietly slid out his rifle. There was a cartridge in the chamber so he pulled back the cocking-piece. Then he turned, holding the weapon in his big hands. Susan was standing next to him. He gave her the fullness of his nighttime smile. 'If you had two teams, The Free Ones against The Unloved Ones, which side would you back?'

She looked steadily into his face. 'I'm not afraid, Lew.'

'I am.' He held the rifle casually, as though it didn't really matter. 'I'm in a blue bloody funk.'

He turned away and began to walk slowly, alone, to the gates.

CHAPTER TWELVE

JEDREN had light-coloured eyes, grey like the skin of an elephant. Beneath indigo *litham* there was a straight nose, a short, clipped greying moustache and a firm-lipped mouth. Like all the Touareg, he was soft-skinned. There was little muscular definition. His wrists and ankles were slender with breeding, his arms, chest and legs relatively hairless.

He sat his camel loosely, his brown sandalled feet crossed beyond the crucifix pommel, interestedly watching the lone Frank carrying a rifle trudge through the sand of the courtyard and stop between the gates. He had, he was aware, to handle this carefully. There were certain things he knew that this man did not. Conversely, the Frank might have the advantage of him in other respects. There was a problem to be faced which needed careful manœuvring, but on that score he was not particularly concerned because of his endless confidence in himself.

The Frank had spread his legs in a straddle. He brought the rifle to his shoulder and aimed it. None of the men in the long line moved, because they could see the low depression of the barrel. A puff of smoke enshrouded the muzzle and in the same second sand was geysered up into a small fountain a few yards away. The bullet fled into the yonder distance with a harmless howling.

Jedren moved his camel forward a few yards. He was smiling under his veil but he made his voice firm. 'Was it necessary to do that?'

The Frank was ejecting the spent shell even while the accentless French crossed the distance between them. The man smiled warily and said, 'After seeing the remains of the Zufra patrol, I think it was.'

Jedren made a gesture of mild irritation. 'The troopers saw us from a distance. All we wished to do was speak with the *Sous-Préfet* who was leading them. Instead he made them draw their weapons and attack us. We were astonished. A handful of men against mine! But we had to defend ourselves against this madness.'

The man put the rifle butt carefully on the sand and leaned on the weapon. He managed to look tremendously casual and Jedren was impressed. The man said, 'That is not the way I understood it. Those men had been massacred. Most of them had not even fired their rifles.'

Jedren was amused. 'There are ninety-one men here who will repeat word for word what I have recounted. Should we waste words?'

There was a small pause. Then the man said, carefully, 'No, I don't suppose so. You would make a good lawyer, Jedren. It is Jedren, I presume?'

'You have the advantage of me' Jedren acknowledged courteously.

'My name is Lassiter.'

'Were you in Libya at one time?'

'I was.'

'I have heard of you.'

'All of it bad, probably.' Lassiter lifted the rifle idly, but only to waist level. 'You make a very conspicuous target, you know.'

'It would be grossly uncivilised to shoot me now.' Jedren waved a hand. Immediately, the ranks of Touareg on either side of him bristled with guns. 'Apart from which it might prove suicidal.'

'But at least it brings us to the meat of the matter.' Lassiter worked another cartridge into the breech with the casual movements of a man winding his watch. 'I think I am entitled to know why you are here.'

'Oh, indeed.' The grey eyes mocked him. 'We are moving south, you understand. There is trouble there and the forces of rebellion need a certain amount of assistance and re-organisation.' He shrugged. 'To put it rather dramatically, the Prophet is ill-represented. I thought I might take a hand. But in the meantime my men and I are tired and in need of shelter. We wish to occupy Fort Masuril.'

Lassiter seemed to sigh. 'I thought you might.' He shook his head. 'I am afraid that is impossible. There simply isn't the room.'

'You could always go, of course.'

'Possibly.' Lassiter nodded sagely. 'That's quite true. But how far? As far as the Zufra patrol?'

'I give you my word you would proceed unharmed to Zufra.'

Lassiter grinned. 'And once there we would radio Fort Lamy. The Legion does not like that little war, Jedren. It was tired from doing boring garrison duty in Corsica. It was looking forward to action. But since it has been in Chad it has largely chased ghosts. It would dearly love to have your band as a quarry. The helicopters would be out, and the halftracks and the spotter planes and behind all this the toughest infantry in the world.' Lassiter shook his head. 'I have heard of you, too. You are not stupid. I am afraid I cannot accept your word.'

'This is distressing.' Jedren sounded apologetic. 'I do not like to threaten, but you realize, no doubt, that I could move in if I wished. To your disadvantage, of course, because by then I might be angry.'

'It could prove costly.' Against Jedren's apologetic tone

Lassiter sounded positively regretful. He simply held a fore-finger aloft. 'Look up there.'

Jedren raised his eyes to the parapets. There was a tremendous glare, so that the parapets and the crenels between them were almost entirely in silhouette against the hot gunmetal sky. But some of the crenels did not show up as naked empty notches between the parapets. They were blocked by human figures. Jedren counted slowly. Seven. He narrowed his eyes, seeing a twinkle of light off a rifle barrel. There were weapons up there. He tried to make out the number but it was impossible. He lowered his glance. There was also the Frank in the gateway, of course, who was quite mad enough to get himself killed while taking a few of them with him.

Jedren's decision faltered. He began to make small estimates in his mind. He and his men were about sixty metres from the walls. In a direct frontal assault they could get in, of course. But he would lose men in the process, perhaps as many as twenty. He could also be assured that he and T'ekmedhin would be killed by Lassiter, who had already picked the boy out nearby Jedren and was looking from one to the other with serious speculation. Almost, Jedren thought, as though he were calculating the range and pondering how long it would take him to swing from the one target to the other.

Jedren brought all these thoughts to a head and smiled. It showed in his eyes. 'Very well. I see what you mean. You realise, of course, that these things can be done at night, and from four different sides? Then it would be a different story.'

'Possibly.' Lassiter shrugged again. 'That is up to you. I am sorry that I have had to be so rude.'

Jedren laughed. The mad Frank laughed along with him. 'For the time being then, *au revoir*. I am afraid you will be hearing from me very soon.'

Lassiter said, 'I am aware of this. But remember that the moon is almost full and I know this tends to make one shoot high.'

Jedren raised a hand. The long line of camels and men began to wheel.

Lassiter's voice stopped them abruptly.

'Jedren!'

The Touareg half-turned. 'There is something else?'

'The money, Jedren. Let us stop bluffing each other. We have not found it yet.'

Jedren shrugged. 'I must accept your word.' Then the movement continued and the blue-clad men merged into the desert, dropped beyond a crest and were gone.

*　　　*　　　*

Goru opened his eyes and looked straight above him at an area of yellowed ceiling. He was weak in body but incredibly clear of mind, as though he had not drunk, or smoked, or eaten rich things in some time. He felt sore, and very tired, but purified. He tried moving his head but his neck hurt him so much that he stifled a groan. Instead he rolled his eyes to the right and saw Lassiter crouched next to him in a chair looking like a friendly gargoyle, his shoulders from this upside-down angle seeming monstrously wide but also terribly thin, within an awful wine-coloured shirt that draped his bony body and flapped when he moved.

'Oh, Monsieur Lassiter.' He found that he could speak quite clearly into this new void of complete clarity. But apologetically, of course. 'I fear that I have been dreaming.'

He watched Lassiter's craggy face break into a grin. I was right, he thought, he is terribly ugly and terribly good looking and women would find him horrible and desirable at the same time, and the crocodile is still there. 'This wasn't the one about the potatoes, and the multiplying Touareg?'

Goru thought for a moment. 'I must have been indiscreet. In my sleep, I mean.'

'I wouldn't say that.' Lassiter lit a cigarette and held it for Goru to draw. It was an English cigarette and Goru found it quite frightful after his Gauloises but he was too polite to say so. 'I'm wondering why it had to be potatoes, out here in the Sahara.'

'I always had a fondness for potatoes.' Goru's stomach spasmed. I cannot be too badly injured, he thought. 'Especially boiled in their jackets, with a lump of cold butter behind, on the fork. Very bad for the heart, they tell me, especially in middle-aged men.' The ceiling had a bulging hole in it and through it he could see the sky tarnishing with the stain of evening's arrival. 'What time is it?'

'Six o'clock.'

'Then it must be last night that I was . . .'

'Yes.' They both dodged the exact truth. 'It was last night.'

Goru frowned at the ceiling. 'Anybody get away, apart from me?' He spoke very carefully and without emotion.

'No. Nobody except you.'

'They're all dead, then?'

'Yes. Hit many times, most of them.'

There was a short silence. Then: 'Poor boys, Simple tribesmen. They really did not know what it was all about.'

'Yes, I know that.'

There was an ache in Goru's abdomen. He had a foreknowledge of further disaster. 'Where is my nephew—Henri, the sergeant—and his trooper?'

'I did not know you were his uncle.' Lassiter's wise eyes, full of the tragedies of the world, considered Goru. Then he told him exactly how both men had met their deaths. There was no other way.

The *Sous-Préfet* took a little time to adjust. Then he said, slowly, clearly, 'Please tell Nailand that he should consider himself under open arrest until I have the opportunity to convene a court of enquiry.'

'All right.'

Goru's eyes followed Lassiter as he got up, went to the open doorway, studied the courtyard and the open gates, came back again and sat down. 'You're restless. Expecting the Touareg, I suppose. After what he did to me it is logical.' He thought a moment. 'I will say this for Jedren: He warned me. So I do not think that he will come with fire and sword, if that is in your mind. It is more likely that he will pay you the most civilized call, first. Jedren doesn't like to waste ammunition or men. In fact he would have made a good lawyer.'

He was unconsciously repeating Lassiter's own words. The wide shoulders rose and fell within the ghastly shirt. 'Oh, he has already made his call.'

Goru's eyebrows shot up. 'Really? What happened?'

Lassiter looked apologetic. 'I spoke to him quite nicely. I told him that there was no room at the inn.'

'And he went away, just like that?'

'With a little persuasion.'

The *Sous-Préfet* stirred restlessly. 'He will be back, of course. You realize that?'

Lassiter nodded. 'Soon. Maybe tonight.'

'He wants the money. He knows about the money-plane.'

'Oh God. Not you, too?' Lassiter regarded him with weary disbelief. 'Everybody knows about that bloody aeroplane. It wouldn't surprise me in the slightest if a group of Rotarians turned up and asked for a percentage for charity.'

Goru gave a grunt of sour humour and then winced from the pain in his neck. 'I doubt that it's quite so bad. My mother-in-law happened to see the Dakota loaded in Fort Lamy. She is about a hundred years old but she remembered.'

There was a short silence. Lassiter stared broodingly across the room. 'Jedren would never have taken the drastic and irrevocable step of annihilating your patrol unless he knew about the money. It's obvious that he knows. I even mentioned it during our conversation. He wasn't remotely surprised.'

Goru was interested.

'What did you say?'

'I told him that we hadn't found it yet.'

'Ahah, that is the point. I have been thinking about it while we talked. Why is Jedren behaving so recklessly, committing murder, threatening to do so again, when *the money has not yet been found?*'

'That's been bothering me, too.' Lassiter got up, more restless even than the *Sous-Préfet*. 'There are all sorts of explanations. Perhaps he has found the money himself.'

'Never!' Goru was adamant. 'If he found it he would be gone—poof—like that, back to Touareg country. He would not bother with us.'

Lassiter ignored him. 'Or he might have found Teefer's plane, and thinks he can take it from there on his own, without us in the road.' He smiled a little. 'Alternatively, he may simply not believe us. Perhaps he thinks we have found the money. I don't think that it is in Jedren's nature to expect anyone to tell the truth.'

'He is a most accomplished liar,' Goru agreed. He let the silence run for a while. Then: 'Whatever his reasons, he wants us out, not so?' He did not expect an answer. 'It follows, therefore, that we must oblige him. We must get out, quickly, before he comes back.'

'We wouldn't last ten miles. You know that.'

Goru considered. 'It may suit him to let us go.'

'So that we can radio for the Legion when we get to Zufra? Talk sense.'

They were both becoming irritable. 'Very well, what then? If we do not run and get killed do we stay here and get killed?'

Lassiter lit another cigarette. 'Moving, we stand as much chance as your patrol. Here, there is at least a very small percentage of hope. Jedren is a clever commander. I doubt very much that he would rush in headlong from all sides. He knows we're armed. He is more likely to probe cautiously, to feel us out.'

Goru said sharply, 'What weapons do you have?'

'My rifle. Bowdrey's Webley. The Lebels from your two men. Your revolver, if we may borrow it.'

'You're welcome.' Irony dripped from his tongue. His stomach was screaming, now. Perhaps, he thought with alarm, I have been hit in the belly and am dying. But he went on doggedly, 'You do not genuinely suppose that three rifles and two hand weapons will keep out a hundred determined Touareg?'

Lassiter was now decidely snappish. 'I said it was a very small hope. But it's better than nothing.' He got up quickly, tense and rattled, went to the door, looked once more into the courtyard. He hovered there a moment.

'Where have I been hit?' Goru moved his left arm with difficulty to wipe at the sweat on his face. The movement made his neck hurt.

'All over the place.' Lassiter was quite cheerful about it. 'In the muscles around the left side of the neck.' He pointed to high up on the trapezius. 'I don't know what one calls it in French. Also your right arm has been smashed. Mrs Bowdrey has immobilized it. Turns out she was a nursing Sister, once. Then, finally, you got a bullet through the flesh at your waist. By and large you seem to have done your best to resemble a colander.'

'I am afraid I cannot be of much help.'

'I'll call you when we get down to the potatoes.' Lassiter

raised a hand, turned quickly and was gone out into the courtyard's gloom.

*   *   *

John-oh skirted the rear of Lassiter's Land-Rover slowly, as though deep in thought. In actual fact his mind was relatively idle. It was his eyes that were busy. They were studying the sand under the tail-gate with deep interest that developed into concern.

He bent, putting his hands on his knees, peering. After a moment he knelt and prodded the sand with a forefinger. He considered the grains that came away, stuck firmly to his skin. Then he nodded, as though unhappily satisfied with his diagnosis. He got on his back and wormed a short distance under the truck, his eyes roving busily over the smooth metal bottom of the water tank. They stopped at a certain point and for a few seconds regarded the small hole there. It was really a ragged indentation with the steel pierced through at one point. While he watched, a teardrop of water made a silver streak as it plummeted to the sand.

The last, he thought. He wriggled from underneath the truck, sat up and lit a cigarette, blowing smoke into the greying light of the courtyard where shadows had collected in the corners.

Lassiter emerged, coming from the room they shared, and where Goru was now ensconced. He came straight to John-oh and fixed him with a bleak eye.

'Why are you sitting on your arse when there are things to be done?'

John-oh simply pointed.

All Lassiter said was 'water?'

'Yes, it's all gone.'

'Leak or sabotage?'

'Leak, I'd say. Wear and tear. A small stone, flung up. It wasn't T'ekmedhin, if that's what you're thinking.'

Lassiter put his hands on his hips. 'There's the tank in your Land-Rover.'

John-oh looked away. 'The first night I went to the *guelta* for water I imagined I saw a Touareg mounted on a Hoggar camel. I got scared. I didn't fill the tank fully. Last night I

215

went again, with Mrs Nailand. We got talking and . . .' He stopped. His eyes met Lassiter's without fear.

'You didn't fill it at all.'

'That's right.'

'How much have we got left, then?'

'About two gallons.'

Lassiter toed the damp ground under the Land-Rover. 'The trip last night. With Lola. That meant something, didn't it?'

'Yes.'

'Then there's nothing more to be said.' Lassiter gave him a brief, almost shy glance. 'Get up on that catwalk, and keep watch with Nailand.'

They parted. Lassiter went to the back of John-oh's Land-Rover, fiddled around amongst the tools there and produced a light camping hatchet, all-metal with a chamfered rubber-bound handle. He walked quickly to the kitchen, swinging it in one hand.

Susan Shields was there. He gave her a friendly but enigmatic smile that was distinctly distant, then began to fling things off the table she had called the French Inheritance. He did this quite casually, breaking the stove in the process, pausing only momentarily when this happened to say, 'Everything has its place in the order of things, and the stove is no longer of importance. Weighed with staying alive, would you eat cold food?'

She said, 'Yes,' and left it at that because she knew it didn't matter, anyway.

'Fine.' Lassiter had hardly stopped moving. With a calm and dispassionate manner he now attacked the French Inheritance with the hatchet, reducing it in a series of smashing blows to bits and pieces of fat-browned wood, the broken edges of which showed a shocked and pristine whiteness. Out of the chaos he produced eight stakes of about more or less equal length and width.

He paused at this stage, puffing mildly, pleased with himself. One long finger pointed to the heap of slashed, petrol-doused cans nearby. 'Get an opener and cut the bottoms out of eight cans about that size.' He singled out a jam tin. 'It's the bottoms I want.'

'Why?'

'Never you mind.' Lassiter dropped the hatchet and fastened two huge claw-like hands on the rickety wall-shelf. His shoulders heaved and the whole unit came crashing to the ground with a screeching of sundered rawlplugs. Dust flew in clouds.

'Nails. It's nails I'm after.' He turned a sweating face. 'Get a move on with those can-bottoms.' Then he turned away, picked up the hatchet and waded into the dust, slamming the shelves apart in a series of swooping backhanded blows.

At the end of five minutes he had eight reasonably straight nails. Susan gave him the circles of tin she had cut from the cans. Lassiter nailed each one of these to a stake, using the back of the axehead, then bundled them under one arm. He said simply, 'Come,' and strode at a rapid pace across the courtyard and out between the gates, where he stopped.

She bumped into him.

'Am I entitled to an explanation?'

'Not yet. Count out aloud while I pace.'

He strode out ridiculously into the desert while she scurried along next to him. At one hundred paces he stopped and hammered one of the disc-topped stakes into the sand with the hatchet, so that its tinned, shiny side faced the fort. Then they went on again and at the two hundred mark he planted another.

She was beginning to understand. 'We do the same thing on the northern, western and southern sides?'

'Lew likes you because you are so clever,' he said. He marched away, letting her follow him until they reached the northern side of the fort where he wordlessly planted two more stakes at the same distances. Then he went on until finally, hitting the last one into the ground, grunting to make sure it was firm, he lifted a slick, expressionless face and said, quite unexpectedly, 'Wish I had some grenades.'

'*Grenades?* What on earth for?'

'Because Jedren and his boys are not coming to play bridge. You take a grenade and pull out the pin and stick it into an empty can so that the lever can't flip up and start the fuse burning. You do this with a whole lot of them, link them together with string and lay them out along the line where your friends are expected. Somebody comes along, kicks the string, a tin falls over, the grenade slides out, the lever flips up—do I have to go on?'

A small smile tugged at her lips. 'Did you learn that in the war, Daddy?'

'Depends which one you mean.' Lassiter actually chuckled. 'First or second?'

There was something very good between them at this moment. She laughed quickly. 'You're not that old. Lew, how can we be so casual?'

'Because we don't care.'

They were walking back. The gates neared, looming ahead of them in the now rapidly gathering dusk. 'You care, Lew, only you won't admit it.'

Without waiting for an answer she walked on between the gates and into the courtyard.

*   *   *

It was full dark, and cold, with a wash of sickly moonlight touching them where they stood on the catwalk. Jane's breath came out from her thin lips in little puffs of smokelike mist. She shivered even bundled in a heavy coat with a thick scarf about her throat. 'Goddam Lassiter, what in hell you trying to do to me up here? I'm gonna freeze to death!'

'No you're not, you're too mean.' Lassiter firmly tugged her to the north-eastern watchtower. 'Now shut up and listen.'

The small bundled form became still. The sightless eyes stared out into the moon-washed desert where Lassiter's two markers glittered like tiny silver gems.

'Hear anything?'

'No. Nothing.'

'Sure?'

'Of course I'm sure!' Her angry, frozen tones filled the night.

'For God's sake be quiet!' Something seemed to strike Lassiter as funny. He laughed and then reached past Jane to the girl, who stood silently behind her employer. 'Give me that bottle I asked you to hold.'

She handed it over reluctantly. 'Do you have to?'

Lassiter swigged and gave the bottle back. All he said now was, 'Got to retain the cutting edge.' He turned away and took Jane by the sleeve. 'Come along, you old coot.' He tugged her away along the catwalk and the girl followed, holding the bottle.

'Jesus, Lassiter, if I didn't——'

'Didn't want to stay alive? Yeah sure, you'd fire me. But you do, so you won't.' They reached the next watchtower. 'Keep your mouth shut and listen.'

Jane hunched up. Her face swung. They watched her, all of them, Nailand from across the other side, John-oh on the west, Bowdrey only a few yards away. They watched her with a solemn and serious intensity as the nose twitched, the head swung in more and more minute degrees and finally settled.

'Out there.'

There was a soft sighing from them, a release of the tension of waiting.

'Sure?'

'Yes, dammit.' She had the sense to whisper now. 'Straight ahead of my nose. I can smell 'em and I can hear 'em. I'm as sure as a pointer is at Grand Junction.'

'Fine.' Lassiter pulled back the cocking piece on his rifle. He said to Susan, 'Take her along to John-oh. Then come back here. But leave the bottle.'

She gave him an expressionless look from the small white face. Then she was gone and Lassiter settled down, kneeling with the rifle cradled in his hands, his left elbow on the parapet. He felt the rock-like steadiness of his body and smiled, looked down at the bottle. Then he shook his head. No. This was the cutting edge. Leave it alone.

He heard a mutter of voices on John-oh's side and then the very soft patter of Sue's footfalls as she returned along the catwalk. But he did not turn his head, even when she crouched down next to him.

'Keep away! Don't touch me! You're shaking!'

He felt her inch away. 'That's okay. And keep your head down.'

Something was moving out there. Three dark shapes had slipped forward in their dark robes almost mantled in the night. But he had them pinpointed.

'There! Lew, why don't you——'

'Quiet. Watch the markers.'

The further disc glittered like a tiny catseye. The shapes

came forward in little rushes, five of them now, moving without jerkiness as though they had been oiled. They reached the marker.

Lassiter said quietly, 'Now.' Then the incredibly loud noise of the rifle exploding, a short tongue of flame from the muzzle. One of the shapes spread out with a lifeless flatness and remained still even as the bolt was coming back, the hot case went spinning past Susan's ear, the bolt rammed back and the rifle banged deafeningly again. Another of the dark figures fell. It uttered a little cry and went still. Lassiter said conversationally, 'Put your money where you put your mouth' and fired a third time. Another night-dark figure sprawled out, actually knocking over the marker. Lassiter said, 'Pity,' but even as he was pushing home the bolt the two remaining attackers were gone back into the deeper darkness. From there revengeful eyes winked yellow and something made a cheeping noise overhead and was gone. Lassiter muttered, 'Sour grapes.' Then he looked around for the bottle. 'We must retain that cutting edge.' He grabbed it and swigged again.

John-oh's voice came quietly out of the night. 'Over here, Lew. Lady Teefer says to come.'

'I'm a travelling man,' Lassiter said cheerfully. He took Susan's hand. 'Come along but keep down. That wasn't a bird that flew overhead.'

They reached the western wall. Jane was kneeling halfway along with John-oh. She was so sure of herself that she pointed over the parapet. 'There, Lew. Follow my arm.'

'Okay.' He settled down in the same position as before. 'John-oh, you keep your nose out of this unless I miss. The thing is to impress.'

Again, out of the darkness, the figures came, seven men spread out and more cautious than the first. They passed the first marker and John-oh began to fidget anxiously but Lassiter only fiddled with the sights on his rifle.

'Let's give them some false confidence.' He went still, head down, his right eye hawklike along the sights.

The men neared, gradually closing up. When they reached the second marker they began to run. Susan could see the glint of their rifles in their hands.

Lassiter said, 'Shit, I wasn't expecting that,' and fired,

worked the bolt and fired again and then a third and fourth time so that the shots seemed to run together and the empty cases rattled in quick succession on the catwalk. Four of the running figures dived forward as though for cover, one after another in half-second intervals. But when they struck the desert they rolled on, arms and legs flapping uselessly, tossed like rag dolls with their robes awry and one or two with their bellies showing in the unrespectful way of the sudden dead.

'Okay, John-oh.' Lassiter rested his chin on the gun and ceased to take any further interest. The other three men were running away, their robes spread out like wings, running in terror of the unnaturally accurate hand of death that was striking from the parapet.

John-oh fired the Lebel. It was deafeningly loud, seemingly louder than Lassiter's rifle. Now there were only two survivors, because one of the three had dropped his rifle in a twinkle of reflected moonlight and spread himself out on the sand as though in an attitude of prayer. But he did not move.

Lassiter grunted. 'Lucky shot.'

'Yes, it was.' John-oh stared at the still body of the man his bullet had struck.

'Let the others go. They'll tell their pals Lassiter is here.' He grinned and found the bottle. 'Take Jane around to Nailand. But I think that's all for this evening.' He swigged. 'It's been a pleasure entertaining you. I'm going to sleep in the watch-tower. Call me if you need me.'

John-oh went away with Jane. Nobody said anything. But they watched him, all of them silently, from their various viewpoints.

Lassiter cocked a ribald eye and found Susan. 'Not amused. That's what Queeny Vic. said. You're not amused are you?'

'You've got yourself canned.'

'That may be, that may be.' Lassiter reached for the bottle. His wrist struck it and it went tumbling off the edge of the catwalk. 'The fact of the matter is that there is such a narrow dividing line between the cutting edge and the blunt one that I only just made it.'

'You sure did.' She knelt against where he had turned away from the parapet and put her head against his chest. 'Lew, sometimes you're a mess.'

'Let's take this mess to bed.' He got up quite steadily and went to the watchtower where they had slept last night. The blankets were still there, a deep nest of them. Lassiter more or less dropped into them. He reached out a cold hand and grabbed hers. 'God, I'm so tired. Don't leave me, kid.'

She knelt next to him. He was asleep, already, holding on to her like a little boy who needed security. She released a hand and gently stroked his face. Then she got up and went to the watchtower entrance.

'John-oh.'

'Over here.' She made out his sturdy figure.

'Take Lady Teefer to bed. The Touareg have gone. I'm staying here with Lew.'

*   *   *

'What are you doing, Mr Franc?'

Lola's voice came out of the shadows so unexpectedly that John-oh jumped. 'I'm loading my truck with jerry-cans. Then I'm going to the *guelta* for water. It's our last chance. The Touareg will be back tomorrow.'

'You're insane. They know where the water is. They will kill you there!'

John-oh tried to sound more confident than he felt. 'It's possible. But a Land-Rover is faster than a camel Mrs Nailand. And the Touareg have taken a licking tonight. Eight dead. I hope they will be quite a distance away, mulling over things.' He straightened and closed the back door. 'Apart from which there comes a time when man has to face up to himself. I must do this tonight or be in doubt for ever.'

She studied him very seriously. 'There is no need for doubt. Tonight, up there on the catwalk. You——'

'Ah, yes. I shot a man.' He sounded bitter. 'Like a cardboard cut-out in a target gallery. It was hard even to realize that they were real, that they were human.' He shook his head. 'No, Mrs Nailand, it's not that kind of doubt that I have. I want to know whether I can take a calculated risk. I want to stand on a girder a thousand feet above the ground, and freeze, and go on again without anyone knowing. That's why I want to go to the *guelta*.'

222

She laid a hand on his arm. She did it gently, as though he might shy. 'I am coming with you.'

He looked into the beautiful green eyes and the lovely face palely lit by the moon which stood now directly above the courtyard. 'Why?'

'Because I love you.'

He quivered. 'You must not say that, Mrs Nailand. It is quite wrong to say that.'

'It might be wrong to say it, but it is true. We both said it last night after all. Are you going to deny it now?'

He gave in all at once. 'No. God help me, I am the same, I burst with it.' He took her and held her and they strained against each other, gasping with a sudden mutual intensity.

When she pulled away her eyes were sparkling. 'Look up there. See that star? It is our star of love and hope. We shall follow it all the days of our lives.'

He touched her. 'If you knew how much I . . . you would not believe it possible that one human being could . . . I cannot express in words Mrs Nailand what I feel about . . .' The tumbling half-sentences trailed away.

'I know, Jean.' For the first time she used his Christian name. 'Don't struggle to tell me.' She took him and held him, gently this time, ruffling his hair. They were like that for more than a minute. Then she said, 'If we are going for the water then we must go now.'

'Yes.' He let her go reluctantly and they got into the Land-Rover. He put his hand to the ignition and then brought it back. 'If we do not come back, people might think that we had run away. I left a note in my room saying where I was going.'

She nodded. The big engine caught instantly and he kept it at just over idling level as he eased the truck out of the courtyard. Then they were out on to the hard sand, swinging north, heading directly for the *guelta*. John-oh brought the speed up, and they travelled in silence. Now and then she touched him, and for a while they held hands until the country became rougher and he had to change gear continuously. But all the time she watched him with a loving tenderness that seemed to radiate from her.

He slowed, at last. 'Here we are. It is in there. You will remember that the first time I came here, I was afraid. I

223

imagined I saw a Touareg. I went on my knees and begged for mercy. Then I came here with you and my place of terror became a place of great beauty, like a sanded garden, a small gem in a dead land.'

'I will never forget,' she said.

They drove in, stopped near the *guelta*. Both of them got out and John-oh produced two jerry-cans. But she made him put them down.

'Jean. There might not be a chance again for long time. Let us——'

He reached out and took her. A great delight filled him, an all-powerful sense of manhood that made him feel in that moment that he was invincible. He strained against her, kissing her fiercely and demandingly. With her full firm body against his he lifted his glance for a moment and saw the Touareg at the entrance, mounted on the Hoggar camel the way he had been the last time, silent, watching him.

John-oh went still and rigid. She detected it. She pulled away, looking up into his face. 'What's the matter?'

He turned his head. There was another Touareg behind, and more of them at the side. These were dismounted. He could see the glint of steel amongst their dark robes. Swords.

'The Touareg are here.' He held her so tightly that she quivered in his grasp. 'Do not be afraid. I will always love you. I——'

Hands came out of the darkness and jerked them apart. A shaft of moonlight struck John-oh's face. He shouted at her. 'Do not be afraid! Remember our star? Think of it. Remember our star which is ours, entirely, our star of hope and love, and that we will always follow it——'

The flat of the sword came out of the darkness, swung in a great circle with tremendous force. He was still talking when it struck him across the face, smashing his nose, splintering the skull beneath his forehead, driving his dark hair into the pulp. The sword came away and she saw the two dead eyes glinting like empty mirrors amongst dark oozing liquid, without mirroring the life that had shone from them so fiercely only a moment ago.

He was drooping dead in their grasp when she began to scream.

224

CHAPTER THIRTEEN

NAILAND stood flatfooted in the middle of the courtyard with the new morning sun beating down on him. He studied the tracks left by the tyres of John-oh's Land-Rover with a grace-less disgust, as though they were the spoor of some huge repulsive night-time quarry that had escaped his clutches.

'They've bloody-well done a bunk! They've run away! Je-sus, that lowly bitch and her dusky cock-hound! By God, if ever I get my hands on either of them I'll kill them so slowly.'

Lassiter emerged from the room he shared with John-oh. He walked right up to Nailand and tendered a piece of white paper, 'John-oh went for water. He left this note behind. Lola, presumably, went with him. If you'd bothered to stretch your addled little brain you might have noticed that all the jerry-cans have gone. John-oh wanted to bring in a supply that would have really lasted.'

Nailand hovered. He snatched sulkily at the paper with his little hands, read it with a thundercloud expression he normally assumed when he was not sure of himself. Finally he said stupidly, 'They're certainly taking their own sweet time about it.'

'Exactly. The penny has dropped. They are in trouble of some sort and I don't know what it is.'

All of them stood in the courtyard, even the children. Only Goru was absent but then he was not really part of them. Susan had dark shadows under her eyes. Bowdrey was un-naturally silent for a noisy man. It was noticeable in the unflattering light of early morning that he was bone-thin, especially about the upper body. Ann, nearby, stood with her strong body held neatly in its usual settled way, the way Lassiter would always remember her. Jane was bundled in the same coat she had worn on the catwalk and although it widened her and thickened her, it actually made her seem smaller and older. The haggard face protruded tortoise-like, lined. She shivered permanently. None of them had slept properly, and now they stood staring at the tracks of John-oh's vehicle as though these could impart something.

Lola Nailand walked in through the gateway at this moment. She walked unnaturally erect, as though the movement of her legs and arms and graceful body were remote-controlled. She held her head high, moving towards them in a world totally devoid of the tiniest sound, giving no indication of pain from feet that were bloodied and lacerated from walking, or of embarrassment from the fact that her dress had been slashed to ribbons and most of her body showed through it, or of concern for the fact that the ivory skin of her legs had been made hideous with a hundred tiny knife-cuts.

'John-oh is dead.' The automaton stopped a few yards away. 'They broke his head in with a sword. They played around with me for a while and then Jedren let me go. He sent me with a message.' Her dry, caked lips framed the words carefully, as though she had been mesmerised. 'He said that he has eight dead in exchange for only one, and that he is now angry. He said I must remind Lassiter that he said he might become angry. He said he will be seeing us soon.'

The words stopped. The silence stretched on. Lola looked at her children and smiled. 'I will be all right.' Then her glance went back to the others. 'Even when they took him, he was encouraging me. He said I must not worry, there was our star, up there, our star of hope and love, and that we would follow it all the days of our lives. He was saying it even when the sword smashed his head open and suddenly he was dead.'

Susan walked out from the others. 'Come.' She took Lola's arm. 'Come on, Lola.' The two of them began to walk towards Lola's room and Susan looked back. 'Mrs Bowdrey, I think I'll need help.'

Ann moved out slowly and joined them. She took Lola's other arm and the three of them disappeared through the doorway of Lola's room.

*   *   *

Goru's condition was much improved. He had a glint to the eye and a testiness in his manner. 'I can get up, I am sure.'

'You are staying put.' Lassiter sat on the chair next to the *Sous-Préfet*'s bed. 'Give it another day, if we're still alive, and you will be that much more use to us.'

Goru grunted. 'What's the time?'

'Eleven. It's as hot as hades outside.'

'No sign of Jedren?'

'No.'

'He's there. Have no doubts.'

'I know.'

'A pity about Franc. It was a brave but stupid thing to do. How is Mrs Nailand?'

'In a state of shock. She rambles. We've got her in bed.'

Goru sighed. 'The world—our little piece of it—is in a mess, isn't it.' He didn't expect an answer. Instead he gazed up at the ceiling and went off on a different tack. 'Why did Lady Teefer wait four years before coming to search for her husband's body?'

'That is one of the imponderables I can't figure out.' Lassiter tapped ash. 'The decision was so sudden. She left the States in a hurry without preparation. I think her idea was to start organizing in Algiers but without contacts it wouldn't have been easy. She found me in London. I found Franc for her after she signed me up. Franc got the vehicles together and then we met in Algiers.'

'To leave all that money for so long.' Goru shook his head. 'I can understand Bowdrey. He was perpetually sick and without funds. He only came because he was driven to it, because he read of Lady Teefer's expedition. He leapt to a very logical conclusion.'

Lassiter chuckled. 'She may, of course, have genuinely wanted to find Sir Peter's body.'

'Do you really believe that?'

'No.'

They sat in silence that was both glum and thoughtful. And in this moment the shot came. It was loud but muffled, rolling and echoing around the courtyard, the sounding flung back from wall to wall.

'God, Jedren!' Goru was trying to come up, gasping and wincing from the pain.

'No.' Lassiter was already at the door. 'It came from one of the rooms.' Then he was gone, running as fast as he could across the courtyard.

* * *

Lassiter knelt in the sand of the courtyard. It was hot, now, and it burned his knees but he did not notice. He put his arms around Neil and Thrin, holding them tight against his broad body.

'Your Mum has gone. She is with Jesus.' He squeezed the two frail bodies. He struggled to speak. 'She is safe with Him.'

They were so expressionless. 'When Daddy died the Vicar said the same thing.' It was Neil. 'May I see her?'

'All right.' He took their hands and led them into the room. He uncovered the face. Lola had shot herself directly through the heart with Bowdrey's revolver which she had taken from the Mess, so the perfect features were untouched. They were, if anything, more lovely than ever.

'Mother has gained peace.' Thrin looked down at the almost serene face. 'After Daddy died she never really had it. If she has got peace, now, then I am glad for her.' Tears sprang from her eyes and rolled down the small cheeks. 'I am perfectly satisfied that she is with Him.'

Lassiter held her tightly. 'Cry, Thrin. It is nothing to be ashamed of.'

Lassiter led them out again. He took them to their room. They stood there silently. He made them sit on the bed. 'You must understand something. Joe has no control over you now. Nor has Jane. I will look after you.'

They nodded. 'Is there anything I can get you? Is there anything you would like to do?'

Neil spoke suddenly. 'I would like to talk to someone.'

'All right.' Lassiter got out their tattered mat and unrolled it on the floor. He sat down at one corner and the children at two others. They bowed their heads. When the girl came in quietly they looked up only briefly. She took the fourth corner, sat down, crossed her legs.

'I think I will be able to answer,' she said.

*　　　*　　　*

With the exception of Goru, all of them gathered in the Mess for a skimpy lunch. It was the last of their food and very nearly the last of their water. The children sat between Lassiter and Susan. Bowdrey slumped in a chair across from them, staring at the floor. Nailand and Jane were together. No one had said anything to him. No one had offered their sympathies. He was as unmoved by Lola's passing as by that of a distant acquaintance.

Ann Bowdrey was the last to enter. She went slowly across to Lassiter and gave him a piece of paper. 'Mrs Nailand left a note. It is not a'—her eyes flicked across to the children—'it is not that kind of note. I have read it, and I cannot make head or tail of it.'

The paper had been folded once across. Lassiter opened it. He frowned a moment at the words, then he read:

> ' "In his last binn Sir Peter lies,
> Who knew not what it was to frown;
> Death took him mellow by surprise,
> And in his cellar stopped him down.
> Thomas Love Peacock: Headlong Hall." '

He put the paper on his lap. 'That's all. John-oh told me that when Lola first read that entry in Sir Peter's log-book she said it was from a poem, and that she was sure she knew it, she'd read it somewhere. It is obvious that she remembered, eventually. Possibly even because of her state of grief and shock, she remembered. And it meant something to her. That's why she wrote it down. To help us.' How typical of her, he thought, that even in contemplation of death she had been obliging. So much like Lola. So much like John-oh, whom she had loved. And both of them were dead.

Lassiter got up. He went to the door and looked out upon the bright blaze of the courtyard. 'It means something to me, too, now. I'm afraid I haven't been very bright, because even without knowing the full verse of which Sir Peter gave us only a line it should have dawned on me that he had found this fort in the course of his wandering while he was stranded. Why else should he write "Shades of P.C. Wren" in his log-book? Wren wrote about the Foreign Legion. Books like *Beau Geste*, *Beau Sabreur*. There're others. And forts exactly like this one figure very prominently in his stories.'

He turned back. He looked at no one while sadness passed across his face, making it homely. Then he went to Thrin where she slumped apathetically in the background. He knelt in front of her and put his hands on her shoulders. 'Poor Thrin. You were one of the unloved ones too, weren't you? You

229

needed someone so much to give you the affection you hadn't had since your father died. And he came, too, straight out of the Arabian Nights.'

Lassiter's face changed. "Thrin. T'ekmedhin never left the fort, did he? He was here until I found him in your room after he'd murdered the sergeant. It has to be that way. He could never have come back, and done what he did, without being discovered.'

He made her look at him. 'Where did you hide him, Thrin, you and Neil?'

She began to weep, quietly and without the throat-tearing agony of a child. She wept, and he could see the beauty of the woman who was dawning. 'I have been so wrong. I thought he liked me. He was so different. I——'

'Where did you hide him, Thrin?'

The tears rolled down her cheeks. Her eyes had reddened. She looked at Lassiter showing the yearning for something that had never really existed. She seemed to sigh. 'There is a cellar beneath our room. We found it when we cleared some of the sand. We never went down there ourselves because it was too dark and frightening. But when the *Sous-Préfet* arrived T'ekmedhin asked us to hide him. We had taught him to play Snakes and Ladders. I did not think he was bad. We let him go down there.'

'Thank you.' Lassiter took his hands away but immediately Thrin's face changed, as though she were losing something for ever. She cried out, 'Oh, Lew! I have been so bad!' and this time the crying came from deep within her and only the child was there, clinging to Lassiter with a fierce and desperate need while he looked at the silent people watching them and said, to Thrin and to them, 'It takes an awfully long time to get to know someone. No one will blame you for what happened.'

After a while the crying stopped. Lassiter smiled, getting up. He cocked an eye at Lady Jane. 'I think I know where Sir Peter, is madame.'

Jane released a long, shuddering sigh. 'I think I do, too.' She got up, paler than they had ever seen her, and sucking for breath. 'Come on, girl.' She put out a hand. 'Lew, let's go and have a look.'

CHAPTER FOURTEEN

THE COLEMAN HISSED QUIETLY. There were ten wooden steps and Lassiter took them slowly with Susan following, reaching back and guiding Jane with one hand.

'It's very d-dark. Four more steps, Lady Teefer. Careful. Here.' The hand let go a moment, then took Jane's right ankle and placed it firmly on the next step. 'There. Two more. Give me your other foot. Okay. Now the last one. Stop pushing her, Nailand!'

'I want to see! I want to see!' Nailand's frantic quacking came from above. Only his lower body protruded below the trap in the floor of the children's room, but his knees were bent, pushing hard into Jane's back, hurrying her on.

'Wait your goddam turn,' the girl said implacably. Somewhere up above Bowdrey was braying with impatience. Susan ignored it. 'There is about a two-foot drop to the sand, ma'am.' She reached up and took Jane's frail body under the arms. 'Relax. Let go. I won't let you fall. All right, You're on the sand now.'

The three of them stood bunched together at the foot of the steps. 'Peter. God, Peter! Is he here?' The words tumbled from Jane's thin snakeskin lips.

'The cellar is big.' Lassiter held the Coleman high. Light trembled out across a sandy floor, pushing away the reluctant darkness. The lamp shooshed and gulped as it swung in his hand. The light retreated timidly, advanced again, dashed back once more in fright to cling to them.

'Hold it steady.'

Susan's hand came up and stopped the Coleman's pendulum motion. 'Is that all right? I think I see something.'

'So do I. Over there. Looks like a row of bundles.'

Jane's hand fluttered to her mouth. 'Peter? Is it him?'

'I don't think so.' Lassiter passed the lamp to the girl. 'Hold it like that. I'll have a look.' On his left was a rough yellow-lit wall. He began to move along it, conscious of the rest of the cellar stretching away in darkness to his right.

'Let us down!' Bowdrey had got his head below ceiling level. He craned it, his furious bellow ringing huge and hollow. 'I've a right, too! I've just as much right as Nailand or——'

Lassiter stopped. He could see what the bundles were, now, they were sacks, stuffed full to their mouths, lying neatly along the wall quite close to the steps. There were other things beyond.

He turned to face back the way he had come. 'If you or Nailand give me any more trouble I'll drag you back upstairs and lock you out until we've finished. And if it means cracking your heads together, I'll do it.'

He was not threatening. He was finished with threats, and they knew it. Bowdrey subsided muttering. Nailand's knuckles popped hideously as he ground his hands together.

Lassiter watched them for a moment. Then he turned and went on. He reached the sacks, bent, pulled some papers from the mouth of each, stuffing them into a pocket.

'Hold the lamp a little higher, there're some other things here.' He was talking for Jane's benefit. He heard her shuddering gasp and added quickly, 'So far nothing, Lady Teefer. Sacks filled with what looks like fifty years of waste paper.'

He passed them and the light followed him. His tone changed. 'An ammunition box.' There was a muffled thump as he removed its lid and dropped it. 'Twenty rounds or so at the bottom. The French must have left in a hurry, or else it's defective ammunition.' Again his voice altered, interest charged it. 'What's this?' A pause. Then: 'Two Lebel rifles. One has no bolt. The sights on the other one have been damaged. And a Bren gun with a magazine in place. It's probably as useless as the rest of this stuff. The French obviously abandoned only what was worthless to them.'

'Jesus, Lassiter, get on with it!' Jane's gasping, fluttering voice reached him from the steps. It lacked the cawing harshness even of this morning.

'Yes, for God's sake!' Nailand's own impatience overrode his fear of Lassiter. 'Are you taking a frigging inventory of the place?'

Lassiter came back with the Bren, which he put down next to the steps. 'This interests me.' Then he fiddled in his pockets and brought out the papers he had taken from the sacks. He studied them in the closer, more intense light of the Coleman, dropping them one by one so that they fluttered to the floor.

'Rubbish.' He remembered that Jane was sightless. 'The

232

paper from the sacks is rubbish, madame. Memoranda. Bulletins. Forms, Requisitions. A letter about whether someone has satisfactorily explained loss of a belt buckle. If not forms A, B, C, D must be completed in triplicate.'

There was a short silence. Then Jane said, 'What lies the other way? You've been talking from nearby, on my left. Is there anything across, over there, to the right?' Her blue hair gleamed in the lamplight as it turned.

'That's what we're going to find out. You and me, with Susan.' He faced Nailand, Bowdrey and Ann. They stood awkwardly, almost ridiculously, one above the other in line up the sharp rise of the steps.

'You three will stay here.' He sensed their wild-dog madness. Their eyes glittered as though with fever. It was a fever of a kind, he thought. 'If you come before you're called, there will be trouble.'

They hated him silently, all three of them. But they said nothing. He turned away and took the Coleman from the girl. They started to walk away from the steps with Susan holding Jane's arm. Almost immediately, though, she stopped again.

'Footprints. Look, Lew.'

They stretched away, two sets, sometimes crossing each other, neatly and clearly etched into the sand.

'Teefer. And T'ekmedhin.' Lassiter pointed. 'Teefer moved around. He backtracked at least once. That would be his first and second visits.'

'Oh God, Peter!' Jane's quavery tones rebounded from shadows off the far wall. They started to walk again, slowly, cutting across the ageless footprints. Silence came except for the gentle whoosh of the lamp and the grunting of Jane's quick agonized breathing. The group at the steps had fallen into lighter shadow, but when Lassiter swung the lamp and looked back he could see their eyes gleam like a trio of silently watching wolves.

It was eerie, here in this place that was a vault below the time-lock of the battered caravanserai above and the vastness of the dying desert all around. It was almost cold, and yet Lassiter felt the sweat running down his cheeks, he sensed the tremble in Susan's shoulder when she touched against him, he listened to the reediness of Jane's breathing and realized that all of them were aware of it, they were half-afraid of the darkened tomb in which they walked and the unafraid savagery of the jackals at the steps. . . .

He held the light so high that his knuckles scraped the ceiling. The light rushed away, pushing at the darkness, and in an instant the far wall leapt into relief, disclosing at the same time the frail flung bundle of clothes that had clearly once been a man, and the harsh unsympathetic rectangularity of the suitcases lying near him, that had destroyed him.

'There he is.' Lassiter was surprised at how calm his voice sounded. 'He's there, madame. And the suitcases too.'

There was a moment when time halted. His words were gone into the far shadows and yet time remained quite stationary, as though even his watch had stopped. He felt frozen like the rest of them, and unable to think.

Then time started again. Life leapt once more into animation in an explosion of movement from behind him at the steps, a ragged cry of exultation from Bowdrey, a bitter and frantic cross-cursing as they barged into each other in their pelting run across the cellar floor. Jane was knocked aside and Susan staggered as Bowdrey and Ann burst past them, rushing for the suitcases. Nailand, a yard or two behind, blundered into Lassiter.

'Christ!' Lassiter nearly dropped the lamp. He reeled, regained his footing and caught Nailand by the collar of his shirt, pulling him back. But the man twisted out of his grasp, off balance, weaving and lurching in a desperate attempt not to fall, headed all the time in a dogged and persistent lunge for the unnaturally flat dark spread of clothing that was Sir Peter Teefer.

Lassiter put the Coleman on the sand. The light lowered, but it was still strong enough for him to see Nailand reach his goal and fling himself astride the body, callously straddling it with an asexual lust, his small hands darting forward like the squirming feelers of a tiny squid. The Bowdreys were clambering about the suitcases on hands and knees, sweat-wet and sand-smeared, scrabbling at the untarnished silver clips that winked white fire from the lamplight, struggling, heaving, forcing their fingers under the overhang of the lids.

Lassiter ran forward. He reached Nailand first, bending over the unheeding figure, his fingers sliding off the sweat-slippery neck until they found purchase on Nailand's shirt. He twisted his hands into the cloth, heaved Nailand to his feet, swung him around and hit him savagely in the face.

Nailand's legs took him backwards in reflex action past Susan, who was helping Jane to her feet, until finally he sprawled in a shower of sand lit like sparks by the lamp. He quivered and lay still.

Lassiter watched him for a moment. Then he walked the few paces across to the Bowdreys who ignored him the way Nailand had except at the last moment, when Ann raised her head and he saw in the blank fanaticism of her expression that the girl in the *brauhaus* at Eichstadt was for ever gone. It was a moment of sadness, for something that could have been. But it did not stop him from aiming quite deliberately, and kicking Bert Bowdrey in the side.

Bowdrey fell over and began to cough. He tried to rise, moving a sand-coated elbow feebly like a damaged fin. But the coughing held him; racking him, until he lay back, his chest heaving and subsiding, watching Lassiter out of staring eyes.

Ann ignored him. She looked up as Lassiter turned towards her. She saw the revulsion in his expression and backed away, scrambling on her hands and knees, her hair hanging loose and partly obscuring her face. Sweat shone on her forehead and upper lip.

Lassiter said nothing. He walked very slowly towards the body of Sir Peter Teefer.

Jane's strange gulping voice came to him across a void. 'Is it him, Lew?'

Lassiter stooped over the body. He looked down, and a face looked back at him, a blue-grey face without eyes, but a still beaky nose, lifeless black hair faintly tinged with grey, foppish even now, lipless lips and bared yellow teeth that sucked like an infant mummy at the muzzle of a rifle that was thrust into the tiny black cave between them, a neck wrinkled with its countless mummy wrinkles down which the rifle barrel made a black bar that shone, unlike the lustreless dead skin. The neck lost itself in the folds of an expensive shirt and neat linen jacket, unbuttoned as though for comfort, but the rifle went on to the shrunken hands that clutched it in a deathly love, to the scarecrow leg bent at an almost impossible angle so that the bare elephant-coloured foot could reach the trigger guard where one grey mummified toe still pressed there in a frozen perpetuity of self-murder.

Peter Adair Teefer, Lassiter thought, would be there blowing a hole through the top of his skull for the next million years, while the desert dried, like him.

'God, Lassiter, is it him, why don't you answer?'

'Yes. It's him. He committed suicide with another of the Lebels. He stuck the muzzle in his mouth and pressed the trigger with his toe. The body is mummified.' His head turned for the first time, to where Jane and the girl crouched next to the lamp. 'Want anything more?'

The milky eyes gleamed like discs. They seemed to bore through him. The Coleman tried desperately to hush them all to sleep.

'I thought he had more guts.' The words came, eventually.

Lassiter considered her. Then he gave a grunt of laughter. 'That's your epitaph, not mine.'

Jane got up, using Susan's shoulder as a prop. 'Take me there, girl.'

Susan trembled.

'I don't want to, Lady Teefer.'

'Take me there, girl!' The voice sharpened, there was a hint of the caw in it.

'I . . . the body is mummified. I don't think I——'

'God, Jesus, I pick her off a garbage heap, she's seen things, she's done things in twenty years one solid million women have never done, and she's scared of seeing a mummy like you get them in a museum because Peter's sand ran out, he lost his guts and blew a hole in himself.'

Pudgy fingers tightened around Susan's arm. The many rings dug into her flesh. The gasping voice rasped in her ear with its fluttering wind of stale nicotine. 'Earn your goddam keep, you crud, it's as ugly as all the other things you done except this time you don't get an orgasm!'

The girl and the old woman came forward together, except that this time the old almost led the young. Only the young's eyes worked, they stopped the old in time, just short of the body.

'Search him.' All the old commanding harshness was back in Jane's voice. 'You know what to look for.'

The girl bent slowly and finally knelt. Her hands came out, trembling like the beating wings of a moth, fluttered to the jacket and felt within the outside pockets while her head remained averted.

'An empty packet of *Craven A*.' The thin hands fled to the pocket on the opposite side. They delved. 'A comb.' It dropped on the sand.

'Go on, go on!'

The girl shuddered. Again, the hands moved slowly, hovering like two white gulls above their beachside carrion. One swooped and lifted the jacket, the other darted to the inside breast pocket, pounced and jerked back so suddenly that the wallet flew away and puffed upon the sand.

'Ahah, that was something, whaddya find?' The blued head tracked. 'Purse? Pocket-book? Envelope?'

'A wallet. I've found a wallet, Lady Teefer.'

'Open it, for Chrissake!'

The girl's fingers fumbled the press-stud. 'There's some money. English pounds.' A short pause while she counted. 'Er-er-s-sixty pounds. A credit card. No, two credit cards. Hertz and Diner's Club. A receipt. A bus ticket. That's all.'

'Sure?'

'Yes.'

'Go on, then. They're other pockets. Go through them all, goddamit!'

She moved gingerly to the trousers. 'A handkerchief.' Metal chinked as it fell. 'Some small change. And two er-er-silver keys.'

There was an immediate, loud silence. Bowdrey's coughing had stopped. Nailand, furthest behind, had come upright on his knees. All their eyes focused on the two tiny keys that shone with a beautiful untarnished and innocent brightness in the light of the lamp.

From nowhere, a hand descended and scooped them up. They chinked as they dropped into Lassiter's pocket. 'That's where they'll stay.' He straightened again.

The eyes silently hated him, waiting now, biding their time.

'Nothing else, Lady Teefer.'

'You're wrong. There's still the back pocket. Try that.'

'It will mean turning him over.'

'Then turn him over.' A thought, and a quick warning. 'I can smell you sweating, Lassiter, I can smell your hate. This is my seeing-eye girl. Let her do it.'

Susan's eyes closed. Her head went back, her neck arched, her lips came back from her teeth. 'I can't. I can't. I can't. I . . .'

A hand went over her mouth. Lassiter bent, shaking his head at her to be still. He took the frail body, gripping the trousers at the hips on either side. With a quick movement, he flicked his hands over.

They all heard, in the silence, the dry crack of Sir Peter Adair Teefer's backbone snapping like a powder-dry twig.

Susan whimpered. She crawled away with her hair hanging down across her face and vomited dryly into the sand.

'Some people just haven't got any sand.' Jane seemed finally to accept that Susan was finished. 'Anything there, Lew?'

'No.' Lassiter's hands had investigated. 'Like to feel for yourself?'

'No.' Jane's voice had gone whispery again. She crumpled. 'Nothing underneath? Feel in the sand. Feel deep.'

Lassiter's fingers probed. 'Nothing.'

The Coleman's lullaby hushed along nearby. Its light was dimming. Then Jane said, 'Ahh, God, why did he do this? All those years. All that money, down the drain. That light, Lew, is it going low?'

'Yes, ma'am.'

'It's like me. Got no spirit left. Here, girl. Quit puking and help me up the stairs.'

Susan stood up. She scrubbed a forearm across her lips. Her exhausted eyes flicked across Lassiter's face. Then she silently took Jane by the arm. They moved very slowly away.

'I'll bring the light.' Lassiter picked up the lamp.

At last, the tableau at the suitcases broke. Bowdrey reared up, shaking, barging into Ann as she also rose. 'The keys. They're mine. Give me the keys!'

'Wait a moment, there.' Lassiter watched until Jane and

Susan stopped. Then he took the keys from his pocket and deliberately tossed them on to the sand.

Ann scooped them up an inch from Bowdrey's grasping fingers. She whirled to a suitcase, fumbled, and fitted a key to one of the locks. It clicked away almost in rhythm as she turned it backwards and forwards, fruitlessly.

'It's the wrong——' Bowdrey snatched at her hand as it came away from the case. She held on and they rose to their feet, swaying, scattering sand, locked in a silent battle made more vicious by the look of incurious, detached blankness on their faces as they moved almost in slow motion in a macabre dance, the bare, slim brown feet, sand-painted so that they seemed coated with a glistening gossamer, stepping with rigidly neat movements between the clumsy canvas boots of her partner, backwards and forwards and sideways to a terrible hidden rhythm until a suitcase intruded and they fell, with Bowdrey underneath.

He had hurt himself. He closed his eyes and gasped. He let go his hold on the keys. Ann came erect, clutching them in both hands, cupping them as though to warm them into her favour, moving without haste now, the strong body filled with power and force as she stooped to the other case. A key penetrated and was accepted by the silver lock, there was a moment of neat intercourse and then the clicking climax of its surrender, the clasp flying up like an ejaculation, the woman shuddering with it as though in sympathetic spasm. Then the other lock was done, neat precise fingers lifted the lid, and she froze into complete statuesque immobility, staring at the sea of notes that seemed to blaze at her in the lowering light of the Coleman.

She turned, at last. She showed Lassiter the crazy triumph in her eyes, the culmination of her want, the knowledge that all her winters were gone for ever.

Bowdrey got up on to his knees. He watched in silence while she opened the other case. It, too, showed a flat face of banknotes, pocked in one single place where a packet was missing.

Susan had come back, leaving Jane standing straddle-legged and slack-faced with the Coleman lighting her from beneath and concealing the milkiness of her eyes so that she seemed to have sight, she seemed to be vaguely watching them.

Lassiter pointed to the second case, to the oblong cavity where the one packet of notes was missing. 'T'ekmedhin. This explains many things. He even put the keys back in Teefer's pocket, the clever little bastard.' He shook his head. 'Jedren is a bloody fool. If only he'd come here and said, "I know about the money, I know exactly where it is, I even have a sample in my saddle-bag. God, I'd have given him the lot there and then, and we would still have John-oh and Lola." '

Bowdrey had recovered. 'Give it to him?' He stared at Lassiter in acute astonishment. 'Give it to him? You must be bloody-well mad! That's my money! It's mine and Ann's. You're not giving one single, solitary cent of——'

'Shut up.' Lassiter turned away with the girl.

'The light! We need the light!' Bowdrey got to his feet. 'And we'll need help, getting those suitcases up the stairs, you can't just walk out!'

'We can, you know.' Lassiter picked up the lamp. Susan took Jane's arm. 'Get your own light. And as for the money, it's yours, as you say. Do what you like with it. Put it where the monkey puts his nuts. It's cost too much already. It's not worth having, any more.'

They went up the stairs slowly, so that the light gradually dimmed. But finally it was very dark, a false blackness deeper than night itself, and the two of them sat quietly in it, lost in it, letting the minutes run by. It was Ann who spoke at last.

'It worked out, in the end. We've got it. We're rich, Bert.' Her voice had a strange tonelessness.

'Aye.' He said it like a sigh.

Again the silence. Then: 'There may not be a great deal of time left. We shall have to work very hard. All night, maybe. The Touareg will be back. You heard what Lassiter said.'

'Aye.' He got up. 'I'll get our light.' He began to move away cautiously, feeling his course through the darkness.

'Bert?'

He was already at the steps, there was a pale square of grey light here shafting down from the trap. 'What is it?' He tried unsuccessfully to put impatience into his voice. All he produced was a hard dislike.

'You don't seem very excited. What were you thinking about?'

He chuckled. It surprised even him. 'You wouldn't like it if I told you.'

He went up the stairs and was gone. She sat a moment in the darkness. Then a slender hand reached out and took a bundle of notes from the nearest case. Flipped like a pack of cards, the tips of the notes were soft. They were like velvet. Spread against her cheek they were soft, like the kiss of the lover she had never had. Gently, she stroked them against her skin.

*   *   *

'Give me a drink, Ayrab.' Jane gave a grunt of laughter and shrugged. 'Hell, I'd forgotten he was dead. Get me a drink, Lew.'

Lassiter said nothing. He went to the table where the drinks were and came back with a strong whisky. 'There is very little water.'

'Who cares? I don't.'

There were four of them in the Mess—Jane and Lassiter, Susan and Nailand. Jane had aged unbelievably and it was not so much the small walnut-wrinkled face as the spirit that had gone out of her, the meanness, the hellishness, the braying voice, the crudities, the obscenities, the jeering insults. It was as though, Lassiter thought, that the rottenness inside her could find nothing to feed on and had dried up and withered away.

He sipped at his drink. 'You never knew about the money, did you?'

'Nope. Uh-uh. Not until Bowdrey told us. How'd you guess?'

'It wasn't so hard. You were obviously surprised when Bowdrey came out with it, that night after he'd found the Dakota. Nobody can act that well, even you. And then, in the cellar, you weren't interested in the suitcases. You were concerned only in finding out what Sir Peter had in his clothes. What was it?'

'Negatives.' She found a little animation within and grinned. But it was without the monkey maliciousness that she usually produced. 'Photographic negatives. Gawd, if only you knew. Want to hear the story?'

241

'If you want to tell it.'

'Sure. Why not? Only Sue here knows. That's because she's my eyes. She had to know. Gimme another drink, though, first.'

Lassiter took the half-empty glass, went to the table and freshened it. 'Thanks. Now let's see. It was in 1943, I think. Yeah, it certainly wasn't earlier. I'm fifty-four now, so I was twenty-eight then. Young, mighty good looking, with a body better than Lola's ever was and eyes that worked. And I'd had me a time. Never married. But brother, had I seen life! Hell, I tell you, I'd been born to see the elephant and hear the owl hoot. Anyway, I'd got bored with life in the States, apart from which I was in trouble in one or two places. So I joined the W.A.A.F. I was posted to London where they gave me a job as a filing clerk. By and large I kept office hours so when night time came along I could whoop it up the way I always had. The night clubs were going great guns, and in one of them I met a guy called Hack Johnson.'

She sighed. 'Do I ever regret that. Hack was an army photographer, a great man with the lens, but otherwise a no good, drunken bum. I doubt I ever saw Hack sober after three in the afternoon, and before that he was usually busy getting over the night before.'

She took a sip of her drink. 'This could be a long story, but I'll try and cut it short. One night Hack and I got in with two other guys. I can even remember their names—Merv Jones and Dick Walley. We got canned in Merv's apartment and one thing led to another. I ended up doing the most incredible things with those two guys, things you'd never believe. And Hack was taking photographs all the time.'

Jane gave another humourless grunt of laughter. 'Can't say I'm particularly proud of that evening. Liquor makes you crazy.' She shrugged. 'It was the end, as far as Hack and I were concerned. I told him a few days afterwards that he had the morals of a randy monkey and he agreed, but reckoned that I was the closest thing to an alley cat he'd ever come across. I asked him for the photographs and he said he'd ruined the whole lot in the developing. I didn't believe him but what could I do?'

She handed out her empty glass. 'Come on, this is thirsty

work. Anyway, we parted company. Jones was killed over Berlin about a month later and within days Walley had a buzz-bomb fell on his head. But Hack saw out the war. I heard about him from time to time.'

Lassiter brought her the drink and pressed it into the small, pudgy, beringed hand. 'So I got out in 1945, and was barely back in civvies when I met a guy, quite old already, a nice old feller by the name of Barnes Marlow. He fell for me like a ton of bricks and I was more than ready to settle down. We got married. I was thirty, he was sixty-eight. Hell of a difference, isn't it? But anyway, suddenly I was Mrs Barnes Marlow with a mansion in Virginia and a husband so rich that he employed a team of accountants just to keep the score. I mixed with the blue-blood of America, I'm telling you, and they accepted me because of my name and because I was straight with 'em. I had a social position I'd never had before and it came to mean a hell of a lot to me.'

She took a generous gulp of her drink. 'Poor old guy died within five years. His heart packed up and one morning I woke up, but he didn't. So now I was still Mrs Barnes Marlow, but a widow. The will didn't work out all that well in my favour. I had plenty, sure, but the main inheritance was bequeathed in trust to some nieces and nephews I'd only seen at the wedding. And of what I got, I could only use the interest, and when I died the corpus—at least I think that's what they call it—would also pass on to these kids.'

She lit a cigarette with her usual dexterity and pocketed the lighter. 'At this stage I lost my eyes. It was a rare thing, this disease I got, and I had a team of specialists working on me but there was nothing they could do. I was blind and that was that. I simply had to adjust to it.'

Jane grinned. 'Now we're getting more up to date. You've probably been wondering what all this is about. Well, enter Sir Peter Adair Teefer who was in the States with a British Trade Mission. So now I'm thirty-five, blind, but still good looking and still rich. He married me and took over the mansion. He was younger, but he liked the life of a country gentleman. He settled down nicely and he was very good to me. He ran the estate, rode horses, went shooting. He even taught me to shoot.' She grinned. 'Think that's impossible for a blind person? Well it ain't. The targets had bells attached to them and when he rang one I fired at the sound. Got so that I hardly missed.'

She shrugged. 'Anyway, I said I'd keep this short. The Teefers had always been broke, but Peter was born to the life. At that stage he was my eyes instead of Sue, here.' She smiled quite warmly. 'We had a good life together. I think in his own way he was fond of me.'

A shadow crossed her face and a small spark of the old meanness came out. 'Course, he used to cheat on me. But I always caught up with him. I'd hear talk about someone's good-looking daughter, and I'd put it to him and he'd admit it, and then as punishment I would cut down on his allowance for a couple of months and he would behave for a while. And I forgave him, every time.'

She held up her empty glass. 'Same again, Lew.'

'Take it easy,' he admonished.

'Gimme the drink.' When he shrugged and poured her another she went on: 'That's the way life was for quite a few years—not bliss, but damn enjoyable, with both Peter and I contented with our situation. I went from strength to strength with the social set; I got to know Joe, here. He wrote to me in 1957, renewing old family ties, as he put it, which was nice. He was about the only living relative I knew, so we corresponded.'

Jane's mouth turned down at the corners. Her face went ugly with hate. 'Then came the day. It was about 1958. Peter always brought the mail to me around noon and we would go through it together. Because he was my eyes he opened everything, of course. Whether it was addressed to me personally, or marked "confidential", he opened the lot. On this occasion he said, "Here's one for you from London" and I heard him slit the envelope. Then he went awful still. I asked him what was the matter and he told me there were some photographs and a letter.'

She swung her blind head around at them all. 'You know after all these years, I suspected straight away what they were. I read the letter. It was short enough. The writer wanted one thousand pounds, or copies of the photographs would be posted to the members of my bridge club, investment planning

244

club, friends—a whole lot of people and organizations meaning an awful lot to me.'

'So you paid,' Lassiter said.

'Sure, What else could I do? Those photos must have been terrible. I think even the unshockable Peter was shocked. All he said was, "I never knew you were so supple in your younger days" but he said it in a subdued, wondering kind of way. I asked him what to do. He said, "Is it you?" and I told him sure, it was me, and I told him how it happened. Then he said, simply, "Pay, Jane. You've no other choice." '

She shrugged again. 'So I paid, as Lew here says. But it was the old story. The guy came back, three months later, and wanted again. More, this time. He started to bleed me, and as the months went by he bled me until I started to show more white corpuscles than red. My resources were taking a knock. So with Peter's help I hired a private eye in London, a guy with a really good reputation, but by God it took him two years to find Hack Johnson, who was a dying alcoholic at this stage. Hack certainly wasn't the blackmailer. He'd parted with those negs. years before. But he must have given the detective some sort of rambling trail to work on because after a hell of a long time while I kept on paying, we got a cable one day. It was from the private eye. It said he'd found his man, he would like a representative of mine to be present when the blackmailer was unmasked.'

She waved her hands. 'I couldn't go obviously. So Peter was the logical choice. He flew a lot and had his own plane. One I'd bought him, naturally. Anyway, he agreed to go and when he reached London he sent me a cable after two days saying simply "Got him. Stop worrying." Then he disappeared on his way back, dashing off into the Sahara without ever telling me that he was going to do it.'

Jane cleared her throat and gulped at her drink. 'This is turning out longer than I expected, but there isn't much more. I can understand now, of course, why Peter detoured for the money he knew had been lying out here for all those years. I was keeping him short whenever he misbehaved and he stood to inherit nothing on my death. He wanted to be independent, and I can't blame him for it. At the time, though, I missed him and grieved for him and cursed him for being a silly hare-brained idiot. Then I got over that and thought well, at least I won't be bled any more, those negs. are lying out in the Sahara somewhere. I did try, out of curiosity, to find out the name of the blackmailer and how he'd got on to me, and the only person who could tell me was the private eye. I wrote to him and got a letter back from his wife saying he'd died of a coronary and there was nothing on file. So that was that.'

'Until the blackmailer started up again.' It was Susan, this time.

'That's right, girl, you know the story. Tell them what happened.'

'Lady Teefer dug in her toes.' Susan said. 'She challenged the blackmailer to prove he still had the goods, and after a while she received some more photographs. She paid up quickly. I had just started working for her. I saw the photographs myself. This was 1967. And so Lady Jane went on paying from time to time—an average of about three or four times a year, but always a large amount—until she decided that the only thing to do was to try and find Peter's body in the pretty certain hope that he would have the identity of the blackmailer on him in some form.' She shrugged. 'Except he didn't.'

'That's right.' Jane got up. Susan rose with her but Jane shrugged her off. 'It's okay, girl. I know the way by now. I feel like being on my lonesome for a while.'

She shuffled slowly out of the room. Evening rolled on into night.

CHAPTER FIFTEEN

GORU'S THICK FINGERS came together to form a neat, ridged platform. They hovered for a moment, then briefly and sharply slapped the top of the magazine. There was a small mechanical click as it slipped precisely into place. Sitting upright in bed with his legs crossed, the *Sous-Préfet* reminded Lassiter of a Buddha, a black unsmiling Buddha who intoned a very different kind of chant; 'Bren, Mark 1. Calibre .303, air-cooled, gas operated, effective accurate range 500 yards, cyclic rate of fire 450 to 550 rounds per minute, weight 22 lb. Box magazine normally contains 100 rounds but this one is half full. Barrel life-time approximately ten magazines. This one has fired many more than that. It is worn. It is useless. It would in fact be about as accurate as a drainpipe except at very close quarters.'

For the first time Goru looked up. He had a way of abandoning a subject and darting off on an entirely new tack which Lassiter found amusing. The chocolate-coloured face broke into a smile making him more the Buddha, but less gravely menacing.

'Where are the Touareg, Monsieur Lassiter?' He was being formal today and the smile was humourless. He was very much in earnest.

'Somewhere. Not far. Watching, I suppose.' Lassiter shrugged. 'You know damn well they are hanging around.'

'Yes.' Goru pretended to renew his interest in the Bren which he had recently expertly stripped and inspected.

'I know. But why do they not come?'

'Jedren is cautious. Why should he come busting in here? He knows that if he waits a little longer we will run out of water because of what happened to Franc.'

'He will be watching the *guelta*. He will be watching the route back to Zufra.' A thick tentative finger explored the slightly bell-shaped muzzle of the Bren where it squatted beyond Goru's knees. 'How much does that money mean to you, *mon ami*?'

'Not a great deal.'

'Why?'

'It wouldn't last. I have had money before.' He smiled. 'In any case, the moment we got to Zufra you would impound that money, wouldn't you?'

Goru turned back to Lassiter. He sighed. 'My friend, I am only human. My wife is *very* human. I did have certain ideas, I must confess.' He wagged his head. 'But they were ill-founded. They were creatures of fantasy.' The decision seemed to injure him. 'Yes. I would in fact impound it, although I fear that my domestic life would not be one of considerable bliss for some time to come.' He prodded the Bren as though

247

it had slightly annoyed him. 'The point is that we are not going to get to Zufra, are we?'

Lassiter studied the down-turned head. 'No. We wouldn't get any further than your patrol.'

Goru's gaze remained fixed on the Bren. 'There is a solution, of course. It is a solution which would ensure our safe withdrawal from this place. It is a solution which does not appeal to me but there is absolutely no alternative.'

'Pierre.' Lassiter flicked the cigarette through the doorway into the brazen glare of the courtyard. 'I know exactly what you have in mind. But it will mean trouble with the Bowdreys. They've worked all night over that money, down in the cellar and backwards and forwards up the steps to their quarters. In fact they have hardly slept. They must have counted every last note. Even their hands are red and chaffed from working with it.'

Goru made disgusted noises. 'Aah! The Bowdreys can be dealt with. This solution. If you're such a good mind reader then tell me what it is.'

Lassiter put his hands in his pockets. 'We find Jedren. It shouldn't be difficult. We invite him here. And then we give him the money so that he will go away.'

There was a long pause. Then Goru said, 'Full marks.' Something seemed to strike him as funny. He began to laugh. 'We give him the money. After all this time, all this trouble trying to keep him away from it. In the end we give it to him. We say, "Here, Jedren, Touareg bastard, here is the money. Now go home." Very droll.'

Lassiter also began to laugh. He sat down on the edge of Goru's bed and they laughed, the two of them, there in the shadow of the room while the sun's new morning heat scalded the deserted courtyard.

*   *   *

Bowdrey blinked sweat out of his eyes. His ragged, outraged tones filled the courtyard. 'I'm doing this at gun-point! I want everyone here to know that Ann and I are being forced into this by threats of death!'

Goru smiled equably. They had carried his bed out into the shaded half of the courtyard. Sitting erect he held a Lebel casually across his body. But it was pointed quite firmly at Bowdrey's middle.

'Zat is quite true.' His horrible English made him even more menacing. 'Any more noises, Meester Bowdrey, an' I shoot you anyway.'

Bowdrey quivered. 'You're insane, all of you! The Touareg will kill us in any case, after we've handed over the money.

'Not the way Meester Lassiter will 'andle things,' Goru said confidently. 'Now shut up.'

The *Sous-Préfet*'s rifle pointed a single eye of death at Bowdrey. Goru pulled back the cocking-piece and had one finger curled rather tightly around the trigger. Bowdrey went silent. He stood with Ann just outside their room. The two suitcases lay baking in the sun in the middle of the courtyard. Lady Teefer, Nailand, Susan and the children were ranged around Goru's bed. Lassiter had finished tying a long white pennant to the aerial of his Land-Rover. He came across to them now, lighting a cigarette, the sweat making huge black patches on his khaki shirt.

'All set. I'll drive until I contact Jedren. Then, if possible, I'll bring him back with me.'

'Good luck.' Goru put out a hand and they shook.

'Good luck, Lew.' Susan's quiet voice reached him, as he began to walk away.

Lassiter stopped. He gave her a moment of attention. Then he smiled, winked at the children, turned and went to his truck. The big engine burst into life and he was gone through the gateway in a running fuse of dust, leaving the two groups watching each other silently, with the suitcases in between.

*   *   *

Lassiter drove for an hour without seeing any form of life. The browns and yellows of the desert rolled on with the endless monotony of a dead planet. At the end of the hour he stopped, got out of the truck and fetched his rifle from the back. He held it loosely and indifferently, its muzzle pointing impersonally at the sky. Then he worked the bolt and fired three shots in rapid succession. He listened to their rolling echoes, like the booming barking of baboons in distant mountains.

Nothing happened. Silence came back quickly, as though

resentful of the intrusion. Minutes ticked by. He checked the time on his wristwatch and had a very small mouthful of water from a canteen that was nearly empty. Then he mounted to the roof of the Land-Rover and carefully searched the aching, frozen landscape. Still nothing. He got down, smoked a cigarette and gave himself over to the bleakness of his thoughts. But the moment did not last. The heat desiccated him and he became drowsy. His mind leapt about in patternless impulses and he knew that he was on the verge of an exhausted sleep.

It was ridiculous. It was absurd that his head should want to nod now, when so much depended on him. He forced himself upright. The old boxer, he thought, falls asleep in his corner before the bell for the last round. God, how they'd laugh, how the crowd would laugh, they would fall out into the aisles. The old blind bitch would be there adding her caw-cackle to the din, Nailand would be guffawing and the seeing-eye girl would be weeping bitter tears out of the knowledge that it was too many years on the bottle, too many thousands of gilded golden nights, too many millenniums of dry vomiting in the morning and the ache of his poisoned body, with the knowledge that the glorious giddiness of the darkness was gone.

He took the rest of the water and drank it and flung the bottle on the sand, staring at its coarse green baize cover minutely sparkling with the tear-drops of what he had spilled. No more.

He seemed to stay like that for a very long time. Then, hearing a sound, he came upright very slowly, and turned. He stood straddle-legged with his hands hanging, fighting an eternal weariness that threatened to engulf him in apathy. Jedren and about half his men were forty yards away, miraculously appearing the way they had to Goru on the sand outside the palm-grove of Zufra. Jedren the magician, Jedren the unconquerable. We should never have fought Jedren, he thought, Jedren was part of the Sahara and the Sahara itself could not be overcome.

There were camel tracks leading from an *oued* two hundred yards away. Lassiter forced himself to study them. Jedren the showman, hiding there until the right psychological moment, waiting the hour that was necessary to dry and wither the man who wanted him. Jedren the desert psychologist. He took a deep breath. A haggard grin broke the surface and he was himself again, at least for this while.

'You have a way of popping up rather unexpectedly.' He gestured loosely at the white-pennanted aerial. 'That is a flag of truce. I would like to talk with you.'

Jedren moved his camel forward until about twenty yards separated them. He studied Lassiter from the narrow slit above his *litham*. Slender brown fingers toyed with the striped quirt, the badge of his nobility, that hung from the saddle pommel.

'Why?'

'Because we have found the money.'

'And?'

'We are prepared to abandon it to you.'

Jedren had lost a deal of his mockery. 'Such a change of heart, Monsieur Lassiter. Two days ago you were prepared to kill eight of my men for that money.'

Lassiter shook his head. 'It was not because of the money.'

'Then why did you oppose our entrance to the fort?'

Lassiter studied him for a moment. Then he said, 'Because I had seen the bodies of the Zufra patrol.'

The silence came again. Lassiter moved restlessly. 'If you had said to me, "I know where the money is. It is in the fort. T'ekmedhin found it. I have some in my saddlebag at the moment, and I want the rest." If you had done that, then I think ten people would be alive today who are unnecessarily dead. The woman who was with Franc, at the *guelta* committed suicide yesterday morning.'

Jedren gave no sign of regret. He said indifferently, 'She was weak, that one.' He thought for a moment, frowning at Lassiter across the wide gap between them. 'Things do not always work out the way they might. It is possible that if I had told you what I knew, you might indeed have given up the money. But it is only a possibility. I, personally, do not think you would have. Your mood was stronger. No one had died at that stage. When people die, the resolution of the living weakens.'

He shrugged. 'That is the past, anyway. Now consider this; you have no water and no food. You cannot return to Zufra—you cannot go anywhere—because I cut you off. Obviously, you will only freely abandon the money on condition that I allow you to go. But why should I? I have everything on my side. A few more days and all of you will be dead or too weak to resist.' He paused a moment and then ended abruptly. 'I see no reason to bargain.'

Lassiter toed the sand. 'There are one or two things you might think about. To begin with, the *Sous-Préfet* survived your ambush. He was the only one, and badly wounded, but he lives nevertheless, and he has told me that he had arranged to contact Zufra—if not by radio then by runner. It would have been done by now. The people there, including his wife, will be alarmed. They will have radioed Fort Lamy.' He shrugged as expressively as Jedren. 'Who knows? By now perhaps the Legion is on its way.'

He produced a cigarette and appeared to light it calmly. The only reason his hands did not shake was because of his desperate weariness. 'Then there are another two aspects. Already we know that time is not on your side, it is actually running against you. In addition, we have more supplies than you think. When T'ekmedhin sabotaged our food he missed things. It was inevitable. We can safely last at least another eight days.'

The lie came out quite fluently. 'One final point.' He pretended to lose interest again, looking down at the marks he had drawn in the sand. 'We have a Bren-gun. The French left it in the cellar where the money is.' He brought his eyes up suddenly, looking directly at the Touareg. He even managed a smile. 'If you don't believe me, ask T'ekmedhin. He was in the cellar for quite a long time. He must have seen it.'

They matched glances for a minute or more, like two statues in the baking heat, one neat and belonging, one ragged and alien. Then Jedren held up a hand. He called sharply. There was a stir in the line of mounted men and T'ekmedhin rode forward.

Lassiter recognized him at once—the narrow, graceful body, the coolly arrogant posture, the ferocity of the light eyes that spat venom across the distance between them. There were no shades to this boy, he was more poisonous than the painted snakes with which he had deceived the children.

Jedren spoke in Rifinak. Lassiter understood none of it, but he caught the word 'Bren' mentioned several times. T'ekmedhin replied at length, angrily, his eyes never leaving Lassiter.

'The boy says he saw the machine-gun. The French had left behind three damaged rifles. The man Teefer had used one with which to kill himself. He says the Bren was damaged too, otherwise it would not have been left behind.'

Lassiter pretended indifference. 'He is an expert on weapons, I presume.' He put a sneer into the words, knowing T'ekmedhin was following the French. 'All I can say is that if you would like a practical demonstration you can have it.'

Deliberately, he flicked the butt of his cigarette, as hard as he could, across the gap towards T'ekmedhin. It landed near the camel, spluttering sparks.

'*Merde!*' The boy's eyes blazed hatred.

Lassiter laughed. He said to Jedren. 'I know you will never believe this, but the Teefer group did not know about the existence of the money. At least, not at first. Only the sick man Bowdrey, and his wife. We did not want the money and we never did. That is why we are prepared to abandon it without any regret. That, and to give us the opportunity of getting Madame Teefer, whose heart is bad, back to civilization.' He shook his head. 'But if you do not wish to negotiate then there is nothing more I can say.' He began to turn away. 'May I go? You can kill me, I realize, but the Bren remains at Mazuril.'

Jedren had already made up his mind. 'In a way, Monsieur Lassiter, time works against both of us. I will bargain with you, but only to this extent; give me the money and I will allow you to leave Masuril and proceed to Zufra.'

'There is opportunity for treachery on both sides.' Lassiter opened the door of the Land-Rover. 'You may come as far as one hundred metres from the gates. There, your men must dismount and put their rifles on the sand. I will come out with one other man, carrying the money. You may inspect it, and if you are satisfied then you must take it and leave immediately for wherever you came from.' He smiled. 'The Bren will be mounted between the gates.'

Jedren put up a hand, making Lassiter hover with one foot inside the truck. 'You are dictating terms, and you have no right.' He was angry, now.

'Only for self protection, and out of a desire to be fair.' He met the Touareg's eyes without any hesitation. 'If I had not seen the dead men of the Zufra patrol I would not be doing this. I would invite you to come into the fort, take the money and leave.' It cost him great effort, because his vision was blurring, his eyes were watering as exhaustion finally gained the upper hand. 'I simply do not trust you, Jedren.'

'Nor I you.' It was unusual for the Touareg to snap back so quickly. Both of them were feeling the strain. He added more slowly, 'I approach to a distance of one hundred metres from the fort. My men dismount and lay down their rifles. At this stage the Bren, if it really works, and I must accept that it does, opens fire and the majority of us are slaughtered. You then depart with the money. How does that sound, Monsieur Lassiter?'

'Not unreasonable.' Lassiter fumbled blindly for a cigarette. 'But there is a solution. Long before you reach the agreed distance, I will be waiting at the hundred-metre mark with the other man and the money. You may then approach in any order you like, because we will be directly in the line of fire of the Bren.'

Jedren fiddled with his quirt again, slapping it idly against the saddle. Then he raised his head abruptly. 'All right. I agree.' He looked briefly at the sky. 'I must gather the rest of my men. I should be at Masuril when it is noon.' He began to turn his camel away and then stopped. The serious grey eyes came around like twin gun barrels and sighted on Lassiter. 'One thing. Do not trick me, Lassiter. There will be no second chance.'

'There will be no tricks.' Lassiter considered him. 'The money, Jedren, is a king's ransom. What good will it do you?'

The Touareg's eyes crackled. 'That is no concern of yours.'

Lassiter nodded. 'I have only one regret about this transaction, Jedren.'

'And that is?' The Touareg was relaxed now.

'That I will not have the pleasure of cutting the throat of that small piece of camel dung you carry around in your entourage.' He fixed his glance on T'ekmedhin.

The boy started to quiver. His eyes shrieked their hatred and his right hand streaked to the sleeve of his robe, clamping on the dagger in its arm-sheath, bringing it out in a curving silver parabola that stopped only on the single barked command of his leader.

Jedren was not angry. He considered T'ekmedhin's furious, raging frustration, then turned to Lassiter. 'That was a foolish thing to say.'

Lassiter began to get into the Land-Rover. 'One can be foolish when one is backed by a Bren.'

The Touareg were lost to view. All Lassiter could see were the legs of all the camels like a sparse, hairy knobbled corpse, turn and begin to lunge away across the desert to the *oued* from which they had come.

He sat a moment, head drooped, seeing the sweat fall on to his already wet shirt from the point of his nose. He shuddered. That last remark had been deliberate, calculated, dredged up to convince Jedren of his indifference and the power of the toothless Bren at Masuril. And it had worked.

Lassiter sat quite still while the seconds ticked by. Then he shook his head. The boxer came out after all, he thought, punch drunk and automatically answering the bell.

After a while he started the truck and drove slowly back, following the twin lines of his tyre tracks home.

*   *   *

At noon the sun hung like a giant gong directly over the courtyard, melting the last little scraps of shade. The suitcases lay as though carelessly abandoned on the sand, as though they had been dropped in hasty flight. But they were in fact imprisoned there by the small black muzzle of the Lebel that rested now across Goru's knees.

The *Sous-Préfet* had caused a makeshift awning to be rigged above his bed. He sat upright and cross-legged, still rather Buddha-like except Buddha was now smoking a Gauloise and had a light linen sheet drawn up over his legs. He looked lazily and imperturbably determined, despite his ridiculous appearance. Whenever the face of Bert or Ann Bowdrey would appear in the shade-gloomed doorway of their room across the courtyard, Goru would smile and waggle the muzzle of the rifle very gently. He was amused at their frustration, at the way they would stare at the gun as though it were animated, drop their glance to the suitcases and then retreat once more into the shadowed interior. It was a ritual that had been going on for a long time and Goru was enjoying it because his dislike of the Bowdreys outweighed his personal discomfort.

Lassiter appeared, sweat-sodden and puffy-eyed, rumpled and creased and in brittle mood. He stooped under the awning, sat on the edge of Goru's bed and lit a cigarette.

'Nothing yet?'

'No.' Goru shook his head. 'I have the children watching.' He raised his eyes to the catwalk and Lassiter saw the small forms of Neil and Thrin each crouched at a parapet, resting heavy binoculars through which they stared out into the desert.

'It's time.' Lassiter looked at his wristwatch. 'Five past twelve.'

Goru flicked away his cigarette. 'The Sahara is not the Metropole, or Paddington Station, or Idlewild Airport. Time-tables are unfashionable.'

Lassiter grunted. Goru studied him for a while. 'You did not sleep well since your return, I take it.'

There was a long silence. Goru wagged the muzzle of the rifle at a face that appeared in the Bowdrey's doorway and it disappeared.

Lassiter had watched the incident. Now he turned blood-shot eyes on Goru. 'What are those two idiots doing?'

The *Sous-Préfet* chuckled. 'Hating. Hating us. They cannot believe that we are going to give their money away. They simply cannot accept the idea. It is impossible for them to conceive.'

'They'd better get used to it.'

There was another silence. The heat was aching, draining the liquid from their bodies. Lassiter's eyes drooped. He studied the Bren where it squatted menacingly between the gates, oiled by Goru so that it gleamed with a lethal promise. Jedren, he thought, could have no better proof than that.

'You across there, Lew?' It was Jane's voice.

Lassiter turned. 'Yes, madame.' He rose wearily because she was alone.

Her radar detected the movement. 'Stay put, I'll find you.' Unsteadily, she crossed the sanded gap, took Lassiter's out-stretched arm fumblingly and perched on Goru's bed. 'Ticker's playing up. Gimme strength, Lew. Gimme some of that rough blood in you, gimme that tough indestructible heart.'

'There's no heart left.' Lassiter stood, because there were limits to the capacity of Goru's stretcher.

'Ah, gwan.' She lit a cigarette shakily.

'You shouldn't smoke.'

'The hell with it. This is the end of the road, Lew.'

'For you it's the beginning. The way home.'

'Nuts. I know. I gotta feeling.'

'Where's Susan?'

'Reading Peter's log-book.' The shrug was just a stir of the newly frail shoulders. 'Beats me, why she should. Especially now. Says it interests her.' The blued head turned. 'That you, Joe?'

'Yes.' Nailand was coming towards them across the court-yard.

'Picked you up by the booze smell.' Jane chuckled. 'Started early, huh, cousin?'

Nailand said nothing. He joined them under the awning, sullenly regarding the Bren between the gates.

Lassiter said, 'Nailand, I'll take Bowdrey with me when I go out with the suitcases. You go and lie behind that weapon. If you don't know how to fire it that's all right, it's useless anyway.'

Nailand nodded silently without changing his position. Silence came back that lasted minutes, and then Neil gave a small cry from the catwalk and waved an arm.

Lassiter moved out into the sunlight. 'How far?'

'About half a mile.' It was Thrin. 'There's a lot of them. The whole group, I should think.'

He walked the short distance to the gates and stood next to the Bren. In the distance appeared a long line of cameleers who seemed to swim towards them in the shimmer of the heat haze.

Lassiter turned back. He walked to the suitcases, bent, picked one up and at the same time called sharply, 'Bowdrey!'

The north-countryman's bony face appeared a few paces away in the entrance to his room. He rubbed his reddened, chaffed hands as though they were painful. 'What do you want?'

'They're coming. Do you still want to take the other case?'

'Of course I do.' Bowdrey emerged, blinking in the glare. He fumbled for the handle of the suitcase and finally picked it up with difficulty.

Lassiter considered him. 'You're sick, man, let Nailand take it.'

'Go to bloody hell.' He was struggling not to cough. His hating eyes were fixed on Lassiter. 'It's my money. I want to see it go. I want to go and see you hand it to those robbers, I want your crime exposed. I've got my rights, you know. I'm going to see my solicitor, I'm going to take legal action when I get home.'

Lassiter stared at him. 'You're mad.'

Bowdrey laughed unexpectedly. 'Some might think so.' He turned and laboured out between the gates. Lassiter shrugged and followed him until they reached the hundred-metre mark which was fixed by Lassiter's tin disc.

'Stop here.' Lassiter put the case down. Bowdrey followed suit. Then he put his hands on his knees and sucked for breath.

Minutes passed. The approaching line had ceased to be a bobbing image of delirium-figures. They had firmed into men, armed, silent, purposeful Touareg swathed alike in indigo and white above the browns and greys of their camels.

At last, excitement overtook Lassiter. He felt a fresh, mounting interest. This was the moment when anything could happen. This was the moment when the useless menace of the Bren between the gates could be the deciding factor. Jedren could take, and depart, or take, leave no witnesses, and depart.

Lassiter turned almost idly. 'Bowdrey, they might kill us. I'm sure they would prefer to. I hope you realize that.'

Bowdrey's bitter lips twisted. 'I'd like to see them kill *you*. You and all your stinking group.'

Lassiter shrugged. He watched the line come closer and finally stop within yards of them. The Touareg seemed so tall above their camels, nearly a hundred pairs of eyes watched him above the blue *lithams* with a calm inscrutability. He thought suddenly, with a quick, dawning realization, I know why you hide your faces and your bodies, it's not the desert, it's not the sand, it's not the flies, it's not the hot wind that blows, it is in fact a timeless knowledge that expression is weakness, the face shows so much and the eyes so little. You look upon us and know that we are afraid, and we look back at you and see invincibility.

'Jedren,' he said out of this timeless moment, 'if the Imo-Chagh were ever unveiled they would be lost.'

A tall Tibesti camel, its ancestors taken on a raid perhaps many years before, shrugged forward. The kohled eyes above the *litham* held nothing, although the face might have. Jedren lifted an arm and the camels sank in a long wavering line to the sand, filling the heated air with their complaints. Their riders dismounted. Each man placed his rifle on the sand, carefully, with the bolt upwards so that sand would not enter the action.

Jedren remained mounted. His eyes slid to the gates of the fort, to the squatting Bren and the man who lay behind it. He seemed to measure the weapon, to weigh its gleaming look of competence against the uncalled bluff of its silent belled mouth. He looked at it for moments, and then tore his eyes from it and looked to left and right along the line of his men. Again, he seemed silently to struggle within.

Lassiter licked his lips. One movement, one nod of Jedren's head, and the desert lions would regain their claws and bound forward. He and Bowdrey would die very quickly, those in the fort a few seconds later.

Jedren's hand came down from the pommel of his saddle. He reached quickly and expertly for the Lebel in its scabbard. The rifle came out with a smooth and ready expectancy, for one moment showing Lassiter its single eye of death. The long line of men were turned, tensed. Then the barrel was pointing at the sky and the butt was coming down towards Lassiter, hovering before him so that he could see the grain in its oiled surface. His hand came out automatically and took it, his body bent as a reflex action and laid it on the sand. He stood up and found himself trembling.

'Do you expect me to dismount?' Jedren's tones were unashamed, unregretful. He had seen what Lassiter had promised, weighed his chances in the balance of his cool and cautious mind, and reached a logical decision. Only madmen charged a machine-gun.

Lassiter shook his head. 'Not if you don't wish to.'

A brown, longfingered hand pointed. 'The money is in those suitcases?'

'Yes.' It was Bowdrey answering, in a strange, unnatural, croaking distortion of a voice.

'Are they locked?'

'Yes.'

'Open them.' The voice was quiet, implacable, even contemptuous of the scarecrow figure struggling with a shaking hand to force its sweaty wetness through the dragging cloth of his pocket. The keys came out, twinkling bright in the sunlight, spun in the air as they jerked from Bowdrey's spasming hand and fell with a tiny clink upon the sand.

Bowdrey fell on his knees. He snatched at the keys, crawled over to one of the cases and fumbled in a world totally devoid of sound until the catches snicked and the lid was flung up.

The notes blazed at Jedren, they blinded him with their richness. His eyes stirred at last. Bowdrey opened the other case and the richness of both cases joined and became one in his mind, they became ten thousand men racing down a slope, they became the clack of a thousand machine-guns competently cocked, they became the blinding brassy sea of a million belts of ammunition.

'Show me the money.' The swathed head turned quickly, confidently to the men ranged along either side of him. They saw the flash of his eyes and began to murmur. Bowdrey thrust two packets of notes in Jedren's hands and the murmur became a sea of talk while the brown fingers flicked the notes so that they blurred momentarily like cards. Then the hand went aloft, it rocketed high above the indigoed head, it waved the notes like a signal flag while the eyes flamed with a blazing triumph and the talk became a ragged swelling roar of acclamation.

Jedren let it last a moment, no more. Then the hand came down, a voice barked one single command, and silence fell. The two packets of notes fell at Bowdrey's feet.

'Put them back in the case.'

Bowdrey went on his knees again, absurdly. He crawled back to the suitcases, replaced the notes with shaking hands. Then he lowered the lids, snicked the clasps into position and fumblingly locked each case in turn.

'Give me the keys.'

Bowdrey stood up. His mouth gaped open, ringed by lips grey and dry and cracked like snakeskin. Two trembling fingers held out the keys.

Another command. Four Touareg broke away from the rest. They rushed in upon the suitcases, pushing Lassiter and Bowdrey aside, taking them and hurrying away with them towards a group of pack camels where more men waited with thongs to lash the cases into place.

'My rifle, please.' Jedren's voice was jeering again, it touched Lassiter with the light brushing feathers of its mockery.

He reached down, picked up the Lebel, gave it to Jedren who held it in one hand with the muzzle nearly touching Lassiter's forehead.

'So easy, Monsieur Lassiter.'

'I do not mind.' Lassiter heard his voice from some distant place. 'You are killing nothing.'

Jedren considered the man below him. Abruptly, he stopped his game. The rifle was scabbarded, a commanding hand raised. Over a hundred camels saturated the air with their woeful moaning.

'It has been a pleasure to have known you, Monsieur Lassiter.' The tall figure was still as the rest of the camels turned. The grey eyes regarded him with interest. 'It is a pity we could not have drunk tea together, if the circumstances had been different. Touareg mint tea is delicious.'

Lassiter said nothing. Jedren watched him a moment more, then he raised a hand, turned, and the camels moved away in line abreast, eating away the desert in their rocking, ground-consuming motion until they became once more delirium-figures in a waterless sea that swam and bobbed and weaved their way towards the horizon.

It was as though a year had passed. Lassiter turned slowly and achingly.

'Let's go.'

Very slowly, they began to walk back towards the gates where Nailand had already abandoned the Bren. It squatted there suddenly devoid of its menace, in forlorn mechanical disgrace.

Bowdrey stopped. He bent over, placing his sweating hands on the gritted, sand-covered boniness of his knees. His shoulders shook. His scrawny neck quivered and spasmed.

Lassiter considered him as a figure apart. 'The money has gone, Bowdrey. It is no use weeping. Weep now, and you will weep for it all the rest of your life.'

The thin man slowly straightened. His head rolled loosely on his shoulders and he showed Lassiter the craziness of his eyes. 'You bloody fool.' He began to cough. Phlegm appeared in a clot on his lips and slid down his chin. He fought desperately against the spasm. 'You bloody fool. I'm not weeping. Can't you see I'm laughing?'

A figure appeared next to Lassiter, a calm figure tanned light biscuit-brown by the sun, a figure of settled purpose holding a stainless-steel box in which lay a hypodermic and an ampoule of liquid.

'Will it help?' Lassiter watched the rock-steady movements of the slender hands as the hypodermic greedily sucked the ampoule dry.

Steady grey eyes met his, eyes without the last remaining dreg of emotion, without feeling of any sort. A robot beautiful mouth framed the indifferent words.

'I don't know.'

Lassiter watched while she bent to give the injection. Then he turned and walked with slow and exhausted steps into the courtyard where the first touch of shadow was beginning to edge the sun from the deepest corners.

*   *   *

Goru let the Lebel fall with a careless thump on to the shaded sand next to his stretcher. It was uncharacteristic of him, and done only because he was torn by relief at seeing the Touareg ride away, and anger that the deaths of his men had not been avenged.

'Zat is all.'

Jane flicked away her cigarette. 'They've gone?'

'Yes.' The *Sous-Préfet* watched Nailand come slowly back from where he had been lying behind the Bren. His face had an unnatural pallor and his movements were stiff, as though the sun had desiccated him. The young seeing-eye girl whose name he could never remember emerged from a shadowed doorway at the same moment, wan-faced and lustreless, trailing dispiritedly across towards them with a book held loosely in one hand so that she and Nailand arrowed from different angles towards the same point. Further out, Bowdrey had collapsed on the sand between the gates and Lassiter was watching him with a detached interest, as though the sick man were two-dimensional. The Bowdrey woman was moving towards them very slowly as though time was of no consequence.

We must go, Goru thought, before we all die. He, too, had been struck by a sudden anti-climactic apathy. It was dangerous, losing one's purpose like this. They had lost the sense of the meaning of things and it could kill them.

Nailand and Susan reached the awning at the same time. The girl said quietly, 'Lady Teefer, I have found another entry in Sir Peter's log-book.'

They stared at her. Jane had lit another cigarette. 'What was that?'

'There is another entry in the log-book. It was written in a blank space between some of the routine entries.' The thin shoulders rose and fell in a disinterested shrug. 'We only looked at the end. But there was no reason, I suppose, why he shouldn't write anywhere he chose, especially later on when he might have had *cafard*.'

There was an unnecessary silence. It was as though they had become stupid, all of them. 'What's it say, girl?'

Susan opened the book. All of them could see the neat firm entries made in blue ballpoint, and the shaky pencilled scrawl in a gap between. She read without any expression: ' "All you want, Jane, seven inches beneath what you treasured most." '

Jane's harsh, cawing cackle filled the air, it rolled about the courtyard so that the two small figures on the catwalk turned and looked down. It was, Goru thought, a return from their present lunacy to a near normality, because complete peace these unloved people would never know.

'God almighty! That's just like him, that's just the sort of thing the old bastard would have written.' Jane got up, filled with a visible excitement. 'Come on, girl, we got things to do.'

'You know what it means?'

'Sure I do, kid, sure I do.' She took the girl's arm. 'C'mon, now! Haven't got all the time in the world.'

They moved off across the courtyard unaware of the sun's beat, walking slowly like dream-figures towards the doorways on the other side.

*   *   *

The Coleman hissed softly in the sand near the scarecrow that was the body of Sir Peter Teefer. Jane sat down beyond it near the two oblong squares in the sand that marked the place where the suitcases had rested for four years.

'You leave me now girl.' She almost primly settled herself. 'I'll be just fine.'

Susan looked down at the small figure. 'I don't fully understand. I think I'd betta stay here with you.'

'Nuts. You get outta here and take the lamp with you. You can leave the trap-door open. I'll be along in a while.'

The girl hesitated. 'I don't like the idea of leaving you all alone.'

Jane cackled briefly. 'Because you like me so much, huh, kid? That's why you want to stay with me?'

The girl was silent. Jane nodded, almost in approval. 'Sure. Of course you don't like me, and you can't kid yourself. I picked you off a garbage heap and dressed you and fed you and paid you a salary and at the same time I insulted you, humiliated you, demeaned you in public. You were my seeing-eye girl and about the most we can say is that we respect each other. At least, now we do. That's about the long and the short of it.' There was a pause. Then the old, fierce tones came out in a rush. 'Go 'way, get outta here. Leave me be!'

Susan picked up the Coleman. She stood for a moment considering Jane. Then she turned and walked slowly across the sand of the cellar to the steps.

She was beginning to climb them when the voice reached her out of the near-darkness.

'Good luck, girl.'

Susan stopped. She held the lamp a little higher. Then she said, 'Thank you, Lady Teefer,' and went on up the steps so that the light diminished and finally died, leaving her in a world of blackness that was her world anyway.

Time passed. She knew that her breathing was acutely short and that her heart was worse than it had been in a long time, but she muttered, 'The heck with that anyway,' and lit a cigarette, becoming lost in a world of speculation that jumped from one thought to another but returned always to the conviction that hers had been the hand that had figuratively cast the net that had enmeshed so many people: Jedren and his People of the Veil, coming out of nowhere with the scent of riches floating on a hot desert wind and returning into nowhere richer than their dreams; the fat, fussy *Sous-Préfet* whose warnings had been so coldbloodedly and deliberately ignored; Lassiter, with his golden night-time moods, and the broken bridge in Zambia and the two dead children locked for ever in an ache within him; Susan Shields, who had lived two lifetimes in twenty-one years and was finding it a burden too great to bear; those two kids who——

Her mind stopped with the fierceness of brakes suddenly and deliberately applied. All her senses leapt to a quivering attention.

She had heard the faint scuffle of a foot on the first of the cellar steps.

Jane's breathing-rate increased to the extent that she had consciously to restrain it. No time now, she thought, to blow that wonky fuse. Quickly she extinguished her cigarette by pushing it into the sand. There was the sound of the trapdoor thudding heavily into place, followed by an immediate angry, but muffled and cautious curse. Jane grinned in the darkness.

A match flared. She heard the sizzle of it. The feet came on down the steps and crunched on the sand. There was the sound of quick, nervous, frightened breathing. The person was moving in a tiny pool of match-light towards the end of the cellar, towards Sir Peter Teefer's body, and her.

'So you came.' She chuckled. 'I figured you would.'

The match went out. She detected even the tiny tick of her dead stick touching the sand.

'That's no goddam use. The darkness doesn't hide you from me, I live in it dammit, I'm in it all the time. You're only hiding from yourself.' A warning note came into her voice. 'But keep the light out. The Bowdreys left a lamp and a gas lighter down here. Don't light it because if you did you might try something silly.'

She listened a moment to the panting of the breathing. To her it was almost loud. 'It's better, this way. Gives me the advantage. This way I can kill you without a hell of a lot of difficulty. Don't you remember my telling everyone how Peter taught me to shoot by sound? I know exactly where you are and I've got Bowdrey's Webley here. And it's the only thing left to do, isn't it? I'm sick and tired of paying.'

There was a long pause. She grinned when she heard the tiny rattle of the matches in their box, the beginning of the scrape of one along the box's side. She was holding Bowdrey's revolver in her hands, the hammer on full cock. She fired and in the aftermath of the deafening thunder of the explosion she heard the terrified gasp of breath.

'Close, huh? Now behave yourself. And I can tell you right now that crawling up to Peter and digging away under his balls isn't going to help you any. Susan and I concocted that entry. I dictated it and she wrote it. There's no evidence. There're no negatives. It's all a gag. We played out a little act under the *Sous-Préfet's* awning but it worked rather well, didn't it, Joe?

Another sharply-drawn intake of breath. Jane grunted. 'Hell, don't sound so surprised. I've suspected it was you for a long time and I've been positive in my mind these past few days. Give me credit for *some* brains, although they've taken one hell of a long time to function. But I've had time to think and on top of that you've made some pretty bad mistakes. The worst, of course, was sending the first blackmail letter in braille. Don't you remember, when I was telling my story the other night, I said Peter opened the letter and *I read it*?'

She sighed. 'There're a whole lot more things. Like you were moving around England at a rate of knots because every business you touched went bust, but the blackmail letters, although they also came from all over the place, *never* came from the same town or city where you happened to be. It was too good to be true.'

There was no answer, just the quick in-and-out breathing. 'Playing it cool, huh? Won't help you any, dear old cousin. You gave yourself away so often that even a blind old fool like me couldn't help but catch on. Like the way you came tearing over to the States the moment you read that I was planning this expedition, all set to help me out.' She gave a disgusted grunt. 'Gawd, all you wanted to do was come along and make damn sure I didn't find the evidence I was looking for.'

Still, there was no answer. Jane chuckled. 'Who wanted to high-tail it when the Touareg appeared on the scene? Good old cousin Joe. To hell with the money Peter had found, you had your own source. You only gave in on that one when you realised you were making a fool of yourself. And then Lola told me the truth about what happened when you found Peter's plane, how crazy you were to be the first to read the log-book, first into the cabin—that's why you shot the trooper, isn't it, Joe? You hadn't had a proper chance to read the log-book yourself and you were dead scared it might give you away. Same reason, when we finally found the money, that you went for Peter's body while the Bowdreys were halle-lujahing around the suitcases. Lassiter had to hit you to get you out of the way.'

Nailand lay in the darkness, grinding his sweating hands together. His heart thundered so within him that he was afraid she might hear it. He got down on his belly while she talked.

'There's no need to do anything rash, Jane,' His voice trembled out of the darkness. 'You know who it is, now. I'm no danger to you any more. I promise. I give you my word on oath, that it will stop. You'll only hang if you kill me.'

'Your word?' Her voice was larded with contempt. 'Listen, you must have hundreds of prints of those negatives, whatever Peter did with them, and whether I know you or not doesn't mean a damn. You can still bleed me. You think I want all my friends and connections to know what I got up to one crazy evening?'

'Jane.' His voice was a desperate drone. 'I promise. I'll go back to England. You'll never hear another word from me again.'

'Nuts. I'm going to make damn sure you don't leave this cellar. And as for hanging, do you think the others are going to give a damn? Do you think a man like Lassiter would report me after what you did to John-oh and Lola? Do you think the *Sous-Préfet* would bother, after what you did to his trooper? Talk sense Joe, don't try and scare me.'

Nailand was desperately afraid. Icy sweat cascaded out of his body and saturated his clothes. He trembled. And he had a knowledge of that deadly gun-muzzle aimed inexorably at him, linked to him like Asdic by his sounds, by the mere waves of his presence.

He said, 'I never meant any harm. I got on to you by sheer chance.' He had a picture in his mind of the Bowdreys' lamp and gas lighter, something he had automatically detected before his match had gone out. They were lying very close to Teefer's body. God, if only he could reach the lighter, it would burn without a sound, one more foot and with a stretch of his fingers he was sure he could do it. I don't want to die here in this cellar with a mad woman, he thought, if I can reach the lighter and get at the Lebel Teefer used to kill himself, at least I can even chances, I can . . .

He forced himself to stop thinking. He began to talk desperately while his body wormed along the sand with the slowness of an infant in new animation.

'In 1957 I bought a photographic studio with all the capital I had left. My previous business hadn't worked out.'

She chuckled without humour. 'They never do, do they? Come on, let's hear it, I want to know how you got on to me. Did you know Hack Johnson?'

Nailand's chin was scraping the sand, he was so flattened out. 'I'd never heard of him until you spoke about him two nights ago. As I've said, I bought this studio. I felt I could make a go of things at last. It was in a mess. The previous owner had obviously made quite a living out of pornographic pictures. I threw most of them away but there was one particular set of negatives put aside in a special place. They were of very good quality, taken by a man who knew his business. I printed them out of curiosity, then I enlarged one or two and got the shock of my life.'

A laugh, this time. 'Recognized cousin Jane, huh?'

He had to fight to keep his voice from trembling, and to keep it low so that she wouldn't detect the fact that he was growing gradually nearer. His groping fingers reached out, fumbled, touched something cold and metallic. Bowdrey's lighter! Trembling, he drew in his hand and held the lighter close to his body. It would light soundlessly, he was sure.

'That's right. My mother had a picture of you at home, taken just prior to the war. I'd seen it hundreds of times before she died. But I wasn't completely sure. I found out your address and wrote to you. You sent me pictures and details of your war-time career and then I was certain.'

He coughed, forcefully and harshly, and at the same time pressed the lighter. It burned instantly with a pure blue flame, beautiful to him in that moment, showing Teefer's ragged body and the shining Lebel so near. Only a few more inches. Beyond, Jane sat like a crone, her knees drawn up and the heavy barrel of the Webley balanced upon them. It was pointing at him, but not directly. She had missed his change of direction. A warm triumph began to fill him.

'Once I was certain, I started blackmailing you. I only wanted one payment, really. In fact if I had thought you would be sympathetic I might have asked you straight-forwardly for a loan. But I guessed you weren't the lending type. So I made it blackmail. And it worked.'

'Worked? By God, it worked.' Jane's lips came back from her teeth in a snarl. 'Only trouble was, you kept going bust, you're such a goddam idiot, and you kept on needing money.'

'That wasn't my fault!' Nailand flared. 'Money is nothing to me. It's a commodity. I can buy and sell money every day of my life. I was duped by fools and tricksters!' He shrugged in the darkness. No need to get upset. The lighter was growing hot in his hand. The Lebel was only inches away. All he had to do was get her to talk while he made his dispositions.

He went on. 'Anyway, they got me in the end. I used a whole series of addresses, as you know, and go-betweens as well, but in the end the detective got me while I was in the act of opening the post-box. Teefer was with him. They took me to their car and got me to admit everything. The detective wrote it all out and I signed it. Then they let me go.' He shuddered, remembering that nightmare scene and the terror of those moments.

'I went home. I went to my study and took out my revolver from a drawer. I had the muzzle to my head when Teefer walked in and stopped me. He showed me the negatives I'd

269

handed over. Don't be silly, he said, you can copy them, can't you? I told him yes, I could. So he said I was to go ahead. I was to make a whole set of prints which I could re-photograph whenever I needed to. He would give you the negatives, he said. Then I should wait six months. After that a new blackmailer would appear on the scene. Those negatives had been kicking around since the war. They could have been printed hundreds of times. Only this time he and I would split the profit.'

'That's a goddam lie!' Jane's furious bray bellowed out of the darkness. 'That's one thing my Peter would never have done. By God, do you really expect me to believe that crap?'

'It's true.' Nailand put out his shaking hand, touching the Lebel, tugging at it, loosening it from the frail grip of the long-dead fingers.

'Never!' Jane was almost weeping with fury. 'You bastard, you've made that up to upset me and it won't work. Peter never did a thing like that——'

He had the Lebel in his hands. The bolt flicked back and thrust home over a fresh cartridge. But she had heard the clack of the action. Even as he was bringing the long barrel around she had thrust the revolver forward and its muzzle grinned at him like the mouth of the person who was aiming it.

Nailand knew in that last fraction of a second that he was too late. He was committed to his movement, there was no time to dodge. He had time only to say, 'Jane . . . I . . .' and then the revolver had thundered and he was lying on his back, knocked over by the force of the big bullet, feeling a numbness creep over his body. Darkness gathered in on him. He said, 'I think the lamp is going out,' and then the darkness was final.

Jane crawled over to him. She felt him and knew he was dead. She chuckled weakly, got unsteadily to her feet and made her way to the stairs. Something bad had happened to her heart in the tension of those moments. She was fighting for air.

'Got to get my goddam pills.' She fumbled for the stairs, found them, made her way painfully upward until her grasping fingers found the trap-door. She pushed. It remained immovable. She worked her way up another step, got her shoulder against the heavy wood and heaved. It remained as unshakeable as before, and the effort had greatly weakened her. She tried twice more until she realized that each push was considerably fainter than the one before.

'Hey, you up there.' It was a call for help, but she realized that the words were no stronger than a whisper. She tried again, but the whisper had possessed her body and her voice had gone.

She remained at the top of the stairs for a minute or two. Her heart was trying to beat its way out of her body now and she was perspiring in streams, icy cold sweat that gushed out of her as though from every pore.

Finally she shrugged. She clambered very slowly down the steps again. Her progress over the sand was a shuffle. When she reached her husband's body she knelt to make sure it was him. Then she lay down next to it.

'I don't believe a word of what he said.' The whisper came out like a cry of confidence four years late. Then she grinned, that old monkey-like grin of hers. 'Move over, you bastard, you're taking up too much of the blanket.'

She lay there next to him, contented, waiting for the last darkness that she knew would not be long in coming.

*   *   *

'The bloody thing is stuck.' Lassiter heaved at the ring. Fresh sweat burst out all over his face. He braced his back and the sinews in his neck corded. With a whoosh of air the trap-door burst open. He staggered back, cannoned into the wall. But there was no time to waste. The Coleman was burning quietly next to the dark rectangle of the opening.

'Stay here. There's no need for you to come.' He said it to Susan, already going down the steps, taking the Coleman off the floor when it was at waist level to him. He said, 'That's cordite I can smell,' and then he was gone.

He was away only a minute or two. He came up very slowly. He stood on the top step so that his head was nearly level with hers and stared at her. 'Nailand's dead. Jane clearly shot him. She's dead, too.'

She looked straight into his eyes. 'It's a long story. I'll tell you some time.'

'I think I can guess most of it.' He came up to floor level and took her arm. 'Come on. We're leaving. Let's go.'

They ran out together into the beating heat of the courtyard to where the two Land-Rovers squatted bumper-to-bumper, nearly ready to go.

CHAPTER SIXTEEN

LASSITER looked at the suitcase on John-oh's bed. Then his glance moved to the small pile of belongings next to it. He picked up a shirt. Light cotton. No name-tab. It could have belonged to anyone. So could all the other things, they were as featureless and as anonymous. A pocket knife. Some coins. A tube of lip-ice. No rabbit's foot, no photographs, no old letters from someone, sometime, when a person like John-oh died it was like blowing out a small candle and trying to remember the flame.

He turned away and picked up his own suitcase. When he looked up he saw Susan standing in the doorway, watching him. She looked briefly back at the bed.

'John-oh's things?'

He nodded. 'Let's go.'

'You're not taking them?'

'No.' He found himself making a small puffing sound with his lips. The candle, going out. 'John-oh's gone. What am I going to do with that stuff, give it to charity in Algiers?' He shook his head. 'Leave it for the Toubou.'

She was still blocking the doorway. He moved impatiently. 'I don't want to miss Zufra after dark. Are you ready?' When she nodded he added, 'The children. Is their gear loaded?'

Again the nod.

'Jane's clobber?'

'No.'

'Why?'

She stirred. Her eyes had a depthless quality. 'The same reason you gave. Leave it for the Toubou.'

There was a stillness between them of reflection. He had to force himself to move, and this time she moved to one side and they went together out into the baking heat of the courtyard where the shadows on the western side had grown longer.

Lassiter was struck immediately by the scald of Bowdrey's furious voice. He found himself looking into the raging face with its over-bright eyes and fevered cheeks.

'The *Sous-Préfet* says he's coming in my vehicle. Has he got sunstroke?' He stood quivering, cocked like a gun, waiting for the answer.

'You know bloody well that he hasn't. There're four of us plus a lot of camping equipment. We have to load Lieutenant Goru bed and all, and you've got the room. It's as simple as that.'

'It is not!' Bowdrey's breath wheezed between sentences from his rotten lungs. 'You talk about room? Christ, man, look at that lot!' He waved a hand towards the open rear of his truck, and Lassiter saw the same graceless assortment of bulging blanket bundles and frayed cardboard boxes that had been brought out the day the Touareg had arrived. While he watched, Ann came from their room with another box and he found himself incongruously reading the stencilled legend on its side. Bully beef. It typified the Bowdreys: bully beef and the heterogeneous collection of morbid-looking containers.

He hung on to his temper. 'I still say you've got the room. And it's only till Zufra, anyway.'

This appeared to incense Bowdrey still further. 'I don't care if it's till Blackpool! You can take that fat black bastard and his half-ton arse and put him in your truck!' He sucked for breath while another idea appeared to take him. 'Why don't you fetch Franc's truck from the *guelta*, anyway? The Touareg have gone, if that's what you're worried about.'

Lassiter shook his head. 'It simply isn't worth the trouble. It's bound to have been smashed. They wouldn't just leave it there.' He hunted for words for a moment, finding difficulty in conveying his own sense of mounting urgency. 'It's the time factor, Bowdrey. The afternoon is wearing on. We have no food at all, no water at all. You're sick, Goru is wounded. The children are showing signs of dehydration. I——'

From across the courtyard Goru's voice called in French. Lassiter shrugged. 'There's an end to it. The *Sous-Préfet* says that if you don't co-operate he will shoot you with that Lebel. He says he hopes that you ignore his warning because nothing would give him greater pleasure than to put a hole in your belly.'

Bowdrey's rage and his caution struggled with one another. He opened his mouth for another braying bellow, then shut it again. He looked uncertainly across at Goru who smiled encouragingly, patting the rifle.

Bowdrey panted his anguish.

'Bert.' The clear, unexcited voice came from the doorway of his room. He turned and saw Ann standing there. He read the decision on her face and Lassiter watched while conflicting emotions shuttled patiently across the bony face.

'She's always agin me.' The thin shoulders hardly stirred the over-voluminous drape of his shirt. Bowdrey had lost pounds in weight over the past few days. 'Do what you like. Put him on the frigging bonnet if you wish.'

Lassiter watched him walk away. He lit a cigarette and put on his sunglasses. Then he went to Goru and perched like a weary and worried stork on the edge of the bed.

'Thank you. It was reaching a point where the only thing left to do was hit him.'

Goru waved a hand. 'A pleasure. I also have this feeling that we should hurry.'

'Would you really have shot Bowdrey?'

'Indubitably.' Goru produced an enigmatic smile, 'Any hesitation on my part would have been only because creatures of such incredible volume are rare.'

Lassiter flicked away the half-smoked cigarette and moved out from under the awning. He whistled and waved a hand. The children came immediately with Susan Shields, the Bowdreys trailing behind with deliberate reluctance.

'Everybody grab some part of the stretcher. Then we'll drag it across to the truck and heave it in.'

The Bowdreys and Susan took one side, Lassiter the other, and the children the top and bottom. In a sort of crabwise movement they struggled across the sand to the Land-Rover. Panting, they slid the stretcher into Bowdrey's truck from the rear, so that Goru faced the back doors. Enthroned there, he smiled at their sweating faces.

Lassiter was puffing. He had borne most of the effort of the final lift. 'For a man who has hardly eaten over the last forty-eight hours you seem actually to have gained weight.' In truth the *Sous-Préfet* seemed oddly bulky under the drape of the sheet that covered his legs.

'I have heavy bones,' Goru said. 'All my family have heavy bones.' He surveyed the stacked jumble of boxes and bundles on either side of him with distaste and tucked the white sheet more firmly about his middle, patently disassociating himself from the mess. 'I suppose it is better than a camel.' Then, almost primly, 'You may close the doors.'

Lassiter slammed them. He lifted his sunglasses and let the accumulated sweat run out from under them. 'Ready?' He cocked a finger at Bowdrey.

Bowdrey had been watching Goru through the window. He turned to face Lassiter and unexpectedly smiled. 'Ready as I'll ever be.'

Lassiter nodded and walked around the truck to his own vehicle. His three passengers were already on board. He started the engine, hearing the grind, whine, and final roar of Bowdrey following suit. He put the Land-Rover into gear but kept his foot on the clutch.

'So much has happened.'

She considered him. 'Here?'

'Here and before.' He was gripped by a feeling of desolation. 'You remember the little green tree? It is dying. I looked at it this morning.'

She looked ahead of her through the windscreen. 'Hope can be tonight's drink, in Zufra. It can be the whore you'll take in Algiers. Or it can be the one you took in Djanet. Drive past the green tree, and don't look at it.'

He let the clutch out and they barrelled between the gates, heading south.

*   *   *

Lassiter chose the defile that Goru had avoided on the night of his ambush, more to avoid the distended corpses of the troopers from Zufra than for convenience. And three hundred yards beyond it he struck soft sand. He tried to bull it through but he was tired, his reflexes had gone. The truck snorted, heaved, slid sideways and stalled.

Lassiter dropped his hands on to his lap. The long fingers lay curled, without tremor. 'That's marvellous.' He turned his head to look at Susan. The children were very quiet, behind. He looked, she thought, as though he were dwelling on some distant, vague problem, that had him, ruminating. But all he said was, 'We will all have to help,' and then he got out.

They unstrapped the shovels and sand ladders. In silence they began to clear the wheels. After a while Bowdrey and Ann came up and joined them. They did nothing at first, standing there whispering, ringed about with enigma, this odd couple who were an eternal and obscure riddle.

It was only when Lassiter looked up at them out of a streaming face and said dispassionately, 'We may miss Zufra in the dark, you know, and there will be no second chance,' that they involved themselves, and all of them worked on in the febrile heat, dream figures far away in a world that was only the chuff of shovels and the phlegmy rattle of breath from Bowdrey's clotted lungs.

It took half an hour. Then the sand ladders were put in and Neil and Susan did the placing, the grabbing and the running while Lassiter handled the truck with the door open, shouting directions, and Ann Bowdrey stood back with a strange, unnaturally calm look of complacency on her smooth face.

They got the vehicle out. Bowdrey avoided the patch and they went on. But only a hundred yards further Lassiter bogged down again.

This time he did not let the engine stall. He accepted the slow, inexorable settling of the big vehicle and switched off. For a time they sat and listened to the ticking noises of the metal. Then he opened the door and swung himself on to the sand and lurched away in it, ankle deep, going forward for more than twenty yards, stopping, looking about, finally coming back and pausing at the window only long enough to say, 'This is a bad one.'

She heard the rattle and clank of the ladders being loosened. She was vaguely conscious of lighting a cigarette and wondering why, when she had no saliva at all left in her mouth. Her legs felt bruised when her feet touched the sand and she walked with an infinite slowness, trailing around to his side of the vehicle with the children silently following her, standing there watching his wide back tighten his shirt as he worked with the shovel.

Into the heat, she said, 'Why is the tree dying, after all these years?'

The sweat slicked his face and made him look quite young. He gave her a look of grieving tenderness and said, 'Because it has lost its hope.'

Goru was calling. They considered each other for a moment and then she said, 'I'll take that,' and grasped the warm round column of the shovel. It bit into the yellow powder, it gulped a mouthful and she straightened, tossing it aside. Lassiter was there, still, watching her, so she said out of the dryness of her mouth, 'Go on, go to him,' and turned away.

He trudged through the sand towards the rear vehicle, passing the Bowdreys as they came up. They stopped, silently studying him as he passed. When he looked back they were watching him still. He stopped and the three people regarded each other expressionlessly until Ann touched Bowdrey's arm and they went on.

Lassiter walked the last few yards to the rear of the Land-Rover and opened the back doors. An oven-like heat, hotter even than the outside air, rolled from the vehicle. Goru was sitting, his knees bent, the sheet still tucked about his waist. He had sweated so much that he was dehydrating. It showed in the shrivelled, prune-like withering of his dark face and the deer-like dullness of his eyes. Lassiter was conscious of only a distant alarm, as though this man was just another of the two-dimensional figures with whom he was associating. He had a thought that if they did not get Goru to Zufra soon he would die.

A voice said out of some place, 'You need salt. I'll get you some.'

It was his own voice.

'Without water?' The *Sous-Préfet* struggled with his dry tongue. He shook his head. 'No.' His mind seemed to wander. He gazed over Lassiter's right shoulder into the leaping distance. The sparkless antelope eyes brushed back over

Lassiter's face, held there a moment, went back into the unseeing distance.

'Those Bowdreys. They whisper all the time. All the way from the fort. It is odd. And Bowdrey laughs, sometimes, as though his senses have gone.'

Lassiter stared at him. His brain thrummed in neutral, not trying. But a picture entered it slowly, of Bowdrey's snake-skin lips and the wheezing voice impelled by the leaky bellows of the dying lungs saying, 'You bloody fool. I'm not weeping. Can't you see I'm laughing?'

He said around the parchment of his tongue, 'Bowdrey is going mad.'

The *Sous-Préfet* did not appear to have heard him. He plucked at his sheet absently with trembling fingers, like an old man unaware of senility, rambling on. 'The whispering and the laughing. All the time the whispering and the laughing. And all about me the bundles and the boxes bound with string, the lunatic *impedimenta* of the mindless. The bundles, I think, the bundles and the boxes will whisper to me of more madness.' The hands plucked the sheet as though in spasmodic weaving. 'So, the last time we bogged down. I open one.'

You opened the plunger box and made sure that the leads were connected. The plunger handle was round and there was frost on it as though it had been garnished with sugar. But your hands were gloved so you took the garnished plunger handle and waited, thinking of the column of explosive lying quivering in the tight virginal passage of the rock face, waiting for the orgiastic throe of its own calamitous self-destruction.

His brain slipped back into neutral. Wrong direction. Try again.

'And you found?' He was right, this time. He blinked. Brain was in first gear, slowly proceeding.

One of the brown hands stopped its nervous plucking at the sheet. It leapt at Lassiter and opened hugely in front of him, with Goru far away at the end of this long telescopic extension of an arm.

Lassiter blinked again, to get the hand in focus. He studied the pink palm that was first a blur. He urged his eyes on, begging them to see. The palm clarified so that he could see the sweat-wetness of it, and what lay there, blinking at him.

A ten-thousand franc note.

There was a stirring within him. His slow heart responded to this message and beat a little faster. It mixed adrenalin with his blood.

'In a blanket bundle?'

'This one.' The other hand moved sideways and indicated.

Lassiter saw the broken string. He pushed in, his shoulder pressing against the stretcher. His hands extended before him and stirred the blanket so that its hot humid folds fell away and the notes lay there like a mound of leaves.

He and Goru stared at them. Lassiter felt nothing. He forced his hands through the dragging cloth of a pocket and brought out a penknife, opened it, and cut the binding on another bundle. More leaves, like a neatly-raked pile next to the first one. A cardboard container, next. Another gathering of leaves.

Lassiter folded the penknife and put it back carefully in his pocket. He met Goru's eyes unblinkingly as the *Sous-Préfet* started to tug at his sheet again. Then he walked away leaving the rear doors apart like welcoming arms.

The Bowdreys were standing next to the front vehicle. They were still, frozen as though for all time, and he moved into the tableau and became one with them in this motionless desert tapestry.

'Why?' They could speak in this state of immobility.

Bowdrey's lips worked like a puppet. 'It's ours. Ours alone. We knew you'd want half, despite what you said in the cellar. So we dummied the one suitcase. We were going to give it to you in Zufra. And we left two genuine packets of notes in it so that we could open it and hand one to you and say see, it's all there. We would be taking a chance, but we didn't think you would be wanting to turn the whole lot out and count it, you're all so . . . so superior. Then we became afraid that we might mix up the suitcases and give you the wrong one, the one with real money in it. So we dummied the other one, too. We left just one genuine note on top of each packet. The rest is paper.' He stared at Lassiter without any interest. His concentration seemed to leave him and his eyes clouded.

'Paper.' Ann Bowdrey said. 'All the letters and memorandums from those sacks in the cellar. Cutting, cutting, all night

279

cutting.' She began to rock slightly from side to side. 'I wasn't going to give any away. Not even half. I wasn't going back to those nights by the telly and the rain rattling in the gutter and my mother pottering with the feather duster. I would not be able to tell them apart, any more, my mother and the duster.'

Lassiter stared at the round 'o' of her mouth, slightly furred by the dryness of her lips. 'That hating you did, this morning when we gave the cases to Jedren, all the time you knew. . . .'

'We knew and we were laughing inside but we had to——'

'You had to pretend because otherwise——'

'You would have suspected something and had a more careful look and then we would have been. . . .'

'So all that standing in the doorway watching Goru was just bluff——'

'And fright. Fright too. It was an enormous chance but I didn't care if I died, you know that yourself, don't you. I'm not his wife at all, I'm Ann Anderson, Sister Anderson from the last hospital he was in. He was there a long time. He guessed that the years were leaving me behind and he came to me in the rain one night, he was wet and I had to give him gin before he would say what it was. . . .'

Silence rushed in upon them. She looked down at her feet. Her tongue protruded and circled her lips. The bent head was blonde right to the roots, to the clean healthy scalp. Then the scalp tilted and he was looking at the eyes again, clean with health but unhealthy with her eternal greed.

'Two thousand pounds It was all I had. Enough for our passages, enough for that old Land-Rover. Enough for a little food. I felt it was a good investment.'

The silence came again. *I felt it was a good investment.* The head was down-turned again, she was staring at her feet re-living something in her thoughts.

When the explosion came the rock face would dissolve water, like a splash from a boulder thrown into a stream. It would come down in cascade, still liquid in its fluid streaming until the dust started to rise and you knew that it was stone. Then you raised a hand, fresh from the plunger, a gloved or mittened hand that was now garnished with the sugar of the frost the way the plunger handle had been, you stared at the sugar frost and thought things while you listened to the roar of the bulldozers moving in.

His brain was back in neutral. Wrong. Go back. Try again.

'Jedren has never owned that much money in his life. He had to be dignified when we handed over the cases. But the compulsion to stop, and look, and count the notes, will be uncontrollable.'

'They are far away.' She said it dreamily.

'Over the hills and far away.' Bowdrey laughed, hugging his arms to him as though he were cold.

'No.' He struggled with his tongue. 'By now, on their way back here. He warned me. He said there would be no second chance.'

'You will have to accept it. You must accept it the way you accepted the bridge at Eichstadt.'

Susan and the children were watching him closely. His feet took him over to them.

'We must dig. John-oh always said that a Land-Rover is faster than a camel. I will try my best.' He looked back at the Bowdreys. He felt a need to explain something to them. 'When Jedren comes, I will tell him what happened. I will offer the two of you to him in exchange for what you have done. I do not think that he will accept part payment. But I must try.'

They said nothing, but the money-love was still so strongly with them that they broke out of their statuesque contemplation of success, they grasped the urgency, and they worked with a sudden desperate purpose until the ladders were in, the truck rumbled along them, the ladders were in again, the big threaded tyres consumed them, the ladders were in again but the third time one ladder was askew. The Land-Rover ran off it on the left side, lurched, swam a little like a blind panting bull and then bogged again.

The shovels slid into the sand. The sand was confetti, the girl thought, they were moving it around aimlessly like guests after a wedding where the bride had not turned up and the groom kept drunkenly falling into the confetti and they had to keep dragging him out of it. She heard the groom calling her but she kept stirring at the confetti until she realized that it was Goru's voice from the rear Land-Rover.

281

Lassiter had heard. He stood up slowly and shielded his eyes from the sun. His smile was very full. 'We dig for life. We have no hope, you and I, but we dig. Why?'

She fumbled with her thoughts. She wanted to answer him but already he was going, calling to them all, swinging an arm in command so that they trailed behind him to Bowdrey's Land-Rover and clustered at the open back doors. They did not need the *Sous-Préfet* to point for them. They could see the Touareg coming in a long blue-clad line, moving swiftly out of the swimming heat-haze and hardening into a needle-sharp focus.

Lassiter blinked, but the Touareg were ever there, growing larger. He turned to the Land-Rover and hauled out the bundles, throwing them ahead of him, splitting the ones that were still bound so that eventually the money lay scattered in its many leaves upon the treeless desert, untroubled in the windless air.

The girl was at his side. Her lips stirred.

'Your rifle?'

'On the catwalk.'

'I am afraid.'

'Then you have hope, don't you? I am afraid, too.' He frowned at the approaching men. It was so important that he explain. He would not die without explaining.

'Jedren.'

The Touareg halted sixty yards away. The tall Tibesti camel moved ahead slightly, out of the line.

'We did not know.' He took the Bowdreys gently each by an arm and brought them forward on either side. They came with a slow, stiff willingness. 'This man and this woman. They deceived all of us. We have only now found out.' He shook his head. 'That is why the money lies there. You can see it is real. You can count every note of it. Take it. We never wanted it. Take them too, if you want them. Take Goru and me. But leave this woman and these children alone.' He strained his eyes at Jedren. 'There is no Bren any more, Jedren.'

Jedren pushed his camel a little further forward. He could see the money. He knew it was real. He could see Lassiter's tired, earnest face, the way the young girl and the two children clustered behind him as though behind a shield.

282

'Reason is the shackle of cowardice,' he said. 'I warned you. I told you there would be no second chance.'

The Sahara showed in his eyes, then, in the stiff movements of his body. The Sahara was hardness and harshness, it was death and Jedren was part of it. He lifted an arm and dropped it. Lassiter heard his voice. It seemed to fly away from him like a bird, it seemed to cry, 'I am sorry, Monsieur,' and then the camels had closed, the long line of the Touareg were moving forward and the camels were coming at a reluctant run towards the back of the Land-Rover.

'Don't be afraid.' Lassiter stood upright. He clustered the girl and the two children behind him, his long arms reaching back, his big hands touching a thin shoulder, a bony rib-cage, once the small soft mound of her breast. 'Don't be afraid. They are not going to hurt us, they will hurt only the Bowdreys.'

He watched the Touareg close in. They moved in from the sides so that they became a solid bunch as they reached towards the small group of people clustered behind the money. He saw the blue-clad arms dip, and lift; he saw the razor-bright flash of the swords, he smelled the sweat of the camels, and saw the fierce eyes, nearly a hundred pairs of eyes with all the death of the desert in them, he cried aloud, he tensed his body as though he could keep the swords away from the clutch behind him. He was filled with the desperate need to tell them something. He called the words on a high note, 'Don't be afraid! It is all right! Lew loves you! Everything is going to be all right!'

They were so near, now, the swords held up, burnished by the bright rays of the sun that flashed points of fire off them, they were thirty yards, twenty, they were crowding in upon each other, bunched, colliding, the points of the swords coming down inexorably.

The muscles on Lassiter's chest had clamped. He waited for the pain of entry and wondered whether it would be like John-oh, whether John-oh had felt anything. But he was calm because he had told them, there was the tremendous satisfaction of knowing. And then he heard a sound, a harsh and discordant rattle like the noise of hail on a tin roof, and the Touareg were being tossed this way and that, falling, swinging off to the left and right of the Land-Rover as Goru staggered forward from the back of the Land-Rover with the Bren cuddled in his arms, its bell-muzzle spitting death from the horn-curve of the magazine, and Jedren stretching out dying on the sand amidst the flung bundles of his men, the dead men and the camels, T'ekmedhin with the hate still in his dead eyes, Jedren's seeking Lassiter with a last look of shocked betrayal, all of them lying like the troopers from Zufra, the apex of the charge, blasted down while the rest became a fleeing cloud that cried in dark shadow towards the horizon and Goru had staggered and fallen on his fat buttocks right amongst the dead, the smoking hell-hot Bren on his lap and the tears bursting out and bubbling down his face like soda water.

'The dream was not true. They fell when I fired, although I did not think they would. Nothing is eternal; no man is immortal.' He dug his fingers into the sand, looking about him, fussing with the sand like a child at the seaside.

Lassiter turned very carefully. He took the children's hands. He swung them around, and forced them out into the open track that led to Zufra. He held their hands very tightly.

'Walk,' he said. 'It is a very beautiful day. It is not really so hot and the sun is shining and in a little while they will catch up with us.' The girl came up, alongside him. He shepherded them all, touching them constantly. 'Walk,' he said, 'don't look back. The day is beautiful and everything is fine.'

They walked for half an hour. And then they heard the distant growl of the Land-Rover, gaining sound as it came up behind them.